PRAISE FOR *HANGMAN*

'Jack Heath's writing grabs you by the throat, gnaws on your bones and washes it all down with a hefty dose of funny. Sick, twisted, violent and oh so good. In Timothy Blake, Heath has created a one-of-a-kind character. I hope.'—Emma Viskic, internationally bestselling author of *And Fire Came Down*

'Blake is a brilliant, complex character . . . this quiet and unassuming figure might just be the most dangerous man in the room. *Hangman* is cinematic and grubby, brimming with pulpy noir.'—Michael Offer, producer, *How to Get Away with Murder* and *Homeland*

'Wild and original, *Hangman* stamps a high and bloodied mark on this dark genre. Hannibal Lecter will be adding Jack Heath to his reading list.'—Ben Sanders, internationally bestselling author of *American Blood*

'A grisly, efficiently written nail-biter packed with riddles and suspense, *Hangman* has bestseller written all over it. It's a dark book, but one with plenty of humour, and a twisty plot that keeps you guessing to the very end.'—*Sydney Morning Herald*

'Compelling . . . Heath keeps the suspense at a high level through to its stunning conclusion. An addictive and suspenseful thriller that will keep you reading well into the night.'—*Canberra Weekly*

'Let's cut to the chase: *Hangman* is a great read! Jack Heath's boundless imagination and singular voice have produced a truly unique thriller. By turns psychologically insightful, wonderfully disturbed and even darkly comedic, *Hangman* will keep you coursing through the pages at a lightning pace. Brilliant! (Probably best read with lights on and doors locked. I'm just saying.)'—Jeffery Deaver, No. 1 international bestselling author

'*Hangman* is ghoulish fun, and fills the Dexter- and Hannibal-shaped holes in our lives.'—*Books + Publishing*

'Blake is a classic kind of hard-boiled hero, mixing cynicism and honour, brutality and sentimentality ... he's a chivalrous knight of the kind we have never seen before.'—*Weekend Australian Review*

'A cracking read full of well-crafted twists and turns ... Heath manages to bring Blake out from behind the shadow of his predecessors and stand on his own.'—*Australian Crime Fiction*

'Heath has given the crime world an anti-hero for this century. Gifted and flawed, Blake will horrify and entrance readers, quite often at the same time. An exceptionally taut novel both in action and execution, this sledge-hammer story is sure to entice fans of serial crime fiction, taking readers into the dark and dirty recesses of Blake's mind.'—*Good Reading*

'*Hangman* is a pulpy and perverse delight . . . Heath makes Blake young, rough, streetwise, and precisely the sort of person Dr Lecter would avoid in the street. This is a gobsmackingly (or lip-smackingly) violent tale, but it is also bizarre, hilarious, and a stealthily astute commentary on post-financial crisis America. Give me more.'—Christopher Richardson (blog)

'Jack Heath has created an extraordinary and original character in Timothy Blake, and I can't wait to read his next book.'—Carpe Librum (blog)

'Richer than Reacher . . . an accomplished and compulsive thriller that kept my appetite to return to its banquet of kidnapping and bloody murder. *Hangman* literally tingles with tension, and Heath injects a healthy dose of dark humour.'—*Sydney Arts Guide*

'*Hangman* is cheerful in its gore, with a knack for unexpected violence that'll leave even the most jaded crime readers at least a little bit impressed . . . It's all the best parts of noir fiction, all the spatter pattern ghoulishness of forensics-focused dramas, and so much fun it might just concern you a little bit.'—Hush Hush Biz (blog)

ABOUT THE AUTHOR

Jack Heath is the bestselling author of more than twenty-five novels for young adults and children. His books have been shortlisted for many awards, translated into several languages and adapted for film. He lives on the land of the Ngunnawal people in Canberra, Australia. *Hangman* was his first novel for adults.

Warning: *Hunter* is unsuitable for children and some adults. It includes descriptions of sexual violence and suicide.

HUNTER
JACK HEATH

ALLEN&UNWIN
SYDNEY·MELBOURNE·AUCKLAND·LONDON

For my family

First published in 2019

Copyright © Jack Heath 2019

All rights reserved. No part of this book may be reproduced or transmitted in any form or by any means, electronic or mechanical, including photocopying, recording or by any information storage and retrieval system, without prior permission in writing from the publisher. The Australian *Copyright Act 1968* (the Act) allows a maximum of one chapter or 10 per cent of this book, whichever is the greater, to be photocopied by any educational institution for its educational purposes provided that the educational institution (or body that administers it) has given a remuneration notice to the Copyright Agency (Australia) under the Act.

Allen & Unwin
83 Alexander Street
Crows Nest NSW 2065
Australia
Phone: (61 2) 8425 0100
Email: info@allenandunwin.com
Web: www.allenandunwin.com

 A catalogue record for this book is available from the National Library of Australia

ISBN 978 1 76052 708 2

Set in 12.5/18 pt Sabon Lt Std by Post Pre-press Group, Australia
Printed and bound in Australia by Griffin Press

10 9 8 7 6 5 4 3 2 1

 The paper in this book is FSC® certified. FSC® promotes environmentally responsible, socially beneficial and economically viable management of the world's forests.

Standing on the corner with a dollar in my hand, honey
Standing on the corner with a dollar in my hand, babe
Standing on the corner with a dollar in my hand
Standing here waiting for the Crawdad Man
Honey
Baby
Mine

—Civil War-era folk song

CHAPTER 1

What has a neck but no head?

If Charlie Warner wants you dead, first she steals your shoes.

Not in person. She has people all over Houston.

One of them is James Tyrrell, a pudgy guy with Coke-bottle glasses and scar tissue on his arm where the number 88 used to be. A coded white supremacist tattoo—H is the eighth letter of the alphabet. The 88 means *Heil Hitler*. 'I'm no Nazi,' I heard him say once, 'but if you want to survive Huntsville prison, you gotta pick a team.'

Tyrrell will open your front door with a police-issue lock-release gun and go to your bedroom wearing latex gloves and a hairnet. He'll steal your most expensive pair of shoes. Usually black, always shiny—the kind you might wear to a funeral. He'll take some socks, too, but won't touch anything else on his way out.

Two more guys will drive a white van with stolen plates to wherever it is you work. Their names are Jordan Francis and Theo Sariklis. They both have thick necks, square jaws and crew cuts. It took me a while to tell them apart. Sariklis is the one with the drooping eyelid and the Ramones shirt. He's been working for Warner longer than me. Francis is new—just moved here from San Jose, California. He's the one who cracks jokes. Even in winter he wears a wife-beater to show off his biceps. He might go to the gym after killing you.

Francis will park the van next to the driver's side of your car. Sariklis will open the sliding door on the side of the van and wait.

You'll walk out of the office and approach your car. When you go to open the door, Francis will grab you and drag you into the van. It takes seconds. He's had plenty of practice—in San Jose he worked for one of the Sureño gangs. You won't even have time to scream before Francis shuts the van door.

You'll know who they work for. Warner doesn't target bystanders. They're here because you stole from her, or lied to her, or informed on her. Or maybe you didn't pay your tab at one of her businesses. An underground casino, a bordello, a drug den.

They'll ask you questions. The first few are a test; they already know the answers. If you lie, Francis will hold you down, while Sariklis forces a water bottle into your mouth and pinches your nose shut so it feels like drowning. They do it like that because they're still in the parking lot and there aren't many quiet ways to torture someone.

Just when it feels like you're gonna die, Sariklis will take the bottle out. You'll throw up. Then he will ask you some more questions. The real ones. Whatever Warner needs to know. *Who have you told? What are their names? Where do they live? Show us the messages.*

The last question is always about the PIN for your bank account. You'll answer that one gladly. You'll think it means they only want money. You'll think they're going to let you go.

After you give them your PIN, Sariklis will stick the bottle back in your mouth. This time he won't let up. He'll drown you, right there in the parking lot. Three minutes until your heart gives up, four until brain death.

Francis will stay in the van with your body while Sariklis takes your car, your phone and your wallet to an ATM. He'll withdraw as much as he can, then drive to a secluded stretch of beach in Galveston.

There he'll meet Tyrrell, who has your shoes. Sariklis will place your shoes side by side on the sand, your wallet and keys tucked inside like frightened mice. Tyrrell will do a factory reset on your phone, switch it off and hurl it into the sea. They'll abandon your car on the side of the road, within sight of the grey ocean, and take Tyrrell's car back to Warner's office to give her the cash.

I've only been to Warner's office once, and I had a bag on my head for the whole journey. But I was memorising the turns, and counting the seconds. Afterwards I got them to drop me off someplace else, and I memorised that journey as well. Later I looked at a map, and narrowed it down to four city blocks near Market Square Park.

They usually take you on a Friday. If you live alone, you may not be reported missing until Monday. The police will find your car and shoes around Wednesday. Some of them will say you drowned accidentally while swimming. Others will suggest that it was suicide. The shoes are too classy for a normal swim, they'll say, and there's no towel. Plus, your bathing suit is still at your home.

Because of the ATM withdrawal, still others will say that you faked your death. You did have some powerful enemies, after all. Your missing phone lends credence to this theory. But anyone who suspects Warner will be smart enough not to say so.

All this is assuming you're one of the lucky ones, and Warner doesn't want the credit for your death. Sometimes she kills someone to send a message. No stolen shoes, no water bottle. The body turns up in dozens of pieces, each removed from a living person.

Once upon a time Warner's men would have just thrown your body into the ocean. The water in your lungs would make sense on the autopsy report. But the bruising around your lips and wrists, plus the damage to your gums, might raise some eyebrows. Now they have a better way.

While Sariklis and Tyrrell bring the cash to Warner's office, Francis will take the van onto State Highway 12, alone. Your body will be in the back under a sheet, slowly going cold. Francis will drive through the dark, watching the buildings disappear and the trees get taller and taller.

Then he'll see a beat-up Toyota parked on the shoulder, miles from anywhere. He'll pull over. Despite what he's seen and done, he'll shudder before he gets out of the car.

Then he'll slide open the van door, and give your body to me.

CHAPTER 2

What flies without wings and cries without eyes?

He's late.

I pace up and down the shoulder, watching the road for headlights. The trees whisper secrets in the gentle breeze. My breath makes clouds in front of my face. It's not snowing, but the sky is seriously considering it. People think Texas is hot, but in early December it falls below fifty.

Normally I'd stay in the driver's seat, working on riddles. Strangers mail them to me, and I solve them for twenty bucks each. This started out as a money-laundering scheme, and surprised me by becoming an actual job. But tonight I have to get out of the car. A diet of primarily meat, stale bread and salted coffee has ugly side effects. I'm having stomach cramps.

I check my phone, squinting at the tiny screen. It's two am. The phone is a burner, small and cheap. Warner told me to keep it switched on and with me at all times. The battery never lasts long, so I know she installed a hidden tracking app. She probably assumed I'd figure that out, but she also knows I'm smart enough to play dumb.

My guts gurgle, twisting in my belly. I need a bathroom break. But if I'm not here when Francis arrives, I don't know what he'll do.

I take deep breaths. That only makes it worse. I try to think about the van instead, cruising towards me with the body inside.

The dead man is named Aaron Elliott. An investment banker. He hit one of Warner's callgirls, leaving her with a busted nose. Now she can't work. Warner said it would be bad business to let something like that go unpunished.

The body is supposed to be big. Six foot, two hundred pounds. Might be a challenge for me to dispose of.

The pressure from my insides is getting unbearable. I take one more hopeful look at the road, but there's still no sign of the van, so I scurry into the woods.

Living your whole life in the city, you forget how dark it gets beyond the edge. Even when I was sleeping on the streets, there was always light around. A fizzing streetlight here, the glow of a gas station there. No trees to block the moonlight. Out here, there's nothing but the smell of earth and the buzz of insects. An eastern screech owl trills somewhere above me. I fumble through the foliage, using the flashlight app to find a good spot.

Then something stops me. The smell of meat.

I've always had a good sense of smell. Starvation does that to you. I turn around, slowly. Taking rapid, sharp sniffs, like a dog. It's not cooked meat, but it's also not a dead animal. There's none of that farmy, furry odour. And it's . . . this way.

Curiosity has taken my mind off the stomach cramps. I push through the brush, branches scratching at my legs and arms, until I reach the source of the smell.

It's a dead body.

The man is naked. Thin, short—not Elliott. Facedown, with one arm outstretched, as though he's swimming. His other hand is trapped under his torso.

I sweep the phone over him. The glow illuminates his face. He's white, mid-forties, with a short beard and grey-flecked hair. His eyes are wide, his teeth bared. Pained, enraged or terrified—can't tell.

People with hypothermia sometimes take their clothes off right before they die. Their body temperature gets so low that the air feels hot around them, and they start shedding layers. But even in winter, it would take at least an hour to die of exposure, and he's barely fifty feet from the road.

In the dark, it's impossible to know which direction he came from. But there's nothing out here—that's why Warner picked this spot—so I assume a car dropped him off. Sometimes the police do that. Take your clothes and kick you out of the car, miles from anywhere in the freezing cold. Murder by weather.

But in that scenario, he would have stayed on the road in case a car came by. He wouldn't have run into the woods.

So he was trying to escape from the driver. Maybe he even threw himself from a moving vehicle, although I don't see any grazes on his palms or his knees. His skin is pristine. I touch it. Soft, too. He hasn't been dead long. A day at the most.

Don't do it. It's the voice of Agent Reese Thistle, my old FBI handler. I haven't seen her in months, but I still hear her in my head. She's what I have instead of a conscience.

Walk away, she says.

Ignoring her, I squeeze the man's upper arm. It's the perfect mixture of fat and muscle. I squeeze it, and lean in close. My heart rate is through the roof. I can hardly breathe.

Are you kidding me? Thistle says. *You don't know who he is, where he came from, how he died or who might be looking for him. Plus, you got another body on the way. You don't need this.*

She's right. But she's too late to stop me. It was too late the moment I saw the body.

Just one bite, I tell myself, and rip a chunk out of his arm with my teeth.

He screams.

I rear back, but it's not him. Something else has screeched—maybe that owl from before.

A flashlight flits between the trees in the distance.

Holy shit. I duck down, gore dribbling from my mouth. I'm not alone in this forest. Someone is here, probably tracking the dead man. Maybe the driver of the car he escaped from. Or a cop, doing search and rescue. Either way, the person with the flashlight will be armed, unlike me. Boots trample the undergrowth, closer every second.

I could run back to my car. But when the tracker finds the body, he or she will notice the fresh bite, clearly made by human teeth. The tracker will start looking for me. If they are with the police, they'll call in reinforcements. The forest will be surrounded, the highway blocked off. The cops will stop me, see the blood on my face, and it's over.

So I can't let the tracker find the body.

I heave the dead man over my shoulder. He weighs maybe a hundred and sixty pounds. Less than me, but still it's hard to walk with him on my back. My feet sink deeper into the undergrowth with every step. Leaves crunch, branches rattle. Hopefully the tracker won't hear me over his own footsteps.

Soon I've reached the edge of the forest. I look around. No sign of any cars on the road other than mine. I hustle out of the forest and run over to my Toyota. My fingers are shaking as I open the trunk, leaving blood on the handle.

Headlights in the distance. Engine noise. If that's anyone other than Francis, I'm in trouble.

There's a thirty-gallon plastic tub in the trunk. I dump the dead man in and slam the lid. I keep my face turned away from the car as it passes.

The car slows down, but doesn't stop. I'm not sure

how much the driver would have seen. Even less sure how likely they are to report anything they did see.

One more thing before I go. I pick up a rock about the size of a deck of cards, and pitch it as far as I can, over the tops of the trees. It crashes down somewhere in the distance. I can't see the flashlight, but I can hear the tracker changing direction, moving with renewed urgency.

I wait until the sound fades. Then I start the engine, release the park brake and pull out onto the highway.

•

My house is a dilapidated two-bedroom, one-bathroom thing in a bad neighbourhood just outside the loop. The rent is surprisingly high for such a crummy place. Ideally I'd split it with someone, but since I ate my last roommate—a drug-dealing rapist—the idea makes me nervous. It's safest for everyone if I live alone.

I reverse the car into the carport, jump out and open the trunk. Contrary to popular belief, it's not always darkest before dawn. Already a cold blue glow is starting to spill across the street. The sun will be up in an hour. I need to get the body inside before someone—

'Morning, Timothy!'

I look up. My neighbour is on the sidewalk, dressed in a tank top and sweatbands. A blond labrador sniffs around his running shoes.

I always feel sorry for dogs, even though I've been bitten a few times. Like me, they're keen observers of body language and have a good sense of smell. Also like me, they love meat, they have poor impulse control and they're usually at someone else's mercy.

'Hi, Shawn,' I say. 'You're up early.'

Can he see the blood on my face and my shirt? Probably not, if I stay in the shadows of the carport. And from this angle, he can't see the inside of the trunk. I casually close the lid.

'New Year's resolution,' Shawn is saying. He does an exaggerated hamstring stretch. 'I'm gonna get into shape.'

Shawn is already in shape. I've often thought he looks tasty. Two hundred pounds, five foot nine, thirty years old, black. There's no sweat in his moustache, so he hasn't started his run yet.

'It's December,' I say.

'I know. I'm *training* for New Year's.'

'Oh. Have fun.'

The dog looks very interested in the trunk of my car. She strains at the chain.

Shawn tugs her back towards him. 'You should come with me,' he says. 'We could make it a regular thing.'

'Maybe another time,' I say.

Shawn has lived next door to me for years, but only started talking to me recently, after my roommate disappeared. I think Shawn was scared of him. He should have been scared of me instead. He seems like a good guy, so I try to avoid him. I don't want him to get hurt.

Shawn finally registers that I'm not in running gear and I don't have a dog. 'What are you doing out here so early?' he asks.

I've been racking my brain for something that won't make him suspicious. 'Packing,' I say. 'I'm going snow camping with my cousin. Figured I'd beat the traffic.'

'I thought I just saw you arrive.'

'Nah, man. Just turning the car around so it's easier to load.'

'Snow camping? Is that a thing?'

'Yeah. You should try it sometime.'

The dog starts tugging the lead again, pulling Shawn closer to me. I take a step back. My camping story doesn't cover the blood. I should have told him that I'd just come home from hospital, or something.

'Where's your camp site?' Shawn asks.

I hesitate. 'Not sure. I'm meeting Jesse—that's my cousin—in Dallas. Then I'll follow him the rest of the way.'

'Did Jesse used to live with you?' Shawn asks.

Damn him and his good memory. 'Different Jesse,' I say.

The dog growls at me, her fur standing up.

'Take it easy, Caitlin,' Shawn says.

'Anyway,' I say, 'I better keep packing. Enjoy your run.'

'Thanks, man. See you.'

I turn my face away as he pulls on the dog's leash. The dog follows reluctantly. Shawn breaks into a jog and disappears down the street.

I let out the breath I've been holding. I need to get the dead guy inside before anyone else comes along.

I unlock the back door of my house, which leads directly into my kitchen. Then I go back to the car, open the trunk and lift the plastic tub out. The body feels even heavier now—or maybe I'm just exhausted. There's always a crash after the adrenaline trickles away.

I drag the tub into the house, triple-lock the back door, and finally make it to the bathroom.

It would be smart to start covering my tracks. Reverse-engineering an alibi for the last few hours. But I can't ignore the body in my kitchen.

When I get back from the bathroom I switch on the lights and crouch over the dead man. The flesh around the bite wound has already gone white. I look for piercings, or gang tattoos. Nothing. There's a line of scar tissue on his chest, like he's had a skin cancer removed. Mud on the soles of his feet, his knees, his palms. But his hair smells of shampoo. All of it, including his pubic hair. He's trimmed his beard recently.

There's a cut on one of his fingertips, like you might get from a thorn or a staple. The blood has been cleaned or sucked off, but it hasn't healed. Probably happened within the last twenty-four hours.

I pull his mouth open. A faint smell of toothpaste over an even fainter smell of red wine. A merlot, I think. He has straight teeth—probably had braces as a kid—and a couple of fillings. I'm no expert, but they look expensive. His eyes have a slightly dull sheen. I carefully scoop out a pair of contact lenses.

He has a wedding ring—a plain gold band. I wiggle it off his finger. It's engraved with a date and two words: LOVE, GABBI.

A twist of guilt in my chest. I always tell myself that

I only eat bad people. Most of Warner's enemies are criminals, like her. This man could be anybody. An innocent, if such a thing exists. But I know that bite mark is the first of many. I won't be able to help myself.

If only he had some gang tattoos or something. I want a reason not to feel sorry for him.

'Who are you?' I ask him.

He stares up at me through grey eyes.

Tap, tap. Someone's knocking on my front door.

CHAPTER 3

When you run, I speed up; when you slow down, so do I. If I stop, so do you. What am I?

I freeze for a moment. Maybe they'll think no one's home. The curtains don't let any light in or out.

Another knock. Whoever is on my porch, they're not giving up.

'I'm coming.' As quietly as I can, I lift the dead man up, lower him into the chest freezer and close it. I dump my bloodstained jacket and shirt in the laundry tub, and twist the faucet slowly so the sudden hissing of water doesn't give me away. Pink water runs down the drain. I use a wet washcloth to wipe my face and neck, and dry myself with a dish towel. Then I approach the door, trying to look sleepy instead of panicked.

I don't make it.

There's the distinctive whirr of a lock-release gun. The door bursts open so suddenly that the handle leaves a dent in the wall. Two big men with crew cuts storm in. Sariklis—the one with the drooping eyelid—and Francis, the gym-junkie who was supposed to meet me on the side of the road.

I open my mouth to scream. Getting arrested is better than drowning in the back of a van.

But Sariklis is too quick. He slaps a hand over my mouth and compresses my throat with the crook of his elbow.

'Jacksonville, Phoenix,' he says.

Warner has a password system. Every message from her begins with the last password she used, and a new one for next time. Last time it was *Santa Monica, Jacksonville*. Next time it might be *Phoenix, St Louis*, or *Phoenix, Fargo*, or *Phoenix, Dallas*. She uses a different password for each employee. She rarely meets people in person, so this system ensures that no one else can give orders, at least not without her finding out. I assume she has a database somewhere of which employees are expecting which passwords. If it was me, I'd memorise them all. But not everyone can do that.

'You're coming with us, Blake,' Sariklis says. 'You want to be conscious, or unconscious?'

I go limp.

'Good call,' he says, and lets me go.

Francis has closed the door and is looking around my dusty living room. His gaze settles on my ratty sofa, the holes in the fabric patched with duct tape.

'You know,' he says, 'I think I saw your house on an episode of *Cribs* one time.'

'Where were you?' I ask. 'I was waiting.'

'Tell it to the boss lady. Maybe ask to borrow some money while you're at it. Her interest rates are very reasonable. Buy yourself a new sofa. Shit, maybe a whole new house.'

'Leave your phone here,' Sariklis tells me.

One exception to Warner's *take-your-phone-everywhere* rule: I'm not supposed to have it when I meet her in person. Or, I assume, when her men are taking me to an unmarked grave in the middle of nowhere.

'Sure. I'll put it on the charger.' I start to walk towards my bedroom.

'Nope.' Sariklis grabs my shoulder. 'Leave it right here, on the floor.'

'Let me grab a shirt, at least,' I say.

'No time. She wants to see you ASAP.'

I put my phone on the floor. Sariklis frog-marches me to the front door. Francis cracks it open. Cold air floods through the gap.

'No one out there,' he says. 'None of these fuckers have jobs. They won't be up for hours.'

Shawn is up. But I don't say anything.

They push me out towards the white van. The cold makes the hairs on my arms stand up and turns my nipples into bullets. When I was homeless I had zero per cent body fat—with a shower and a haircut, I could have been a model. But being half naked in this weather would have killed me in minutes. These days, I figure I can survive about an hour.

They bundle me into the van. Something is on the floor inside, wrapped in a blue tarp. I can't resist lifting part of the plastic. Yup, it's another body. Six foot, two hundred pounds. Probably Aaron Elliott. His face is slack and gentle. He doesn't look like the sort of person who would beat up a callgirl. But death has a way of erasing your sins, or at least making them invisible.

Warner could be lying to me. Making up criminal backstories for the dead, so I feel less guilty about what I do to them. I've avoided investigating this possibility.

Francis climbs into the driver's seat.

'Were you really late?' Sariklis asks him, almost too quiet for me to hear.

'Five minutes, if that.' Francis is lying. Interesting.

No time to think about it. The van lurches into motion. No bag on my head this time. Means we're not going to Warner's office.

'Can you turn up the heat?' I ask, shivering.

They both act like they can't hear me.

We drive through outer suburbia, where poverty has landed like a hurricane—and so has an actual hurricane, come to think of it. Car parts, rotting furniture and broken TVs litter the lawns. Kids pedal bikes back and forth, no helmets, ready to sell meth to the first tweaker to wake up.

An hour later, we're on the west edge of Bayport. Most of the warehouses and factories look abandoned, some halfway through construction. I've been wondering something for a while: *Once you've killed your body-disposal expert, how do you get rid of his body?* Maybe I'm looking at the answer. You take him to a place like this, and pour a slab of concrete over him.

The van pulls up in front of a diner called The Crack of Noon. I can't imagine many people working around here, or starting this early. But, against the odds, the diner is open, and it's half full. A server is carrying a pot of coffee from table to table.

Sariklis hauls the van door open. 'Out.'

I look down at my bare chest. Are they really expecting me to go out there like this?

Apparently. Francis drags me onto the street and pushes me towards the diner.

Some of the customers glance up at me as I stumble in. A young black woman's eyebrows go up, and a middle-aged white guy smirks. But then they turn back to their breakfasts, like it's not so weird to see a half-naked man get strong-armed into a diner at dawn.

Charlie Warner is in a booth with her back to the wall and a clear line of sight to the exit. I've heard cops call that 'the Clint chair', because of *Dirty Harry*. She's dressed in jeans, boots and a flannel shirt, all tailored to fit. Cowgirl chic. Her blonde hair is pulled back in a tight ponytail. A Stetson rests on the seat next to her.

Warner is sipping an espresso, while everyone else here has brewed coffee. The bacon on her plate looks perfectly crisp, and the eggs neither too sloppy nor too dry. I wonder if she left a huge tip last time she was here, or threatened the owner, or just got lucky.

Wordlessly, she gestures to the seat opposite. The seat from which the exit and the rest of the room are invisible. I wonder if there's a name for that. But they won't kill me in front of all these witnesses.

Not that any of those witnesses seems to be looking my way. When I was a street beggar, I developed a keen sense of being avoided. I have it now—a feeling of being *not* watched, of gazes placed anywhere but on me.

Francis and Sariklis hustle me forwards. Hands on shoulders, they press me down into the seat Warner indicated.

'Francis was late,' I say.

Warner dabs at her lips with a napkin, leaving a little lipstick on it. She clears her throat. 'Let me tell you a story,' she says.

A server brings me a cup of coffee. Brewed. She leaves without saying anything. I don't touch the coffee. Thallium sulfate is tasteless. So is botulinum. Amatoxin. Compound 1080. Any of these would kill me. Some of them would even kill anyone who ate my body afterwards.

'There was a girl who used to work for me,' Warner says. 'Indigo. She was a stripper, and a skilled one. It was amazing, how quickly she could get a man to the point where he would do absolutely anything. She didn't even need to talk—she just had a really authentic smile. Sweet kid. Anyway, her husband had some debts, and Indigo wanted to pay them off. So she requested a promotion to active duty.' She means prostitution.

I say nothing.

'I thought she'd earn me a fortune. I changed her name to Sindy—with an S—and put her to work.' Warner skewers a piece of bacon with a polished fork. 'She was really good at getting the customers from the entrance to her room. Once they were in there, she was not so good, but I thought that would improve over time.'

I'm surprised that she's talking about this in public. No one else in the diner seems to be listening, but I'm not sure what the point is.

'Instead, it got worse,' Warner continued. 'It took her longer and longer to recover after each client. They seemed less and less satisfied. Eventually she freaked out and hit one of them. My boys thought he was trying to leave without paying, so they beat the shit out of him.'

'Wasn't us,' Sariklis put in.

'We know you have to pay up-front,' Francis added.

Warner looks at them, and they both shut up.

'Indigo tried to run, too,' Warner said. 'We caught her. I saw straight away that she'd never work again. She wasn't injured, but some people can't handle it, psychologically. So I let her out of her contract.' She smiles like the Dalai Lama, pleased with her own generosity. 'Her husband was pissed, but no harm came to her. She moved away and never came back.'

'If you're looking for a replacement,' I say, 'I doubt people would pay much to have sex with me.'

In addition to being scarred and haggard-looking,

I'm a virgin. I can't get close to anyone without endangering them.

Warner ignores this. 'Sometimes people apply for a job. When they start doing it, they realise it doesn't suit them. But they're too scared to quit. They don't want to own up to their mistake.' She swallows a mouthful of eggs and leans back in her seat. 'I'm wondering if you have the stomach for the work I've given you.'

My guts rumble. That bite of the mystery man didn't touch the sides. 'I do,' I say.

'Are you sure? Because I won't tolerate another failure.'

This is your way out, Thistle says in my head. *For fuck's sake, take it.*

'I was waiting for forty-five minutes,' I say.

This is an exaggeration, and it provokes the desired reaction. 'Bullshit,' Francis says. 'It was fifteen minutes at the most.'

Warner's eyes flash over to him, and he closes his mouth. I wonder if he has a tracking app on his phone, like me.

'At least twenty,' I say. We're both losing her trust, but he's losing it faster.

Warner holds up her hands. 'Enough. Where were you, Blake?'

'I drove home,' I say. 'He'd never been late before. I thought he must have been caught, and the cops might figure out where he was going.'

She considers this. I can't tell her about the dead man. She'll worry that the cops who are looking for him might find me. Then I'll accidentally lead them to her. Safer to kill me before they get to that point.

'I need this job,' I say.

'Why didn't you call me?' she asks.

'That could have screwed us both. If I got caught, there would be a record of me calling you. And if you were caught—'

'Nice of you to worry about me. Next time, don't. You call me the second something goes wrong.'

I let the air out of my lungs. She's letting me live, for now. 'Sure.'

'And if you decide you can't handle the work,' Warner says, 'let me know, and we'll figure something out.'

'Sure,' I say again.

'Don't try to run,' she says. 'You have no family and no friends, which limits the number of ways I can threaten you. But don't assume that makes you safe. There is nowhere on Earth you can go where I won't find you.'

I realise that everyone in the diner is staring at me. The young woman, the middle-aged man, the server, everybody. The same cold, level stare, like a room full of androids.

They all work for her.

'Do you understand?' Warner asks.

I nod.

She signals to Sariklis, who drags me out of the booth.

'Take him home,' she says.

Francis goes to follow us.

'Francis,' Warner says. 'Don't go anywhere.' She points at the seat I've just vacated.

Francis slowly sits down, suddenly old, as Sariklis takes me out the door.

•

After Sariklis leaves my house, the adrenaline wears off and the sleepless night comes crashing down. I'm like a zombie, yawning and shuffling as I throw some of Elliott in the fridge and the rest in the chest freezer on top of the mystery man. The freezer isn't quite big enough for both men—first world problems. I have to break Elliott's neck to make him fit.

I scrub the blood from my clothes and hang them over the heater to dry. Then I stay crouched in front of the heater for a while, letting my bones thaw. While I wait, I check the weather on my burner phone. Lake Bob Sandlin State Park isn't far from Dallas, and it's had record snowfall.

'I was driving to Dallas,' I say out loud. 'I was supposed to go camping near Lake Bob Sandlin with my cousin, Jesse. But the weather was bad, so Jesse called to cancel. I was driving to Dallas. I was supposed to go camping.'

It's not a perfect cover story, but it fits what I told Shawn earlier, and it's the best I can come up with in this state. I microwave some meat and eat until my stomach hurts.

When I can't take another bite, misery seeps in, like the cold drafts under the doors. Just after a meal is the worst time. That's when I'm not eating, or looking forward to eating, so I have nothing to distract me from what I am.

A bad guy who does bad things for bad reasons. I'm not religious, but the word *damned* seems to cover it.

I clean up, lock the house. I don't want Shawn to come home and see my Toyota still in the drive, so I reverse out and head for Dallas.

Houston is waking up now. The roads are getting crowded. Drowsy office workers going one way, petrochemical engineers the other. Soccer moms taking surly kids to school. Long lines at every drive-through, headlights blurred by the haze of exhaust, drivers exiting with huge throwaway coffee cups in their hands and mouths already full of bacon. The radio shouts at me, on and on, like it's afraid I'll fall asleep at the wheel if given half a second of quiet.

Eventually rush hour ends, and everything settles. I escape onto the highway, the only traffic a truck blasting past. Just music on the radio now, something with slide guitar over a hip-hop beat.

Sixty miles out of Houston, I pull over at a rest stop. It would be safest to go the whole way to Dallas, make my alibi authentic. But I can't afford the gas, and it's not really today I need the alibi for. Last night is the issue. Plus, what if Warner happens to check where my phone is? Not a good look to go far from Houston so soon after the meeting.

I kill the engine and sit, thinking. About the dead guy, about Warner, about how much longer I can live like this. I was hired just over three months back. The traditional probation period is over, but my position only feels more tenuous.

I tell myself I'll stay at the rest stop for two hours, but I get hungry again after one. It's not the sort of hunger a roadside diner can fix, so I start the car and head home. Shawn is unlikely to notice that I wasn't gone long enough for a round trip to Dallas, and I can always tell him Jesse called when I was halfway there.

It's almost six pm when I tumble into bed after another meal. I'm too exhausted even to dream. A small mercy—my subconscious would have made Freud vomit.

A ringing phone wakes me.

I squint at the old clock radio by my bed. It reads 7.02. An hour of sleep is nowhere near enough, but it could be Warner. She'll be pissed if I don't pick up. I drag myself out of bed and hobble towards the landline. My stomach still aches.

By the time I get there, I'm awake enough to remember that Warner wouldn't use my landline. For some reason, I pick up anyway. 'Yes?'

It's a voice I haven't heard for a long time. The voice of my conscience.

'Timothy? This is Agent Reese Thistle, FBI. I need you to come to the Houston Field Office, right away.'

CHAPTER 4

My square house has four walls, and they all face south. How is this possible?

I should refuse. Thistle and I have known one another since we were in foster care together. My parents were shot in a home invasion, hers drove off a bridge with her in the back seat. We lost touch after she was adopted out, but when I was consulting for the corrupt director of the FBI Houston Field Office, she became my handler. We were drawn to each other in a way that was dangerous for both of us. There were only two possible outcomes for our relationship: me getting arrested, or her getting eaten. So I pretended I wasn't attracted to her, to keep her safe.

She didn't take it well.

'What do you need?' I hear myself ask.

'I'd rather not discuss that over the phone.' Her voice is flat. Hard to read.

Spiders of paranoia crawl across my scalp: *She knows.* About why I really rejected her, or about the gruesome work I do for Warner, or both.

Except if she knew, she wouldn't be calling me. She'd be breaking down my door with a SWAT team for backup.

Maybe she suspects, but doesn't have enough for an arrest. I should tell her I'm coming, and then grab everything I own and skip town.

'Is this a personal call?' I ask hopefully.

'Very professional. You coming or not?'

'I'm coming,' I say. 'Tomorrow?'

'What, you got yourself a nine-to-five? Riddles stopped paying the bills?'

Thistle knows about my side hustle solving puzzles and riddles. She doesn't know that it started out as a way to sell memorised credit card numbers.

'No,' I say.

'Then why not come right now? You're up. I'm here.'

Up? I check the phone in my pocket. It's seven am, not pm. I've been in bed for thirteen hours and change.

Or have I? I'm a sleepwalker. I look around the room for signs that I wandered during the night. Nothing seems to have moved.

'Fine,' I say. 'I'll be there in an hour.'

'Great. See you soon.'

I love her voice, even when it doesn't sound like it loves me. I open my mouth to say goodbye, but she's already hung up.

•

The Houston Field Office of the FBI isn't an imposing sight on the horizon. It looks like the office of a telecommunications or insurance company. Eight storeys of dull green windows and grubby concrete. Just the same, I'm nervous as I climb out of the Toyota.

It's not even a stolen car, for once. It belongs to Warner, or to a company owned by someone in her employ. I assume she's low-jacked it so she can track my movements. That's why I've parked it a couple of blocks away. Unfortunately, I can't ditch the phone. Warner might call. But yesterday, it seemed like she didn't often monitor the feed from the tracking apps. She had me dragged me into that diner without even checking where Francis had been. I figure my odds are good.

I shouldn't be here. I should be halfway to Mexico. But it's possible that Thistle doesn't want to arrest me. She might just need some information about one of my old cases. And if so, I can't pass up the chance to see her in real life, not just in a fantasy.

The dreams don't come every night, but they're not getting any less frequent. Sometimes it's a good dream, where Thistle and I live together like an ordinary couple, with a house and a dog and occasionally even kids. Other times it's a nightmare, where I hurt her.

In the good dreams, I'm not me. I'm some other guy, with a regular job and normal hobbies. Even my subconscious knows that Thistle couldn't love a person like me.

I scurry past some cafes and hotels and offices, head bowed against the cold like I'm at the north pole. Soon

I reach the front entrance of the field office. There's a new receptionist behind the desk—an older guy with a heavy brow who watches me with great suspicion as I come in.

'I'm here to see Agent Reese Thistle,' I say.

His gaze flicks down to my missing thumb. That often happens. It's not as though you count the fingers of everyone you meet, but somehow people notice.

'She's expecting me,' I add.

The guy grunts and picks up the phone. I strain to hear Thistle's voice as she tells him to let me in.

He buzzes me through the security door. Thistle doesn't come down to meet me. Probably a good sign. But I still take the stairs rather than the elevator, just in case this is some kind of trap—the cops could shut it down between floors, literally boxing me in.

The *Die Hard* escape method only works in movies, in case you were wondering. The trapdoor in the ceiling of an elevator car is always padlocked closed from above.

Walking along the grey corridor towards Thistle's cubicle, I pass the director's office. There's a new name on the door. The soft muttering of a female voice inside.

I knew the old director pretty well. He was a corrupt ex-cokehead, willing to falsify evidence, torture a suspect or even smuggle death-row cadavers to a cannibal if it would close a case. I don't know anything about the new director. Hopefully she doesn't know anything about me, either.

A muffled word catches my ear: 'Warner.'

My skin prickles. I lean closer to the door to listen. The new director could have said 'warn her'. Or it could be a coincidence, her discussing the notorious crime boss Charlie Warner at the exact moment that I arrived.

Someone's coming. I straighten up.

It's Maurice Vasquez—the head of comms intelligence. He's as handsome as a Bernini sculpture, with a straight nose, trimmed nails, slicked-back hair. He spends his time listening to wire taps, decrypting hard drives, reading hacked emails and text messages.

'Blake,' he says, 'what are you doing here?'

'Hi, Vasquez. Long time,' I say. 'How are you?'

He doesn't look pleased to see me. Maybe he caught me eavesdropping.

'I thought you were all done with this place,' he says.

'So did I. Thistle called me in.'

He raises his eyebrows. 'For a new case?'

That hadn't occurred to me. 'Not sure.'

'I'd advise you not to take it,' he says. 'You of all people know how dangerous this work can be.'

'I was thinking it might be about an old case.'

'Well, whatever it is, don't do anything dumb. Let me handle anything you're not sure about, okay?'

I'm oddly touched. 'Thanks, man. I'll see you around.'

He nods briskly, and strides away towards the elevators.

When I get to Thistle's cubicle, I see an unfamiliar man behind her desk. Comb-over, blue polo shirt, big watch. He looks me up and down.

'I'm looking for Agent Thistle,' I say.

He snorts, either at her or at me. 'You a lawyer?'

What? 'No. I'm—'

'Blake,' Thistle says from behind me, 'thanks for coming.'

My heart kicks as I turn. 'Any time.'

Thistle is wearing a crisp white blouse and a necklace of imitation pearls, bright against her ebony skin. Her hair is tied back in a ponytail, revealing earrings that match the necklace. The clothes and jewellery are cheap, but she looks good in them. I feel a moment of hope—maybe she's dressed up for me. Or, more likely, she's trying to prove that she's doing great without me.

She sees me looking at her outfit. 'I'm giving evidence in court later,' she says.

Oh. Nothing to do with me at all.

'This way.' She turns around and strides away. I keep my gaze on the back of her head as I follow.

Thistle's new cubicle is a little bigger than her old one, and closer to the windows. It's not a corner office, but it looks like a small promotion. Not too recent, though. She's unpacked all her stuff. A photo of her Jack Russell terrier, a framed bravery medal, a curved ergonomic keyboard that doesn't match the others in the building.

For the first time, I wonder why she was originally tasked with babysitting me while I was consulting. Not much of an assignment for a twelve-year veteran of the FBI. From what I saw, she was smart, hard-working and incorruptible—but she must have done something to piss off the old director. Maybe the new one likes her better.

She smooths down her skirt and sits at her desk, gestures to a swivel stool in the corner of her cubicle. I sit.

'How you been, Reese?' I ask.

She forces a smile. 'Fine, thanks. How about you?'

'Yeah, good.' I'm an addict with a steady supply, so I'm not unhappy, but not exactly happy either. I'm numb, which is the next best thing to non-existent.

'Glad to hear it,' Thistle says. 'Got a case I thought you might be able to help us with.'

'Oh.'

'I know you like the weird ones.' She taps her keyboard and the computer screen lights up. She types in a password. I watch her fingers: *DollyParton84*.

'Weird how?' I ask.

'Day before yesterday, a math professor at Braithwaite University leaves work,' she says. 'He calls his wife, tells her he's running late. Then he makes a withdrawal from an ATM.'

I stiffen. If Thistle is investigating one of Warner's victims, that's bad news. Either she'll solve the case and I'll be out of a job, or Thistle's shoes could show up on a beach somewhere. The latter is more likely. It wouldn't be the first time Warner has killed a cop.

'How much?' I ask.

'Huh?'

'How much was the withdrawal?'

'Two hundred and sixty bucks,' Thistle says. 'Why?'

'Did he have more than that in his account?'

'Yes. Don't tell me you've solved the case already?'

Warner's men would have withdrawn more. 'No,' I say. 'Sorry—just wanted to know if it sounded like run-away money.'

'Don't think so, but it's more than just day-to-day money, wouldn't you agree?'

'I would.' Theories are already bubbling up in my brain. I push them away. It's always tempting to come up with a solution too early.

'So after the withdrawal, the professor never comes home. His wife reports him missing the next morning. The Houston PD traces his phone signal to a garbage dump in Louisiana and throws the case to the FBI since it crossed state lines. But we went to the dump, and the phone itself is nowhere to be found. Believe me, we did some digging.' Thistle grimaces. 'No phone, no car, no body. No one at the dump knows anything. No one at the college knows anything. None of his friends or family members know anything.'

This doesn't sound like an especially weird case. Maybe Thistle just wanted to see me. I feel a dangerous little glow at the thought.

She looks at me expectantly. Apparently she's ready for my input.

'Are any of his contacts already known to the authorities?' I ask.

'None.'

'Does he gamble?'

'Everyone who knows him says no. I've been calling casinos, but no one has a record of him.'

'Drugs?'

'I found some pot at his home. Only a small amount—no sign that he was dealing. Nothing else suspicious in his apartment.'

'Was it his birthday?'

Thistle sucks in air through her teeth. 'How the hell did you guess that?'

Because I know how greedy people think. 'Okay,' I say, 'he's middle-aged, I assume, because he's a math professor. Maybe having a mid-life crisis. Thinking about all the things he never got the chance to do before he got married and had kids—does he have kids?'

Thistle nods. 'A daughter. Twenty-one.'

'Right. So the message to the wife means he was going to do something after work, something he didn't want her to know about. I thought it might be a birthday present to himself. If it's not gambling or drugs, it's sex. The amount of the ATM withdrawal narrows it down. Too large for a night out with his mistress, but too small to get far with a sex worker, too small to pay off a secret debt or to have someone killed—'

Thistle's eyebrows go up. 'Hold on, Blake. How many crimes are you planning to pin on our victim, exactly? And what kind of psycho has someone killed as a birthday present to themselves?'

'I'm just showing you why I ruled those things out,' I say. 'My bet is he went to a strip club. Got drunk, bought himself a couple of lap dances. After the cash ran out and the booze wore off, he was disgusted with himself. Maybe started thinking about how the strippers are the same age as his daughter, or his students. Then he committed suicide.'

Thistle leans back in her chair. 'That's an inspiring story,' she says. 'Let's leave aside for the moment that there are plenty of hitmen or sex workers who will perform their services for two hundred and sixty dollars—'

'Not discreetly,' I say. 'He was well-off, right? He would have wanted discretion.'

'But if it all went down like you say, where's his body?'

I shrug. 'The bay somewhere?'

'And his car?'

I open my mouth and shut it again.

'And how do you explain the phone trail to the dump?'

I'd forgotten about that part, too.

A voice behind me says, 'Mr Blake, I'm guessing?'

I look up. A woman is standing outside Thistle's cubicle. White, mid-forties, ash-blonde hair. Grey pantsuit. Make-up and high heels—someone not dressed for field work, but always prepared to go on camera. From that and the way Thistle has tensed up, I'm guessing this is her new boss.

'Timothy, this is Marianne Zinnen,' Thistle says. 'The new field office director.'

'Thank you for coming in, Mr Blake,' the director says, extending a hand with nails painted a subtle shade of maroon.

'You're welcome.' I shake her hand. She doesn't seem to notice my missing thumb.

'I do hope you can help us with this case. Gabriela Biggs is a close friend of mine. She and her daughter are frantic. And Kenneth's colleagues at the university, too.'

This isn't unnecessary detail. She's telling me to tread carefully when it comes to the family. But a missing university professor is more obvious than a missing cab driver or store clerk, so Zinnen is probably under political pressure to solve this case quickly.

'Mr Blake thinks it might be a suicide,' Thistle says.

'Oh, how awful,' Zinnen says. But there's relief in her eyes, too. The media loves pointing fingers, and if it's a suicide, those fingers will be pointed at the underfunded mental health services in Texas. A high-profile unsolved murder, on the other hand, could be blamed on her. 'Well, I hope you can help us find his remains,' she continues. 'The former director's notes indicate that you're the best man for the job.'

She's buttering me up. The last director hated me—the best his notes could possibly say is that I had a good solve rate. But . . .

Oh. I shrivel a little inside. Thistle doesn't want me here at all. Her boss pressured her into calling me.

'I'll do my best, ma'am,' I assure her.

She beams. 'Thank you. Let me know if there's anything at all you need.'

This is an empty offer. I'm only here because the FBI's budget is, as always, stretched to breaking point. But I play along.

'Will do,' I say.

'Agent Thistle,' Zinnen says, 'you have everything you need for this evening?'

'Yes,' Thistle says. 'Thanks.' I get the feeling she doesn't want me to know what this question is about.

Perhaps sensing this, Zinnen shakes my hand again and disappears back towards her office. She doesn't ask any questions about the evidence for my theory. This makes me think she was never a cop—just an administrator who rose through the ranks.

Thistle sighs heavily. 'All right. We'll check the strip clubs. What else you got?'

'I'd like to meet his wife, and his co-workers.'

'I don't want to use up too much of your time,' Thistle says, knowing my time is worthless. 'We still don't have the budget to pay you. So just tell us what you'd like to know about them, and I'll find out.'

I ask her point blank: 'You don't want me on this case, do you?'

Thistle keeps her voice low so the cops in the neighbouring cubicles won't overhear. 'Do you really want to be on it?'

Thistle is wrong about me in a lot of ways. She thinks I helped the FBI out of a sense of justice, when really I just liked the free food. And she thinks I don't like her—there's no way I could explain that I was rejecting her for her own safety. Now she has no idea why I would want to take this case when working with her would be so awkward.

'I do,' I say. Not ready to say goodbye.

Thistle looks neither pleased nor displeased by this. 'Fine,' she says, picking up her keys and a black coat, polyester made to look like wool. 'Where are we headed?'

'Wait,' I say. 'I need more information about Biggs.'

'You can read the file on the way.' Thistle leans back over her computer, selects a document and hits print. Papers start chugging out of her printer.

'I need the file to decide where we're—'

I stop dead. Because I've just seen Biggs's face come out of the printer. Skinny, greying hair, hollow cheeks. I know exactly where he is.

My freezer.

CHAPTER 5

What goes up and down without
moving or changing?

'You okay?' Thistle asks.

It's like standing on the deck of a tilting ship. 'Huh? Yeah. What?'

Thistle looks from the picture of Biggs to me and back. 'You know him?' she says.

'No. I expected him to be older, is all.'

'Why?'

'Well, he's a math professor.' My mind is racing. I'm in deep trouble. I've just volunteered for a case I can't allow myself to solve.

'Blake, if you know this guy . . .'

'I don't.'

'You knew it was his birthday.'

I look her in the eye. 'I guessed.'

My heartbeat is through the roof, but I'm good at keeping my face slack.

After a long moment, Thistle raises her hands. 'Okay. You were about to tell me where we were going.'

'The university,' I say quickly. His home is the best place to start, but I need to buy some time.

Thistle puts on her coat. 'Fine. Let's go.'

Down the staircase, out the door to the parking lot. Thistle unlocks a white Crown Vic. Different plates from her last one, sleeker interior. The FBI bought thousands of these when Ford discontinued them. No CD player in this one. I'm sure Thistle is missing it—she's a musician.

I open the case file, but it's hard to focus, knowing the information I need won't be in there.

Why were you naked in the woods, Biggs? The only mark on your body came from me, so who or what killed you, and how? And what the hell do I do now?

Maybe Biggs ate some poisonous mushrooms out in the woods. He could have been starving, or, since he was a pot user, maybe he thought they were hallucinogenic. I didn't see or smell any vomit, but maybe he kept them down. Do poisonous mushrooms make you feel hot, so you take off your clothes? I don't know. It's strange that he was so close to the road. He didn't get far at all before something happened to him.

I've been chewing my nails—now my hand freezes halfway to my mouth. If Biggs did eat toxic mushrooms, it's possible that I poisoned myself when I bit him. I remember hearing that certain types of mushrooms—death caps, they're called—cause your DNA to unravel. Your body withers away as though under attack from the world's most aggressive cancer.

That would serve me right.

Thistle doesn't speak as she drives us towards Braithwaite University. The silence is tense, but it gives me some time to scan the file. Biggs was an associate professor of mathematics who'd worked at the university for twelve years, tenured after seven. Before that he was a high school math teacher in Tennessee. He was fifty-one. Briefly hospitalised a couple of years ago, though the file doesn't say what for. Gabriela, his wife, is a forty-eight-year-old warehouse manager. His daughter, Hope, dropped out of college to do graphic design jobs for a bank on Lamar Street. She mostly works from home. They all live together in Southampton. I can't see any red flags, other than a professor's daughter being a dropout.

'Anyone else gone missing from the university?' I ask.

'A young woman named Abbey Chapman vanished, but that was about seven months ago,' Thistle says. 'And five weeks back an early-morning jogger was assaulted on a bike path near the campus.'

'A teacher?'

'No. Unconnected to the college, although he said the three perps—all men—looked young. Might have been students screwing around. They punched him in the head, took his phone, ran off. He couldn't describe them well enough for us to ID them.'

'How many students at the college?'

'Twenty-eight thousand undergrads, eleven thousand graduate students. Most of them won't be there today, though. Classes ended last week.'

I spend a minute calculating odds. With that many people, it would be unusual if there wasn't a disappearance and an assault within the last few months. Probably not relevant to my case. But I stir the information into the batter anyway.

'Vasquez seemed kind of tense,' I say.

'No doubt,' Thistle says. 'He's on the Warner task force.'

Uh oh. 'The what?'

'It's an organised crime case. Only a small group of agents are working it, because they're worried about corruption. So the workload is huge, and Vasquez is still supposed to manage incoming communications for other cases.'

The FBI is investigating Warner again. Maybe I should try to get close to Vasquez, find out what the group knows. Or maybe I should stay as far away from him as possible.

'You're not on the task force?' I ask.

'I wasn't invited,' Thistle says.

She has suddenly become very intent on the surrounding traffic, deliberately discouraging further questions.

'I need to know that you can be professional,' she says finally.

I look at her. She keeps her eyes on the road.

'You know I can,' I say.

'I mean it. If working with me is going to make you uncomfortable, I don't want your help.'

I need to be on this case so I can sabotage it. Thistle is resourceful. Without my interference, she might follow Biggs's trail all the way to my freezer.

'You need me,' I say.

'I don't, actually. I was solving cases just fine until you turned up. I've been solving them fine since you left, too.'

'Your boss thinks you could use my help.'

Thistle's nose twitches. 'She doesn't know you like I do.'

'What do you mean by that?' That fear again: *She knows.*

'You "solved" our last case by accidentally wandering into the killer's house,' Thistle says. 'If I hadn't identified him with actual detective work, you'd be dead. I signed an NDA, so I can't tell my boss about that. But if I could, she might not be so keen on your help.'

'Maybe,' I concede.

She says nothing. If I can't mollify her, she might find some way to kick me off the case, or start working it when I'm not around.

'Look,' I say, 'I get why you don't want me here. I was an asshole.'

'Yup.'

'I'll work this case with you, and then I'll disappear. Next time the director asks for my help, I'll tell her I'm unavailable. What do you say?'

Thistle spins the wheel, taking the Crown Vic into one

of the campus parking lots. She glances down at my mutilated hand. A thin smile.

'I give that plan two thumbs up,' she says.

•

The campus is huge, with square lawns separating the sprawling yellow-brick buildings. There's no one around, maybe because there's nowhere to shelter from the cold wind, and only a few cars in the parking lot when we pull in at eight forty-five.

'What kind of car did Biggs drive?' I ask.

'A blue Prius. Security footage shows it leaving this parking lot at six pm on the day he went missing.'

I look around, noting the position of the cameras. They don't cover the road, so we can't tell which way he turned. The missing car wouldn't be odd if he skipped town—but I know he didn't. So where is it?

I stick my numb hands in my pockets. 'Who did you talk to last time you were here?'

'All his students, and all the staff in his department.'

'Including cleaners?'

'Correct.' Thistle points. 'Math department's this way.'

'Let's go to the cafeteria first.'

'I'm not buying you breakfast.'

A shame. 'It seems likely that our victim spent time there. I just want to get a look at it.'

'Whatever.' Thistle follows me into one of the buildings.

There are three food shops inside—a sandwich place for those who like to eat healthy, a fried food place for those who don't, plus a coffee shop. Not many students around. Most are probably studying for exams, or they've gone home for the winter break. A few young people are at tables, eating waffles or eggs one-handed while they scroll through their phones. A couple of others lounge on bean-bags in the corner.

'No teachers,' Thistle observes. 'Seems unlikely that our victim ate here.'

I grunt, and approach the sandwich place. From Biggs's build, I'm guessing he ate mostly healthy stuff.

As I pass the students, I get a flash of the relationships in each group. A girl is talking about her accomplishments in a video game she's been playing, while the kids around her pretend to care. Five other teens are sitting in a circle, close enough that they must know each other, but they're all looking at their iPads, so they must not like each other that much. A chisel-jawed guy who looks like he's here on a football scholarship is talking to three wide-eyed girls who could be freshmen. He's trying to impress them, and it's working on two of them.

When I reach the sandwich place, the woman behind the counter—blonde hair under a white hairnet, latex gloves, pitted skin—watches me like a TV show she's not interested in.

'My name's Timothy Blake, and I'm a civilian consultant for the FBI,' I say. 'This is Agent Reese Thistle. Have you seen this man?'

I pull out the picture of Biggs from the file.

The woman looks at it and blinks slowly, like a sloth.

'Egg salad sandwich,' she says finally. 'On low-sodium bread. He comes in on Wednesdays and Fridays. Always gets a diet soda, too.'

Thistle and I look at each other. Witnesses aren't usually this good.

'You know his name?' I ask, testing.

The woman shakes her head. 'Sorry.'

'Seen him since last Friday?'

'Not here. Around the campus maybe.'

'Maybe? You're not sure?'

'No.'

Thistle speaks up. 'Did he usually eat with anybody?'

'Yep. A younger guy. Ham and cheese sandwich on white bread.'

'Seen that guy lately?'

The woman looks around. 'He was here a second ago,' she says. 'Can't see him now.'

I scan the room. The crowd has changed since we walked in. Six more people have arrived, and three have left. Only one of the missing people was male—the chisel-jawed guy. The girls he was talking to are still here, holding identical business cards.

'Thanks for your help,' I tell the woman, and walk over to the girls. They regard me much more suspiciously than the last guy.

'Excuse me,' I say. 'Can I have a look at that?'

I snatch the business card from one of the girls—a short redhead wearing a pink sweater and hoop earrings.

'Hey!' she says.

The name on the business card is Shannon Luxford. He's a grad student/teaching assistant. Wondering what kind of narcissistic TA orders business cards, I memorise the phone number and email addresses, then I hand the card back.

'Thanks,' I say, and walk away before she can make a thing of it. I push through the doors out into a freezing courtyard.

Thistle catches up to me quickly. 'How about you let me take point next time?' She sounds annoyed. 'You remember that you have zero qualifications, right?'

A few people are walking back and forth. I turn around and around, looking for the missing man.

'What are you doing?' Thistle asks.

'I saw Biggs's dining partner before he left,' I say. 'He's a white guy with dark hair. Muscular build. Looks like Clark Kent, but without the glasses.'

'So he looks like Superman,' Thistle says dryly. 'Was his name Shannon Luxford?'

I frown. 'How did you know that?'

'Because I've already interviewed him. He's a TA in the math department.'

'Well, I want to talk to him.'

'Sure. Come on.' Thistle starts walking. 'But I don't know what he'll tell you that he didn't tell me.'

As we walk past a vending machine, I note that the prices are high. 'What does tuition here cost?'

'About ten grand per year, or thirty for students from out of state.'

I whistle through crooked teeth. 'A pretty good scam. Do these kids know they can just look stuff up in the library?'

'Not if they want jobs at the end of it,' Thistle points out.

'Exactly. The college has convinced companies not to hire people without degrees, so they can squeeze tens of thousands of dollars out of parents who don't want their kids to be unemployed. It's a scam.'

'Uh-huh. How would you like to get open-heart surgery from a doctor without a degree?'

'Doctors learn at actual hospitals,' I say. 'The university only provides the piece of paper.'

Thistle glares at me. 'I learned a lot at college. Made some friends for life, too.'

I want to remind her that those friends had parents who could afford the tuition fees. The kinds of friends I never got to meet. College is where the walls go up, stopping the rich and poor from ever knowing one another in more than a superficial way. But it looks like I've already pushed her too far.

'Your view might be coloured by your personal experience,' Thistle says. 'Or lack of it.'

I feel a stab of disappointment. She was supposed to be on my side. We both grew up poor in the foster system, before she was adopted out. I knew she'd made something of herself since then, but I didn't think she'd forgotten what it was like to be hungry.

'Maybe,' I say. 'Sorry. I was just wondering if there might be a money angle to this. What's Biggs's salary?'

'Eighty-eight K.'

He'll never be a billionaire, especially not now that he's dead. But his income was well above the average in Texas. Maybe someone thought he was worth robbing.

We reach the math department, which looks more like the art department. A garden of native shrubs surrounds the building, the windows have frosted patterns, and a teal sculpture shimmers out the front, metal twisted into smaller and smaller spiral patterns. I get the feeling that the shapes might represent fractals, but I only half know what fractals are.

Thistle leads me upstairs towards Biggs's office. The building is quiet—I can feel how dense the concrete walls are, under a coat of pale yellow paint.

We pass a row of study nooks in the corridor. A stunning woman hovers near one of them talking to a female student. She looks like she just came from a photo shoot with *Vogue*. Thirty-something, her porcelain face partially curtained by gleaming blonde hair, her Barbie-doll figure wrapped in a high-waisted grey skirt and chocolate blouse. She bends over like a 1950s flight attendant, straight spine, hips back, showing a picture on her phone to the student. The student seems unable to resist a peek down the woman's cleavage.

The woman glances at me then quickly looks away, alarmed. We're about the same age, but I'm withered by hard living and missing a thumb—I feel suddenly guilty for even occupying the same dimension as her.

Thistle and I walk past her. When we're out of earshot, Thistle says, 'Was she your type?'

She keeps her voice level, but I don't think I'm imagining the bitterness in it. I'd much rather be with Thistle than with the blonde, or with anyone. But I can't tell her that.

'She didn't look like a teacher,' I say instead. 'Or a student, or a cleaner, or a parent. You think this place gets many visitors from outsiders?'

'You think a teacher can't look that good?'

'I think a teacher that age can't afford those clothes.'

We've reached a door with a sign on it. SHANNON LUXFORD.

'Is it normal for a teaching assistant to have his own office?' I ask Thistle.

She shrugs, and knocks on the door.

I didn't expect him to be in—most people don't close the door if they are—but he is. The lock clicks, and Shannon Luxford appears.

Up close, he looks less like a superhero. His eyes aren't quite symmetrical, and he has a pimple under one ear. But he's taken care with his appearance. His hair is curled perfectly at the front, and it's short enough at the back to indicate that he's had a haircut within the last two weeks. He smells of expensive aftershave and fabric softener. I'd guess his age at twenty-two or twenty-three.

'Can I help you?' His eyes flick from me to Thistle, and a smile spreads across his face. His gaze lingers on her breasts. 'Agent . . . Thistle, right? Nice to see you again.'

'This is my associate, Timothy Blake,' Thistle says. 'We just had some routine follow-up questions. Do you have a minute?'

'Sure.' Luxford opens his office door wider and steps back. '*Mi casa es su casa.*'

There's a new stiffness in his neck, and the tendons are standing out in his wrists. This could mean that he's nervous. Maybe he's expecting bad news about his boss. Or maybe he's always nervous around cops, like I am.

'Can I get you anything?' he asks. 'Coffee? Tea? Water?'

'No thanks,' Thistle says. 'We—'

'I'll take a coffee,' I say.

Thistle grits her teeth.

'Uh, sure,' Luxford says. 'Cream? Sugar?'

'Both, please,' I say. 'And salt.'

He blinks. 'Salt?'

'Just a pinch,' I say.

He nods. 'Reduces the bitterness, right? They drink it that way in Japan. I go skiing there every winter.'

I prefer salted coffee because it tastes like blood. I doubt that people drink it in Japan. But he came up with the story almost instantly. Either he's a practised liar, or someone in Japan has played an excellent prank on him.

He calls out the door, 'Liz, can you grab a Japanese coffee for my guest? Sugar, cream and salt. You heard me.'

He closes the door without waiting for a response. I assume teaching assistants don't have secretaries—he might be in the habit of using students like servants.

He sits down on the other side of his desk, which is too big for the room. His office is on the second floor, and his window overlooks the courtyard we just walked through. A wi-fi router blinks in the corner. There's a bookshelf, the books themselves hidden behind trophies and tchotchkes. A small, tacky statue of a fish with dull red scales looks particularly out of place on the top shelf.

Thistle and I sit on two squishy swivel chairs, possibly stolen from other departments. Mine has JOURNALISM scratched into one of the arms. The framed photos on Luxford's desk—him with some skis, him getting a trophy in high school—are all facing outwards. They're designed for visitors. No family in them. A Zippo lighter with a satin finish sits near a silver ashtray, despite the non-smoking signs all over the building and the smoke detector right above.

There's a strange wooden device on his desk next to the printer. A horizontal rod with thirteen discs impaled on it, capital letters carved into the outside of the rims.

Luxford sees me looking.

'You like that?' He doesn't wait for a response. 'It's called a wheel cipher. Thomas Jefferson invented it in 1795. Each disc has all twenty-six letters in a slightly different order, and a unique number. So you can spin the discs to make a row of letters which spells a message. Then you write down the letters from a different row, which will look like gibberish. Only someone else with the same discs in the same order will be able to decode it.'

'Interesting,' Thistle says convincingly. 'Where'd you get it?'

'A thankyou gift from the professor.'

'Thanking you for what?'

He smiles modestly.

'Seems like a lot of work,' I say. 'Couldn't you do the same thing with a pen and paper? Just write down A equals F, B equals X, or whatever?'

'That's the clever part,' Luxford says. 'With a wheel cipher, A can equal a different letter each time it shows up. So you can't just look for the most common letter and assume that it's E. Although if you sent enough messages using the same sequence of discs, a computer could still use letter frequency to crack it.'

Now that I understand, I automatically scan the letters on the discs. Just nonsense, in its current configuration. I look away when I realise I've started memorising the rows. Wasting brain space.

'Who has the other one?' I ask.

'No one,' he says. 'It's decorative.'

'Oh.'

The light fades from Luxford's eyes as he realises we're not going to ask any more questions about the cipher.

'So,' he asks, 'any progress on the case?'

'We're still interviewing witnesses,' Thistle says. 'I don't suppose you've remembered anything else about Professor Biggs's movements on Tuesday?'

'Sorry,' Luxford says. 'Like I said, I was helping students all day.'

I glance at Thistle. She nods slightly—she's confirmed this with the students.

I let the silence linger for a moment, to see what he fills it with. Maybe he'll ask how Biggs's family is doing. Maybe he'll ask which angles we're looking at.

He does neither. 'It'll just be brewed coffee, I'm afraid,' he says finally. 'I have an espresso machine at home. Nineteen bars of pressure.'

So he's rich, and keen to show it.

'Those girls you were talking to this morning,' I say, 'were they your students?'

'Which girls?' He looks honestly perplexed.

'In the cafeteria. You gave them business cards.'

He laughs. 'Oh! No, I don't know them. I was just being friendly.'

'You try to befriend all the students?' I ask. 'Or just the girls?'

He shrugs, not looking embarrassed. This could mean that he's honest to a fault, not caring or unaware how he comes across to people. But the aftershave, the hair and the outfit don't fit with that. It's possible that he's not embarrassed because hitting on students isn't so bad compared to other things he's done.

There's a knock at the door. Luxford says, 'Come.'

A young woman walks in, holding a cup of coffee. It's the same student I saw talking to the blonde beauty in the study nook outside. She has braided hair and a nose ring, and is in a summer dress despite the weather. She wears black leggings underneath, like a dancer. She looks faintly confused, as if Luxford has never instructed her to get coffee before, and she's just now wondering if it was in the job description.

'Thanks, Liz,' Luxford says without getting up. He points at me. 'Right here.'

Liz hands me the coffee with a glare, apparently deciding that this is all my fault. Then she leaves without a word.

I sip the coffee, watching Luxford. Most people wince when they see me drinking coffee with salt in it. He doesn't.

'Do you know what Professor Biggs does on the weekends?' I ask.

Luxford looks as though he's never really considered it. Like his boss just ceases to exist between Friday and Monday.

'Just reads books, I guess,' he says. 'About math.'

'What area of math does he specialise in?'

'Geometry.'

'Does he go hiking?' I ask, still looking for a connection to the body in the woods.

A smug smile. 'That's geography.'

'Oh.' I let him pretend that I misunderstood. 'The wheel cipher doesn't look like geometry.'

'Geometry was his job; cryptography was his hobby.'

'Did he have friends who shared this hobby?' Thistle puts in. 'A club, maybe?'

'Not that I know of.'

'What about shooting?' I ask. 'Has he ever talked about hunting buddies, or trips?'

Thistle sends me a sidelong glance. Maybe I've been too specific. I need to find out why Biggs was in the woods without revealing that he was there.

'I don't think so,' Luxford says.

I put the coffee down, and chew a fingernail. Then

I deliberately rip a chunk out of it, and suck some air through my teeth. A show of pain. 'Ow.'

'What's wrong?' Thistle asks.

'Just broke a nail. See?' I show her my finger, where the missing piece has left a small part of my raw flesh exposed. Then I show Luxford.

Again, he doesn't wince. 'Nasty,' he says.

Blood starts to well up. 'You got a bandaid, or some gauze?' I ask. 'I don't want to bleed on your carpet.'

That gets him moving. 'I'll find something,' he says, and hurries out the door.

Immediately I go around to the other side of his desk and start opening drawers.

Thistle jumps up. 'Blake—what are you doing?'

I keep rummaging through Luxford's stuff. Pens. Notepads. Two keys on a small ring. Phone chargers. Glossy photo paper for his printer. An address book, probably for passwords. 'He's a sociopath,' I say, 'and he's hiding something.'

Thistle grabs my arm. It's been so long that her touch is electric. 'Stop! You can't do this without a warrant.'

'We won't get one. Do you want to find Biggs, or not?'

I've uncovered a bottle of vodka. Probably against the campus rules, but not illegal.

'I can't let you do this,' Thistle says.

'Then arrest me.'

She hesitates. And in that moment, I find what I'm looking for.

CHAPTER 6

What was the first invention that could be used to see through walls?

One of the drawers feels wrong. It's heavier than it should be, and shallower than the others. There's a little groove on one side of the bottom, just wide enough for a thumbnail.

All my nails are bitten to the quick, so I use one of Luxford's pens to lever out the false bottom. Underneath I find a photo, printed on glossy paper. It's a picture of Luxford's office. A young woman is sprawled across Luxford's desk, chestnut hair fanned out, skirt hiked up, panties around her ankles.

Again, Thistle tries to stop me. 'Blake, you—'

I hand her the photo, and she stops talking. There are more pictures underneath. The same young woman in different positions. She's not supporting herself in any of the photos. She looks half-asleep, or drugged.

Underneath those pictures, there are even more. A different woman this time—Asian, naked except for high-heeled shoes. After her, there's a redhead with a torn dress exposing the freckles on her stomach.

I hand the photos I've found to an increasingly alarmed Thistle and keep digging. There are dozens of women in hundreds of photos. All the women look semi-conscious, and all the pictures were taken in this office from the same high angle.

I look around the room and walk over to Luxford's bookshelf. The fish on the top shelf catches my eye. The glass eye is swollen and dark. I can see the camera lens behind it.

The lens expands as I get closer, adjusting to the changing light. I look back at the photos in Thistle's hands. I don't think they're photos—I think they're screenshots. This is a video camera. And it's running.

In the corner, the lights on the router are flickering furiously. Information is being transmitted.

And Luxford should have been back by now.

I glance out the window just in time to see him walking across the courtyard towards the parking lot.

'Thistle! He's on the move.'

'On it.' Thistle runs out the door.

I don't follow her. By the time she gets down the stairs, he'll be gone, and we won't see which way he went.

The window is locked. I open one of the desk drawers, where I saw the two keys. One of them fits. I push the window open and climb out onto the ledge.

The drop is maybe fifteen feet. No time to think about it. I push myself off the ledge and plummet down towards the garden of shrubs. There's a moment of sickening weightlessness, the air rushing in my ears. I hit the ground hard and collapse, the shock numbing my legs. The branches take deep gouges out of my arms. I scramble to my feet and take off after Luxford.

He has a head start, but he's not running as fast as I am. He doesn't want to call attention to himself, and doesn't yet know he's being pursued.

He turns a corner into a wide tunnel between two buildings, breaking my line of sight. When I turn the corner, there he is again, headed for the parking lot. Faster now.

At first I'm fifty feet behind his back. Then forty feet, blood dripping from my arms. Thirty. My heart is going to burst. I'm not in the best shape.

He may not have noticed me yet, but someone else has. 'Yo, Shannon, watch out!'

Luxford turns his head, sees me, and says, 'Oh, shit!'

He puts on a burst of speed. I'm older than him, and malnourished—I don't have a hope of catching him. Especially when someone else comes out of my blind spot and crash-tackles me.

I slam into the cold concrete, hard. The impact pulps the flesh of my left shoulder, but my head doesn't hit the ground.

My attacker keeps me pinned down. He's a student, big, white, with close-set eyes and bleached hair in a Caesar cut.

'Stay down,' he snarls.

His thick, veiny neck is within reach of my teeth. Blood pulsing just beneath the surface. So many vulnerable tubes in there. The carotid, the jugular, the trachea, the oesophagus. Instinct takes over. Without thinking, I open my mouth and—

'FBI. Get off him, right now.'

The guy looks over at Thistle, who has a stun gun levelled on him. He climbs off me and raises his hands. 'Whoa! I didn't do anything. I was trying to help.'

The bloodlust recedes back to low tide. I stand up, shaking. I almost killed that guy.

A crowd of onlookers has gathered. A few are filming with their phones from a safe distance. Luxford is gone.

'Shoot as much video as you like,' Thistle shouts, 'but uploading even a single second of it will be considered obstruction of justice. You got that?'

It's a misdemeanour at worst, punishable only by a fine. But the grumbling students put away their phones. No point filming something if they can't show it to anyone.

'You all right, Blake?' Thistle asks.

'He went that way,' I say, and start to run towards the parking lot.

Thistle overtakes me quickly. Her breathing doesn't sound as ragged as mine; all FBI agents have to pass a fitness test where they run three hundred yards in fifty seconds.

When she gets to the parking lot, she doesn't pause

to scan the parked vehicles—she keeps running up the campus driveway, maybe hoping to spot a retreating car.

I can taste my own blood at the back of my throat, so I stop running when I reach the lot. I look around at the parked cars. No one in any of them. I flop down on the asphalt. No one hiding behind or underneath. I can't see any clues to identify Luxford's vehicle.

This is a disaster. If the police don't catch him, I'll never get to find out what he knows. If they do, they'll find out his secrets, which could lead them to where Biggs died, which might then lead them to me.

Assuming he knows anything at all. I can't see a connection between his collection of homemade porn and Biggs's death.

Thistle's coming back. 'He's gone,' she says.

•

We're halfway to Biggs's apartment when my phone starts buzzing in my pocket.

It's the burner Charlie Warner gave me. The one I'm supposed to keep on my person at all times.

I don't want Warner to know that I'm working for the FBI again, and I definitely can't let Thistle realise that I'm working for Warner.

'You gonna get that?' Thistle asks.

'No.' I pull the phone out of my pocket. Private number, but it can only be Warner or one of her goons. I reject the call, pocket the phone and hold my palms in front of the heater. Cold like this brings back painful memories of when I was homeless. Some days I worried about losing fingers to frostbite. Seems ironic now, since the room I lost my thumb in was plenty warm.

'When we worked our last case together,' Thistle says, 'you told me you didn't have a cell phone.'

'It's new,' I say.

'Sure.'

I change the subject. 'Did you put a BOLO out on Luxford's car?'

'I can't,' she says. 'Not without probable cause.'

'None of those young women looked like they knew they were on camera. They barely looked conscious. Some might even have been underage. That's probable cause of three crimes right there.'

The photos themselves are in an evidence bag on the back seat. But I don't think the forensics team at the field office will find anything useful. We already know who took the pictures, and where.

I wonder why Luxford kept printouts of the photos in his office. Seems risky. I'd like to examine them right now. But with so much flesh on display, Thistle might notice how it affects me. She could misinterpret my interest. Or, worse, interpret it correctly.

'This is why you don't open a suspect's desk without a search warrant,' Thistle says through gritted teeth. 'We can't use any of the photos you found. I can get some agents watching his house, but I can't get authorisation to search it. Without other evidence, we can't charge him. Another predator goes free. Nice work, Blake.'

'He would have gone free either way,' I say. 'No one suspected him.'

'One of those women would have come forward eventually,' Thistle says. 'And then so would the others.'

'How many more women would he have exploited in the meantime?'

Thistle squeezes the steering wheel like she's trying to crush it. 'There's no point solving crimes if you can't charge the perps, Blake.'

For me there is. I take cases not because the bad guy gets punished, but because I get so wrapped up in the puzzles that my hunger disappears. When I was searching Luxford's desk, I completely forgot that I was supposed to be sabotaging this case rather than solving it.

I remember the enthusiasm in Luxford's voice when he talked about the wheel cipher. It was the only time in the conversation when he didn't seem like a narcissistic asshole. Maybe, like me, he's a monster except when he's focused on something that really interests him.

'We can leave one of the photos out in the open,' I say. 'Let them be discovered by Liz. She'd recognise his office.'

'Now you're talking about evidence tampering.'

'But he couldn't prove we did it.'

'You don't get it, do you? I am *law enforcement*,' Thistle says. 'I don't get to make up my own rules, and nor do you.'

She's crossed that line before—admittedly not as far as I have. Maybe something happened between now and then that has made her stricter.

Maybe that something was me.

'You didn't bring me in to catch a sleazy TA,' I say. 'I'm here to find a missing math professor. Now we have some leverage over Luxford. We can use it to find out what he knows, even if we can't charge him.'

'For all we know, Luxford has nothing to do with Biggs's disappearance.'

'You think it's a coincidence that there was a sexual predator in his department?'

'It's college. There's probably a sexual predator in every department,' Thistle says. 'If you're so sure Luxford is involved, we should be going to his house, not driving to Biggs's place.'

We should—except I don't want Thistle with me when I find Luxford.

'He'll turn up,' I say. 'But Biggs is my priority. I want to meet his wife and daughter.'

'Fine. But so help me, if you touch a single thing in their apartment without asking for permission, I'll arrest you.'

'That might not inspire much confidence with Biggs's family.'

'I mean it, Blake. I'm *this* close to kicking your ass off the case. To hell with the director.'

'Okay, okay.' I turn to the window, and watch the crummy parts of Houston disappear as we drive towards Southampton. The houses get bigger, the lawns greener, the cars shinier. Most of them even have four wheels, which is a nice change from where I live. Apartment buildings on the horizon.

'I want to know if Biggs's prints are on any of those photos,' I say.

'You think he and Luxford might have worked together?'

'I'd like to rule it out.'

Thistle nods. 'So would I. But Biggs doesn't have a criminal record, so we don't have his prints on file. No DNA, either.'

'Can't we get both those things from his house? Prints off his keyboard, DNA off his toothbrush?'

'Toothbrush DNA is hit and miss. Hairbrush, too, unless you get a follicle. It would be more reliable to get a cheek swab from his wife and his daughter, compare the two samples and extrapolate Biggs's genome from that. But we don't have much of a budget for this, and there's a huge backlog at the field office. It'll take us a day or two to get someone to analyse the prints, and DNA will take even longer. Remember, this isn't a homicide investigation.'

'Yet,' I say.

CHAPTER 7

*Three people fall out of a boat.
Only two get their hair wet. Why?*

Mrs Radfield never told us that potential parents were coming to visit, but I always knew. She'd ask more questions than usual. 'Have you brushed your teeth? Change that shirt. Where are your shoes?' Things she didn't care about, most days. And she always fiddled with my hair, trying to push down that bit at the side, and sometimes snipping off the hairs she'd missed last time I was shorn.

Thistle—or Arty, as I knew her then—always sensed it too. She looked amazing on those days. Clean clothes, jewellery she'd found somewhere and hidden from the other kids. Hair pulled back into a neat bun, exposing her bare neck, like she was trying to seduce a vampire. No wonder she got out.

I would sit on my bunk, taking deep breaths, while the

other kids played outside. I didn't want to risk joining them, because I might trip over. If the parents didn't take me, and I had muddy knees, Mrs Radfield would assume that was why they'd turned me down. She'd hit me. Only once, and only with her hand—but she was bigger than me, and it was scary.

After hours of waiting I heard voices downstairs. 'Come on up,' Mrs Radfield said. 'I'll introduce you to Timothy. He's quiet, but he's a sweet kid. I think you'll get on well.'

'Timothy?' a woman's voice said uncertainly.

'Timothy,' a man's voice repeated.

'You could always change the name if you wanted to,' Mrs Radfield said. She was pretty desperate to get rid of me, and wasn't doing a good job of hiding it.

The government was paying her to feed and clothe us, and she was making quite a lot of money, because she never bought any food or clothing. Our outfits came from donation bins, and the food had been thrown out by local supermarkets when it reached its sell-by date. But now I was stretching the limits of Mrs Radfield's scam. I ate too much. And the taller I got, the harder it was to find free clothes that fit me.

The door creaked open. 'Timothy?' Mrs Radfield said. 'Are you in here?'

'Yes, ma'am,' I said, standing up from my bunk and smoothing down my shirt. I suddenly wished I had been pretending to do something. Reading Charlotte Brontë, or even just staring out the window. Now I looked like a weird kid who sat around doing nothing.

'Can I introduce you to someone?'

'Of course. I like meeting new people.'

Tone it down, I told myself. For Christ's sake, act normal.

'This is Mr and Mrs Veerhuis,' Mrs Radfield said. 'They're visiting today.'

'Call me Bob,' the man said. He was a big guy with thinning hair and a neat little moustache. 'And this is Lillian.'

His wife, a narrow-waisted brunette in a yellow sundress, nodded to me, but said nothing.

'Really nice to meet you.' I shook Bob's hand. His grip was limp, like he was afraid of breaking my fingers.

I wanted to wipe my sweaty palm on my pants before shaking hands with Lillian, but it would have looked like I thought Bob's skin had been unclean. I held my hand out for Lillian, and she took it.

'Hello, Timothy,' she said. Her smile didn't reach her eyes.

She's scared, I thought. She can tell there's something wrong with me.

We all stood in awkward silence for a moment. I wondered what to say. What were the magic words that would make Bob and Lillian take me with them when they left?

'What do you do, sir?' I asked, not really caring. I knew people liked talking about themselves.

Mrs Radfield winced, and I knew I'd misstepped. Bob and Lillian would think I was choosy. Looking for a rich couple. But I wasn't. I'd take anyone who would get me out of there.

'I'm in landscape architecture,' Bob said. 'Do you know what that means?'

I nodded.

'And I'm a dispatch operator,' Lillian said. 'We might have talked before. Have you ever called 911, Timothy?'

'No.'

A beat.

'Timothy solves puzzles,' Mrs Radfield said finally. 'Don't you, Timothy?'

The couple looked at me expectantly.

'I love puzzles,' I said, which was an exaggeration. I was just good at them. 'Want to see?'

'Sure,' Bob said. He followed me over to my bunk, and Lillian reluctantly fell into step behind.

I showed them one of the puzzles I had been working on—a loop of thick wire threaded through two holes in a piece of polished wood. I had found it among the donations. None of the other kids had been interested.

There were no instructions. I assumed the goal was to remove the piece of wood without breaking the wire. It was a hard puzzle—much harder than jigsaws, Rubik's Cubes or riddles—and so I thought it would impress Bob and Lillian.

Except that I hadn't solved it yet. Suddenly my cheeks flushed. What if the solution was obvious to Bob and Lillian? What if they thought I was stupid for not seeing it? They wouldn't adopt a stupid child.

I jiggled the wood back and forth against the wire. The rattling echoed around the big, cold bedroom. I could feel them watching me as I struggled to figure out the puzzle. Tears stung the corners of my eyes.

'It's okay, Timothy,' Bob said. 'You don't have to—'

'No! I can do it.'

I fiddled for another frantic minute, dismissing idea after idea. Then, at last, the answer became clear. As with all good puzzles, once you saw the solution, you realised it couldn't be any other way. I tipped the puzzle upside down, and bent the wire just enough that two loops fit through one hole. Then I slid the wooden piece the entire way around, and watched as it came loose, just like a magic trick.

I brandished the piece at my future parents. *Love me*, I thought. *Please.*

But they weren't impressed. Their eyes were wide with alarm. Clutching the puzzle like a weapon, red-faced and sweating, I must have looked obsessive. Maybe dangerous.

'Perhaps you'd like to take Timothy out for a hot chocolate?' Mrs Radfield suggested. 'There's a lovely little cafe just—'

'Maybe another time,' Lillian said. She worked in law enforcement. She had probably seen dangerous obsessives before.

They were leaving. My stomach churned. 'How about tomorrow? We could—'

'Tomorrow's not good for us,' Bob said, picking up on his wife's unease. 'Some other time.'

Mrs Radfield shot me a glare—*You fucked up again!*—and then led them to the door.

'Nice to meet you, Timothy,' Lillian lied, as they walked out.

As soon as they were gone, I pressed my ear to the door. Maybe I would hear them saying that they secretly liked me. Or that they might come back to see me in a different setting.

Instead, I heard Bob say, 'We're still thinking. In fact, we were wondering if a daughter might suit us better.'

A few days later, Thistle was gone. She even got to keep her name.

Mrs Radfield didn't hit me in the end. But I agonised for weeks, convincing myself that Bob and Lillian had been the perfect parents—rich, smart, kind—and I had screwed up my chance.

Now I'm looking up at Biggs's apartment building. Modern, with four storeys of polished glass. A doorman. Probably a pool on the roof and a gym somewhere inside. A roller shutter protects the underground parking lot, but there are a few empty visitor spaces out front. It's the sort of place the wealthy live if they're afraid of the poor. If an uprising happens, they're ready to wait it out in style.

It's exactly the sort of place I used to imagine Bob and Lillian lived in.

'How are your folks?' I ask Thistle. 'Bob and Lillian?'

'I don't talk to them much,' Thistle says. 'My divorce pissed them off.' She looks at me. 'How did you know their names?'

'They almost adopted me.'

'Really? Jesus, that's weird to think about.'

'A *Sliding Doors* moment,' I say.

'We were nearly siblings.'

'Or I was nearly you.'

She gives me a withering look, as if I couldn't possibly have been her.

All the windows have open curtains except for one. I bet that's Biggs's apartment. A home in mourning.

Thistle pulls into one of the visitor spaces. 'Let me start, okay?' she says. 'They're hurting. They think Biggs either abandoned them or is dead in a ditch somewhere.'

I wonder if my freezer would be considered nicer than a ditch. 'Okay.'

To get to the front entrance of the apartment building we have to walk along a winding path through a well-manicured garden. Yellow roses everywhere, the bushes carefully pruned. A discreet steel box where frost-blankets are probably kept. We pass a fountain carved into the shape of a child, a handful of seeds in his outstretched palm. No water.

The doorman is a hulking guy in a puffy black wind-breaker. Plenty of meat on him to shield him from the cold. He doesn't look like he's feeling it.

'Which number?' he asks, reaching for a buzzer. Like he's here to push buttons for people instead of keeping them out.

'One two one,' Thistle says, and flashes her FBI badge for good measure.

The guy looks more closely at us both. He seems particularly interested in me. A man used to staring. Big enough that no one would pick a fight with him.

'Something wrong?' I ask.

'No, sir,' he says, and pushes the button.

As we wait, I check his shoes. Cheaper than the rest of his uniform. Probably the only part he paid for himself. When the poor eventually rise up, I wonder if the people who live here are dumb enough to think he'll be on their side.

'You see Kenneth Biggs last Friday?' I say.

'Left at eight o'clock,' the doorman says. 'Didn't come back. Like I told you.'

He says this last part to Thistle. Her resigned look tells me that it wasn't her he talked to last time. Probably another black police officer of about her age—I make a mental note to find out who.

'Anything unusual about his demeanour?' I ask. 'He seem worried?'

'No. If anything, he seemed happier than usual.'

'Like, happy excited?'

The doorman thinks about it. 'Yeah, maybe. I'm not sure.'

So Biggs didn't expect to wind up dead and naked in a remote forest that day.

'He say anything to you?' I ask.

'Left me a tip, which was unusual. Most people don't, unless it's Christmas. He told me to have a nice day. That's it.'

The intercom says, 'Hello?' A female voice, young-ish. I'm guessing the daughter, Hope.

'The FBI is here,' the doorman says.

'Okay. Send them up.'

The doorman opens the door. I can sense him watching me as we walk through the faux-marble lobby towards the elevator.

•

Apartment 121 has a heavy wooden door. That makes three layers of security—I've been counting. If someone wanted to abduct Biggs, they wouldn't have chosen this location. Thistle knocks. A young woman in a grey turtleneck and sweatpants opens the door. Looks like pyjamas, even though it's ten-thirty am. Her eyes are wide with fear. She's five foot nothing, with darker skin than Biggs. She mostly got her mother's genes, I guess.

'We haven't found your dad yet,' Thistle says quickly. 'I'm sorry, Hope.'

The young woman deflates. She looks both relieved and miserable. 'Oh. Okay.'

'My associate, Timothy Blake, would like to ask some follow-up questions,' Thistle says. 'If that's all right with you.'

'Sure, I guess. Come in.' As Hope turns away, I notice a small bald patch on the back of her head. Maybe she's been pulling her hair out.

The apartment is larger than you'd think, but dark. Two levels. Smells faintly of air freshener. Plenty of framed photos on the walls—not just Hope, Biggs and a Latina woman who must be Gabriela, but extended family, too.

Cousins, uncles, grandmas. Mostly on Gabriela's side, going by skin colour. I wonder if Thistle has called all these people already.

Around the corner to the living room where Gabriela is sitting on an expensive leather sofa, like she's in therapy. In place of a therapist there's an ultra-HD TV with the sound turned down. The news comes out as a faint muttering through surround-sound speakers discreetly built into the walls, as though the apartment is haunted.

Unlike her daughter, Gabriela is dressed formally in tailored pants and a silk blouse. A crucifix hangs from a gold chain around her neck.

She stands up when we enter. Four foot five at the most, even in her polished heels. Possibly Guatemalan—after centuries of poverty and war at the hands of US-backed dictators, the average height in Guatemala is much lower than Mexico, or anywhere else in Central America. She has the hollow-eyed look people get after a flood, or a terrorist attack.

'Agent Thistle,' she says, in slightly accented English, 'any news?'

Thistle shakes her head. 'Nothing yet, I'm sorry. Do you have a moment to answer some questions?'

'Of course. I will do anything to help. Can I make for you tea or coffee?'

'No, thank you.' Thistle shoots me a warning glance.

I actually think making tea or coffee might help her— sometimes having something to do with your hands can ease trauma. When my dark thoughts get the better of me, I solve Rubik's Cubes. But I take the hint.

'No thanks,' I say. 'My name's Timothy Blake. I'm a civilian consultant, assisting with the search. I was hoping you could tell me a little about Kenneth's home life?'

Gabriela fiddles with a gold chain around her wrist. 'Of course,' she says again.

It looks like she doesn't want to sit down until we do, so I lower myself into an armchair. The cushions are so soft they threaten to swallow me. Thistle sits on a nearby chair. Gabriela descends back to the couch. Hope lingers in the doorway.

It's hard to decide which angle to target first. 'What was Kenneth's mental state like in the last few weeks?' I ask.

'Good,' Gabriela said quickly.

I wait.

'He had suffered from depression in the past,' she finally admits. 'But not lately. He had been happy. Like he had much to look forward to.'

Hope nods, confirming this.

'Okay. How does he usually spend his free time?'

'He works a lot,' Gabriela says. 'Even when he is at home, he is usually reading scholarly papers on the internet.'

'What about on weekends? Does he go camping, or hiking? I know someone else in his office is a skier.'

'You mean Shannon? Kenneth is fond of Shannon. I think it was his endorsement that got Shannon the job.'

I resist the urge to glance at Thistle. Luxford is a bad

guy. If Biggs liked him, that could make Biggs a bad guy too. At best, he's oblivious.

'But they never went skiing together,' Gabriela continues. 'My husband, he is not very . . . outdoorsy.'

'How much cash did he usually carry?'

'Oh, I don't know. Not very much. A hundred dollars? Perhaps two hundred?'

Strange to think of a world where that's not much money. But it puts the ATM withdrawal in context. Definitely not run-away money.

But if he had two hundred on him already, and withdrew two hundred more, *that* would be suspect. I'll have to ask Thistle when he made his second-last withdrawal.

'Does he own a gun?' I ask.

Gabriela stiffens. 'He has a permit for it.'

'A hunting rifle?'

'No. A handgun. He has never fired it. I would like to get rid of it, except they are hard to dispose of safely, and . . .' She gestures at the TV, looking tormented. 'Every night there is a story about a home invasion or a kidnapping. I wanted to install a panic room, but we couldn't get approval for the renovations. The building's management is very strict.'

It's hard to blame her. My parents were killed by a would-be burglar, and I nearly was too. It's not as common as the news makes it seem, but it does happen.

'Anyway,' she finishes, 'Kenneth does not go hunting.'

Hope turns, walks away towards what I guess is the kitchen. As she passes me, some of her hair shifts and I get a better look at the bald patch on the back of her head.

It's scar tissue. It looks to me like an exit wound.

Some statistics flash through my head. Of those who are shot in the head, five per cent survive the injury. And in the USA, most gunshot wounds are self-inflicted.

It no longer seems strange that Hope works from home, even though the company she works for has an office not far from here. It's so her parents can keep an eye on her. She and I have something in common. We've both survived a suicide attempt.

I wonder if she, like me, has mixed feelings about it.

CHAPTER 8

Jon comes home to find Cleo dead,
surrounded by broken glass.
He accuses Tom, who doesn't deny
killing her. Why is Tom never arrested?

'Have you checked that the gun is still here?' I ask Gabriela.

'Yes,' she says. 'Agent Thistle asked me to confirm that none of my husband's belongings were missing. I checked that the gun was still in the safe.'

'Any bullets missing?' I ask.

She hesitates. 'I didn't check.'

Hope returns with a glass of water. She doesn't drink it. I guess she just wanted to be out of the room while the gun was discussed.

'Do you mind if we have a look now?' Thistle asks.

'That is okay. You stay here, Hope.' Gabriela

stands—again I'm struck by how small she is—and leads us to the stairs.

A wrought-iron spiral staircase leads to the upper level of the apartment. Christmas lights are wrapped around the bannister. They must throw parties sometimes.

Gabriela climbs slowly, looking more reluctant with every step. I suspect I know why.

When we reach the top, she leads us into the master bedroom. There's a king-size bed with a thick mattress and high thread-count sheets. Cat hair on the duvet, white. Bedside tables with thick books piled atop them. Some of the books on one side are in Spanish. The ones on the other side are popular science. I don't see anything about cryptography, though. Nor is there any sign of a wheel cipher to match the one Luxford has on his desk.

Gabriela opens the walk-in closet, revealing dozens of dresses, several suits and a gun safe. I've only seen Biggs naked—strange to think of him in one of these suits.

Gabriela punches in the combination, retracts the bolts and heaves the door open.

Like she said, there's a single handgun in there. A Ruger LCP—inexpensive, reliable and compact, although I've heard gun enthusiasts say the trigger-pull sucks, whatever that means. There's a box of .380 ACP cartridges.

'You see . . .' Gabriela begins.

I pick up the box and open it. The bullets are lined up in rows and columns like lipsticks in a department store. One is missing—I assume it's the one that went through Hope's head. Bullets are easily replaced in Texas, but I can see why Gabriela and Biggs wouldn't go out and buy a new box right away.

I cover the missing cartridge with my thumb and show Thistle. 'All still there,' I say. Then I close the box and put it back in the safe.

Gabriela looks at me questioningly. I give a slight nod. She doesn't have to talk about her daughter's suicide attempt if she doesn't want to.

She gives me a grateful nod in return, and closes the safe door.

When we get back downstairs, Hope has turned off the TV. 'You think Shannon has something to do with what's happened to my dad?' she asks.

'We interviewed him this morning,' Thistle says carefully. 'At this stage we have no evidence that he did. Why do you ask?'

'Just not sure who to trust,' she says.

A grandfather clock ticks softly in the corner.

'Can I make a private recommendation?' Thistle asks. 'Off the record?'

Hope crosses her arms. 'What kind of recommendation?'

Thistle looks like she's struggling to find the words. She can't warn them about Luxford without getting into trouble.

But I can.

'Stay away from Shannon Luxford,' I say. 'We don't have any evidence that he's connected to your husband's disappearance. But he didn't strike me as a good guy. If you hear from him, I think you should call us.'

Gabriela looks shocked. Hope doesn't. I wonder if she's heard rumours about what he does in his office.

'Was Kenneth especially close to anyone in your extended family?' I ask.

'Most of his family, they live in Tennessee,' Gabriela says. 'We never hear from them.'

'Was there a disagreement?' Thistle asks.

'They thought I was marrying Kenneth for a green card. They tried to talk him out of it. After the wedding, we lost touch.'

'Hope,' I say, 'can we talk to your mother in private for a second?'

'Why?' Hope asks. A challenge.

'Suit yourself,' I say, and turn back to Gabriela. 'How are things in the bedroom? With your husband?'

Thistle winces. Gabriela's cheeks redden.

'You think he abandoned us,' Hope says. 'Ran off with some woman.'

'No,' I say. 'In fact, I'm pretty sure he didn't. A few more questions and I can rule it out entirely.'

Gabriela clears her throat. 'We have been married for many years,' she says. 'We do not . . . make love as frequently as when we were newlyweds. But still sometimes.'

'He never cheated on you in the past?' I'm sure Thistle already asked this, but I want to look her in the eye when she answers.

'No,' she says, and I'd bet my life she was telling the truth. 'He is a wonderful husband. He stood up to his family for me. He throws the most wonderful surprise parties for my birthday—every time he convinces me that this year there will be no party. He often leaves lovely messages around the house for me to find. He loved Tennessee, but when I said I wanted to move to Texas, immediately he started looking at houses here, and jobs. Ever since Hope was born, he has been the most wonderful father to her.'

I realise that Hope is quietly crying.

Gabriela looks uncomfortable. Is she hiding something, or just feeling her daughter's pain?

'I saw a very glamorous woman in his department this morning,' I say. 'A tall blonde, in her thirties, large breasts. You seen anyone like that hanging around?'

I bring this up mainly to see if she looks suspicious about it.

'No,' she says, open-faced and anxious. A woman used to trusting her husband.

I look from her to Hope and back. I can't tell them Kenneth will be okay, because he's dead and in my freezer. There's only one worry I can help erase.

'Kenneth sounds like a good man,' I say. 'He didn't run away.'

They look relieved, until they realise what this means.

I stand up. 'Can we borrow his computer?'

•

Not even lunchtime yet, but I'm desperately hungry by the time we get back to the field office. It isn't the sort of hunger a normal meal will solve. My favourite food is waiting for me at home, and I can't get to it.

You'd think that knowing so much about Biggs might stop me from wanting him. But it doesn't. Most people know that pigs feel stress and that cows grieve when their calves are taken away. People might feel guilty, but they still eat bacon and drink milk.

So what use is the guilt?

'I have to tell you something,' I say to Thistle as we carry the computer inside. I have the tower, she has the keyboard and router. No prints on the monitor, so we left it behind.

Thistle raises an eyebrow.

'Hope attempted suicide,' I say. 'That bald patch on the back of her head was an old exit wound.'

Thistle frowns, maybe picturing Hope's hair. 'With whose gun? There were no—'

'I lied. One bullet was missing. Mrs Biggs looked like she really didn't want to talk about it, and I didn't want to push her over the edge, so I pretended they were all there. But I also wanted you to know all the facts.'

This is true. I may want to sabotage the case, but I also need to know what happened to Biggs. And I'm fast running out of leads. We're nowhere. I need Thistle's help.

'Since when do you care about hurting people's feelings?' Thistle asks.

'I guess I felt sorry for her. For both of them.'

This statement hangs in the air.

'You picked a hell of a time to go soft on me,' Thistle

says finally. 'Don't do that again. I get it—but don't. Okay?'

She's right. I don't know what got into me. It was easier to be a monster when Thistle wasn't around, reminding me that I could have turned out differently.

'Okay,' I say.

We take the elevator down to the basement. Vasquez has an office, but as usual it's empty. We find him wandering around the forest of desks, checking the work of his subordinates. Vasquez is a stickler for grammar.

I'm uneasy. I don't like basements. Nothing good has ever happened in a basement.

'Maurice,' Thistle says.

Vasquez says, 'Agent Thistle. Didn't expect to see you today.'

'Well, here I am,' she says evenly.

He forces a smile. 'What brings you down into my lair?'

I'm uncomfortably aware of his perfect teeth and muscular arms. When Thistle looks at him there's a flicker of jealousy in my gut. Which is unfair. I pushed her away, after all. Just the same, I find myself selfishly hoping she realises that he's gay.

'The Biggs disappearance,' Thistle says ominously, like it's the title of a Ludlum novel. 'Got a minute?'

'Sure.' Vasquez turns to me. 'Blake. You working a new case after all?'

'Looks that way,' I say, lifting the tower. 'Got someplace I can put this?'

'What is it?'

'Victim's computer.'

'Okay. Right this way.'

He leads us through the basement to an empty desk in the corner and helps us put everything down. He takes a bunch of small blocks—they look a bit like power adaptors—out of a drawer, and puts one on the end of each cable before he plugs it into the server under the desk.

'What are those?' Thistle asks.

'We can't plug an unknown computer directly into our systems,' Vasquez says while he works. 'These stop any viruses from getting through.'

'Like a computer condom,' I say.

Thistle stifles a laugh, giving me a warm feeling in my belly. But Vasquez doesn't look amused.

'You're the fifth guy to make that joke, Blake,' he says.

The monitor lights up. A login screen. The password field fills up with a long string of dots. A message flashes up on the screen—POLICE BYPASS ACCEPTED.

'What exactly are you looking for?' Vasquez asks.

'I want his emails and his browsing history,' I say.

'We'd like his text messages as well,' Thistle says. 'I already filed a request upstairs.'

'You got a warrant for all this?' Vasquez asks.

'We got the wife's written permission.'

'How long will it take to get all this stuff?' I ask.

Vasquez is already hunched over the keyboard as if preparing to dive into the screen. 'Depends on a lot of things,' he says. 'Which web browser he uses. What his privacy settings are like. If he uses a password manager.

If he sends normal text messages or uses an encrypted messaging app.'

'He was a math professor. Cryptography was his hobby.' As I say this, I realise we only have Luxford's word for it. No evidence at the house.

'Then it could take forever. That's not hyperbole. I could use all the world's computers until the heat death of the universe and not get through.' Vasquez gestures around the room. 'I'm sure half these computers are filled with unspeakable videos. But if the suspect used the right kind of encryption, there's no way I'll ever prove it.'

'Just get us what you can,' Thistle says.

Her phone rings. She moves away to answer it.

A flash of paranoia. The voice on the phone could be another cop, saying, *We found Kenneth Biggs. He was in Timothy Blake's freezer.*

Or it could be nothing.

Vasquez is still tapping away.

'You gonna work this personally?' I ask.

'For a while. If it looks like it will *actually* take until the end of the universe, I'll farm it out to an intern.'

'Got it.'

Vasquez glances up. 'It'll take even longer with you looking over my shoulder.'

'Okay, okay.' I back off.

Thistle ends the call and comes over.

'Blake,' she says. 'We have a problem. A second guy has gone missing.'

CHAPTER 9

I have four legs at dawn, two legs at noon, three legs at night. What am I?

Thistle is driving as fast as she can get away with, no siren. It's hard for me to read the file with the car bouncing around. But she wants to get to where we're going—she hasn't told me where that is—before the leads dry up.

So do I. A second victim turns this whole thing upside down.

'Daniel Ruthven,' I say, reading the missing persons report aloud; Thistle didn't have time to look at it before we jumped in the car. 'Thirty-one years of age. Unmarried. Last seen two days ago. He's a low-level construction worker, currently building a fast-food place in Hendrix.'

'How long has he been doing that for?'

'Doesn't say how long he's been building the fast-food place. But he's been with the company six years.'

It's strange, reading to Thistle while she drives. Feels like the kind of thing a husband would do for his wife. The thought would leave me melancholy if she weren't driving so terrifyingly fast.

'There's a picture, right?' she says. 'Does he look like the last victim?'

The last case we worked together involved victims who looked nearly identical. I turn the page, revealing Ruthven. He's tall, fat, balding, and a decade younger than Biggs. I'm strangely relieved that he's not the other guy in my freezer, not this that would have made any kind of sense.

'They're both white males,' I say. 'But different in every other way. How do you know the cases are connected?'

Thistle takes another corner like a Nascar driver. 'His phone signal,' she says. 'The trail goes to a landfill and then just stops. Five days ago.'

So he's been missing longer than Biggs. There's a stirring in my bones. 'The same landfill as Biggs's phone?'

'Right. Someone is using it as a dumping ground.'

'Is that where we're going?'

'That's where we're going,' Thistle confirms. 'What else does the file say?'

'Uh, born and raised in Houston, father died of prostate cancer, mother still lives here. Went to Waltrip High School—'

'He didn't go to the college Biggs taught at?'

'No college at all.'

'And yet he still managed to get a low-level job building a fast-food place,' Thistle says. 'Your kind of guy.'

I ignore the gibe. 'He was reported missing by his roommate, Ian McLean. McLean works for a software company.'

'We'll have to talk to him, too.'

'Hey, do you know how much Biggs took out in his second-last ATM withdrawal?'

'A hundred,' Thistle says. 'Same as the one before that. Further back, I don't know. But two-sixty is a lot, for him.'

'Hmm.'

Ninety minutes later we drive past a blue sign with a fleur-de-lis: WELCOME TO LOUISIANA—BIENVENUE EN LOUISIANE. Thirty-six hours now since I found Biggs in the forest. The trail is cold and getting colder.

It's just gone two o'clock when we slow down and turn a corner. Thistle says, 'This is it.'

Up ahead are mountains of trash as tall as skyscrapers. It looks post-apocalyptic, the landscape jagged and bleak, all the colours faded and stained and scraped to sewage-brown.

We drive up a dirt road to a big steel gate and a sign—SULPHUR RESOURCE MANAGEMENT CENTER. Sulphur is the name of the nearest town, and it could also describe the stench. I'm gagging even before Thistle rolls down the window to show the security guard her badge.

Once, at the group home Thistle and I grew up in, someone knocked over a plate of food and it landed upside down. I would have picked it up and eaten it, but it was asparagus with ranch dressing. Not my thing.

For whatever reason, no one else picked the plate up either—it was in a corner, out of the way and half hidden. Weeks later, when it was my turn to vacuum, I noticed that the plate was still there. I unstuck it from the floor and flipped it over. Beneath it was a seething mess of maggots and congealed dressing.

This whole place smells like that plate did.

The security guard—a broad-shouldered man with aviator sunglasses—sees us grimacing. He grins, showing a mouth of crooked teeth. 'You get used to it,' he says, and waves us through.

'He's right,' Thistle says, as she drives through into a small parking lot. 'After a day searching for Biggs's phone, I barely noticed the stink.'

I grunt, and get out of the car.

Up close, I can see the content of some of the garbage piles. Dressers, TVs, blenders, toy trucks, a walking stick. A lot of it still looks workable. Unwanted, not broken.

There are huge hills of magazines and DVDs. As Thistle and I walk closer, I realise that almost all of them are porn. An endless mosaic of cupped breasts and spread ass cheeks. After they've been used, most DVDs and magazines end up collecting dust on shelves, but I guess porn isn't like that. Once people use it, they're ashamed of it, and they just want it gone. Straight in the trash.

A row of shipping containers have been concreted into place, with windows cut in the sides. They're being used as site offices, I guess. As I watch, a moustachioed man with no neck emerges from one of the containers. He's wearing a checked shirt under a hi-vis vest. Thin, greying hair peeks out from under his hard hat. He's fortyish, with skin like leather.

'Agent Thistle,' he says, as he approaches. 'Back so soon?'

'Different case this time,' Thistle says. 'Bevan Edwards, this is my associate, Timothy Blake.'

Edwards shakes my hand, and does a double take at my missing thumb.

'We're here looking for a man named Daniel Ruthven,' Thistle says.

Edwards makes a big show of trying to remember, raising his eyes to look at the sky. 'Doesn't ring a bell,' he says finally.

'We have a picture of him,' Thistle says. She clicks her fingers. I hand her the file, and she shows the guy the photo.

He peers at it, but also keeps glancing at us. Like he wants to gauge our reaction to his words.

'Sorry,' he says. 'I haven't seen anyone like that around here.'

This is clearly untrue. Several employees are visible from here, and half of them are pudgy white guys. The other half are lean Latinos.

'Well, we're tracing a phone signal,' Thistle says. 'Same as last time. Maybe we could talk in your office?'

'Uh, sure,' Edwards says.

As he leads us over to his shipping container, he keeps glancing at one of the others. One with no windows.

The back of my neck is prickling. Something's going on here, although I don't know what.

Edwards's office has a single chair, a small desk, two filing cabinets and a plastic fern. Through the small window, I can see the mountains of garbage, but not the road, the vehicles or the people. From in here it looks like the whole world has ended.

'Like I told you last time,' Edwards is saying, 'we don't inventory everything that comes here. If one of my boys sees a gun, or drugs, we call it in. Anything else just goes on the pile.'

'So no one's handed in a suspicious phone lately?' Thistle asks.

'No. But to be honest, if it was a new model in working order, someone might have just kept it. Especially the new guys. The first couple of weeks, they're amazed what people throw away, and they take a lot of stuff home. Then they get over it. Or their garage fills up, and they realise why the stuff got thrown away in the first place.'

The phone trail ends here. If someone took it, they haven't switched it on. Unless they swapped out the SIM card first. I'll have to remember to ask Vasquez if there's another way to trace it.

'What about things that could be recycled?' I ask. 'You have to separate that out, right?'

'The recycling centre is a half mile that way,' he says, pointing east. 'Things are here because people can't recycle them, or don't want to for whatever reason. Not much sorting happens.'

'When the pile gets too big,' I say, 'then what?'

'Then it gets buried, so it doesn't get scattered by animals. Or the weather,' he adds. 'During Hurricane Harvey it rained trash over half the town. Now City Hall says we gotta bury twice a month, not just once.'

'Does the name Shannon Luxford mean anything to you?' I ask.

He puts on the same show as before—raised gaze, pursed lips. 'I don't think so. Why?'

'No reason,' I ask. 'What's in the other shipping container?'

His expression shifts. I can almost sense his blood pressure rising. 'Just files and stuff.'

'You don't keep your files here?' I gesture to the filing cabinets.

'Only the new ones,' he says. 'Old stuff gets archived.'

Thistle leans forwards. 'We'd like to take a look, if that's okay,' she says.

'The phone trail dead-ends there,' I add. This isn't true, as far as I know. But it gives us a plausible reason to want in.

A bead of sweat trickles out from under Edwards's hard hat. 'I'm not really sure where the key is.'

Thistle looks at me. 'I guess we could come back with a full forensic team,' she says. 'They always bring cutting equipment.'

'Just... hang on,' Edwards says. He starts opening and closing drawers in his desk. Eventually he produces a key. 'Here we go. You can have a quick look.'

He's hoping we'll be less thorough than a forensic team. He's wrong.

Thistle and I follow him out the door and over to the windowless container. Thistle stays a few feet behind him. Not so close that he could suddenly turn and attack her, but close enough that he couldn't destroy or hide any evidence without her seeing.

Edwards unlocks the container. The keys jingle louder than you'd expect. I think his hands are trembling.

The door creaks open. It's dark inside. As my eyes adjust, I see more filing cabinets and some archive boxes.

'See?' Edwards says, half blocking the doorway.

'Are there lights?' Thistle asks.

'Oh. Yeah.'

Edwards reaches in and clicks a switch. Fluorescents flicker on above, casting more light across the cabinets and boxes. There's also a folding chair, a little desk lamp and a wall planner.

A well-adjusted person might not have noticed the splotches, but my gaze is drawn to them straight away.

I walk over to the wall planner like a moth approaching a bug zapper. Twelve red spots are scattered across it. Each one has a faint whorl pattern. Fingerprints.

With my back blocking Edwards's and Thistle's sight-lines, I scratch off a tiny fragment of red with a fingernail and touch it to my tongue. A familiar copper tang.

When I'm certain, I turn around. 'Agent Thistle,' I say, gesturing to the wall planner, 'does this look like blood to you?'

CHAPTER 10

J. A. S. O. N. D. J. F. M.
What is the next letter?

'Mr Edwards,' Thistle says, 'do you want to tell us why there's blood on your calendar?'

'Blood?' He looks perplexed.

'Red stuff. Usually kept inside the body, rather than on the walls.'

Edwards swallows. 'I don't know.'

'You don't know,' Thistle repeats.

'Maybe . . . maybe someone got a papercut before they wrote on it.'

'Does that seem likely to you, Mr Blake?' Thistle asks.

'It does not, Agent Thistle,' I say.

'How many people have access to this container?' Thistle asks Edwards. 'Just you?'

'My office isn't locked during the day. The key was in

the drawer. Anyone could have—'

'Could have what? Broken in here, given themselves a papercut, dabbed some blood on the wall planner and then left again?'

Edwards's eyes are wide. I get the feeling he honestly didn't know about the blood. This isn't what he was worried we would find.

Thistle's playing bad cop, so I play good. 'You seem like a nice guy,' I say. 'I'm sure you didn't expect anyone to get hurt. If you just tell us what happened, we'll be able to—'

'Nothing happened. I don't know how that got there.'

I open the least dusty archive box and start digging through the contents. Just employment records, like Edwards said, plus some receipts and bills for utilities. None of them less than three months old. No references to Biggs, Ruthven or Luxford. All the surnames in here sound like occupations—Tailor, Smith, Cook, Mason, Post. I'm checking phone numbers and addresses as I go, and so far nothing matches either victim. Got to work quickly. Soon Edwards will wake up and realise we need a warrant for this.

'I want to call my lawyer,' Edwards says, like he's reading my mind.

'Go ahead,' Thistle says. 'But you know you're not under arrest?'

Edwards clenches his jaw and says nothing. He pulls a phone from his pocket, checks the screen and walks out of the container.

Thistle checks her phone, too. 'No service in here,' she says. 'What are you thinking, Blake?'

'Not sure yet.' I close the archive box and go back to the wall planner, chewing my lip.

'I've never seen a spatter pattern like that,' Thistle says, looking at the blood.

'It's not exactly spatter. There are prints in it.'

'How fresh do you think it is?'

'Day before yesterday, I figure. No older.'

'Okay. You be the victim, I'll be the killer.'

I turn to face Thistle. She takes a pen out of her pocket.

'I come at you with a knife,' she says, and slashes at me with the pen. I raise my hands instinctively, and the nib swipes across my palm.

'So you're hurt,' she says. 'Your hand is bleeding. Do you trail it across the wall planner as I push you backwards?'

She steps forwards, and I step back, like we're dance partners. I leave my arm outstretched, keeping my fingers an inch away from the planner. 'Doesn't feel right,' I say. 'And it's not a trail of blood. It's just spots.'

'So maybe you lean against it.'

'Twelve times? With only finger each time?'

'Is it the same finger?' Thistle asks.

'The print looks the same, yeah.'

'Okay, forget that for now. But let's pretend that you're already bleeding.'

'All right,' I say.

'I come at you again, and you push back.' She comes at me with a slow-motion stab to the sternum. I put my hands on her shoulders and give her a half-hearted push back.

'You fall,' she says, and pushes me over. I slowly tumble to the floor.

'I keep coming,' she says, and mounts me. I try to think about absolutely anything other than how close to me she is. My saliva glands are in overdrive. Other parts, too. I hope she doesn't notice.

Thistle raises the pen, and goes to stab me in the heart. The nib stops an inch from my shirt. Her hair hangs almost low enough to touch my face. I can smell mint on her breath. I wonder if she's teasing me.

'So where's the rest of the blood?' she asks.

I look around. 'They cleaned up.'

'But they missed the calendar? And it's not like you can wash those archive boxes.' She touches the floor. Her finger comes back dusty. 'This place hasn't been cleaned. At least not within the last two days.'

'Okay,' I say. 'So no one was murdered here.'

'Then why the blood on the wall planner?'

Edwards comes back in. He wordlessly hands his phone to Thistle.

Thistle puts it to her ear. 'This is Agent Reese Thistle,' she says.

After a pause, she says, 'Can't hear anything. No service.'

'Oh. Well, it was my attorney,' Edwards says. 'He was gonna tell you to get out and come back with a warrant.'

•

Thistle and I walk out of the container, blinking like newborns in the harsh sun. As the security guard promised, I'm already used to the smell. I nibble a fingernail, still tasting the sliver of dried blood from the calendar. According to the file, Ruthven was a blood donor. Maybe I could track down one of his donations. Confirm by taste that the blood in the container is his.

This is ridiculous on several levels, but fun to think about as Thistle argues with Edwards about *probable cause*. Tells him he's not a suspect *at this time*. Gives him one last chance to cooperate. I already know he won't take it. His jaw is clenched, his tasty veins bulging. He's angry, maybe at us.

I turn back towards Thistle's Crown Vic—and then realise I'm not the only one staring at it.

A group of workers are wading through debris between two hills of trash. One of them, a Latino man in his late thirties, slows down when he sees the car. He's wearing a dust mask and carrying a milk crate filled with what looks like broken PVC piping. He finally stops, like a clockwork toy that needs winding. The other workers trudge on, oblivious.

I watch him from the corner of my eye, not wanting to spook him. He looks from Crown Vic—clearly a police vehicle—to Thistle, in her pantsuit and dark sunglasses. His eyes skip over me completely. I probably blend in with the garbage.

He starts to back away. I walk towards him, slowly,

like a cat approaching a bird. He doesn't notice. He's still watching Thistle.

Then, suddenly, Thistle is watching him, too.

The guy drops the milk crate and bolts.

'Blake!' Thistle yells, but I'm already running, sloshing into the river of trash as the man with the dust mask disappears between the two rotting mountains. The other workers watch me wide-eyed as I approach. One of them, an apple-cheeked white guy I've seen somewhere before, steps into my path.

'Hold on there, fella,' he says. 'Where you headed?'

I remember him now. He pulled over to offer unwanted roadside assistance once. Nearly caught me eating a Tanzanian triple murderer. Hopefully he doesn't remember me.

'Move,' I say. 'Police.'

'You don't look like police,' he says, which is true. But Thistle is behind me now, waving her ID. He reluctantly steps aside.

'Sorry for the delay,' he says, but we're already past him. We race through the trash, looking for signs of the man with the dust mask.

We're looking down a long vista between two walls of trash. Plastic slurry, bullet casings, mouldy cow bones, coffee pods, more porn. Can't see the guy—he must have turned off somewhere. We keep running, looking for his trail.

There's a narrow side alley between hills of shredded polyester clothes and shattered iPhones. Too much of this trash is probably mine. I reuse a lot, but I don't recycle. One of my many bad habits. After you've eaten a few people, none of your other flaws seem important enough to fix.

'I'll check that way,' I say, puffing. 'You keep going.'

'No,' Thistle says. 'This whole place is fenced off. We should go back. Guard the exit.'

'The guy looked like he could climb a fence. Especially if someone threw away a ladder.'

Thistle hesitates. She doesn't trust me. Usually a good choice.

I don't give her time to decide. I run down the side alley. She doesn't follow.

The path is narrow and dark. Probably only gets sunlight at noon. Mushrooms grow from deep gashes in the trash. A crust of moss is swallowing an old fridge. There are footprints in the damp cardboard, but it's impossible to tell how recent they are.

A diesel engine rumbles somewhere up ahead. Seconds later there's a screech and a metallic crash. Maybe a mountain of broken toasters collapsed. I hope our suspect wasn't under it. This deep in the maze of garbage, like the ruins of a freshly dead civilisation, it's impossible not to think about being buried alive.

The smell makes it hard to run. It feels like each breath I take is one-third air, one-third fungus, one-third plastic confetti.

I'm exhausted by the time I turn a corner and find a clearing. The first thing I see is a car crusher—not switched on, not the source of the noise. The next thing I see is a chain-link fence, topped with cruel coils of razor wire. The fence has been knocked down and flattened against the patchwork mud. Huge tyre tracks tell me that our suspect has stolen a tractor, or maybe a bulldozer. Those things have a top speed of maybe twenty-five miles per hour, but I won't catch him on foot.

I'm about to yell out to Thistle when I see something else. The crusher looks like a giant sandwich press. A car is clamped between its mighty jaws, the roof caved in and the doors prolapsed out.

The plates have been removed, but I'm sure it's the blue Toyota Prius that once belonged to Kenneth Biggs.

CHAPTER 11

Lovers circle each other where guilt is found, freedom lost and rackets heard. Where am I?

'It could be a coincidence,' Thistle says.

'You think it is?'

'No.' Thistle takes another sip from her banana milkshake. She glared at me after ordering it, as though daring me to criticise her for ordering like a kid.

'It's the same make, model and year as Biggs's car,' she continues. 'And it was found at the same dump where his phone was last switched on. We just need to remember that, legally, it's not proof. Not until the VIN number is confirmed, anyway.'

We're at a diner around the corner from the courthouse. Sun's setting out the window. It's the kind of place with harsh fluorescent lights, cloudy water bottles, and cherry pie congealing in an unrefrigerated glass cabinet. Thistle didn't have time to take me back to the FBI—she's supposed to be on the witness stand in an hour, and she still has to change. Her blouse is stained with sweat, and we both smell like trash. The other customers keep glancing at us, and I can tell the staff want us to leave.

'You said you pulled the dump apart looking for the phone yesterday,' I say. 'How come you didn't see the car then?'

'Because it wasn't there. I may not be a "genius" like you, but when a trail goes cold at the dump and the vic's car is missing, I'm smart enough to check the crusher.'

Unlike me, Thistle is smart enough to hold down a proper job, to lead an ethical life, and to avoid getting involved with organised crime. But she's not fishing for a compliment, and I don't give her one.

'So the perp has been to the dump since yesterday,' I say. 'I saw cameras—are they real?'

'Yeah, but useless. The insurance company mandates that there be cameras, but it doesn't require them to be recording, so they weren't. And no one saw anything suspect on the live feed.'

'According to who? Edwards?'

Thistle slurps up the last of her shake. 'Right. Who I don't trust at all.'

The diner starts to disappear around me as I become more and more immersed in the puzzle. In my head, I'm still at the dump, looking around. 'He's hiding something, for sure. But if the perp *doesn't* work there, then someone would have noticed him trashing a car and two phones, right?'

'Him?'

'Even if the perp isn't Luxford, Edwards or the guy who stole the tractor, I reckon we're looking for a man.'

'You mean statistically.'

'Not just that. Ruthven is a big guy. Two hundred pounds. Not easy for a woman to overpower him.'

'You might be surprised,' Thistle says. 'I was on my high school wrestling team. Sometimes the weight doesn't matter—you just gotta find the right angle.'

'The point is that our perp either works at the dump or has teamed up with someone who does,' I say. 'We're getting close.'

Thistle checks her watch. 'I have to go. My lawyer will be shitting herself.'

'*Your* lawyer? I thought you were just a witness.'

Thistle ignores this. 'How are you getting home?'

Stealing cars is harder than it used to be. 'The bus,' I say.

'Okay. I'll see you at the field office tomorrow.'

'Let me give you my new cell number,' I say, 'in case you find anything out before then.'

Warner told me not to tell anyone about the phone, but I want to emphasise to Thistle that it's new. I want her to know that I didn't lie to her before, when I told her I didn't have one.

It's stupid, because I lie to her all the time. My whole life is a fabrication. But I don't like her thinking I'm dishonest.

'Sure.' Thistle gets out her phone and types in the number I give her. 'Welcome to the twenty-first century.' She leaves some cash on the table and walks out the door, not even staying long enough to get a receipt.

I sit, sipping my salted, sweetened coffee for a minute. Thinking.

I should go home. Keep working the case. Do something about the bodies in my freezer.

Instead, I follow Thistle to the courthouse.

•

When I pictured the inside of Herbert W. Gee Municipal Courthouse, it always looked like a grand old hotel. Lots of wood panelling, marble floors, maybe even a chandelier. I figured there would be people in expensive suits—and me in chains.

Instead, it looks more like the place where I used to collect my welfare cheques. A line of cheaply dressed, dejected-looking people stand behind a nylon strap stretched between two silver poles, waiting for their turn at the counter, which is protected by shatterproof glass. A sign says, OPEN 8 AM TO 10 PM. Too much crime in Houston to deal with in normal business hours.

When I reach the front of the line, I explain my situation to a gaunt white lady. I'm a friend of Reese Thistle's, here for moral support, but I've forgotten which room—

'You want Bucetti versus Thistle,' the woman says, her voice muffled by the glass. 'Court 3.'

Apparently this isn't confidential. And it's Bucetti,

not the state of Texas—so not a criminal matter, which makes sense. If it was, Thistle would be suspended from working cases.

'Hey,' a man says, walking in. 'You here for the Bucetti trial? Come on, I'll show you the way.'

He's thirty-something, black, and dressed like a lumberjack in a flannel shirt and jeans. His shoes—polished leather, pointed-toe, thin laces—give him away as someone with a desk job, though.

'Which side you on?' he asks as we walk.

'Thistle,' I say cautiously.

'Aw, that's too bad,' he says, smiling like we have opposing baseball teams. 'How do you know her?'

'We work together sometimes,' I say. 'But I've been away a while. I don't even really know what the whole thing is about.'

We walk through a metal detector, like at the airport. A guard with a vacant stare waves an explosive residue wand over me before he lets us pass.

'You didn't hear about the shooting?' the lumberjack says.

'Shooting?' I haven't seen any sign that Thistle has been shot, which means she shot someone.

'Oh, man.' The lumberjack shakes his head. 'Sorry to be the one to tell you, but your girl, she fucked up.'

I don't know if he means she *did* fuck up, or she *is* fucked up. Either way I don't believe him.

'Big time,' he continues. 'She's going down. How well do you know her?'

I should act like a casual acquaintance, but I can't help but stick up for Thistle. 'Well enough to know that she wouldn't have done anything wrong. If she shot Bucetti, I'm thinking he had it coming.'

I expect the guy to be pissed off, but he just laughs. 'Man, you got no idea. Your friend? She has a cold streak. You'll see.'

I could bite your face off, I think. But he walks into court 3 before I come up with something I can say out loud.

It's a wide room with a low ceiling over a tiled floor, maybe for ease of mopping up tears. There are pews rather than seats, mostly full. I take a seat up the back, so Thistle won't notice me. The lumberjack, inexplicably, sits next to me. Boxing me in. Which is bad, potentially for both of us. Now that I've thought about eating him, it's hard to stop.

CHAPTER 12

I am an odd number. Take away a letter and I become even. What am I?

'Please state your name for the court.'

Thistle leans in close to the microphone. 'Reese Catherine Thistle.'

She's changed into a suit that doesn't fit her very well; it probably belongs to her lawyer—a tense-looking white woman with narrower shoulders and a lesser bust.

Thistle doesn't look nervous, but she's highly alert. Aware that she's under attack.

Bucetti, whoever he is, hasn't turned up. His lawyer is an old man in a brown suit—from here I can only see the top of his liver-spotted head. It seems strange that the lumberjack came along for moral support when his friend isn't even here.

After Thistle—who's an atheist—swears on a Bible, the bald lawyer stands up. He's taller than I expected, and his voice is louder.

'Miss Thistle. Let's pick up where we left off last week, shall we?'

'Let's,' Thistle says.

'When you shot Anthony Iuculano, was that the first time you'd fired your service weapon?'

'No,' Thistle says. 'I go to the range every week.'

'But it was the first time in the line of duty, correct?'

Thistle's lawyer is on her feet already. 'Objection! Leading the witness.'

The judge is a middle-aged black woman with sagging cheeks and a head which hangs low, as if weighed down by decades of bullshit. 'Sustained,' she says wearily.

The bald lawyer rephrases. 'Miss Thistle, was this the first time you'd fired a gun at an actual suspect?'

'Yes,' Thistle says.

'It must have been hard,' the lawyer says, 'lining up a shot on an actual human being, putting your finger inside the trigger guard for the first time . . .'

He lets the words hover in the air for a moment.

'Was that a question?' Thistle asks.

'Meanwhile, Iuculano was lining up a shot of his own, taking aim at your partner, Agent Mario Bucetti.'

'I'm still not hearing a question.'

'Miss Thistle,' the judge warns. 'I strongly discourage you from being flippant in my courtroom.'

Thistle clenches her jaw. 'Sorry, Your Honour.'

I'm starting to understand why Thistle is here. Not because of who she shot, but who she didn't.

'Unlike you, Iuculano didn't hesitate,' the lawyer says. 'He—'

'No, but my aim was better,' Thistle says.

'He shot Mario clean through the arm,' the lawyer says. 'The bullet shredded his triceps and chipped the bone. My client nearly bled to death in that stairwell. According to this affidavit from Dr Van Spreeuwel—' he waves a document in the air '—Mario may never regain the use of his right hand.'

'Lucky he's left-handed.'

The mention of shredded triceps makes my stomach gurgle. It's six pm. I'm hungry again. The lumberjack gives me a funny look.

The lawyer is humanising Bucetti by using his first name. Making Thistle seem incompetent by always referring to her as 'Miss' rather than 'Agent'. He must be used to performing for juries rather than judges, who presumably don't fall for those tricks.

'If I hadn't given him first aid, he'd be dead,' Thistle says.

'That could very well be true,' the bald lawyer says. 'But if you hadn't hesitated, if you had fired earlier, what do you think—'

'Objection,' Thistle's lawyer snaps. 'Calls for speculation.'

'Mrs Fletcher,' the judge says, 'please let Mr Simmons

finish his questions before you decide whether to object to them.'

All eyes are on the action up the front, including mine—until I realise someone is watching me. A young white man, no eyebrows, dressed in a dark blue tracksuit. He's on the other side of the courtroom. He doesn't look away when I spot him. Instead, he holds up a piece of paper, angled so I can read the scribbled words: COME WITH US.

My heart is loud in my ears. I nod to the man in the tracksuit. *Message received.*

'If you had fired sooner,' Simmons is saying, 'then Iuculano wouldn't have had the chance to shoot your partner.'

There's a pause. Someone sneezes in the front row, and Thistle flinches.

'Mr Simmons,' the judge says, 'it's late. Other cases are waiting to be heard. We're all familiar with the basic facts of the case. Ask your question.'

'Yes, Your Honour. Miss Thistle, do you regret not taking the shot earlier?'

The man in the tracksuit tucks his homemade sign into a satchel. Then he makes eye contact with another man—Asian American with spiky hair and an ear stud. The lumberjack seems to notice none of this. I try to work out if he could be with them—whoever they are. It felt like an accident, him running into me outside the courtroom. But experienced con men are used to manufacturing accidents.

No one moves. I guess they want me to go with them after the court session has concluded.

'That would have been irresponsible,' Thistle is saying. 'I wasn't sure the suspect had a gun. It could have been a phone or a wallet.'

Simmons picks up a photograph from his desk. He shows it to the judge, then to Thistle. 'Does this look like a phone, or a wallet?'

'From a yard away in a well-lit courtroom?' Thistle says. 'No.'

'Especially since Iuculano had already used it to murder his wife.'

'We'd heard reports that shots had been fired in the building,' Thistle said. 'But at the point when we first saw Iuculano, we didn't know who had done the shooting, or who had been shot.'

Simmons places another document in front of her. 'According to Mario and the neighbours, this is what you said *before* Iuculano opened fire. Read it for the court, please.'

Fletcher stands up. 'Your Honour, this was in my client's official statement. The facts are not in dispute. Mr Simmons is—'

'I'll allow it,' the judge says.

Thistle clears her throat. 'I said, "Drop the weapon. Do it now."'

'I take it you didn't mean a phone or a wallet,' Simmons says.

'It could also have been a knife or a Taser,' Thistle says.

'It could have been anything. My hope was that he would put it down no matter what it was.'

'Well, he didn't. He shot your partner. A man who—'

'At which point I determined that it was a gun,' Thistle says, 'so I put him down with two shots to centre mass.'

'He shot your partner,' Simmons repeated, 'a man who entrusted you with his safety.'

'Hence the first aid,' Thistle says. 'Instead of blaming me for Bucetti's shooting, maybe you should blame the guy who shot him.'

'I'm inclined to agree, Mr Simmons,' the judge says. 'Care to tell me why I shouldn't throw this case out of court?'

I can see Thistle holding her breath.

'Iuculano may have caused the damage to Mario's arm,' Simmons says, 'but Miss Thistle is responsible for his emotional pain. He put his trust in her, and she failed to protect him.'

'Do you have any evidence of that emotional pain?' the judge asks dubiously.

'He's been in therapy,' Simmons says.

'Already paid for by the FBI, Your Honour,' Fletcher puts in eagerly. 'Standard after a shooting.'

'He doesn't feel like he can go back to work,' Simmons says.

'Well, not after suing his partner,' Thistle says.

The judge silences her with a sharp look. Then she says, 'Even if there were adequate evidence of emotional harm, *Agent* Thistle wouldn't necessarily be responsible for it. It sounds like she has fulfilled her duty of care, and

I don't want to set a precedent that encourages police to fire on potentially unarmed suspects, even to protect other officers. Case dismissed. The plaintiff will pay the defendant's costs.'

Thistle looks at her. She can't believe it.

'Your Honour—' Simmons begins.

'I've made my ruling,' the judge says. 'Case dismissed.'

She bangs the gavel and starts the slow process of getting out of her chair.

Thistle sags with relief. It's only now that I realise how well she was hiding her anxiety. She's not rich—losing this case might have ruined her. She gets up from the witness box, shaking. Her lawyer hugs her. A twinge of envy—no one in my life is close enough to hug me and, even if they were, I couldn't do it without endangering them.

Then Thistle sees me.

Her eyes narrow. She notices who I'm sitting with, and her annoyance turns to fury.

I glance at the lumberjack. Does she know him?

The lumberjack turns to me. 'Well,' he says, 'that's that.'

'Like I said,' I tell him, 'she's a good cop.'

'I'm sure she is.'

'You'd like her if you got to know her.'

For some reason this seems to make him mad. Teeth clenched, he says, 'I never got your name.'

My phone is buzzing angrily. It can only be Warner. The Asian guy and the tracksuit man watch as I stand up. Both are still hemmed in by other people, but they won't be for long.

'No,' I say, 'you didn't.'

I walk calmly out of the courtroom and turn the corner, breaking the line of sight between me and the two men.

Then I start running.

The corridor is wide, with a gradual curve to the right and lots of light coming through the big windows on my left. Nowhere to hide. No sign of a fire exit. I dart around other people, sprinting towards the front entrance.

'Hey, man, watch it,' someone says.

I keep running.

I turn one more corner, and now the entrance is visible up ahead. I see my reflection in the glass. Already red-faced, my hair glued to my forehead by sweat. Behind me, I can see the two men. They've spotted me. They're walking quickly, but not running. Not calling attention to themselves.

The tracksuit man is walking stiffly, spine rigid. He has something in the back of his pants, probably a knife. Carbon fibre, since he got it through the metal detector.

A bottleneck ahead. I won't have to go through the metal detector to get out, but I will have to walk through a one-way security exit. There's an automatic door, followed by a short airlock-like corridor, followed by a second automatic door. The crowd is slowing down as it approaches the exit. I push through, angering more people. 'Sorry, sorry.' My phone is still vibrating like a hornet trapped in my pocket.

A security guard is looking at me. Rotund, black, with a thick moustache and a wedding ring. Maybe I should tell him the guys behind me have a gun, or a bomb. He wouldn't believe me, because of the metal detector. But enough people in the crowd would fall for it to create mass panic. Dozens of people running. The confusion might help me slip away.

Or it might give the two men the freedom to stab me with a carbon-fibre blade and disappear into the crowd, leaving me gasping on the floor like a fish as I bleed out through a punctured liver. I meet the guard's gaze and then look away.

The first automatic door opens for me, making a squeaking sound like on *Star Trek*, and I'm running through the airlock. Quieter in here. I can hear my breaths reverberating off the walls, the clopping heels of the woman ahead of me. She looks like a lawyer. Grey skirt, jacket over one arm, gold earrings. She senses me behind her and turns, alarmed. I overtake her and hurry through the second door.

Out through the foyer and onto the courthouse steps. I trot down them like a dancer, my legs a blur. Across the road is the diner where I ate with Thistle. There was a multistorey parking lot on the other side of it. If I—

Someone grabs my collar and I miss a step. My legs fly out from under me, but the hand keeps me from falling down the stairs. It's like I'm being dangled over a cliff in the cold night air, although the next step is only six inches below me.

'Phoenix, Cleveland,' the tracksuit man says, in a voice with at least two generations of Texas in it. 'Now answer your goddamn phone.'

•

'When we met yesterday,' Warner says, 'I don't remember you mentioning that you were working for the FBI again.'

She doesn't sound pissed off. Instead, there's an ominous flatness to her voice. It takes me back to Mrs Radfield at the group home. *I'm not angry, Timothy, I'm just disappointed.*

'Where did you hear that?' I ask, still pretending not to know about the tracking app.

'Please,' Warner says. 'Are you going to pretend that you're not with Special Agent Reese Thistle right now?'

Actually, Thistle is still inside. I'm with the tracksuit man on the courthouse steps, the streetlights stretching our shadows to a surreal length. But I take her point.

'You never said you wanted me to work exclusively for you,' I say. The plastic phone creaks in my hand as I squeeze it tighter and tighter.

'I figured that was strongly implied,' Warner says. 'And given the nature of the work you do for me, I thought you'd be smart enough to stay a mile away from the feds.'

She's not wrong. 'I'm not investigating you,' I say. 'It's an unconnected case. Unless you murdered someone named Kenneth Biggs?'

I said 'murder' deliberately. Maybe she'll ask me how I know he's dead. If she does, she's involved.

But there's just silence at the other end of the line. Impossible to read.

The Asian guy is at the kerb at the bottom of the steps, smoking a cigarette and spinning a car key in one hand.

I'm guessing it's for the black SUV parked nearby. The lumberjack is still inside.

Tracksuit man is adjusting the back of his pants, where the knife is. I don't know if he's willing to use it. He and the Asian guy would both have been recorded entering and leaving the courthouse. If he stabs me and runs, the police could probably ID them both with facial recognition. He might be too dumb to realise that, though. And Warner might consider them both expendable.

'You don't know as much as you think you do about my business,' Warner says finally. 'But you know enough that I don't want you hanging around cops.'

'It's a one-off,' I say. 'Just this case, then I'm done.'

'It won't surprise you to hear that I'm a big fan of Bill Clinton.'

Actually, that surprises me quite a lot, not least because it seems to have nothing to do with what we were talking about.

'I liked his three-strikes law,' she continues. 'It was nice and easy to understand. Get caught three times, that's it. Life sentence.'

The law was more complicated than that, but now I see what she's getting at. 'You must have lost a few customers.'

'I'm a minority shareholder in a few private prisons. I make money off these guys whether they're on the streets or not. The point is, you didn't call me when Francis missed the drop-off yesterday. That's one. You took a case for the FBI. That's two.'

I say nothing.

'You're not gonna solve this case,' Warner says. 'You're gonna drop it. Or else that's three. And then I find a new waste-disposal guy and give him his first assignment.'

The Asian guy is watching me from the bottom of the steps.

'You understand?' Warner asks.

I cough. 'Yeah.'

'You're gonna drop the case?'

'Yes.'

'Good. I've got another delivery for you. Be waiting at one am. Now put Tane on so I can tell him not to kill you.'

I hand the phone to tracksuit man. He puts the phone to his ear. 'Yeah?'

There's a pause.

'He tried to run,' he says.

I can hear Warner laughing. Then she says something else.

'Understood,' Tane says. He ends the call and hands the phone back to me. 'Lucky break, asshole.'

But I can see signs of relief. An unclenched jaw, slackened shoulders. Some people go through life hunting opportunities for violence. You find them in bars, police forces, armies. Looks like Tane isn't one of them.

Nor am I. But I've done terrible things anyway, things I can't take back. I'll never be able to look at a stranger without knowing, in a flash, what their insides look like. I'll never hear a knock at the door without wondering if it's the police. I can never have an unguarded conversation with anyone.

Tane doesn't have to live with any of that, at least not yet.

'Lucky break,' I echo, wondering how long it will take Warner to realise that I lied to her.

CHAPTER 13

Without me, you cannot live.
But when I'm broken, you do not die.
I'm often paired with diamonds. What am I?

Dinner is reheated Biggs. It's a dangerous meal, since I still don't know how he died. He may have been poisoned. But Aaron Elliott smelled off. Must have been left unrefrigerated too long, which means he'll have to be cooked, and I'm too hungry to wait. Eating people is dangerous anyway, because of blood-borne viruses. Doesn't mean I can make myself stop.

Don't judge me. Heart disease is the number-one killer in the USA, but you still eat doughnuts. Your diet is killing you, too.

While I'm chewing, I find myself looking at Biggs's left hand. The right is in my freezer. I'm saving it so I can plant it in the home of his killer, once I've worked out who it is.

The cut on his index finger is bugging me. When I was homeless I donated plasma every two weeks, because they'd give you free food after. Cheese, crackers, juice, a milkshake. But I couldn't help watching the people in the other chairs, leaning back like fat kings on thrones as the blood trickled out of their arms—so I always left hungrier than I arrived.

Before each donation the nurses would stab my fingertip with something a bit like a stapler, taking a single drop of blood to check my haemoglobin levels. I'm type O negative, universal donor, so my blood was in demand. If the levels were too low the first time, they'd keep stabbing fingers until they got an acceptable reading. The wound on Biggs's fingertip looks a bit like the ones I used to have.

Or . . . I look closer. That *could* be a bite mark. Not one of mine. I don't take little nibbles like that. I take huge chunks, like a great white shark.

On a hunch, I lift Biggs's floppy arm, bending his elbow so his hand is near what's left of his face. I'm no forensic expert, but his teeth seem like they might match the divot in his finger.

I think back to the bloody prints on the wall planner in the shipping container. A tingle ascends my spine as a half a theory emerges from the shadows in my mind.

I swallow and clean my face, as though Thistle will be able to see me. Then I make the call.

She picks up the phone quickly. 'Yeah?'

'Imagine you're a math professor,' I say.

'You wanna explain what the hell you were doing in that courtroom?'

I hesitate. Right. The courthouse.

'Were you trying to put me off? Get me sued?'

'No,' I say. 'I sat up the back so you wouldn't even notice me.'

'That's worse, you creep. You think you have the right to keep tabs on me? Were you and my asshole husband comparing strategies?'

'Your husband?' Oh. The lumberjack. *Man, you got no idea. Your friend? She has a cold streak. You'll see.*

'Don't come in tomorrow,' Thistle says. 'I can solve this case without your help.'

It's the perfect way out, but I don't take it. 'I'm sorry,' I say. 'I was worried about you. When you said you had a lawyer, I thought you were in trouble. I just wanted to know what was going on.'

'If I wanted you to know, I would have fucking told you.'

'And I didn't know that guy was your husband,' I say. 'He didn't tell me. And he's not what I pictured.'

She doesn't respond.

I keep talking. 'I get that you don't . . .' *Like me anymore.* The words are too hard to say, so I finish with: '. . . want to see me. But you're my oldest friend.' *Only friend.* 'I care about you.'

Thistle hesitates, making it clear that she doesn't think of me as a friend.

'You can show it by respecting my privacy,' she says.

'I will,' I say. 'I'm sorry. I shouldn't have followed you.'

'You had the chance to be a part of my life,' she says. 'You turned it down, remember?'

'I know. I'm sorry about that, too.'

Another pause. I can feel her wondering what I mean. Do I regret my choice, or am I just sorry for hurting her?

The answer is both. Something else has been bubbling away in the dark recesses of my brain. I rejected Thistle because I was afraid of hurting her. But now Warner is providing me with a steady supply of bodies. My ugly desires are sated. Does that mean a relationship between Thistle and I could be . . . safe?

But there are two problems. One, Thistle hates me now. Two, Warner will stop supplying bodies—and maybe kill me—if I keep seeing Thistle.

'So,' Thistle says, 'I'm imagining I'm a math professor.'

I exhale, relieved to be back on safe ground. 'Right. Say you were locked in a shipping container at a dump site. You're expecting your captor to move you soon. You want to get a message to the cops—a warning, about something happening on December ninth—but you don't have a phone. What do you do?'

'You think that was Biggs's blood at the dump? Not Ruthven's?'

'Biggs went missing more recently than Ruthven, and the blood wasn't old. Not fresh, but not old.'

'And why December nine?'

'Those splotches of blood weren't random spatter. He was marking specific dates. The last one was the ninth of December. Tomorrow.'

A beat.

'Okay,' Thistle says. 'So Biggs pricked his own finger and decided to write with his own blood, rather than doing something more obvious and less dramatic.'

'Like what?'

'Like using the whiteboard marker right under the calendar.'

'We wouldn't have paid attention to that,' I say. 'Random dots of marker on a wall planner.'

'We would have, if he added a message explaining what they meant.'

'His captors would have seen a message when they moved him. They would have cleaned it up. Blood was the only way to get our attention without getting theirs.'

'So what happens tomorrow?'

'I don't know,' I say. 'But whatever it is, it happened at least eleven times before. There was a date marked on each month. January ninth, February thirteenth, March nineteenth—'

'I have the dates. I took a picture. So if we work out what happened on all of those days . . .'

'Then we can guess what's supposed to happen tomorrow.'

'I don't even know what to look for,' Thistle says.

'Get Vasquez on it. Maybe he can use software to look for similarities.'

'We don't have much time. I'll call him now.' A pause. 'Good work, Blake.' The line goes dead.

A flutter of pride, but also guilt, as I look down at Biggs.

Thistle wouldn't be congratulating me if she knew whose finger had 'tipped' me off.

She's more right than she knows—we don't have much time. I need to solve this case quickly so I can stop working it before Warner kills me. Which means I can't just wait around for Vasquez to find an answer. I need to go back to where I first found Biggs. If the killer dumped *his* body there, then maybe I'll find Ruthven there too.

Texas has a drive-through culture, and I'm not immune to it. I can't resist carving some more off Biggs to eat on the way. As I slide the knife under his pectoral muscle, I see something strange beneath his ribs.

I have to crack them with a hammer to get to it. When I finally pull it out and wash the gore off, I don't recognise it. A little silver bulb, topped by wires contained in transparent plastic.

A pacemaker—it must be. Which turns this whole thing upside down.

Heart failure. The number-one cause of death in the USA. I still don't know how Biggs ended up naked in the woods, or why his car and phone ended up at the dump. But it's possible that he died of a heart attack while fleeing from his abductor. If that's the case, the person who took him—the one who sealed him in that shipping container, who presumably also abducted Ruthven—might not even realise he's dead.

•

I'm getting into my car when Shawn opens his front door. Probably not coincidence. More likely he's been waiting for me to leave.

Sure enough, he waves to get my attention as he jogs over. He's holding an empty plastic tray. The dog is watching from the window, paws against the glass.

I wind down the window, teeth chattering in the cold.

Shawn twists his face into a grimace and puts on a funny voice as he approaches. 'Hey, buddy. You got a dead cat in there, or what?'

'Excuse me?'

He drops the voice, looks disappointed. 'It's from *Terminator*. You haven't seen it?'

'No.'

He shrugs. 'So anyway, I smelled something funny near your place. Caitlin smelled it first, led me right to your doorstep. Thought I'd let you know. You used rat poison lately?'

'Nah,' I say. 'Gives me hives.'

He hesitates for a moment before laughing. 'Okay. Well, maybe you got a dead rat under your fridge, or a racoon died in your trash can or something. Or there's a dead body under your floorboards.'

He laughs again. I laugh too, thinking about the off smell from Elliott's body.

'Thought I should tell you,' he says. 'You know how you can't smell your own house? You wouldn't want your new lady friend smelling it like that.'

Thistle would certainly recognise the smell of death. 'No, sir, I would not,' I say. 'Thanks.'

'No problemo.' He sees me looking at the plastic tray. 'Oh, I gotta take this with me whenever I leave the house. So Caitlin thinks I'm taking the recycling out, and not going for a walk without her.'

The dog starts barking at the window. Maybe she heard her name through the glass.

'Gotta go,' Shawn says. 'Hasta la vista, baby.'

CHAPTER 14

I am fatally wounded with a blade before I am given away as a gift. The receiver keeps me alive as long as possible, but I always die. What am I?

Francis isn't due to deliver the next body until one am. It's ten pm now—I have some time to kill.

I park further off the road than usual, bumping down the grassy slope and waiting until the hood is nudging the shrubbery before I kill the engine. I don't want everyone who drives past getting a good look at my car.

My trail through the woods is only two days old, but hard to find in the dark. Up close, the trees are seething with life, insects devouring everything that isn't made of stone, and plants slowly smothering everything that is. My footprints are half buried in a layer of patchy undergrowth. Ten steps in and I can't see my car through the wall of dark green, speckled with white flowers. I flick on my flashlight app, but keep the beam at a low angle.

Soon I think I've reached the spot where Biggs's body was. My footprints become indistinct here, and then reappear somewhere else, less deep without Biggs's weight. The blood is gone, consumed by the forest.

I turn slowly, thinking back to the moment when I realised someone was moving through the woods towards me. They came from . . . this way. I now know it wasn't the police, who still don't know Biggs was here. I trudge in that direction, looking for someone else's tracks.

It doesn't take much searching before I realise this is hopeless. I could find my own path only because I knew where it was. The tracker's footprints are impossible to find.

But soon I stumble across a trail. Dirt, just wide enough for a single pair of tyre tracks, rutted deep over the years.

Not a trail. A driveway.

I imagine Biggs, naked in the passenger seat. The car stopping, maybe to let a deer pass. Biggs making his move, opening the door and leaping out. He sprints into the forest, and . . . dies of a heart attack after twenty yards.

Possible. Maybe. Either way, I want to find out who lives out here.

I walk up the drive. A slight upward slope, enough to leave my thighs burning after a while. I occasionally stop and listen. Too far from the main road for traffic noise now. The silence is crushing.

Eventually I spot a cabin. Bigger than a standard hunting lodge—my guess is three bedrooms. The pine logs are recently oiled, and the windows cleaned of cobwebs. No lights on. I hide the flashlight and slow down as I approach. When I reach the edge of the trees I stay still for a moment, listening. Can't hear any voices or movement from inside, but it's almost midnight now. The occupants could be sleeping, unaware that a monster is lurking in the dark right outside.

I weave through the trees in a slow circle, wanting to examine the back of the cabin from a safe distance.

The other side has big windows, clean gutters and a rainwater tank. I can't see anything through the windows other than lacy cream curtains. The place seems too backwater to be a holiday rental. No mailbox. Maybe it's one of those doomsday prepper places, a hideaway for the apocalypse. The inside might be stuffed with canned food and batteries.

When I'm almost back where I started, I take a nearly fatal misstep. I put my foot down on some fallen branches and find there's no ground beneath them. My arms windmill as I try to shift my weight back onto my other foot. After a moment of wobbling, I crash down loudly onto my ass next to the hole.

I lie still for a full minute, then two. The smell of decay washes over me. No sounds from the cabin, or anywhere else. Seems like I got away with that moment of clumsiness. I'm guessing no one's home. There's no sign of a car anywhere around, and this place is too remote to easily reach on foot.

I pick up my dropped phone and shine it into the hole.

It's a little more than two feet wide, dug deliberately by someone. Can't see the bottom. I think it's a hunting trap. A deer steps in, breaks its leg, and screams until the hunter comes to shoot it. Doesn't seem very sporting to me, but I used to eat death-row inmates, so what would I know?

The hole is only twenty yards from the cabin. It seems likely that the owner dug it. And this isn't too far from where I found Biggs, either. Maybe there was no car. He could have been running away from this cabin when he died of a heart attack.

Time to have a look inside.

I walk up onto the porch. A little square of glass is set in the front door, but it's too dark inside to see anything beyond.

If I'm going to break in, I want to be damn sure no one's home. Home invaders get shot in Texas. So I knock. Three loud taps echo out.

No response.

I knock again, and call out. 'Hello? I need help! My car broke down, and I have no service out here. Can I use your phone? Please.'

Nothing.

When I was homeless, sometimes I'd be lucky enough to find somewhere to squat. Houston keeps spreading outwards, so there are thousands of vacant half-finished houses on the edges of town. Finished ones, too. Investors buy them, wait for the value to go up and then sell, often without bothering to rent them out in between.

Unfortunately, most of the neighbourhoods are patrolled

by private security teams, because rich assholes don't like giving free accommodation to homeless people. The few houses which have no security also have no insulation to keep the heat in or out. By law the renter pays the heating bills, so there's no incentive for investors to build the houses efficiently. I spent a lot of nights shivering on a stolen yoga mat while the cold seeped up from the concrete below.

But I got good at breaking into houses.

Step one: you check if any of the doors or windows are unlocked.

The front door isn't. I do another quick walk-around. No back door. None of the windows will budge.

Step two: look for the spare key. Everyone has one.

The front porch is bare except for a rocking chair and a doormat. Nothing under either one. I run my fingers across the top of the doorframe. Just dust. No potted plants around the cabin. Everyone has a spare key, but you can't always find it.

At this point a burglar would take the hinges off the door, or kick it in. But a squatter will go to step three.

I stand on the rail that surrounds the porch so I can reach the rain gutter, and then I scramble up onto the roof itself. There's a chimney, too narrow to climb down. But the roof is tiled, not sheet metal. Some luck, at last. It's pretty easy to lift one tile just enough to unhook the one next to it, making a square hole of blackness. After removing four more tiles, the hole is just wide enough to worm through.

The flashlight in my phone illuminates a crawlspace

stuffed with fluffy yellow insulation panels. This would be a great place to squat in. I wriggle through the insulation, the fibres sticking to my clothes. I'm going to be itchy as hell tomorrow.

Eventually I find a trapdoor. I open it and drop down into the cabin.

When I dust myself off and stand up, someone is watching me.

I leap backwards, survival instinct taking over. The eyes watching me from the shadows are big and far apart, like something out of a nightmare, gleaming almost too brightly to be real.

I raise the phone, hoping to dazzle the demon with the flashlight. The beam falls on dark fur and long teeth. A wolf!

Or, more precisely, a wolf's head. It's a hunting trophy, mounted on the wall.

The wolf is not alone. I look around, taking in all the animal heads as they stare at me through glass eyes. They're everywhere—above the fireplace, between the cluttered bookshelves, watching over the leather armchair. There's a rug which used to be a deer, its head still whole, mouth agape.

Even my house isn't this creepy—and it contains two human corpses.

A hunting rifle hangs by its strap from a hook beside the door, next to a candle lantern and a flashlight. The wood stock shines, recently polished.

A new image forms in my mind. Biggs, stripped naked on the deer rug, while the owner of this place points the rifle at him.

In my head, the owner has no face. But he's big, and dressed like a hunter, in boots, khakis and a wool-lined cap.

'I'll give you a twenty-second head start,' he says, as Biggs trembles. 'Now run, rabbit!'

I don't have much evidence for this scenario. So it's time to find some more.

I start walking through the house. The floorboards barely squeak under my weight. Whoever built this place knew what they were doing.

The kitchen has no fridge. No power here, maybe. There's canned food in the pantry, but not so much that the owner might be expecting the end of the world. A well-stocked liquor cabinet, with several varieties of whisky and rum.

I was wrong about the three bedrooms. Just two, and only one of them has a bed in it—a queen-size, neatly made. That room has some clothes in the closet, men's and women's. The men's clothes are long of leg and broad of shoulder. A good fit for my imagined hunter. The closet of the other bedroom is empty.

Two bathrooms. One has a single toothbrush and some make-up. The other is bare. Both bathrooms smell bad. Presumably something to do with the plumbing. I don't know how a toilet that isn't connected to the grid even works.

I walk back into the main living area, hoping the books

on the shelves will give me some clues about the people who live here. But as I'm crossing the deerskin rug, I feel a little bounce in the floorboards.

I lift the rug.

A trapdoor. Padlocked shut. The padlock was hidden under the deer's head.

I knock on the wood, trying to get a sense of the space below. A cavern, or a cupboard?

I can't tell. I suddenly wonder what I'll do if someone knocks back.

No one does.

The poker in the fireplace would make a good lever; I could break the padlock off the trapdoor. But that's something I can't fix. When the owner comes home, he or she may decide to report the break-in. That would draw police attention to the woods in which I recently took a bite out of a dead body.

But it's worth the risk. I put the flashlight down and grab the poker. I try to wedge the tip under the padlock, but it's hard to see in the dark.

Then the room lights up as car headlights sweep across the windows. Someone's here.

CHAPTER 15

What breaks but never falls?
What falls but never breaks?

Time seems to slow to a crawl, the space between the moments expanding like dark energy stretching the universe. I scan the room, noting all the signs of my intrusion. Then, as the headlights go dead, I quickly pocket my phone so no one sees the flashlight through the windows.

I roll the rug back over the trapdoor. The poker is my only weapon, but it's also the thing most likely to give me away. I prop it back up in the fireplace, and immediately feel defenceless.

I look out the window. A man and a woman are walking towards the cabin. The man looks anxious, but excited, too. He's black, mid-twenties, with horn-rimmed glasses and a slim build. Too small to be the owner of the clothes in the house. He's wearing chinos and a cardigan—not dressed for a hike.

The woman is white, with long black hair and a matching dress. Her hips swing as she walks. She looks much calmer than the man. She has all the power in this situation, or she's doing a good job of faking it. She's saying something, but quietly. The distance and the crunching of their footfalls make the words impossible to decode.

I can't go out the door; they'll see me. And there's no time to climb back up into the crawlspace. I need somewhere to hide.

I duck into bedroom number two—the one with no bed. Then I stand in the empty cupboard and hold my breath, hunched over to keep my head clear of the hanging rod.

The lock clicks, and the front door swings open on quiet hinges. The gas lantern hisses. Faint light flickers in the cracks around the edges of the closet door.

The man yelps, and then laughs nervously.

'Sorry,' the woman says. 'I should have warned you.'

'What is that, a wolf?'

'Yeah. A Mexican grey. It was a big one, too—ninety pounds.'

Footsteps moving around the living area.

'So,' the man asks, 'where, uh . . .'

'I'll show you.' The woman's voice hovers on the border between friendly and flirtatious. 'You want a drink first?'

'Okay, sure.'

More footsteps, heading towards the kitchen.

I slowly open the closet door. I can hear the liquor cabinet opening. Glasses clink.

I creep over to the bedroom door. Look out. No one in the living room. Where's the man?

'I have to tell you something,' the woman is saying quietly. The man must be in the kitchen with her.

I dart out of the bedroom, cross the corridor and pad across the living area. The front door isn't locked. I turn the handle, wincing at the faint *snick* of the mechanism. Then I slip out onto the porch and carefully close the door behind me.

Heart pounding, I crouch down beneath the windows. No sound from inside. Could mean they're drinking. Could mean they heard me, and they're staring at each other. A silent look of *Did you hear that?*

After a moment, the man says, 'I'm ready.'

The woman laughs. 'Yeah, you are. Bring your drink.'

I tiptoe off the porch and across the undergrowth towards the car. It's a boxy Buick, a few years old. I can't tell in the dark if it's grey or blue or black. I conceal myself in a cave of branches not far from the cabin and finally let the air out of my lungs. That was too close.

I check the time on my phone. I still have a while before Francis is due to drop off the next body. Whoever owned those oversized hunting clothes isn't here—I might wait a while, just in case he shows up to join the other two. This looked and sounded like a tryst, but it could be a party. Or something else entirely.

No one turns up. Minutes pass. The adrenaline fades. My legs start to cramp up.

Midnight comes. Silently, the eighth of December becomes the ninth. It's the day Biggs marked on the wall planner, and I still don't understand why.

About half an hour later, the front door of the cabin opens. The woman walks out, followed by the man. He looks dishevelled. She doesn't.

I'm getting a weird vibe here. If they were married, they would have stayed the night. If they were having an affair, they would have been holding hands or pinching one another's asses on the way in. There's nothing like that, although the man does look guilty. Actually, it's worse than that. He looks disgusted with himself, as though he knows he's just done something it will be hard to live with. A feeling I know too well.

The woman wears an expression of intense serenity. Like a Buddhist sniper. For an instant she looks familiar, but then she turns her head as she climbs into the Buick, and her jet-black hair curtains her face. She's gone before I can place her, like a whisper of perfume on a crowded street.

The man gets into the passenger side of the car. The engine turns over and the brakelights turn the woods bloody red. I keep my head down as the car rumbles away.

Once they're gone, I climb back up onto the roof and replace the roof tiles, not wanting to be given away by a leaking roof. Then I jump down and sprint along the drive towards the highway.

I get to my car just in time. Francis's van pulls up less than a minute later. I pop the trunk of my car, trying to look casual.

Sariklis gets out of the driver's seat.

'Where's Francis?' I ask.

He avoids my gaze. 'Shit, Blake. Did you have to park so far off the road?'

'You think it's unnecessarily cautious? I've seen where lazy criminals end up.'

He shoots me a glare.

'What?' I say.

'Come on,' he says, turning back to the van. 'Give me a hand with this.'

He checks the horizon for cars. There's nothing, six hours before daybreak. He opens the back of the van. I can't see the body through the plastic sheeting, but I can tell it's another big one. I don't have room for three corpses in my freezer, let alone in my stomach. Of course, Warner only knows about two of them.

'You reckon there'll be a gap after this one?' I ask.

'Don't know. You get his feet.'

I can't tell which end is the feet until Sariklis lifts the head. He handles the heavy corpse with surprising gentleness, like a pallbearer, as we carry it down the hill. He's more respectful than Francis ever was.

As we lower the body into the trunk, I realise that my clothes are still covered with insulation fibres. It seems impossible that Sariklis has missed this, but he says nothing.

'Thanks,' I say.

He nods. 'Goodbye, pal.'

I shut the trunk and watch him trudge back up the hill towards the van. He never called me 'pal' before. After a minute, I realise that he probably wasn't talking to me.

I open the trunk again, and peel back some of the plastic. Just enough to reveal the bloodied face of Francis.

CHAPTER 16

By countless teeth is all my body lined, the forest sons I touch with bite unkind, and yet as I eat, I throw it all behind. What am I?

Two hours before dawn I'm at the college campus, hands in my pockets. Three hands. My left, my right, and Biggs's left.

It's December 9, and I'm out of time. I need to speed the investigation up, and that means changing Biggs from a missing person to a homicide victim.

I'm outside the fence line, well beyond the range of the security cameras at the corners of every building. My car is parked a long way from here. My breath comes out of my nose as puffs of steam. My fingers have gone numb. The hoodie does nothing to protect my ears from the biting wind.

I walk along the cycle path, hunched up like an armadillo. Another hundred yards and I'll be able to see the math department on the other side of the chain-link fence. The campus looks different in the early morning. There are floodlights here and there, but all the windows are dark. With no young people around, it looks more like a deserted business park than a school. The classrooms could easily be conference rooms; the study nooks in the libraries could be cubicles. I wonder if the students suspect that they're being trained for life as office drones.

The plan is to throw Biggs's hand over the fence, somewhere within range of the math department. Even during the break, enough people are around that a severed hand won't go unnoticed. Soon it will be connected to Biggs's disappearance, especially since his wedding ring is on it, with the engraving inside the band: LOVE, GABBI. After that, it's a homicide investigation, which gives Thistle and I more resources. We'll even have Biggs's prints and DNA, if the lab hasn't confirmed them yet.

But if anyone sees me do it, I'll become the number-one suspect in the murder I'm supposed to be investigating. I have to be careful.

Soon I see shapes through the fog. Three young men, maybe on their way back to their dorms after a party. Two are staggering like zombies. Drunk. The other guy is practically skipping, still full of energy. Probably on Adderall.

According to Agent Richmond, my former partner at the FBI, practically every college student is on Adderall. It helps them study all night without losing focus. Some take it to get ahead, forcing others to take it to keep up.

It screws with your liver and pancreas over the long term, and you need to take more and more to get the same effect. But by the time the negative symptoms show up, these kids will all have their degrees. They'll be lawyers and politicians. People who can afford a drug habit, an up-market rehab facility, a liver transplant.

Some kids, though, don't take it for study. They just want to be able to party all night and still hear what the teacher is saying in class the next day.

I think this guy is one of those. I hadn't counted on seeing anyone sober enough to remember me later.

I don't know if they've spotted me yet. I can't turn and run, just in case they have. That would be so suspect that I'd have to abort. Go home.

Instead I bend over, as though I'm out of breath, or stretching. I surreptitiously pick up a dented beer can. Then I straighten up and keep walking towards the three men. Not stumbling, that would be too obvious. Just walking.

As the three men come within facial recognition range, I raise the can, like I'm saying, *Cheers*.

One of the two drunkards says, 'Eyyy!' like the Fonz. The other hasn't seen me at all, and says, 'What?' The third guy just nods.

I keep walking.

I'm not sure exactly what tips me off. Maybe it's the scuffling of feet behind me. Maybe the movement of the air. Maybe it's what Thistle said about the jogger who got attacked around here. But I duck.

Too slow. A fist glances off the top of my skull, hard enough to send me stumbling. As I fall, my hands fly out of my pockets.

All three of them.

Biggs's hand hits the path and lands on its back, like a dead crab. I crash down next to it and grab it, hoping they didn't see. I stuff it into the pouch at the front of my hoodie and try to stand.

One of the drunkards kicks me in the chest, and I roll back, tucking my head just in time to avoid cracking it on the path.

'See what he's got,' the other drunk says. He sounds sober now. I can't believe I fell for the act.

The Adderall-looking guy—I wonder why he didn't pretend to be drunk like the others—pins me down with one hand while he searches me with the other. His forearm is like a steel bar across my chest. My arms are trapped. He's done this before.

But this time he gets a surprise.

His hand comes out of my pocket holding Biggs's fingers. For a second the guy doesn't know what he's looking at. Then he says, 'Oh, holy fuck!' and flings it aside.

The pressure on my chest loosens just enough.

I rear up and bite his cheek.

He screams then, turns his face away. But I don't release my grip, so the movement tears a strip of flesh from his face.

He punches me, a desperate but surprisingly well-aimed blow to my left eye. I flop back down, my head full of stars and my mouth full of blood. The meat is so fresh and tender. I need more.

I sit up. The rest of my meal is running away, screaming. So are his two friends.

I'm about to give chase when a light turns on in one of the buildings behind the fence. Someone is here, and awake. As I watch, another window goes bright.

Panic suppresses the hunger. I look around frantically for Biggs's hand. Those guys saw my face. Soon I'll be wanted for assault. If I leave the hand here, that assault could be connected to Biggs's murder.

But the weeds on either side of the path are lush. I don't know where the guy threw the hand, and I don't have time to comb through the grass.

'Hello?' a voice calls.

I break into a sprint, in the opposite direction from the three would-be muggers. For the second time in two days, I find myself wiping gore off my chin with my sleeve as I hurry through a public place, hoping to get to my car before anyone spots me.

I'm losing it. One day I'll make a mistake that gets me killed.

What scares me isn't the idea that I just made that mistake. It's the idea that I did it yesterday, or a month ago. Maybe I've been doomed for years and I just don't know it yet.

I reach my car and jump in. There are flashlights somewhere behind me. Too soon for cops; probably campus security, armed with Tasers.

I drive just above the speed limit. Anything less is considered suspicious in Texas. A passing patrol car might conclude that I had been drinking.

Finally I make it home, and lock the door. Safe, for now. An hour later I've showered and washed my clothes, then showered again. I've brushed my teeth so hard the enamel hurts. I've shone a UV torch over the interior of my car, the radiation unravelling any DNA left behind. But I'm still on edge. I messed up, badly.

You're getting out of control. I push the thought away.

I'm scrubbing the dirt off the soles of my shoes when my phone rings. I answer, forgetting to sound sleepy: 'Yeah?'

'Good, you're up,' Thistle says. 'I'm on my way to the field office. Want me to pick you up?'

Probably a good idea, so Warner doesn't track my car to the office. 'What's going on?' I ask.

'I'm hoping you can give me a *hand* with something,' Thistle says.

•

I stand at the window, waiting for Thistle's car. I don't want her walking up to my front door. She might smell Elliott's corpse. Even after dissolving most of him in acid and freezing the rest in airtight containers, I still can't get rid of the smell. Despite the cold, I've been leaving the back door open to air the place out. It hasn't helped. In fact, the smell seems to be getting worse. *You got a dead cat in there, or what?*

Maybe it's getting worse because it's only in my head. When I was a kid, all my clothes came from charity. Most of them smelled like urine no matter how many times I washed them, and I was never sure if anyone else could smell it. I don't know much about brains—I don't even eat them—but I think knowing about an odour might be the same thing as smelling it, neurologically. Like how hearing the word 'vomit' puts a trace of it in your nose.

On the phone, Thistle didn't give me much information. Just that a severed hand had been found at the college, and she thought it belonged to Biggs. I got the feeling she knew more than she was saying. Hopefully that's only because she wanted to tell me in person.

Her Crown Vic slows down on approach, like she's reluctant to stop. Can't blame her, in a neighbourhood like this.

I slip out the front door, triple lock it behind me and run down the path to the car. Thistle pushes the door open and I jump straight in.

'Good morning,' she says.

I clear my throat. 'Good morning. I'm more awake now—you said something on the phone about a severed hand?'

She zooms up my street and does a U-turn at the end. 'I'll let Dr Norman fill you in on that. First let me tell you about Vasquez. He's been digging through the data on Biggs's computer. There's some weird porn in the browsing history, but so far nothing else suspicious. No significant correspondence with anyone outside our suspect pool, no email receipts from transactions we didn't already know about, no google searches for *how to fake your own death*.'

'How weird is the porn?'

'Vasquez only said there was nothing illegal.'

'But potentially embarrassing? Worthy of blackmail?'

'I assume so. Biggs was married, with a daughter and a senior position at the college. The porn wouldn't have to be too weird before it could be used for leverage. What are you thinking?'

I rub my eyes. 'Not sure. Probably nothing. How did Vasquez go with the dates marked on the wall planner?'

'Nothing so far.'

'Too much data to sift through?'

'Too little.' Thistle takes a turn-off towards the field office. 'He's got some kind of deep-learning algorithm working on it. It's supposed to be good at spotting patterns, but only works with huge swathes of data. Twelve dates doesn't give it much to work with.'

She seems more relaxed today. Maybe she's decided that me following her to the courthouse wasn't too bad. Or maybe she's just hiding her anger better. She could be counting down the hours until this case is solved and she never has to see me again.

The thought is painful, and I force it out of my mind. 'Well, we can't give it more dates,' I say. 'But can we give it clues for the sort of thing we're looking for?'

'I assume so. What *are* we looking for?'

'Missing persons or violent crime within a hundred miles of the dump.'

'If you're thinking that Biggs was trying to tell us what was happening to him by pointing to similar cases, there's no reason to assume they'd be local.'

I drum my fingers on my knees. 'If it was just similar cases, he wouldn't know the exact dates offhand. And that wouldn't help us identify his abductor.'

'I know what you're thinking,' Thistle says. 'But if Biggs was pointing us to the past crimes of the perp, he wouldn't know those dates either.'

'Not unless he and the perp were very close,' I say. 'And had been for more than a year. Where are we at with Shannon Luxford?'

'No sign of him anywhere—including in travel records. So he hasn't left the country, but he might have left the state. His car hasn't, though. Licence plate tracking hasn't seen anything.'

'Are his parents alive?'

'Yup. His father installs security systems, his mother's a homemaker. Some agents went to visit, but saw no sign of Shannon.'

'Okay. What about the guy who fled the dump?'

'Well, I've never had to put an APB out on a tractor before,' Thistle said. 'So that was fun. Houston PD found it abandoned in a field near the edge of the city. We're still looking for the driver, but I'm thinking he's in the wind. We don't know his name, and he's had time to change clothes by now.'

'You can't get his name from Edwards's employment records?'

'Oh, that's the other thing. The records are bogus. Full of made-up names and addresses.'

I remember noticing all the Anglo-Saxon names in his files. Half the workforce was Latino—I should have figured the records were fake.

'Let me guess,' I say. 'A bunch of his workers were undocumented—including the guy who ran. Edwards is claiming he didn't know, and that those were the details they gave him.'

'Bingo,' Thistle says. 'Half his employees didn't show up for work today. We must have scared them off. Most of them were smart enough not to run in such an obvious way, though.'

Maybe the guy ran because he thought we were from Immigration and Customs Enforcement. For undocumented workers, ICE is as frightening as the Gestapo in Nazi Germany. But it's possible that this particular man had more reason to flee than the rest.

'Serves Edwards right,' she continues. 'The pay records are pretty shady-looking. Best guess, he was paying those workers much less than he said he was. The IRS is interested.'

'And Biggs's car?'

'The crusher made it pretty much impossible to get fingerprints off the inside, and a lot of people have touched the outside. But the CSI techs found some blonde hairs stuck to the headrest of the driver's seat.'

Interesting. 'Long or short?'

'Long.'

'DNA?'

'Most of the hairs seem to have been cut off rather than fallen out,' Thistle says. 'But we got lucky with one strand—the follicle was still attached. We're testing it now.'

'Cut off' sounds like planted evidence to me. I stare out the window at the other cars. SUVs with no passengers, drivers staring like zombies at the brakelights ahead. A woman doing her make-up while she's stopped at a light.

'So I talked to Zak,' Thistle says after a pause.

'Who's Zak?'

'My ex-husband.' She keeps her eyes on the road. 'He didn't introduce himself?'

'No,' I say. 'In my head I was calling him "the lumberjack". You know, because of the shirt?'

She fights back a smile, but still doesn't look at me. 'So anyway, he thinks you're my boyfriend.'

'I didn't tell him that.'

'No. He assumed it because of how you stuck up for me.' She looks at me.

'Oh,' I say.

'So I'm sorry,' she says. 'I shouldn't have accused you of colluding with him.'

'It's okay,' I say. 'I shouldn't have been there at all. I should have mound my own business.'

It's something we used to say as kids—*mound* rather than *minded*, *sprunt* instead of *sprinted*. She laughs, and my heart thaws a little.

•

'Agent Thistle,' Dr Norman says. 'You always bring me the best cases.'

Norman is tall and pale, with a dry sense of humour and an unsettling way of looking at people, particularly me. I always feel like she can read my mind. She doesn't like me much, but that's okay. No one does.

Today her strawberry-blonde hair is mostly tucked into a blue shower cap. As usual, she shows no sign that she can feel how cold it is down here in the morgue.

The air smells bad. This meat is all too old to eat, and a lot of it has been pumped full of chemicals to preserve it.

'What can you tell us, doc?' Thistle asks.

Norman takes a steel tray out of a big fridge and places it on a workbench. It's covered with Saran wrap, like a plate of leftover sandwiches after a party. She removes the plastic wrap, unveiling the hand. The wedding ring is gone.

'Left hand of an adult male,' she says. 'Mid-forties, judging by the elasticity of the skin. No tattoos, no burns and no calluses on the fingertips, which would suggest a white-collar job. Removed with a serrated blade. Possibly a hacksaw.'

It was a bread knife, but whatever.

Thistle glances at me. 'At least we have Biggs's prints now.'

Looks like my plan worked, sort of. 'How do you know it's the right hand?' I ask.

'It's the left,' Norman says.

Hilarious.

'How do you know it belongs to Biggs? Plenty of men in their forties work white-collar jobs.'

'Get this,' Thistle says. 'A security guard at the university hears screaming from somewhere outside at four-thirty this morning. She has a look around. Finds nothing. Then, about two hours later, a jogger sees a pool of blood on the cycle path.'

'I didn't see a cycle path when we visited the school,' I say.

'It's outside the fence,' Thistle says. 'But not far from the math department.'

'So, no cameras?' I say. 'That's a shame.'

Norman gives me a strange look. I fight the urge to touch my hair, checking it for crusted blood.

'The jogger slows down,' Thistle says, 'and sees a severed hand half buried in the grass a few feet away. She calls the cops. When they show up, they can't find the rest of the body. But they do take a wedding ring off the hand. The engraving on the inside says, *Love, Gabbi*. And it has the date of Biggs's wedding engraved next to that.'

'That does sound fairly conclusive,' I say.

'It's theoretically possible the perp put the wedding band on someone else's hand,' Norman says. 'I'd advise against telling the family until we've confirmed prints or DNA.'

'I'd say they have a right to know,' Thistle says.

'They also have a right to not be jerked around,' Norman responds.

'What do you think happened?' I ask Thistle. 'Best guess.'

Thistle folds her arms across her chest. 'I figure we're being manipulated. The perp planted Biggs's hand and his blood there to lead us off-track—or maybe he thinks he deserves to be caught, since he's clearly unhinged. Violent impulses he can't control, and maybe a loose grip on reality. There are a bunch of other possibilities, but that's my gut feeling about what we're dealing with here.'

Thistle has caught plenty of killers, and she's getting close to profiling me. Luckily, Norman distracts her.

'Two things to note, Agent,' she says. 'First, the hand was removed post-mortem. So whoever screamed, it wasn't Biggs.'

'Huh.' Thistle deflates. 'Well, this just officially became a homicide investigation. Can you get time of death?'

'No more than a week ago. I can't be more specific than that. Lividity is useless without the rest of the body, and I'm thinking the killer may have refrigerated the hand, though I'm not sure for how long.'

It worries me sometimes, how good Norman is at her job.

'What about the blood?' Thistle asks. 'How fresh was it?'

'Very,' Norman says. 'And that's the other thing. I compared it to a sample from the hand. They don't match.'

Makes sense. The blood was from the guy whose face I bit.

I can sense Thistle getting excited. 'Different DNA?'

'I don't have DNA results back yet. But blood group is a much simpler test—it takes ten minutes. The hand is

A positive, the puddle is A negative. They came from different people.'

'The victim and the killer,' Thistle says. 'It's gotta be.'

'Maybe,' I say, thinking fast. I don't want us chasing the wrong guy, but I also don't want to implicate myself.

Thistle ignores me. 'If the killer was the one screaming, then who attacked him? And why?'

She looks at me expectantly, but I don't know what to say.

'It was a lot of blood,' Norman adds. 'Whoever left it behind is likely to need stitches.'

Thistle nods. 'Okay. We'll start checking hospitals. Anything else we should know?'

Norman passes her a manila folder. 'It's all in here, but I've given you the essentials.'

'You taught at Braithwaite, didn't you?' Thistle says.

'Briefly,' Norman says. 'Go Panthers.'

'Can you tell us anything about what Biggs was like to work with?'

'I taught med science. I don't think your victim and I ever met.' Norman turns to me. 'What happened to your eye, Blake?'

'Huh?'

'Your eye.' She makes a circular motion at her own eye, as though I'm not sure what eyes are.

'Oh.' My bruise must be starting to show. 'It was the dumbest thing. My neighbour, Shawn—he has this dog. I was trying to get to my car, and she ran under my legs, and I tripped. Hit my face on the side mirror.'

'Where were you going?' Norman asks. 'In the car.'

'To the library.' It's just the first thing that pops into my head.

'At four am? That bruise looks about six hours old.'

I hold her gaze. 'I'm not supposed to use my bathroom today. Someone came to clean off the mould yesterday, and there are still chemicals in the air. There's a public bathroom just outside the library. It's the closest one.'

Norman nods. But I still can't smother the feeling that she knows I'm lying.

'If a man goes to his doctor with an injury like that,' she says, 'you know what the doctor writes on his chart?'

'Black eye?' I guess.

'DFO,' she says. 'Drunk, Fell Over.'

'I don't drink,' I say. 'But thanks for your concern.'

CHAPTER 17

You're in a room with a concrete floor. You have nothing other than an egg. Can you make the egg fall six feet without breaking?

'Blake,' Vasquez says, 'you still working this case?'

'Why wouldn't I be?'

Thistle and I are in the basement, the air stifling thanks to the humming computers and the AC keeping the mould in the walls alive. No space above our heads, the ceiling only seven feet up.

'I heard both suspects fled,' Vasquez says. 'It's up to the Houston PD to find them now, right? Your job is done.'

'I'm done when we find our missing men,' I say.

'What happened to your face?'

'Dr Norman called it DFO. How's your algorithm going?'

Vasquez gestures at the server humming in the corner of the basement. 'So far it's determined that all the dates you gave me were slightly cooler than average, that overall internet traffic was marginally higher, road congestion was a bit lower, and, most interestingly, that visits to hospitals were up by a tenth of a per cent. Is any of that useful?'

'Not to us,' I say.

Thistle asks, 'Can you program it to look for missing persons or violent crime?'

'I tried that. Nothing.'

'Statewide? Nationwide?'

Vasquez just shrugs his movie-star shoulders.

I wish we could find out what was on Shannon's computer or phone. But we still don't have a warrant out for him.

'How are you going with Ruthven?' I ask.

'Got his phone and his computer. Still working through the data. Nothing promising. He used a dating app, and we're trying to track the most recent person he met.'

I say, 'Can you get us a list of everyone he met with?'

'Why?'

'If I was a killer, I wouldn't want to be the most recent person on an app like that. I'd use the app to make a few fake dates.'

'Okay,' Vasquez says. 'I'll look into that right now.'

'First,' I say, 'show me this "weird porn".'

Vasquez boots up Biggs's computer. He brings up a list of websites and offers me the chair.

I sit down. I don't have a computer at home so my exposure to pornography is limited, if you don't count advertising and music videos. Back at the group home, a kid named Stephen Stattelis had a tattered *Penthouse* magazine that got shared around a lot before Mrs Radfield found it. When it was my turn, I did find all the flesh exciting, but not for the same reasons as the other boys.

'Biggs didn't know how to clear his browser history?' I ask.

'This all came from his ISP. He used private browsing, but not a VPN.'

I click through to one of the websites. I'd been expecting gay porn, or maybe pictures of women's feet. What I find is something entirely different.

'Jesus,' Thistle says, looking over my shoulder. 'That's . . . unusual.'

Biggs's genre of choice seemed to be 'giantess' porn. Videos of women filmed from a low angle to make them look huge, crushing toy cars and action figures under their stiletto heels. Photoshopped images of models in bikinis stomping through cities like Godzilla. Computer animations and cartoons of huge women crushing tiny men against their bulging breasts, suffocating them.

'So he was a feminist,' Vasquez says dryly.

'I don't want to oversimplify things,' Thistle says to me, 'but did you notice the size of Biggs's wife?'

'Was she huge?' Vasquez asks.

'No. Tiny.'

'Huh. Guess that means he loved her for real.'

'This is all fantasy.' I keep scrolling. 'People don't fantasise about what they already have.'

Buried under the pic and video sites, I find a database

of user-submitted short stories. I find the ones Biggs liked enough to click through to page two, and I skim them. They all involve a man being seduced by a woman at least twice his size. Sometimes he fucks her, sometimes she breastfeeds him, and in one case . . .

She eats him.

My mouth goes dry as I read the description of the man disappearing headfirst into the woman's huge mouth, of her gagging as she swallows him whole. Then he's slowly digested, still alive as her stomach acid dissolves him.

'Some people out there fantasise about being eaten?' I say, my voice cracking.

'Yup. They're called vores.' I can hear the grin in Vasquez's voice. 'You haven't heard of that?'

I shake my head, too entranced to speak.

'Doesn't look like Biggs was one of them,' Thistle says, pointing to the screen. 'This is the only story in his history with the "vore" tag. Hey, what's "unbirth"?'

'You don't want to know,' Vasquez replies. 'So are you thinking he was blackmailed, or what?'

I scroll down to the comments section. Lots of very supportive perverts. *Great story! Well done!*

One comment catches my eye. *Anyone want to try this in real life? DM me.*

I highlight the text. 'There are people who *volunteer* to be eaten alive?'

'There's no vore tag on that story,' Vasquez points out. 'Probably just a giant roleplay, however that would work. But, yeah, there are some sickos out there.' He checks his gold watch. 'I'm gonna tweak the algorithm, looking for connections to the dating app.'

He goes away. I just sit there, staring at the words. *Anyone want to try this in real life?* There's plenty of meat at my house. But none of it is fresh. I can still taste the cheek of the man who attacked me.

Would someone let me eat them?

Thistle touches my shoulder, and I flinch.

'You okay, Blake?'

I stand up and back away from the computer like it's radioactive.

'Yeah,' I say. 'I'm fine. Vasquez is right. Sickos.'

'Uh-huh.' Thistle takes over the keyboard, scrolling through the porn. 'Is this the kind of stuff that turns you on, Blake?'

'Definitely not.'

I get the feeling she's not even listening to the answer. She's just enjoying making me uncomfortable. I wonder if I should tell her that she *is* my type—that I only rejected her for her own safety.

Somehow this doesn't feel like the right moment.

'Found Biggs's username,' Thistle says. 'Shortcomings7. Classy.'

'He could be expressing remorse for his tastes,' I suggest.

'Or he just likes a dirty pun. Let's see if he was corresponding with anyone on this forum.'

She taps and clicks around for a while. 'I can't get into his inbox without his password. But he visited the profiles of several other users, and one of them hasn't posted any public content. SleepingBeauty319. Seems like he might have exchanged private messages with Biggs.'

'He?'

Thistle rolls her eyes at my naivety. 'You really think there are any real women on these giant-lady porn forums, Blake?'

She's probably right.

'Can I see his profile?' I ask.

Thistle clicks through and leans back in her chair, frustrated. '404. Profile deleted. All I have is the username.'

'Wasn't Sleeping Beauty the user who posted that comment? Asking who wanted to try this in real life?'

Thistle checks. 'That was SleepingBeauty320. Common username.'

'Or the one person,' I say, 'creating and deleting profiles to avoid leaving a lasting trace. Like burners.'

Thistle nods slowly. 'So you think Biggs might have been honey-trapped? By someone pretending to be a giant woman?'

'He was a math professor. I doubt he believed in giants. But . . .' I trail off, thinking.

'What?'

'If you wanted to simulate a sex act with a giant, how would you do it?'

'I sure hope that's rhetorical,' Thistle says.

Before I can explain, Vasquez is back. 'Guys,' he says, 'I got something.'

We both turn. Vasquez doesn't look excited. In fact, his face is grim.

'I programmed the computer to include Ruthven's dating app in its search patterns. It couldn't find anything on the dates you gave me. But something else came up.'

'What?' Thistle asks.

'Sixteen missing men over the last eleven months, all from Houston, all using the same app.'

I quickly count the bodies I've disposed of for Charlie Warner. It's easy to lose track, since I destroy all evidence of each one—I think this is why some killers keep trophies—but I don't think it's sixteen yet.

'How popular is the app?' I ask. Sixteen sounds like a lot, but Houston is a city of more than two million people.

'Forty-six thousand users in the city. But these are all white, heterosexual males of the same approximate age, height and weight. The computer thinks it's significant.'

Those don't sound like Charlie Warner's victims. This is something entirely new. Thistle and I look at one another.

'Holy shit,' she breathes. 'We have a fucking serial killer on our hands.'

'And he has a type,' I say.

CHAPTER 18

What is the only organ that named itself?

'How long can we keep this quiet?' I ask.

Thistle and I are in the world's slowest elevator, on our way back up to the ground floor. Vasquez is on the phone to the director, telling her what he's found. A serial killer is a major hassle for the FBI. I'm glad I'm not the one who has to break the news to her.

If the victims were women or children, we wouldn't be assuming that they were dead. There are 46 million slaves in the world, 58,000 of them in the USA. Many missing people are eventually found in illegal brothels, small factories or private dungeons. But few of those slaves are white adult males. No one at the FBI thinks these seventeen men will be found alive, especially not the civilian consultant who's currently digesting one of the victims.

When Vasquez ends the call, he'll adjust his algorithm,

looking for other connections between the victims. Maybe we'll get lucky and find a clue about where the perp lives, or where he works. Or, if it's Shannon, where he is now.

'We can't keep it quiet,' Thistle says. 'We have to make a statement.'

'Legally?'

'Ethically. People have a right to know if there's a serial killer around.'

'But then he'll know we're after him,' I say. 'He'll skip town.'

'If it's Luxford, he already knows.'

'Luxford knew one of the victims and fled from the police, but that doesn't mean he's the killer.'

'Even if he's not,' Thistle points out, 'the cat is out of the bag. We've been asking around about Biggs and Ruthven.'

I stare at the screen as the elevator clanks and whirs. 'Not the other disappearances, though. They've only been investigated by local police.'

'We have to take the risk,' Thistle says. 'Imagine you're a tall, overweight, straight, white male in your twenties. And there's a killer out there targeting tall, overweight, straight, white males in their twenties. Don't you have a right to know about it?'

I can't believe this. 'Catching the killer is a better way of protecting those people than warning them.'

'The public is a resource. They can help us catch him, if we tell them what to look for. Did you think of that?'

'Great.' I put on my best newsreader voice. '*Welcome*

to Fox News. First to Houston, Texas, where an unarmed black man has been shot by a tall, overweight, straight, white male who assumed the man was a serial killer.'

'Don't be an asshole, Blake,' Thistle says drily. 'We both know that wouldn't make the news.'

I don't laugh. 'What if the killer already has his next victim? He could be holding him captive, but hasn't killed him yet. The vic would be a loose end. If the perp realises we're closing in, he'll kill him before he runs.'

Thistle looks at me. 'You really think that's a risk?'

'It's possible,' I say. I can't tell her the real reason that I don't want this on TV. Once it goes to air, it's only a matter of time before Warner realises I'm still working the case.

'Well then,' she says, 'we'd better catch the killer fast. Because Zinnen will make a statement either way. Probably today.'

Something connects in my brain. 'Did Biggs use the app?' I ask. 'He was married.'

'You're sweet,' Thistle says. 'I hate to break it to you, but some men occasionally cheat on their wives.'

The idea slips away before I can grasp it. Her voice echoes through my mind, around and around like a carousel. *You're sweet.*

Focus, I tell myself.

The elevator doors open and we walk out towards the lobby.

'Biggs doesn't fit the rest of the profile either,' I say. 'He's older, shorter, less heavy-set than the other victims.'

Thistle chews her thumbnail for a minute. 'What are you thinking?' she asks finally.

'Maybe they're not connected.'

'Even though their phones were dumped at the same place?'

A young woman stands up and approaches us across the lobby. Biggs's daughter, Hope.

'Miss Biggs,' Thistle says, surprised. 'Are you okay?'

Hope nods. 'I was, um, wondering if I could talk to Mr Blake.'

•

Thistle offers to take us to a conference room. But I convince Hope that she'd be more comfortable in the staff cafeteria. I can't focus when I'm hungry.

The cafeteria is a large, bright room with long tables under a low ceiling. A TV babbles quietly in one corner, the screen reflecting the glare from the windows opposite. I grab my lunch from the fridge, even though it's only ten am, and steal a Nespresso pod from someone else's stash to make Hope a coffee with a rattling machine that has probably never been descaled.

Thistle has gone to interview the cops who originally investigated the other disappearances. She looked grateful to be leaving. Thistle is naturally honest—I guess it's easier to withhold the information about the severed hand if she doesn't have to talk to the family.

I'd rather not miss the interviews with the other cops, but second-hand observations have limited value. And the other victims were all just like Ruthven. Biggs is the odd one out. Hope's story could be key to this whole thing.

'Here you go,' I say, putting a paper cup of thin brew in front of her. 'You want cream? Sugar?'

'No. Thank you.'

'Okay.' I sit down and take a bite out of my sandwich. 'You hungry?' I ask, my mouth full. 'I can get you something.'

'I'm fine.' She looks at my lunch. 'What is that?'

I realise it's actually her father. 'Chicken,' I say.

She takes a deep breath. 'I wanted to thank you,' she says. 'My mom, she doesn't like talking about what happened last year. Going over it again, without Dad there, it might have been too much.'

I assume *what happened last year* is her suicide attempt. 'Why'd you do it?'

She looks taken aback for a second. Most people probably ask more carefully than that, or not at all.

'There's this study,' she says. 'Scientists—I assume they were scientists—snipped the connection between left brain and right brain in a few people. Then they showed instructions to the left eye only, like *stand up* or *walk*. The subjects didn't realise they'd seen the instructions, but they obeyed anyway. When the scientists asked why they were standing up or walking, the subjects made up a reason. Like, *I was bored*.'

I take another bite of Biggs.

'So I can tell you why I think I did it,' Hope says. 'But I wouldn't necessarily be right. Dr Rosen said I was just ill. He talked a lot about "risk factors" for suicide, like it's something that happens to you.'

'It doesn't have to be one or the other,' I say. 'It can be something you did *and* something that happened to you.'

To some people this would sound like Confucian gibberish. But it's not. I know what it's like to do something terrible because something terrible has been done to you. Karma in reverse.

Hope gets it. She relaxes a little, the tendons in her neck going soft, her palms spreading flat on the table.

'You want to tell me what happened?' I ask. There are sixteen more victims to investigate—I'm keen to get to the point.

She nods. 'I . . . I guess that's the other reason I'm here.'

I wait. She opens her mouth, half purses her lips, as though she's not sure how to pronounce the words. I can see her growing more and more distressed by her own silence.

But I've already figured it out.

'Why don't you start from when you met Shannon Luxford,' I say.

Then the whole story comes rushing out.

CHAPTER 19

You throw away the outside and keep the inside, then you eat the outside and throw away the inside. What am I?

He gave her a business card in the library on her first day of college. No job title, just social media links and his name—Shannon Luxford. A handsome guy with the Ben Affleck chin, twenty-one, a cute curl of black hair and shoulders like a footballer.

'The first few weeks are hard,' he said. 'Fun, but hard. Get in touch if you need help, okay? Or advice, or just someone to talk to. I mean it.'

'I have a boyfriend,' she said. Which was true. Peter was small and pale, perpetually hunched like Gollum over some arcane thing. He often tried to explain what he was working on—yesterday a new kind of cryptocurrency, today a method for synthesising guitar sounds—and she never understood his explanations. Peter was a skilled programmer, but a poor communicator. He didn't realise this, however, and Hope could tell he thought she was stupid.

'Lucky guy,' Shannon said, with an easy smile. 'Don't worry, I have a girlfriend back home. Anyway, the offer still stands, okay?' He checked his gleaming watch. Hardly anyone Hope knew wore a wristwatch. 'I gotta go to class. See you round, Hope.'

'See you round, Shannon,' she said, copying his tone. She wondered if she sounded like she was mocking him in a flirty way, or if she just seemed like a parrot.

He didn't approach her again, not directly. The next few weeks of classes passed in a blur of confusing paperwork and bullshit introductory lectures full of things she already understood, hidden behind a cloaking device of buzzwords and nonsense. When her communications professor started talking about 'structuration', she nearly walked out.

But Shannon was always there in the background. He'd be laughing with similarly handsome young men, or playing Ultimate Frisbee on the lawns, and then he'd notice her looking at him, and wave. She'd wave back, and then pretend to be on the phone so he didn't notice that she was alone, and that she had no friends here.

Her dad sometimes suggested having lunch together on campus. She always turned him down, saying she was too busy. She wanted him to think she was having the time of her life at college, just like he had.

Then there was the party. It was Kira Schwabe who

invited her. Kira was a first-year English-lit major with an empty birdcage tattooed on her wrist. She was in one of Hope's media tutorials, which she spent scrolling through Twitter on her laptop. Without looking up, she had said, 'You know the party at Natasha's house?'

It was the first time they had ever spoken. 'No,' Hope replied.

'Oh.' Kira looked taken aback. 'Really? I was hoping you could give me a ride.'

It was that stunned look which made Hope say yes. Kira was surprised that Hope hadn't been invited. Hope wasn't fitting in at Braithwaite, but Kira had thought she was. If she didn't go, she would be exposed. Loner. Weirdo. *Target.*

The party was held in a sprawling three-storey McMansion just off campus—four levels if you counted the basement, where giant speakers made rhythmic thumping sounds which filtered up through the whole house, making the walls vibrate and the double-glazed windows rattle. Conversation was impossible. Every now and then the basement door would open and the volume would become deafening. Laser beams and smoke would pour out, and a drunken teen would emerge from the haze like a visitor from the future.

A stranger handed drinks in red cups to Kira and Hope. 'Wooo!' he said simply.

Kira downed hers in a single gulp. Hope sipped with more caution. She couldn't identify the ingredients. Maybe Mountain Dew spiked with vodka.

'Two parts battery acid, one part hand sanitiser,' she said. But Kira had already vanished somewhere into the throng. Another young woman, walking past with a bottle of rum, topped up Hope's drink. Hope sipped it, just because it was in her hand and it was something to do. Standing there doing nothing made her feel conspicuous. Vulnerable.

She went upstairs, where she thought the volume would be more bearable. She saw two men rolling blunts in one bedroom. Through the next door she saw a woman on her back on the bed, either laughing or crying. A man's head was up her skirt. In the same room, another woman was blowing one guy and getting fucked by another, trapped between them like corn on cob-holders. Hope averted her eyes and started to walk back down the stairs.

She bumped into Shannon Luxford coming up.

'Hope!' he said. 'Hey, how are you?' His smile faded as he saw the look on her face. 'You okay?'

'I'm fine. What are you doing here?' It came out more bluntly than she intended.

'I know, right? I'm way too old for this party.' He smiled, as though he knew he was exaggerating. 'A student I've been helping, he asked me to come. But now I don't think he even showed up. Anyway, no big deal. You have friends here?'

'No.'

His voice became more gentle. 'Don't take this the wrong way, but I often see you on your own. Are you sure everything's okay?'

'I'm fine, I just . . .' She hesitated, torn between 'don't know anyone here', 'don't like the noise', and 'don't belong here'. The alcohol made everything fuzzy. She was on the verge of tears.

'It's okay,' Shannon said. He wrapped an arm around her, like a concerned big brother. 'Let's get you out of here, okay?'

She nodded, and he held her hand and helped her down the stairs. Only later did she think he'd held it a little too tight. Possessive, not protective.

She walked back to his car, huddled into him for protection from the wind. He rested his hand on her leg on the drive home, and she didn't want to offend him by pushing it off.

'I'll come up with you,' he said, when they'd parked near her dorm building. He made it sound like it was for her safety.

'You don't need to do that,' she told him.

'It's okay.'

As soon as the room door was closed, he was kissing her. His breath tasted like cheap beer, and this made her feel like he wasn't taking advantage of her—they were both drunk, not just her.

She was drunker, though. Too drunk to fight him off, if she tried.

'We shouldn't,' she said, when he broke off the kiss. Later, she hated herself for saying that instead of 'you can't' or simply 'don't'.

He was already unbuttoning her jeans.

'Please,' she said. But he just tore at her clothes with renewed energy, as though he'd misunderstood.

In the end, she let him do it. She even made encouraging noises, just wanting it to be over. She didn't even allow herself to think the word *rape* until days later, alone at an STD clinic, her vagina still sore, a bruise fading on her upper arm where he'd grabbed it.

Hope didn't tell anyone right away, and the longer she waited, the more impossible it was. It would have been so much simpler if he had been a stranger in a dark alley, or if he'd slipped something into her drink. But she knew him. People would say she had been attracted to him, and they would be right. She had deliberately left the party with him, had let him into her room. She hadn't screamed for help.

Soon it was too late. *If it really wasn't consensual*, she imagined people saying, *then how come you didn't go straight to the police?*

She couldn't even tell her boyfriend, Peter. She was afraid he would think she had cheated on him. It kind of felt like she had, the moment she had taken Shannon's business card.

Later, Peter sent a text to tell her the relationship wasn't working out. He said it felt like they had drifted apart.

Hope decided to do nothing. And that was what she did. She stayed in her dorm with the door locked, skipping classes, eating almost nothing. She looked at the words in her textbooks without really reading them. When her teachers eventually called her, she told them she was sick, and she sounded so zombified that most of them actually believed her. Over and over again, she asked herself what sort of pathetic person just lets this happen and does nothing. Over and over again, the answer was: *Me. I did that.*

And then he sent her a video.

It came from an unknown phone number. She wouldn't have opened it at all except for the thumbnail, which clearly showed her face in profile, eyes squeezed shut.

Feeling sick, she opened it. There she was, facedown on the mattress, her jeans tangled around her ankles. She was making encouraging noises. Shannon had been filming with a phone. The most disturbing part wasn't even watching Shannon violate her. It was seeing things literally from his perspective. She looked so willing.

She wrote back, *Who the fuck is this?* Desperately hoping that it was Shannon. The idea that he might have sent this to someone else was horrifying.

He didn't answer the question. Instead he wrote: *Be nice. We had such a good time.*

Her fingers trembled as she typed. *What do you want?*

His response: *I want you to talk to your dad.*

•

Hope doesn't cry as she tells me this story. She's probably cried enough. Every experience is less potent each time you relive it. Like Adderall—less kick the more you use it.

Her story doesn't move me much, for the same reason. I've watched people die, sometimes by my own hand. I've chewed their insides. Nothing shocks me now.

So Hope and I sit opposite each other, both dry-eyed, as she tells me the rest of the story. She started talking Shannon up to her father, who promoted him to a teaching assistant role and got him his own office. After that, Shannon let her delete the video off his phone, but she has no way of knowing if he made copies.

'He probably didn't,' I tell her. 'The video is evidence of his crime. He would want it gone.'

'Unless he wants me to do something else for him.'

'No. If he wants you to do something else, he can just pretend he had copies.'

'And if I asked to see them?'

'He thinks you're not the kind of person who would ask that.'

'He's wrong,' Hope says. 'I'm not scared of him anymore.'

I nod. Luxford targeted her because she seemed vulnerable. But now that she's survived a bullet through the head, she's probably not so easy to intimidate.

'So you dropped out of college,' I prompt.

'Right,' she says. 'It was too hard to concentrate on the work, and there just didn't seem to be any point. A stupid, spineless person like me, getting a degree.' She holds up her hands, assuming I would object to this. 'I'm just telling you what I thought at the time.'

'Was your father pissed off?'

'Very. He kept encouraging me to spend some time with Shannon. Because I'd spoken so favourably about him, and he thought Shannon would encourage me to get back into my studies. I couldn't tell Dad the truth, but I hated myself for lying. He was angry at me, and Mom was confused. I started to think they'd be better off without me around. And I felt guilty—what if Shannon had done the same thing to other girls? If so, it was my fault. I could have done something at the time, but now it was too late.'

I think of all the photos in Luxford's desk.

'Every time I had to drive anywhere,' Hope continues, 'I'd imagine a car crash. The kind no one walks away from. And the thought became comforting. It was weirdly fast—I went from worrying about dying to hoping I'd die. Then one day Dad left his gun safe open.'

'When? You know the date?'

'May twenty-third last year.'

Not one of the dates marked in blood on the wall planner. 'Do you know why he had the gun out?'

'Mom screamed the same thing at him. Apparently it was an insurance thing. Anyway, he was out, and I saw the gun. I ignored it at first, and went back to my room. Then I kept thinking about it. Eventually I went back. I put it in my mouth, just to see what that would feel like.'

I ask the obvious question. 'How did you feel?'

She's been avoiding my gaze for most of this conversation. But now she looks right at me. 'Awake,' she says. 'For the first time in months.'

I know what she means. I've had a gun to my head more than once. You're never more aware of the sensations in your body. The whole world goes sharp, like that ultra-HD TV in Hope's living room.

'So I put a little bit more pressure on the trigger,' Hope continues. 'Then a little more. Playing chicken with myself.'

She takes a sip of coffee.

'Then what?' I ask.

'Then I woke up in hospital.'

An FBI agent laughs quietly in the corner. Nothing to do with us—he's in his own conversation.

'Let me give you some advice, Mr Blake,' Hope says. 'If you ever want to kill yourself, put the gun to the side of your head, not the front or the back. Apparently the brain can take a lot of damage to the left or the right brain, but not both. The doctor was thrilled. Apparently I'm a medical miracle. People like me advance neuroscience by decades. Mom and Dad, uh . . .' She looks down at the table. 'They were pretty disappointed in me. They didn't understand. They couldn't, because I still didn't tell them about Shannon. It was way, way too late. Since then, they don't leave me alone. It's like I'm a prisoner. If Dad hadn't gone missing, I wouldn't even be here.'

'Who found you?'

'With a hole in my head? A neighbour heard the gunshot. The front door was unlocked.'

I feel a jab of sympathy for Biggs. He was tricked by his TA, lied to by his daughter, blamed by his wife for his daughter's suicide attempt, and eventually abducted. Even his pacemaker let him down, in the end. And the guy who found his body didn't report it—he took a bite out of him instead.

I don't blame Hope, or Gabriela. The only bad guys here are Luxford and me.

'Listen.' Hope leans forwards. 'Do you think Shannon killed my dad?'

She's dreading the answer. She thinks she could have prevented her father's murder.

'If he did,' I say, 'then I can't work out why. You're sure he didn't know about the rape?'

'Positive. Like I said, he was always talking about how great Shannon was.'

'Are you willing to go on the record about all this?'

'Yes,' she says.

'Can I ask you a personal question?'

She raises an eyebrow. 'Like this wasn't a personal conversation already?'

'I've been looking through your dad's web search history,' I say. 'There's some weird stuff in there.'

'What kind of . . . Never mind, I don't want to know. Not if . . .' She doesn't say the rest, but I hear it anyway. *Not if he's dead. I don't want to tarnish his memory.*

'Did anyone strange come to the house?' I ask. 'Any large women?'

She looks confused. 'Large like fat?'

'Large like tall.'

'No. Not while I was home, which has been pretty much always since I got out of hospital.'

I think back to the honey trap idea. 'What about men? Big enough to overpower him. Anyone suspicious at all?'

'We've had no visitors except the mailman. My dad

was a good guy. A little oblivious, maybe, but good. He wouldn't be mixed up with anything bad.' She takes a shaky breath. 'Do you think we'll ever find him?' she asks.

I look down at my sandwich.

'I wouldn't count on it,' I say.

CHAPTER 20

A man calls his dog from the other side of a lake. There are no bridges, and the dog doesn't walk around the lake. When it arrives, it is dry. How?

'I want to know everything,' Thistle says, when she picks me up.

'Shannon Luxford raped her,' I say. 'He filmed it. Then he used the video to blackmail her into talking him up to her father, who hired Luxford as a TA and gave him his own office—'

'Where Luxford could rape more students and take more videos,' Thistle says. 'Holy shit.'

'Right. I didn't tell her about that part.'

'Uncharacteristically tactful of you. Is that why she tried to kill herself?'

'It couldn't have helped,' I say, 'though it sounds like

she was already depressed. Her parents basically haven't let her out of their sight since the suicide attempt.'

'Did her father know about Luxford? Does her mom?'

'She says no. But we don't know about Biggs's final days. Maybe he found out.'

'Well, we just got probable cause,' Thistle says. 'Hang on.'

She pulls out her phone and makes a call to a judge. It takes her a few minutes to explain what we know, leaving out the part about the photos in Luxford's desk. But the remaining facts sound persuasive: Luxford's boss is missing, and Luxford ran from investigators even before the boss's daughter accused him of rape. Thistle glosses over the fact that no agents were present when the accusation was made.

Eventually she hangs up.

'He go for it?' I ask.

'He's deliberating. Let's go to Luxford's house. I'm thinking the search warrant will arrive before we do.'

I nod. Thistle takes West 43rd Street, and soon we're speeding along Clay Road.

'I don't suppose Hope saw any giant women come by while she was under house arrest?' Thistle asks.

'I asked. She said no. But whatever Biggs was doing, he would have done it somewhere else.'

We drive in silence for a minute. The radio burbles quietly over the humming of tyres on blacktop.

'How did you go with the local cops who worked the other disappearances?' I ask.

'Mixed. Some of them went straight into ass-covering mode—they should have connected these disappearances earlier. Others didn't want an FBI agent and an algorithm telling them how to do their jobs. A few were openly hostile. All of them shared their case files in the end, so we have a lot to work with. But I'm not convinced any of it will be useful.'

'Because the cops didn't seem competent?'

'Because it's a serial killer. The files mostly looked at suspects the victims knew well, and their potential motives. Serial killers often target strangers, and their motives can be incoherent.' She honks at a slow-moving BMW in front of us. 'Fortunately for us, they also tend to have low IQ.'

This is a misleading statistic. Psychologists only test the ones who get caught. I watch snowflakes land on the windshield, and get swept away by the wipers.

'What did you say?' Thistle asks.

'I didn't say anything.'

'Something about a misleading statistic?'

I hadn't realised I was talking aloud. How often do I do that?

'They only test the ones they catch,' I say. 'The world could be full of serial killers who are too smart to get arrested.'

'Yeah, well, let's hope it's not. Hypothesis—Biggs found out Luxford had raped his daughter. He confronted Luxford, who killed him to keep the secret.'

'Why wouldn't Biggs just go to the cops?'

'If my dad found out that I'd been raped, he wouldn't have gone to the cops. He would've just shot the motherfucker. Hell, he sometimes threatened to do that even when I consented.'

I remember Bob, the big man who nearly adopted me. The landscaper.

'Your dad wasn't a math professor,' I say.

'You think math professors don't shoot people?'

'Statistically, violent criminals don't have that level of education.'

'Well, look who's pro-college all of a sudden,' Thistle says. 'And remember what you said a minute ago about serial killers. Anyway, maybe he didn't go to the cops for the same reason his daughter didn't. No proof. Fear of humiliating her.'

I nod slowly. 'Possible,' I say. 'Like I said, Luxford's a sociopath. He wouldn't think twice about killing Biggs to save his own skin.'

'He could have been blackmailing Biggs at the same time,' Thistle says. 'Hence the cash Biggs took out of the ATM.'

'Why kill him, then?'

Thistle chews her lip. I try not to remember how good those lips tasted. We kissed four times, and I remember them all vividly.

'Okay,' she says finally. 'Let's say Luxford tried to blackmail Biggs. Biggs pretended he was gonna pay. He even withdrew the cash. But actually he was planning to kill Luxford.'

'Two-sixty isn't blackmail money. And his gun was still in the safe.'

'Maybe there was another gun. A knife. A car. For all we know, Biggs was a black belt in karate. Or thought he was.'

I think of Biggs's muscles. Soft, fatty. Not accustomed to exercise. 'Go on.'

'But it goes wrong somehow,' Thistle continues. 'Luxford overpowers him, or brings a gun of his own. Then he buries the body somewhere, leaves Biggs's car and phone at the dump, and then goes home.'

I chew my nails for a bit. 'Not bad,' I say. 'How did he access the dump, and get the car into the crusher?'

'He might know someone there. Maybe the same guy who ran away from us.'

Her theory covers everything. Except how Biggs's body ended up naked in the forest. The part she doesn't know about.

She glances over. 'You're supposed to ask how his hand ended up back on campus.'

Whoops. Keep it together, Timothy. 'That's him trying to lead us off-base, right?' I say. 'We already know he didn't leave the state.'

Thistle's phone rings. She answers. 'Yeah?'

After a pause, she says, 'Thank you, Your Honour.' She ends the call. 'Our warrant just came through.'

•

It isn't hard to figure out which car belongs to the plain-clothes surveillance agents. It's parked facing Luxford's house, close enough for a clear line of sight to the front door, but far enough away that it's unlikely to be noticed. There's a frozen puddle under a nearby tree, and given the topography of the land, that only makes sense if someone has pissed on it. The driver, a black woman in her forties with army-short hair, is sitting there with her hands in her lap, like she's texting—except her gaze stays on the house. The passenger seat is tilted all the way back, like someone is asleep in it. Probably a man, judging by the piss puddle.

The house itself looks surprisingly up-market for a TA. Two storeys, brick veneer, big windows covered by drawn curtains. And Westbranch is a good neighbourhood. Maybe Luxford shares it with somebody. Or maybe he inherited some money.

We walk up to the car, and Thistle raps on the passenger-side window. A fifty-something white man with a moustache sits up, rubs his eyes and wipes some drool off his chin. He looks around, sees Thistle. I watch him take note of my clothes and Thistle's race. 'Get lost,' he says, his voice muffled by the glass.

His partner nudges him.

Thistle flashes her badge. Embarrassed, the man fumbles with his window for a bit. Eventually it buzzes down.

'Sorry, agents,' he says. 'What can we do for you?'

I wait for Thistle to tell him I'm not a real agent. She doesn't.

'Anyone in or out?' she asks.

The other cop speaks up. 'No, ma'am. And no lights on or off during the night. If Luxford's in there, he's keeping his head down.'

'Someone else watching the other side?'

'The house backs onto a big fence. No gate. You'd have to be Spiderman to get over it. And we'd see him from here when he reached the top.'

I notice an open garbage bag on the back seat, half full of coffee cups and Chinese takeaway boxes. These guys have been here at least twelve hours.

'Well, we're about to find out,' Thistle is saying. 'Our search warrant just came through. You ready?'

'You bet,' the woman says.

The man nods. 'Yep. Hey, you're Thistle, right?'

'That's me,' Thistle says. 'This is Blake.'

'I'm Terracini,' the man says. 'She's Albrecht. Are you carrying?'

'I am,' Thistle says. She draws back her jacket to reveal the Beretta on her hip. 'Blake isn't.'

'If Luxford pulls a gun, are you willing to shoot?'

Sounds like Terracini has heard about Thistle's lawsuit. Thistle's eyes narrow. 'I am.'

'I'll go in first,' I say. 'Luxford might panic if he sees a gun.'

I'm trying to relax Terracini by showing that I trust Thistle. Doesn't look like it's working.

'No,' Thistle says. 'I'll go first, then you. Albrecht and Terracini will cover us. Are we good?'

Terracini and Albrecht exchange a glance.

'That works,' Albrecht says.

'Okay. Let's do it.'

We all walk up the path to the front door. The windows are dark, curtains closed, the corners cobwebbed. A sign above the doorbell says NO DOOR-TO-DOOR SALES. Thistle rings the bell.

No answer.

After a long, tense moment, Thistle nods to Albrecht.

With three sharp taps from a hammer and chisel, Albrecht separates the security mesh from the metal frame. Then she reaches through the gap and disengages the deadbolt.

The wooden door behind isn't locked. Gun raised, Thistle enters the house, as fast and precise as a wary school of fish. I follow.

We clear the hall quickly, then move on to the main living area. Thick carpet deadens most of the sound, and the windows are double glazed, so there's no traffic noise. The house is smaller than it looked from outside, and more modern. My guess is it was built fifty years ago, and the interior has been substantially renovated in the last five. The white-blue paint still looks fresh. There's a big TV, a surround sound system and a coffee table with too many remotes lined up on it. When we get to the kitchen, there are signs that the renovators stopped here. Faded linoleum floor, lacy curtains on the windows, an oven with coil-shaped hotplates on top.

There's a study, with a desktop computer. Two monitors. The whole set-up looks pretty new—not many cables to the back. Power only. Must do everything through wi-fi. A string of thirteen seemingly random letters that could be a password is written on a post-it note.

'Ground floor clear,' Thistle hisses. Then she heads for the stairs.

I follow her up. The staircase slows us down, and it's narrow. No room to dodge. If anyone was planning an ambush, this would be the place.

We reach the top unharmed. There are two bedrooms and one bathroom. No renovations up here. The bathroom has old-fashioned curved fixtures, and a little mould in the corners of the ceiling. Not uncommon in Houston, where the winters can be as brutal as the summers. People shut their doors and windows, closing off the outside world. Bad things grow in the resulting stillness.

One bedroom is being used for storage. Boxes of summer clothes, crates of sports gear, a stepladder. The sort of thing Luxford would probably keep in his basement, if he had one.

Thistle checks the wardrobe. 'Clear,' she says. I wonder why he leaves all this junk on the floor when his wardrobe is empty. No clothes, even.

The other bedroom has a large bed with a thick mattress. Winter clothes hang on hooks in the closet. Neat rows of non-fiction line the shelves.

'Upstairs clear,' Thistle says. Then, when there's no response, she yells, 'Upstairs all clear!'

Albrecht's voice seems to come from a long way away. 'Roger that.'

I start flicking through Luxford's books, looking for notes tucked between the pages. Nothing. A modern trade-off. These days, if you have a suspect's phone, you know basically everything about him. But without it, you know nothing.

In his bedside table, I find a Taser.

I go through the pockets of his clothes. The Blu-rays on his shelves. I can hear an air-conditioner running somewhere. I walk around until I find it, a large unit with pipes disappearing into the ceiling and the walls. I open the unit and check the inside. But there's no journal, no gun, no secret hard drive.

In the ceiling of the closet of the storage room there's a trapdoor. I use the stepladder to push it up, and then push my head through.

It's a fairly roomy crawlspace. Nothing here, not even insulation. No indication that Luxford has ever been up here.

When I climb back down, Thistle is waiting. 'Anything?'

I shake my head. 'Maybe Vasquez can get something off his computer. But he has a lot of cryptography books, so maybe not.'

'I'm starting to wonder if he was telling the truth about Biggs having cryptography as a hobby,' Thistle says. 'I think it was his.'

'Why lie about that?'

'I don't know.'

I look around. I feel like there's something here I'm not seeing. But staring at it won't make it obvious. Like

Vasquez's algorithm, I need more data, so I know what to exclude.

'Let's check out his parents' house,' I say.

CHAPTER 21

What gets wetter the more it dries?

'He's a good boy,' Joseph Luxford insists.

Joseph looks a lot like his son. Square jaw, cobalt eyes. His hair has remained black, but it's thinning at the front. His nose has gone blotchy in a way that might suggest alcoholism.

'What were his grades like at school?' Thistle asks.

She already knows that they were good. Shannon got As in math, science, gym and shop, Bs in everything else. Thistle is trying to get Joseph off defence, talking about something he's comfortable with. Hoping to get a clue about whether or not Shannon is hiding here.

But Joseph glances at his wife. He doesn't know the answer.

'His grades were good,' Francine Luxford says quietly. She's younger than her husband, with a neat bun of hair that would probably be grey if not for an expensive blonde dye job. She sits down carefully, as though she once had an abdominal injury and learned how to move without aggravating it.

'Right,' Joseph says, turning back to us. 'They were good. This girl you're talking about—she might have changed her mind afterwards. That doesn't give her the right to tarnish my son's reputation.'

'Girls,' I say. My turn to play bad cop. 'There were several.'

But Joseph just tilts his head, too dismissive even to shrug. 'He's a good-looking boy.'

An old dog trots over and sniffs my shoes. It can probably smell my neighbour's dog—or meat.

'Max, back,' Joseph says.

The dog slinks away and sits next to the La-Z-Boy, looking guilty.

The living room has a big TV and several framed photographs of Joseph and Shannon. None of Frances, who I guess was usually holding the camera. A potted plant is withering in the corner. No books. An old reverse-cycle air-conditioner dominates one wall.

The kitchen and dining area are immaculate. I'm looking for dirty dishes, or other signs that Shannon is secretly living here. But I haven't found anything so far.

'Anyway, they might be making the whole thing up for the attention,' Joseph says. He talks mostly to me, even though Thistle is the one in charge. 'Don't pretend that doesn't happen.'

'When was the last time you saw your son?' I ask.

'On Sunday, at church,' Joseph says, holding my gaze.

'How about you, Mrs Luxford?' Thistle asks.

Frances looks at her husband, and then says, 'Monday. He dropped off some laundry here.'

'Was there anything unusual among the clothing?' I ask.

'Like what?' Joseph asks.

'Condoms. Blood. Drugs.'

Thistle winces.

'Of course not,' Joseph says. He doesn't bother to check with his wife.

'We're sorry,' Thistle says. 'We have to ask these questions in a missing persons case—we want to find your son before any more harm comes to him or his reputation.'

Joseph looks at her, reassessing. Like a GPS working out the new best route after a missed exit.

'What kind of harm?' he asks.

'We do everything we can to keep these cases quiet,' Thistle says. 'But the longer the investigation goes on, the more time the witnesses have to talk, potentially to the media. The sooner we can get Shannon's side of the story, the sooner we can shut this whole thing down. The last thing we want is for Shannon to become a target, or to hurt himself.'

Joseph nods slowly.

'Can we see his bedroom?' Thistle asks. 'Sometimes it helps to get a sense of the missing person.'

Francine sends an anxious glance in Joseph's direction.

'I guess that would be okay,' he says. 'Follow me.'

He leads Thistle and me up the stairs. The dog follows like a junior agent. Francine stays in the living room.

The top floor of the house is dark and claustrophobic. A narrow, low-ceilinged corridor leads to three bedrooms and one bathroom.

'Does Shannon have siblings?' I ask.

'No,' Joseph says. 'I wanted him to have plenty of individual attention.'

'And IVF can be expensive,' I say.

He and Thistle both look at me, shocked.

'Indeed,' Joseph says finally, reluctant to admit that he can't work out how I know. 'But we could afford it.'

'You didn't think about adopting?' Thistle asks. There's a dark edge to her voice. I wonder if she, like me, is thinking of the group home. Getting all dressed up, being polite to strange adults, heartbroken when they didn't want us.

'It seemed risky,' Joseph says, opening the door to one of the bedrooms. 'You never know what you're going to get, raising someone else's kid.'

The words would once have stung. We were all so desperate for someone to adopt us, especially someone rich enough to get us out of the dirt. When we were kids, IVF was already available to the wealthy. Why take someone else's rejects, when you could buy a kid that was genetically your own?

It's hard to be angry now, though. Joseph is right; you never know what you're going to get. Adopt the wrong kid, and you might find yourself raising a cannibal. Not that Joseph's own flesh and blood turned out much better.

The bedroom is large, with a good view of the neatly trimmed grass in the backyard. The shelves are lined with trophies, and the walls hold several framed posters of football stars from ten years ago. Again, no books. The bed is a queen-size. I wonder if Shannon brought girls home here when he was in high school.

Thistle examines one of the posters. 'Who's this?' she asks.

Joseph walks over and starts telling her about the stats of the guy in the photo. I use the opportunity to slip back into the corridor, looking for places Shannon might be hiding.

I check the bathroom first. Only two towels on the rack, both dry. Just two toothbrushes. Lots of make-up stuff, but nothing fancy. Mostly foundation, blush and eyeshadow. No eyeliner, lipstick or mascara.

It's the kind of make-up cabinet a woman might have if she's used to hiding bruises.

Uneasily, I check the master bedroom. King-size bed, two bedside tables, rows of suits and dresses hanging in the walk-in. Nothing suspicious.

The last remaining room is locked from the outside with a bolt. I quietly slide it back and open the door a crack. This room has a single bed, neatly made, and not much else. Old mystery novels line the shelves. I check under the bed. Nothing. There's a bedside table. In the drawer I find a Bible, like at a motel.

Whose room is this? And why would it have a lock on the outside?

'Please.'

I whirl around. Francine is standing right behind me. I get a whiff of her rose perfume.

'Will you please just leave?' she whispers.

CHAPTER 22

One door leads to death, the other to freedom. One guard always tells the truth, the other always lies. You get one question. What do you ask?

'You think Joseph is abusing Francine?' Thistle asks.

'I think there's a ninety per cent chance that's what's happening,' I say. 'It looked like a time-out space. Like somewhere he would put her when she disobeyed.'

Thistle glances in the rear-view mirror at the shrinking house. 'They could be in a consensual BDSM relationship.'

'There would have been other signs. Handcuffs in the dresser, or a paddle under the bed.'

As I talk, I'm going through sixteen fat files about the other missing men. Learning about their jobs, their families, their friends, the jobs of their family and friends . . . Speed-reading isn't always good for comprehension, but it's useful for spotting connections. It brings all the facts closer together.

So far, though, all I've noticed is that none are married, which makes sense, given that they all used the same dating app, nTangle.

Thistle's voice is grim: 'Do you think Shannon knows?'

'That lock looked like it had been there a long time. He knows.'

'If I were to ask the Houston PD to investigate, not much will happen. Not without more evidence. But I'll file a report anyway. Any sign of Shannon?'

'None,' I say. 'And neither parent seemed nervous enough to be hiding a fugitive, wouldn't you agree?'

'I would.' Thistle takes the exit off the loop back towards the FBI. 'How did you know about the IVF?'

'I didn't, really. Just a feeling. Rich couple, only one child. Did you see the size of that air-con? It looked about Shannon's age, and hot flushes are a common side effect of IVF. Plus, Francine was moving like she'd had abdominal pain in the past. Although now I'm thinking Joseph may be hitting her.'

'Well, you rattled him, that's for sure,' Thistle says. 'Did it piss you off, what he said about adoption?'

'No,' I say, 'that's ancient history.'

She knows what I mean. 'Not for me. I remember getting all dressed up whenever couples came to visit. It was like the world's worst job interview. And you'd meet them, and you'd think it was going really well and that they liked you. You'd start thinking of them as Mom and Dad.

Then you never hear from them again. You wonder what you did wrong, and that makes you self-conscious with the next couple... I wanted a mom so badly. But the Luxfords would spend tens of thousands of dollars rather than risk "raising someone else's kid". It pissed *me* off.'

For a moment, the only sound is the humming of tyres on blacktop.

'Sorry,' Thistle says. 'I know no one picked you.'

I look out the window. 'It's okay. It might have been easier for me, in a way. I could always tell the couples didn't like me, so I wasn't left wondering if they'd be back.'

'Scary Timmy?' Thistle says.

The nickname takes me right back to the playground. 'Right. Scary Timmy.'

'For what it's worth, I think it was their loss,' Thistle says. 'You would have made a good son, if anyone had been smart enough to take you home.'

She's wrong, but I'm touched. 'Thanks. Anyway, seems like we both ended up better off.'

'How so?'

'It could have been either of us behind that locked door.'

I've reached the final file—Daniel Ruthven, the victim we started with. The one who worked in construction, and whose phone ended up at the dump. I've read the file before, but this time I notice something I ignored before.

'nTangle,' I say. 'The dating app they all used.'

'Yeah?'

'It's made by a company based in Houston,' I say, 'in the CBD. Ian McLean works there.'

'Daniel Ruthven's roommate?'

'Right.'

'That connects him to all the victims.' Thistle sounds excited. 'Let's go talk to him.'

My stomach growls. 'Drive-through first,' I say. 'I'm starving.'

CHAPTER 23

What two things can you never eat for breakfast?

Ian McLean is in his twenties, bearded, with kind eyes in a gentle face. The red sweater adds to the illusion that he's a young Santa, not yet grey or fat.

'Took you long enough,' he says, but the words sound exhausted rather than aggressive. He sounds like a smoker. 'You know I reported Danny missing five days ago?'

Thistle and I follow him into the open-plan office. I was expecting the Silicon Valley startup aesthetic—beanbags, pool tables, pets—but instead it's more like the control room of a nuclear submarine. The only light comes from dozens of monitors filled with statistics and pie charts. Headphoned workers tap urgently at their keyboards. Some are eating a late lunch at their desks.

'How long has Daniel lived with you?' Thistle asks.

'Uh, he was at the apartment when I moved in, three years ago,' McLean says. 'I guess maybe five years? His old roommate might know.'

'We'll need contact details for him.'

'Her. I'll have to talk to the real estate company. They'd have those details.'

McLean leads us into a glass-walled meeting room. No one else in there. A big TV in the corner with a camera on top, for video conferencing. We sit on swivelling chairs with mesh backs.

'What do you do here?' Thistle asks casually. 'For nTangle.'

McLean looks wary. 'What does that have to do with Daniel?'

Thistle backpedals a little. 'I mean, do you work long hours? How often do you see Daniel?'

'Oh. I'm in charge of cyber security, so I work late if there's ever any kind of major attack on nTangle. But that hasn't happened in a couple of weeks, so I saw Daniel every day. We used to play *Madden* most nights.'

'Your app is free, right?' I ask. 'So no one's bank accounts are attached to it.'

'Yes, but there are still attacks,' Daniel says. 'If they ever got in, hackers could steal users' photos, their email addresses, their names, data about the places they've been, the people they've met, their desirability score—all that is worth money. People can use it to create real-seeming profiles on social media, and those profiles can disseminate information for companies, or for political purposes.'

'Desirability score?' Thistle says.

'The ratio of winks to profile views. The app uses this score to pair up people who are equally desirable. If an attractive user keeps getting paired up with ugly users, they might uninstall the app. And if the attractive users leave, the unattractive ones won't hang around for long. Users can't see desirability scores, not even their own—unless they work here, obviously. I'm a point one eight.' When neither of us looks impressed, he says, 'Anything over point one five is really good for a man.'

'Different people have different tastes, though,' Thistle says.

'The app learns each user's preferences,' McLean says. 'But it turns out everybody wants basically the same thing. Someone thin but not too thin, young but not too young, and rich.' He doesn't add *but not too rich*. 'Users can pretend to be less shallow than that, but the data tells a different story.'

I'm thin, at least. 'Were Daniel and his old roommate romantically involved?' I ask.

'I don't think so. Danny didn't talk about her much. And I don't think he'd ever had a serious girlfriend.'

'He was dating, though, right?' Thistle says. 'With your app?'

'Well, trying to,' McLean says. 'I recommended it to him, helped him take a good headshot. But he mostly didn't get very far. Women would click *wink* on his profile, but when they met him in person, it would never go any further. He'd buy them dinner or a drink, and then they'd part ways.'

'Did that make him angry?' Thistle asks.

'It made *me* kind of angry,' McLean says. 'Daniel is a sweet guy. It seemed unfair to reject him just because he was carrying a few extra pounds.'

'Yeah, that's harsh,' Thistle says.

She doesn't let the sarcasm slip into her voice, but I can hear it anyway. A fat woman is judged much more severely than a fat man. And I heard somewhere that white people get many more clicks—or swipes, or whatever—than people of colour. I wonder if Thistle has been dating since I last worked with her. I wonder if she's tried an app.

'But did Daniel take it personally?' Thistle asks.

'He was actually pretty upbeat about the whole thing. I mean, he'd seem disappointed when he came home, but the next day he'd just try again. Plenty more fish in the sea, he'd say. As though that was a good thing.'

'It's not?' I ask.

'No—that's the whole problem. Why would a woman date a guy who looked like Danny when her phone tells her there are millions of more handsome guys within range?' He shakes his head. 'Too many fish. Great for nTangle, but bad for Danny. That's why I was so relieved when he didn't come home that night.'

I'm interested now. 'You last saw him when?'

'December 2. He'd met someone—I mean, a woman had sent him a wink—and he was going out on a date with her.'

'Where were they going?'

'He didn't say. In fact, I think he didn't know. She came to pick him up.'

'From your place?'

'Yeah. We tell users not to give out their home addresses, but he was pretty desperate. He said he didn't give her the apartment number, just the building number. He thought that would be safe enough.'

'So you didn't see her.'

McLean hesitates. 'Not exactly.'

'Not exactly?' Thistle says. She manages to sound curious rather than eager. 'Tell us what you did see.'

'I wasn't spying,' McLean says. 'I was just washing the dishes. But I looked out the window, and saw Daniel get into a car.'

'What kind of car?'

'I think it was blue, maybe? Dark, anyway.'

'What brand?'

He looks apologetic. 'I'm not really a car guy, you know?'

'Expensive? Cheap?'

'Uh, mid-range, I guess. But I saw the driver, kind of. Through the windshield.'

'What did she look like?' I ask.

'Blonde hair. Red lipstick. Nice jawline, no double chin. She looked older than him—thirty, or maybe a good-looking forty.'

He might not be a car guy, but he's definitely a woman guy.

'I thought that was a good sign,' he said. 'Maybe she would be willing to date a chubby guy, because she was a bit past her sell-by.'

Thistle chokes on something, and coughs.

'You okay?' McLean asks.

She waves away his concern with a hand.

'The woman used the app,' I say, 'so you can tell us who she was?'

'I can't,' McLean says. 'But the company can, if you get a court order.'

'How was Daniel's demeanour?' I ask. 'When he got in the car.'

McLean shrugs. 'Normal, I guess. Like he was meeting her for the first time. They didn't kiss or anything.'

Thistle has recovered. 'You see which way they went?'

McLean shakes his head.

'What kind of porn did Daniel like?' I ask.

McLean looks taken aback. 'Excuse me?'

'You guys have been roommates for years,' I say. 'You must know what he's into.'

McLean looks at Thistle. *Now* he's worried about offending her.

'We've heard it all before,' she says. 'It would have to be pretty weird to shock us.'

'Well,' McLean says, still uneasy, 'we never really discussed it. I guess just the normal stuff?'

'Normal?' I ask.

He looks even more uncomfortable. 'You know. Blowjobs and anal, and . . . look, I don't even know. We didn't talk about it.'

'So,' I say, 'if I mentioned giants . . .'

'Like, uh, giant cocks?'

'Giant women. That wouldn't ring any bells for you?'

He just looks confused. 'What? No! He was a sweet guy, like I said. He wasn't even dating for the sex. He just wanted someone to love him.' He stares through the glass at the army of coders, refining the app. 'Everyone needs that.'

'You know, Danny isn't the only one missing,' Thistle says.

'What do you mean?'

'There are fifteen others who match his physical description.'

He stares at us, puzzled.

'Sixteen men in total,' I put in. 'All white, heterosexual, carrying a few extra pounds—and users of your app.'

McLean is starting to go pale. 'Wait. You're talking about a killer? Using nTangle?'

I lean forwards in my chair. 'And you lived with one of the victims,' I say.

'You're very connected to this, Ian,' Thistle adds.

McLean is breathing faster. 'Oh God. I don't understand. What are you saying?'

Thistle and I look at each other. McLean definitely looks nervous. But is that because he's guilty, or because he's not?

'We're not saying anything at this point.' Thistle slides a business card across the table. 'But do me a solid—call us if you're planning on leaving the state.'

•

'Thoughts?' I ask as we head for the car.

'I don't think I'd send him a wink,' Thistle says.

'No. But is he hiding anything?'

'Not enough, in my view. Like Shannon.'

I climb into the passenger side. 'How's that?'

'Talking about attractive users, and his own desirability score. It reminded me of how Shannon admitted to hitting on those freshmen. How he made that girl fetch you a coffee. I hate this fucking "be yourself" culture. If you're an asshole, you should at least have the decency to hide it.'

I never thought of my dishonesty as a character strength. It's a shame I can't tell her about it. 'But do you think he might be our guy?'

Thistle starts the car. 'No. You saw him—he was shitting his pants. If we're right, our perp has killed seventeen people, including Biggs. He would have done a better job at acting calm.'

'Maybe the anxiety was the act.'

'You think?'

'I think it's worth going to his house,' I say.

'We don't have a warrant.'

'We don't need one. I just want to see if his story stacks up. What he said about the woman he saw out the window.'

McLean and Ruthven's apartment building isn't far away. It turns out to be two-storey, brick, with narrow windows that wouldn't let in much light. Bird-crap trailing down the sides. Not the kind of place with a doorman, though all the ground floor stairwell doors are locked.

I know from the file that we want number eleven. I push the buzzer.

'You expecting an answer?' Thistle asks.

'Shh.' A buzzing is faintly audible from one of the apartments above our heads. I point. 'Sounds like it's coming from up there, wouldn't you agree?'

'Push it again.'

I do. The buzz is coming from the top-level apartment on the right.

'Yeah, you're right,' Thistle admits.

I walk back to the car and turn to look up at the window. A dark square of glass, turned into a parallelogram by the angle. A bottle of detergent balanced on the frame, probably above the kitchen sink. If there was a woman, and she did park here, McLean might have seen her face as he washed the dishes. Maybe.

'With a court order, we can find out who the woman was,' Thistle says.

'Right.' I get in the car. 'But I think we should treat any information from nTangle as though it's coming directly from McLean.'

Thistle nods slowly. 'He could have made up a fake profile to go with his story.'

'Right.'

I buckle my seatbelt. Thistle starts the engine.

'Where are we headed?' she asks.

I give her the address of a factory in Deer Park. It's after four, but we should still have time to investigate my idea.

Thistle starts driving. 'I don't have a sense of what Ruthven was like,' she says. 'Although when a man like McLean describes someone as "a sweet guy", I'm inclined to be sceptical.'

I swallow the urge to defend the two guys. McLean came across as a prick, for sure. But he doesn't eat people. I want to imagine Thistle could see *me* as having a high desirability score. That's hard when she's looking down on better men.

'For McLean to see the driver with that level of detail, the car would have had to stop in exactly the right spot,' I say.

'You think it was shady that he couldn't remember anything about the car?'

'Maybe. Except a good liar would have come up with a common make or model. And if he's lying about the woman, then he *is* a good liar.'

Thistle nods slowly. 'Okay, let's say he's a suspect. Motive?'

'Well, housemates get mad at each other all the time.' I'm searching on my phone, looking for more information about the factory we're headed to. 'Maybe it was a fight over the dishes that escalated.'

'What about Biggs and the other fourteen victims?'

'Unrelated. Different killer. Or maybe McLean killed the others for money, and then Ruthven found out about it, so he killed Ruthven too.'

Thistle doesn't look convinced. Nor am I.

'It's a tiny apartment,' she says. 'No backyard. How would he get rid of the bodies?'

I dissolve skeletons in the bathtub, but I don't want to appear too knowledgeable about that.

'Maybe he dumps them out in the woods,' I say, thinking of Biggs's half-frozen corpse.

'Well, I'll get someone to check his financials for anomalies, and see if he rents any other spaces. Plus I can get a warrant for his ISP, check out the porn angle. But I've gotta tell you, I don't think he's our guy.'

I grunt. She's right. But I don't like the other possibility that springs to mind.

Charlie Warner is a good-looking blonde woman in her forties. Known for making people disappear. Known to use the woods where I found Biggs.

But if it's her behind these disappearances, then I'm in trouble. I don't want to catch Warner. If she's arrested, that means no more food for me. Which means I can't be around Thistle. I'll get too hungry. I'll hurt her.

Also, it means Warner already has a new body-disposal guy. She can kill me at any time.

We're in Deer Park now—a landscape of petrochemical plants, chain-link fences and towers of shipping containers. No parks or deer to be seen. 'Turn off here,' I say, pointing.

Thistle does. 'So what's the connection to this factory?' she asks. 'Was it in Biggs's search history?'

'Not exactly,' I say.

'Then why are we here?' She squints at the approaching building.

'It's a sex doll factory,' I tell her.

Thistle considers this for a moment.

'I don't think that answers my question,' she says at last.

CHAPTER 24

You can drive it, but it's not a car. You can bank it, but it's not money. The rich have blue, the cruel have cold, many Americans have red. What is it?

The reception is a narrow room not unlike that of the FBI Houston Field Office, except for all the framed pictures of nearly beautiful women. Nearly beautiful because if you look closely enough, you can tell the women aren't real. It's something about the eyes. Slightly too big, and none are looking exactly at the camera, or at anything. Other parts of the women are slightly too big as well.

    A glossy sign above the desk has the company name in cursive font: *She's Alive!* It's a case of hopeful naming, since the women clearly are not alive. Like calling your son Rich or your daughter Chastity. Maybe deceptive naming rather than hopeful, like how North Korea is officially the Democratic People's Republic of Korea. Or the United States of America, which aren't especially united.

The receptionist is a young Latino man with a fade buzzed into his hair, slouching in his chair as he plays a game on his phone. I can hear the crunching and blipping as he smashes digital crates for coins. He looks up as we enter. 'Help you?'

Thistle flashes her badge. 'We're with the FBI. Can we speak to the managing director?'

'Alexandra Howard,' I add—one of the things that popped up in my search.

The kid looks alarmed. He picks up the phone, and says, 'Uh, hi. The, um, police are here.'

A minute later, a gaunt middle-aged woman with freckles emerges through some sliding doors. 'Lexi Howard,' she says, taking off a pair of work gloves to shake Thistle's hand, then mine.

'I'm Agent Reese Thistle, FBI. This is Timothy Blake.'

'What can I do for you?'

'We won't take up too much of your time,' I say. 'Is there somewhere private we can talk?'

'I'm in compliance with all the relevant laws,' Howard says, loud enough for the worried-looking receptionist to hear.

'Frankly, I'm not even sure what those laws would be,' Thistle says. 'You're not being investigated for anything. We were hoping you could help us with a case.'

She nods warily. 'Okay. My office is this way.'

She leads us back through the sliding doors and out onto the production floor. Thistle and I are both taken aback by the sight. Hundreds of bodies hang from the ceiling, hooks lodged through their bloodless necks. Most have no faces, just bare white skulls which look like hockey masks. Severed heads are mounted on one wall, some bald, some with wigs. It reminds me of the cabin in the woods, with the wolf head and all the other trophies.

From here I can see baking trays where nipples and fingernails are laid out like candy. Workers are mixing chemicals in buckets and pouring them into moulds. A dumpster in the back corner is filled with individual body parts. The smell of silicone is overpowering.

And they say American manufacturing is dead.

'It looks like a serial killer's home,' Thistle breathes.

I think about my own house, which looks pretty normal.

'Everyone says that.' Howard shoots us a wry smile. 'Sorry, I should have prepared you. Sometimes I forget how jarring it can be to outsiders.'

'What's the process?' I ask. 'How is one of these things made?'

'It's pretty straightforward, but every step has to be done carefully. Our customers are discerning. We assemble the titanium skeleton, put it in one of those moulds over there and fill it with silicone. Then we do make-up and put on the extraneous bits—nails, nipples, heads.'

'*Heads* are extraneous?' Thistle says.

Howard smiles wryly. 'I know, right? Some men just buy the ass on its own.'

She leads us into an office, which has a window overlooking the production floor. There's a desk, a computer, a filing cabinet—and a plastic tub filled with body parts. I'm already getting used to it.

Howard sits behind her desk. Thistle and I take the two stools opposite.

'To be honest,' Thistle says, 'I'm a little surprised to see a woman running this place.'

'A man used to run it. But he made the breasts too big, the waists too narrow. The results didn't look like real women anymore. My dolls are much more convincing, so they sell better. Men only *think* they know what they want. No offence,' Howard adds, glancing at me.

I just nod. None taken.

'You don't think it seems kind of . . .' Thistle looks like she's hunting for a less offensive word than *misogynistic*.

'First,' Howard says wearily, 'there are plenty of male dolls down there too. Second, this isn't objectifying women. It's womanifying objects. This is the least harmful part of the adult entertainment industry. You know how much physical damage is done to a porn actress over the course of her career? You know how many have been drugged or threatened just before the cameras start rolling? You know how many cam girls are prisoners in those little rooms?'

'There are laws . . .'

'In the USA, sure. Laws that are impossible to enforce in the age of the internet.' She picks up a breast from her tub and starts absent-mindedly squeezing it like a stress ball. 'Plenty of my customers are lonely men with social anxiety who form a genuine romantic bond with the doll. Sometimes they don't even fuck. They watch TV together. She reads him the news. She—'

'She *what*?' Thistle interrupts.

'Oh yeah. The new ones have a computer in their heads, so they can talk. Like a Google Home or an Amazon Alexa, but nicer to look at.'

'I'm sure some of your customers have wholesome, chaste relationships with the dummies,' Thistle says, one eyebrow raised. 'But aren't most just looking for a woman who won't say no?'

Howard nods. 'Yep. Most customers buy them for rough sex. Some actually beat the shit out of the dolls. I've even heard they turn up at the dump with stab wounds. But, ultimately, wouldn't you rather that happened to a doll than a real woman? Not that it's easy to tell the difference.' She tosses the breast to me. 'Tell me that doesn't feel like a genuine boob.'

'He wouldn't know,' Thistle mutters.

Howard is looking out the window. 'In Japan,' she says, 'some men form romantic attachments to apps instead of women. They take their phones out on dates to restaurants and parks. You know what women call those men? *Soshoku*. It means *herbivore*.' She looks back at us. 'Because normal men are predators.'

The opposite of *herbivore* isn't *predator*; it's *carnivore*. But I don't point this out.

'Do you take requests?' I ask, keen to get to the point.

'Our whole business is requests,' Howard says. 'Customers choose the face, the wig, the colour of the nails, the type of nipples. Sometimes customers get bored, and they buy new faces for old dolls. You can peel off the face and swap it out.'

Thistle shudders.

'We don't make anything criminal-adjacent, though,' Howard adds.

'Criminal-adjacent?' I repeat.

'Customers sometimes ask me to make children. Animals, too. I used to pass those requests on to the police. But it turns out it's not illegal to request a sex toy shaped like a child or a dog. Doesn't mean I'm gonna make one, though.'

She seems to have forgotten her argument from before. I think about asking her, *Wouldn't you rather that happened to a doll instead of a real dog? A real child?* But we're not here for an ethical debate.

'I was thinking something different,' I say. 'Giants.'

'Giants?'

'Yeah. Women more than, say, seven feet tall.' On the forums where Biggs had been browsing, Sleeping Beauty had asked if anyone wanted to have sex with a giant in real life. A huge sex doll was the only way I could think of that the offer might be genuine.

Howard nods thoughtfully. 'You know what? I do remember something like that.'

Thistle looks at me, impressed.

She starts to scroll through emails, talking as she goes. 'Someone did ask me to make a giant. I assumed it was some kind of art project. I couldn't help them, though. The moulds and skeletons are a standard size. I can't make big women.'

I sigh. Another dead end.

'Who was it?' Thistle asks.

Howard hesitates. I can tell by the movement of her eyes that she's found the email. 'Confidentiality is crucial to my business,' she says. 'I can't just give out customer details.'

'We're FBI,' Thistle says. 'And this person wasn't a customer, if you didn't make the doll.'

'You got a warrant?'

Thistle and I look at each other.

'I didn't think so,' Howard says. 'Get one, and I'll be glad to help.'

'If we come back with a warrant,' Thistle says, 'we'll end up with access to your whole database. Surely it's better to tell us about just one customer rather than all of them?'

'Sorry. But our privacy policy is clear on this. I could be sued if I give away more than I have to.'

'Can you at least tell us if the customer was Kenneth Biggs?' I ask.

Howard glances at the screen. 'I can tell you it wasn't Kenneth Biggs.'

I sigh, frustrated.

'How about Shannon Luxford?' Thistle asks.

'Also wrong. Now, I can't keep playing twenty questions with you. I have work to do. Come back with a warrant.'

•

'Well, that was a bust,' Thistle says, as we walk back to the car. 'But it did give me a million-dollar business idea.'

'Really?' I ask.

'Yup.'

'Let's hear it.'

'You'll have to sign an NDA first,' she says, deadpan.

'I'll do it back at the field office. Spill.'

She spreads her hand wide. 'Sex doll brothel.'

I laugh.

'Seriously. Did you see the catalogue on Howard's desk? Those dolls cost upwards of two grand each. I can't imagine many perverts have that kind of cash to splash around, and if they're married, they wouldn't want the thing in their house. But there must be plenty of guys willing to pay a hundred bucks for an hour with one. Or six minutes, or however long these guys last.'

We climb into the car and she starts the engine.

'You think they'd be willing to have sex with a doll someone else has just used?' I ask.

'Well, they fuck human hookers, don't they? And we'd obviously wash them between customers. Plus, a doll can work twenty-four hours per day, seven days a week.'

'I thought you were against the whole concept.'

'What can I say? Howard was very convincing.'

'You think a guy would spend two hundred and sixty dollars to rent a doll?'

'That sounds too much for . . . Wait. You reckon that's why Biggs took the cash out?'

'No,' I say. 'Just thinking out loud.'

Thistle stops at a red light. Pedestrians shuffle across in front of us. An old man with a walking frame, a lady with a briefcase, a teen on a scooter. Something on the radio catches my attention. I turn it up.

'*—at least sixteen victims from around the Houston metropolitan area. The killer, nicknamed the Crawdad Man, seems to target white males between the ages of twenty and forty. The FBI has not named a suspect at this time.*'

'There goes our head start,' I say. How long have I got before Warner realises I'm still on the case?

The director's voice comes through the speakers. '*We're devoting all available resources to the investigation, and we'd encourage any members of the public with information to come forward.*'

'Why "the Crawdad Man"?' I ask.

'Maybe all the good names were taken. You know the Grim Sleeper killings were originally called the Strawberry Murders?'

'The dump is in Louisiana. Maybe that's why?'

'Or because it's a dump,' Thistle says. 'Don't crawdads eat decomposing matter?'

The radio host is reciting a phone number. '*And we'd like to hear from you. This just in on the text line:* What a surprise that the police are focusing all available resources on a killer of white men. *Hmm, interesting. Thanks for your feedback, Vanessa.*'

The light goes green. Thistle waits for the last few jaywalkers to hurry off the road, and then we're moving again.

'Do a U-turn,' I say. 'Quickly.'

Thistle flips her blinker on. 'Why?'

'I just saw the guy who ran from us at the dump. The one who stole the tractor.'

CHAPTER 25

If five dogs can eat five bones in five minutes, how long does it take four dogs to eat four bones?

Thistle heaves the Crown Vic into the U-turn, scanning the faces of pedestrians on the sidewalk. Other cars slow right down to avoid colliding with us. Someone honks. 'You're shitting me,' she says. 'Where?'

'He's driving a white Mazda,' I say. 'He went that way.'

'You sure it was him? The traffic's doing fifty.'

'Ninety per cent sure,' I say. It was a split-second glimpse, but it was enough. I'm good with faces.

Thistle reaches for the siren.

'Don't,' I say. 'Let's see where he goes.'

'I can't see the car yet.'

'Me neither, but it's there. Eight cars ahead. Overtake this guy.'

Thistle swerves into the other lane and zooms past a black Toyota. The driver sticks his hand out the window and flips the bird at her. Without even looking, Thistle presses her badge to the window. The guy blanches and slows right down. His car gets smaller and smaller in the rear-view mirror.

'Is that it?' Thistle asks, pointing to the white Mazda.

'Yeah.'

'Can you see the plates?'

I can't, but I did when he passed us the first time. I recite the numbers, and Thistle punches them into her dashboard computer. A registration pops up on the screen.

'The car is registered to Hector Gomez,' she says. 'Not listed as stolen. Was that one of the fake names in Edwards's files?'

'No,' I say. 'Doesn't mean it's real, though. Let's see where he goes.'

'We should call it in.'

'Not yet. He'd hear our backup coming.'

We follow the old Mazda west on the I-10, out of Houston. We pass through Katy—trees on our left, places selling tractors and RVs to our right—and then we start to see signs to San Antonio, a hundred and sixty miles away. A short drive by Texas standards. Another sign says NUEVO LAREDO, MEXICO.

'You reckon he's headed for the border?' I ask.

'The I-69 would have been faster,' Thistle says. 'And if so, why didn't he do it yesterday? Maybe he lives down this way.'

'He worked at a dump in Louisiana,' I say. 'Two and a half hours east. He would have found a job closer to his house.'

We drive in silence for five minutes or so. I watch the scrub rush by out the window. Out here, you can see why some people still think the world is flat. Beyond the wasteland of stunted trees and dying grass on our left, refineries are coughing black smoke into the sky, their spires and stacks like a futuristic city. A forest is approaching on the right.

If the guy doesn't live out here and isn't headed for the border, there's another possibility.

'Or,' I say, 'he's on to us. He's trying to lead us as far away from—'

Just then, the Mazda swerves off the road into the forest without signalling.

'Shit.' Thistle hits the brakes, but not fast enough. She's missed the turn—because there was no turn. Just a gap in the rotting fence which lines the road, invisible unless you know it's there. The Mazda is already gone, hidden by trees.

Thistle backs up, talking into her radio. 'Dispatch, this is Agent Reese Thistle.'

The radio hisses. '*Go ahead, Agent.*'

'I'm in pursuit of a suspect driving a white Mazda, registration . . .' She tosses the radio to me and manoeuvres the Crown Vic into the gap in the fence line. I recite the number and pass the radio back.

'Requesting backup,' Thistle says. She floors the accelerator, and the Crown Vic bounces through the undergrowth, crushing shrubbery and startling birds. Police vehicles have overinflated tyres and modified suspension, but even so I'm worried the car will shake itself to bits. Every lurch throws me against my seatbelt or crushes me into my seat. There are two thick ropes of muscle inside the front of the neck, on either side of the windpipe; I'm not sure what they're called, but I can feel them straining to keep my head attached.

'*Understood, Agent,*' the radio says. '*Cars inbound to your location. ETA six minutes.*'

Not a bad response time, but not good enough. Now that he's off-road, there are an infinite number of directions Gomez could be headed in. Roadblocks won't help. If we don't get eyes on this guy again soon, he's gone for good. I should have let Thistle call for backup earlier.

Thistle yells over the screaming engine: 'Anything?'

I'm frantically scanning the trees, but I can't see any sign of the Mazda. Nor is there any crushed vegetation ahead of us to indicate which way he went. Which means—

'He doubled back,' I say. 'We already missed him. Turn around.'

Thistle does exactly what the other driver must have done. She shifts into reverse and backs into the forest at an angle, far enough that someone else driving past wouldn't see us. Then she spins the wheel, switches to drive and zooms out of the brush, jolting back towards the highway.

'Left or right?' Thistle asks.

I still can't see the Mazda. But unless the guy is a master

of double-bluffing, he won't have pulled that trick only to keep going the same way he was before.

'Left,' I shout. 'Back towards Houston.'

Thistle sends the car careening back onto the road and puts the pedal to the metal. The engine roars, and the scratched-up Crown Vic hurtles up the highway. She flicks on the siren. I notice a trail of splotches on the tarmac, like old chewing gum stains on the sidewalk.

'He's leaking,' I say, shouting over the siren. 'Gas, or maybe oil. His car isn't designed for off-road.'

Thistle swerves around a rusty pick-up. 'How long can he keep going?'

'No clue.' I'm not a mechanic. Even if I was, I don't know how much gas or oil he started with.

Then I see the Mazda up ahead. It's still going fast, but we're gaining. The Crown Vic has a more powerful engine, and it's not leaking.

'I see it,' Thistle says. She pulls out the radio and presses the loudspeaker button. 'This is the FBI. Pull over.'

Her distorted voice bounces back off the other vehicles. The Mazda doesn't slow down.

'Can you side-swipe him?' I ask. 'Knock him off the road?'

Thistle is about to reply when a police car coming the opposite way swerves across the dividing line into the Mazda's path, lights flashing. The backup came early.

The Mazda goes into a skid as the driver tries to avoid a collision. The front wheels tumble off the side of the road and spin in the dirt. The engine stalls.

Thistle slams on the brakes and leaps out of the Crown Vic. She draws her Glock and advances on the car, head low, perfectly even footsteps keeping her aim steady. 'Show me your hands!' she shouts. '*Levante las manos.*'

The other cop climbs out of his car. He's old, but in good shape, with clear blue eyes buried in his sun-weathered face. His pistol is already up.

The driver of the Mazda gets out. I can see him more clearly now—full lips, angled brows under a long fringe. Definitely the guy from the dump. He's wearing jeans and a loose T-shirt. He's terrified.

I've done some bad things in my life. Consequently I don't experience fear the way normal people do. It's the same calculation I did with McLean, but the stakes are higher—*if this guy had murdered sixteen people, would he look so scared?*

I get out of the car.

'*Manos arriba,*' Thistle says, getting closer to the guy. 'Hands up.'

The other cop stays behind the open door of his car. A car door won't stop a bullet, but it will slow one down.

The Latino guy doesn't put his hands up. He looks from Thistle's gun to the other cop's and back. He swallows.

'Don't shoot,' I say. 'He's unarmed.' No side holsters, no room in his pockets. And given that he just got out of the driver's seat of a car, he doesn't have a gun tucked into the back of his pants.

Thistle ignores me. 'Hands in the air!' she says. 'I won't ask again.'

The guy still doesn't move, his brow beaded with sweat.

'He wants you to shoot him!' I say. 'Hold your fire.'

The guy hears me. Before the police have time to process what I've said, he suddenly reaches behind his back, as though he does have a gun.

Thistle doesn't shoot.

The other cop does.

CHAPTER 26

Who was the president of the USA before
John F. Kennedy was assassinated?

'How did you know?' Thistle asks.

We're in the waiting room at the hospital, drinking crappy coffee out of paper cups. The doctors have told us nothing. But at the scene, the wound looked superficial. Like the first little wedge an axe takes out of a tree. The blood flowed from the guy's upper arm, but didn't squirt out of it.

His hand, when it came out from behind his back, had been empty.

'You ever try driving with a gun in the back of your pants?' I ask. 'Me neither—because it would be a stupid thing to do.'

'Not that,' Thistle says. 'How did you know he wanted us to shoot him?'

I look down into my coffee, which is somehow swirling even though no one stirred it. I think of the way the guy stared at those two guns. Looking for a way out, then finally seeing one. Taking a deep breath, like he was about to jump into a cold river.

'I'm not exactly sure,' I say finally.

'Hell of a risk for not sure.'

'I was sure—I just don't know *why* I was sure.'

Thistle leans back in her chair.

'Thanks for trusting me,' I add.

'You've never been wrong before.'

I grimace. 'Actually, I'm wrong all the time.'

'Now you tell me,' she says, with something that's almost a smile.

A doctor emerges from the double doors. But it's not Gomez's doctor, and she ignores us.

'So you don't know why he did it,' Thistle says.

I shrug. 'Didn't want to go back to Mexico?'

'I've been to Mexico,' Thistle says. 'I did some training in Cancun with an anti-cartel unit. Mexico isn't *that* bad. I can imagine risking my life to stay here, but I can't imagine killing myself to avoid going back.'

Her phone rings, and she answers. 'Yeah?'

I watch her from the corner of my eye. As always, I'm worried it's a call from Vasquez. *We're pulling Blake's house apart. There are bodies in his freezer. Arrest him, now!*

'Thanks,' Thistle says. 'See you soon.'

She hangs up. 'That was Vasquez.'

My heart speeds up a little. Maybe I feel normal fear after all. 'Yeah?'

'The guy's name is indeed Hector Gomez,' she says. 'He's undocumented. But he has family here. A wife, a brother and two kids. Five and seven.'

'What are you getting at?'

'His kids were born here. They're US citizens. ICE won't deport the parents of an American-born child.'

'You think he knows that?'

'For sure,' she says. 'Undocumented immigrants know the law better than the politicians do.'

'So when he ran from us the first time, he wasn't scared of getting deported.'

'No. He was scared of something else.'

A doctor appears. Tall, with a JFK haircut and hooded eyes. 'He says he doesn't want a lawyer. You can go in.'

Hector is sitting up on his hospital bed with a handcuff around one wrist. His other arm is bandaged up and hanging from a sling. He looks up at us fearfully when we walk in, but seems almost relieved when he recognises us. Makes me wonder who he was expecting.

'Hector Gomez?' Thistle says. 'I'm Agent Reese Thistle, and this is—'

'You have to go to my house,' he says. 'Please.' His Mexican accent has faded into the background. I'd say he's been in Texas at least ten years.

'First let's talk about why you ran,' Thistle says.

'There's no time,' he says. 'They will kill my boys. I can't protect them from here.'

'Who threatened your kids?' I ask.

Groaning with frustration, Gomez pulls at his cuffs. 'I will tell you everything, okay? I swear it. But you have to send someone to my home, right now. My family is in danger.'

Thistle looks at me, eyebrows raised in a question.

I nod slightly. I'm pretty sure he's telling the truth.

'Okay,' Thistle says. She pulls out her phone and calls Vasquez. 'Hi again. You got Gomez's address there? Great. I need you to send a patrol car to his house . . . Right. No, not at this stage. Sounds like a potential retribution thing . . . Sure. Let me know.'

She hangs up. 'The police are on their way to your house. You want to tell me what they'll find?'

Gomez relaxes. 'Hopefully nothing. They are probably not even home.'

'Tell us who threatened you,' Thistle says.

Gomez takes a breath. 'Okay.'

•

She was pretty, for a white lady. A tall blonde, thirties, with clear skin and full lips. He thought she had a great figure, too, under her narrow grey skirt and that silk blouse. But he didn't look directly at her. He didn't want to be rude. And anyway, he had been married for nine years.

Here at the dump, she looked incredibly out of place. Like a flight attendant who had walked out of a crashed aircraft, unscathed. Hector was headed back to his pick-up—it was sunset—when she waved to him.

'Hector Gomez?' she said.

He shook his head. 'I'm sorry, Miss. You have me confused with someone else.' His name at work was Greg Post.

She smiled, showing perfect teeth. 'It's okay,' she said. 'I'm not a cop. I have a job offer for you.'

'Thank you, but I already have a job,' he said. 'Excuse me.'

He tried to keep walking towards his truck, but she stepped out in front of him. 'A former employee of mine, Judah Price, he said you could use some extra money.'

Hector hesitated. Judah had worked at the dump with him until recently. A big white guy with an army tattoo on his shoulder. He spoke a little Spanish, and he and Hector got on well. Judah had left unexpectedly, and Hector wondered if he'd found better pay elsewhere.

'You know Judah, right?' the woman said. 'A wide gentleman? Army tattoo?'

'I really have to go,' Hector said.

'My boss will pay you an extra hundred dollars per day,' the woman said. 'For less than two hours' work. Sound good?'

Hector did need the extra cash. He was about to have to buy some more school books for his boys, and Cesar needed a new uniform. Hector's car had a rattle which was getting worse, and he couldn't fix it himself. Plus, the rent was going up at the apartment.

But something Hector's mother used to say came back to him. *If it sounds too good to be true, it probably is.* Back in Cancun, the only people who offered such 'easy' money were the cartels. If the lady had offered him twenty bucks he might have taken it. But a hundred? Every day? He didn't want the risk.

'Thank you for the offer,' he said. 'But I'm not looking for more work right now.'

He got in his pick-up. The woman let him do it. Then she tapped on the window.

Reluctantly, he rolled it down.

She passed him a fat envelope. 'This is just for considering the offer.'

Then she started to walk away.

Hector could have chased after her, made her take the envelope back. But he thought about the school books. The rent. The rattle.

The woman got into a dark blue sedan and cruised out of the parking lot.

Hector sighed and opened the envelope.

What was inside wasn't what he had expected. No money. Just printed photos. Dozens of them.

They were all photos of Cesar and Miguel. Some had been taken from outside the front gates of their school. Others were shots from the soccer field. A couple were from outside the church.

With shaking hands, Hector reached the final photo. It showed his boys sleeping. The picture had been taken from right outside their bedroom window.

There was one more thing in the envelope. A flap, thin and pale, like parchment, but as soft as good-quality leather. Hector didn't know what he was holding until he saw the army tattoo.

CHAPTER 27

*Forwards I'm heavy, backwards
I'm not. What am I?*

The clock ticks in Gomez's hospital room.

'You should have taken the money,' I say finally.

He looks at his feet. 'You think I don't know that, now?'

'What did she actually want you to do?' Thistle asks.

He swallows. 'She wanted a key to the container, the one with the filing boxes. I had to steal it from my boss's desk, then copy it. I was supposed to add her licence plate to the database so the gate would open for her automatically. I parked a truck in front of the security camera whenever she entered or left. And sometimes she gave me something to get rid of, like a phone. I was supposed to break it up and bury the parts so deep they wouldn't be found for a hundred years.'

'How often did she come?'

'Most nights. Twice, maybe two hours apart.'

'For how long?'

'The last few months.'

I exchange a glance with Thistle. Is it possible that there are more victims we don't know about? Maybe hundreds?

'Did she bring a phone every time?' I ask.

He shakes his head. 'That was rare. One every two or three weeks.'

'On these dates?' I recite the twelve dates that Biggs highlighted on the wall planner.

'I don't think so,' Gomez says. 'The last time was last week—the second.'

I'm guessing that was Daniel Ruthven's phone. 'What about cars?'

'Just the one car. It was still in the crusher when you guys showed up.'

'Tell me about the shipping container,' I say.

'I don't know why she wanted to go in there,' he says. 'There are just files. After the first time, I went in to look around. It didn't look like she had touched anything.'

I think of the bloody fingerprints on the planner. Biggs, trying to tell us something.

'You should have come to us,' Thistle says.

'The next time we talked—the day after she gave me the envelope—she told me not to talk to the police. She said her boss would skin my boys. She told me Judah had disobeyed him. That is why I ran, the first time you saw me.'

'We could have protected you. We still can.'

'I mean no disrespect,' Gomez says, 'but police don't always take the side of the undocumented. Even legal aliens, they are treated with suspicion.'

'The woman didn't threaten your wife?' I ask. 'Just your children?'

'*Just* my children? I take it you're not a father, Mr Blake.'

'You realise you've assisted with a range of homicides?' Thistle says.

'No, no!' Gomez shakes his head vigorously. 'When she arrived, she usually had a man with her. One of them, I knew his face. On my son's birthday, I had seen him working in the kitchen of the T-Rex.'

T-Rex is a Tex-Mex restaurant in Houston's south. I've never been inside.

'The day after the woman took him to the dump, I went to the restaurant,' Gomez continues. 'He was there. I was relieved to see him alive. So I thought she was using the container just for sex. Not murder.'

'A shipping container at a dump?' Thistle says doubtfully.

'Some people, they have strange tastes,' Gomez says.

'Do you still have the skin?' I ask. 'With the tattoo?'

'At home. Hidden in a Ziploc bag under the carpet. I didn't know how to get rid of it.'

This reminds me of all the body parts hidden in my house, waiting for me. It takes effort to bring the hospital room back into focus.

'This man at the restaurant,' Thistle says, 'was he white? Big?'

'No. He is Latino, skinny. With a moustache, and an earring. Gold.'

'Which ear?'

He thinks about it. 'Left.'

'You know his name?'

'No.'

I want to show him a photo of Charlie Warner. She's blonde, tallish. Capable of skinning people.

But Thistle will want to know the connection, and other than the fact that Biggs's body turned up right near our usual drop-off point, I don't have one. As I'm trying to come up with a plausible excuse, something else occurs to me. Charlie Warner isn't the only good-looking blonde I've seen hanging around since I started working on this case.

'Please,' Gomez says. 'I've answered your questions. I need to go home to my family. They'll be scared.'

'You resisted arrest,' Thistle says. 'Twice. We can't just let you go home.'

'Agent Thistle,' I say. 'A word?'

Thistle follows me out into the corridor.

'I think we should send him home,' I say.

Thistle looks incredulous. 'Our only suspect?'

'He's not a suspect. He's a witness at best.'

'He hasn't given us a sliver of evidence that his story is true. He works at the place where all the phone trails end, and where the blood of one of the victims was found. He fled from us. Twice. No one else has seen this woman.'

'Ian McLean has,' I say. 'She picked up Daniel Ruthven in her car on the night he disappeared.'

'That could have been anyone.'

'We've seen her too. She was outside Shannon Luxford's office.'

'She . . .' Thistle trails off, remembering the tall, glamorous blonde we saw in the math department. Who saw us, and turned quickly away.

'It's a stretch,' Thistle says finally.

'Is it? She looked like she was doing the same thing we were doing. Asking if anyone had seen Biggs. She was showing a picture on her phone to a student.'

'But if she killed him, she knows exactly where he is.'

No, I think to myself. Because I took the body. She may not even know he's dead.

'Let's say she was driving him somewhere,' I say, 'and he escaped. Jumped out of a moving car and ran into the woods, for example. So she went to his work looking for him.'

'There are so many things wrong with that I don't know where to start,' Thistle says. 'Leaving aside the fact that there are thousands of attractive blonde women in Houston—'

'But only one hanging around our victim's office.'

'If Biggs escaped, why didn't he contact us?'

'Didn't his file say he had heart surgery?' I ask. 'Maybe he had a heart attack while he was running away.'

'But the killer didn't notice the body?'

'Maybe he fell down a hole or something,' I suggest, thinking of the deer trap near the log cabin.

'This is a metric fuck-ton of speculation,' Thistle says. 'Even if I bought it, why would I let Gomez go?'

I still think there's a chance that Warner is behind this. But if she is, I'm screwed—so I'm desperate to make this theory work.

'Because if you don't,' I say, 'the killer will find a new stooge at the dump, or a new dump. We'll be back to square one. But if we put Gomez back into play, eventually the killer will call him for help with her next victim. Or maybe she'll try to kill him, now that she knows we're onto her. Either way, we have a chance to catch her. She told Gomez she was approaching him on someone else's behalf—if that's true, I'd like to know who it was.'

Thistle looks appalled. 'You want to use Gomez as bait?'

'Yes,' I say.

'And how do I explain to the director that we're letting our only suspect go?'

'He's not our only suspect, we don't have the evidence to hold him, we're worried about him suing the state because we shot him while he was unarmed.' I shrug. 'Take your pick.'

Thistle takes a long, deep inhale, like a drag on an imaginary cigarette.

'We'll keep him under surveillance, obviously,' I add. 'The risk to him and his family is minimal.'

'Fucking hell, Blake,' Thistle says finally, 'you better be right about this.'

Her phone rings. She answers. 'Thistle.'

A long pause.

'Okay. We'll be sending a covert surveillance team. Stick around until they arrive.'

She hangs up. 'Gomez's family is fine,' she says. 'Shaken, but fine. Forensics found the skin flap. They're taking it to Dr Norman.'

'Was the wife worried about getting deported?'

'She sounded more worried about her husband. The kids protect her, for now, as long as she can prove they were born here.'

We walk back into the hospital room. Thistle unlocks Gomez's cuff.

'You're free to go,' she says. 'You and your family will be monitored round-the-clock by plainclothes agents for your own protection until further notice.'

'Thank you,' Gomez says, clasping Thistle's hand.

'Let me be clear,' Thistle says. 'We're hoping this woman will contact you again. When she does, you're not going to alert her that you've spoken with us. You're going to do everything she says, and pretend you don't know about the surveillance. If you fail to comply, the protection will be withdrawn and you may be treated as an accessory. Understood?'

Gomez nods vigorously.

'Your car's at the impound,' Thistle says. 'We'll get it fixed. In the meantime, here's some money for a cab.'

After he's gone, Thistle turns to me. 'I still can't figure out the connection to those dates.'

'Yeah.' I rub my eyes. 'We're missing something.'

Just saying those words, *missing something*, makes me pause. It's a feeling rather than a thought. That strange tingling as my subconscious starts making connections. Connections it should have made much earlier.

The size of the rooms at Luxford's house. The half-finished renovations. The air-conditioner still running. The extra remote on the coffee table.

'We need to go back to Luxford's house,' I say.

'What?' Thistle looks incredulous. 'We have independent witnesses confirming the existence of this blonde woman. Now you want to focus on Luxford?'

'Yes,' I say. 'I know where he is.'

•

When we get back to Luxford's house, I walk right in the front door. I want to see Luxford before anyone else does. I want to watch the moment he realises he's been caught. Because that will tell me if he's a serial killer, or just a rapist. Different animals, with different defensive behaviours. A rapist will put his hands up and deny everything. Start trashing his accusers. But a serial killer will confess, because he wants the publicity. Or because he's relieved to be caught, and he's afraid they'll let him go if he doesn't.

As frightened as I am of getting arrested, sometimes I'm more frightened that I won't be. That the eating and lying will go on forever.

Thistle is close behind me. The other two cops, Albrecht and Terracini, are behind her.

'He's not here,' Terracini says, but he keeps his voice low. 'We searched the place thoroughly last time. No one's been in or out since then.'

I'm already walking into the living area. 'You know our soldiers didn't find Saddam Hussein in that hole until they'd already searched the area, given up and called the helicopters to extract them?'

Albrecht looks down. 'You want to rip up the floor?'

'No.' I listen. Again, I'm struck by how the room seems smaller than it should be. No sound except the rumbling of the air-conditioner. I can't even hear the traffic outside. This is a well-insulated house.

But why would the owner of a well-insulated house leave the air-con running when he went out?

I go to the coffee table and look at the remotes. Too many.

One is Sony, which matches the game console. One is Samsung, which matches the TV. One is LG, which matches the Blu-ray sound system combo.

On the final remote, all the buttons but two appear to be fake. The two real ones are green and red. The green one features a picture of a key. The red one has a padlock logo. The brand is BHI.

I show it to Thistle.

She nods. 'That's Joseph Luxford's security company. They install security systems.'

'Including panic rooms,' I say. 'Right?'

I push the green button, and listen. Nothing. I walk around the ground floor, pushing it over and over, hoping to hear a beep.

'Let's check upstairs,' Thistle says.

We go up the narrow staircase—narrow because the wall had to be expanded during the renovation, reinforced to take the weight of all the steel and concrete above. We run into Shannon's bedroom and I push the button again.

This time I do hear a beep—but not from this room, from the storage room.

'This way,' I say. But something's bothering me. If Luxford is in the panic room, shouldn't the remote be in there with him? Maybe this one is a spare—but it seems like an obvious oversight.

Thistle has other concerns. 'Why would he install his panic room in the bedroom he doesn't use?'

'Don't know. Maybe the structure of the house couldn't take it anywhere else.'

'Then why not move his bed?'

We've reached the storage room. I open the wardrobe—the one Luxford keeps empty. The rear wall has automatically slid sideways, exposing a foot-wide gap.

Thistle raises her pistol. 'Luxford! Come out with your hands up.'

There's a second of silence.

Then the screaming starts.

CHAPTER 28

A man is stabbed in the heart. No one tries to save him, and yet he doesn't die. How?

I don't wait for Thistle. She has the gun, but we don't need it. The scream has told me exactly what we're going to find in Shannon Luxford's panic room. We've already wasted too much time. So I walk right in. As I pass through the doorway, I notice how thick the door is—there's hardened steel behind the plaster, with huge automatic bolts.

Half of the space behind the closet is a standard panic room. Poured concrete walls, floor and ceiling. There's a bank of small monitors, so the occupant can observe the rest of the house. All switched off, and probably useless, since I didn't see any cameras downstairs. There's a phone line, but no actual phone. Overhead, a narrow vent pumps recycled air around, droning like an idling truck. A hole in the wall next to the door probably used to be the emergency exit button.

The other half of the room could have come from a parallel universe. It has painted walls, a small bed and a fake window, letting in some approximation of daylight. An antique bedside table has a plastic lamp on it. A mirror. Clothes are scattered all over the floor. A skimpy nurse's uniform. A police outfit, but not the kind a real police officer would wear. They're like Halloween costumes, half buried under mountains of heels and lingerie.

Thick plexiglass separates the bedroom from the rest of the panic room. The glass is scratched but not dented from weeks or months of battering. Air holes have been cut in it, and there's a transparent door. Four hinges on one side and three padlocks on the other.

A camera is mounted on a tripod on this side of the glass. Through the lens, this would look more or less like a normal bedroom, except for the two paint buckets in the corner.

Thistle's voice: *A doll can work twenty-four hours per day, seven days a week.* And Howard's: *You know how many cam girls are prisoners in those little rooms?*

A young woman in a schoolgirl's skirt and sweater is slapping her palms on the glass. Her cheeks are hollow after days of starvation. I assume she hasn't eaten or drunk since Luxford fled. Her bloodshot eyes are wide with desperation and terror.

'Get me out of here!' she shrieks. 'Please, just get me out of here! Help me!'

'Holy shit,' Thistle breathes.

I rattle the padlocks. I didn't see any keys when we were searching the place. 'We'll need Albrecht's tools,' I say.

'On it.' Thistle runs back out of the room.

'No! Don't leave me, please don't leave me!' The woman is sobbing with terror. 'Come back!'

I've only been in here for fifteen seconds, and already I know how she feels. Even with the remote in my pocket, it's hard to suppress the panic. What if the door closes? What if the batteries in the remote die and we get trapped? No daylight. No fresh air. No one would be able to hear us shouting for help.

'It's okay,' I say. 'We're gonna get you out of here.'

The woman doesn't even seem to hear me. 'Please, just let me out. Let me out. He could be back any minute.'

I stick my fingers through the air holes. 'There are two more police officers downstairs. He can't hurt you anymore. It's over.'

The woman is shaking, long dark hair falling all over her face. Wheezing like an asthmatic. Now that rescue is so close, she's freaking out. I bet she wasn't this scared when the situation seemed hopeless. The mind is a funny thing.

I understand what she's been through. Not just because I've been starved. Not just because I was once bound and gagged in the trunk of a psycho's car and later chained up in his basement.

It's because I'm a bad guy. As bad as Luxford. So I can imagine everything he would have done to her.

'Hey,' I say. 'He's not coming back. Ever. Okay? If he does, I'll rip his throat out.'

She looks at me uncertainly. 'You'll what?'

'I'll rip his throat out, like a mad dog. I'm not even kidding.'

She grips my fingers through the air holes. 'Please don't leave me.'

'I won't, I promise. We're walking out of here together. You and me. Okay?'

'I want my mom,' she says. 'Can you call my mom?'

'We will. You're Abbey, right?'

She snatches her hands away, suddenly suspicious. Like I'm in league with Luxford. 'How did you know that?'

'You're listed as missing,' I say. 'People have been looking for you.'

Albrecht and Terracini enter the room. Albrecht looks grim. She hurries over to the door and starts punching out the padlocks with the chisel. Terracini takes in the glass, the buckets, the camera, and goes pale.

'Catch him,' I say. 'Catch him!'

Thistle whirls around in time to grab Terracini as he faints. Puffing, she lowers him to the ground. He'll never live this down.

•

Abbey lived in Columbus, Ohio, before she came to Houston for college on a scholarship. Her mom came to Texas when Abbey went missing, but went home again a few months later when the money ran out.

We don't want to wait for an ambulance, so I help Abbey into the car while Thistle calls her mom. 'We found Abbey. She's alive. She's with us.'

I can hear crying down the other end of the line.

'I'm putting her on, okay?' Thistle says.

Abbey takes the phone with a skeletal hand. She's wrapped in Thistle's jacket, which makes her look tiny, even though I know she's nineteen. Dehydrated, but the tears start anyway. 'I'm here, Mom. I'm okay.'

Thistle starts driving us to the Texas Women's Hospital, which isn't far from the field office. I can't hear what Abbey's mother is saying, but she sounds angry, like any parent who's been worried sick.

'Hey,' Thistle says. 'You all right?'

It takes me a second to realise I'm the one she's talking to. Thistle doesn't know everything I've done, but she knows everything that's been done to me. As a kid and as an adult.

I look out the window. 'Fine.'

After a second, she squeezes my hand. I let her.

'You did good,' she says.

'Not who I expected to find,' I say.

'Maybe not. But if you hadn't figured it out in time . . .'

She doesn't need to finish the sentence. Abbey would have died of thirst in that little room. Luxford wasn't coming back for her.

Thistle doesn't let go of my hand until she needs to change gears.

Abbey keeps saying, 'I'm okay,' into the phone, over

and over again. I don't know if she's telling herself or her mom. Eventually she passes the phone back to Thistle. 'She wants to talk to you.'

Thistle assures Abbey's mother that the Bureau will cover her flight to George Bush airport, and she'll be picked up as soon as she gets there. The director might kick Thistle's ass for that, the budget being what it is. But it seems to soothe the mom a bit, and eventually she ends the call.

As we approach the hospital, I can see Abbey getting nervous. When we drive into the parking lot under the building, she looks like she's on the verge of a panic attack.

'You okay?' I ask.

She nods, teeth clenched.

Thistle parks, and we all get out of the car. Thistle and I start to walk towards the gleaming steel doors of the elevators, but Abbey slows right down.

'I can't go in there,' she says.

'It's safe,' Thistle promises. 'The doctors just want—'

'I'm sorry. I just can't.'

I get it. After I got out of that basement, I never wanted to be indoors again.

'Okay,' Thistle says. 'We'll take the stairs.'

Abbey is backing away from us. Towards fresh air, and the twilight at the entrance to the parking lot.

'I can't,' she says again.

'I'm sure we can get a doctor to come outside,' I say.

Thistle looks around doubtfully at the freezing parking lot.

I take off my coat and hold it out. Abbey reluctantly puts it on over the top of Thistle's jacket.

'Maybe you can get some blankets?' I ask Thistle. 'And coffee?'

Abbey's teeth are chattering. 'Tea?' she says hopefully.

Thistle nods. 'Okay. I'll be right back.'

She goes into the lifts and disappears.

I sit on the hood of Thistle's Crown Vic, fidgeting in the cold. It's not too bad being alone with Abbey—not much temptation. Hardly any meat on her.

'You'll have to go indoors eventually,' I say. 'It would be a shame to freeze to death at this point.'

Abbey looks at me. 'Was that a joke?'

'Was it funny?'

She thinks for a moment. 'Not yet.'

'How about you tell me what happened?' I say.

She just shakes her head.

'The more we know, the faster we catch Luxford,' I say.

Abbey sits on the hood next to me. 'You wouldn't understand.'

She thinks she can't let it out. It's so bad that just knowing about it would hurt people. She thinks that once I know what she had to do to survive, I'll look at her like she's a different species.

'I might,' I say. I show her my missing thumb. 'You see this?'

She looks. Doesn't seem shocked, just curious. 'What happened?'

'A very bad guy chained me up in his basement. He was

someone I'd thought I could trust. I was sure I was gonna die, and no one would ever know what had happened to me. I had to chew off my thumb to get out of the handcuffs.'

She keeps looking, examining the scar tissue.

'I tell people it was an accident with a hedge trimmer,' I say, 'because I don't want to have to deal with their feelings on top of mine.'

She turns her head away.

'I wasn't down there for long,' I admit. 'I don't want to say that what happened to me was as bad as what happened to you. But I'm a good listener.'

Abbey takes a deep breath. 'I didn't really know anyone at Braithwaite,' she begins.

CHAPTER 29

A man is found shot to death inside his car. The car is undamaged, the windows up and the doors locked, but the police find no gun inside the car. How was he shot?

At first, Abbey's story sounds like Hope's. A young woman, freshman year, isolated. A party. Out in the parking lot, an offer of a ride home.

But Abbey declined.

And Shannon smiled. 'You have some spine,' he said. 'You're perfect.'

Abbey was bowing her head to take the compliment when she saw the knife.

'Give me your phone and get in the truck,' Shannon said.

Later, she would wish she had screamed and run. He might not have chased her. If he had, he might not have caught her. He might not have used the knife. Or the wound might not have been fatal. There were so many ways she might have escaped.

But like all young people, she thought there would be more chances later. She gave him the phone and got in the truck.

He drove fast, so she couldn't grab the handbrake or the steering wheel without risking both their lives. He drove in silence, apparently feeling no need to justify kidnapping her. When they got to his house, she felt oddly safe. She knew where he lived now. If anything bad happened to her, she would be able to lead the cops to his doorstep. Therefore, nothing bad was going to happen. This was all some kind of joke. A hazing ritual, maybe.

He parked behind a convertible on a quiet street and led her up to his front door, the knife still in his hand. She looked around, wondering if one of the neighbours might be looking out the window. But it was the middle of the night. All the curtains were drawn.

He was on her right. The knife was in his left hand. She could have grabbed it, but her fingers were likely to grip the blade directly. It would hurt, and she would bleed.

This was another chance she would hate herself for missing, later.

She had thought she was scared already. But she didn't really understand what fear was until she saw the room. The camera. The padlocks on the open door.

She lost it then, screaming, thrashing, trying to claw his eyes out. But now it was too late. He grabbed her upper arms hard enough to leave bruises and threw her onto the bed. Then he braced the door shut with his foot as he engaged the padlocks, one by one.

There was no adjustment period. At college there had been an Orientation Week. Not here. Shannon was excited. More excited than she had ever seen a man.

'Say hi for the camera,' he said, his voice slightly muffled by the plexiglass. 'And maybe blow a kiss, or something.'

Still nursing her bruised arm, Abbey told him to go fuck himself.

He seemed delighted to hear this. Like he'd been waiting for the excuse to do something terrible. She fought the urge to shrink away from the glass—if she stayed close to the door, she might just be able to force her way through when he came in to beat her or rape her.

He didn't come in. He just switched off the lights.

Suddenly blind, she fumbled her way over to the glass wall, looking for the door. But he didn't open it. There was complete silence.

As a little girl she had gone to the Ohio Caverns with her older brother. They had driven fifty miles to see the huge limestone stalactites, protruding from the roof like alligator's teeth. But what made a more lasting impression was a smaller cave, left unlit to show city slickers what real darkness looked like. Abbey had only spent a minute in there, but it was enough to make her stomach churn. Even though she knew other people were right outside, it was impossible not to feel the weight of all that stone above her head and think, *What if I never find my way out*? She could hear her brother's breaths quickening beside her. She held his hand as they left, and it was as damp as the walls.

In Shannon Luxford's homemade prison, the silence and darkness were so much thicker. Her heart raced until it felt like she was going to die.

'Okay,' she said finally, 'I'll do it.'

There was silence.

'I said, I'll do it! Turn the lights back on.'

Nothing.

'Are you still there? Hello?'

He must be gone, she thought. He wouldn't just sit there, speechless in the dark. Would he?

She screamed until her throat was raw. Pounded the concrete walls until her palms throbbed. Somehow being alone was even worse than being stuck in there with a psychopath. Eventually she collapsed.

Shannon didn't come back.

To pass the time, she counted all the people who would be looking for her. Tara, her roommate with the hooded eyes and the volleyball obsession, must have reported Abbey missing by now. They didn't know one another well and rarely spoke when their paths did cross, but Abbey came home every night. So Tara would have noticed she was gone, and would do something about it. Right?

So that meant the police would be searching. And her mom, and her brother. Who had seen her leave the party with Shannon? No one whose name she knew. But maybe someone who knew hers.

The dark seemed to be inside her now, nibbling at her lungs. Her breaths grew tighter. Her pulse was deafening. She could feel the panic growing. Was it possible for a nineteen-year-old to die of a heart attack?

This thought led to another nightmare scenario. What if Shannon had a heart attack? What if he was the only one who knew this room existed, and he died? She might starve to death in this little room. No, she would die of thirst first. She'd taken a first-aid course, and heard the rule of three: you can survive three weeks without food, three days without water, three minutes without air.

Oh God—what if there was no source of fresh air? She wouldn't even feel herself running out of oxygen. She would get confused, pass out and suffocate.

Eventually the silence grew too much and she started screaming again. She yelled that she would do anything he wanted if he just turned the lights on. She told herself she was lying. That she wouldn't have to do anything—as soon as there was light, she would see a way out. Something he had overlooked.

It didn't matter. She screamed for hours—or what felt like hours—and no one came. She realised the sun could be up by now.

She got thirsty, and hungry. She sat on the floor, quaking. The adrenaline had exhausted her, but every time she got drowsy, she worried she was running out of oxygen, and suddenly she was wide awake again.

Eventually she slept, right there on the concrete. Using the bed would have felt like accepting his terms, whatever they were. She woke up disoriented and alarmed, thrashing like she was drowning.

After a thousand years the lights came back on. Suddenly she was blind for an entirely different reason.

'Hello, Dolly,' Shannon said.

'Please,' she said, 'just let me out of here.'

'That was two days of lights-out,' Shannon said. 'No one's even looking for you yet. Are you gonna do what I want?'

She nodded vigorously.

He sighed. 'I'm not convinced,' he said, and turned the lights back off.

•

The next blackout lasted only three hours. Or he said it did. Later Abbey would start to suspect he was lying to her. Her hunger gave her a sense of time passing, and it didn't seem to line up with what he said. Sometimes it felt like days between his visits, but he said it had been only hours. When he eventually told her she had been missing for two weeks, she was sure it had been more like nine days. He always smiled when he told her what day it was. Like he enjoyed having control over time itself.

Shannon had thought of everything. There were no sharp objects in her cell. Nothing electrical. Nothing heavy enough to break the glass or use as a weapon, except the bed frame, and she had no tools with which to disassemble it. There was no plumbing to sabotage. She was expected to piss and shit in an old paint bucket, which she kept sealed in one corner. Another bucket had clean water, with a washcloth. The bedclothes were polyester, which she thought about setting fire to—but she couldn't work out how to create enough friction, or what she would do once she was trapped in a burning room. Several times per hour she would reach for her phone to Google something like this, and then remember that Shannon had taken it.

She started to wonder if he'd done this before. And, if so, what had happened to the last woman who lived in this little room.

If she'd been a 'good girl', she would be fed. A TV dinner would be passed through the slot cut in the bottom of the door, with bottled water. No cutlery. This slot—barely wide enough to put her hand through—was also used to deliver outfits and sex toys. The sex toys came in increasingly disturbing shapes and sizes. She was told where to put them, and to act like she enjoyed it. If her performance wasn't good enough, lights out.

Sometimes he left the lights on for what felt like weeks, and that was almost as bad. The colours were slowly bleached out of her prison. It was like jet lag, making her feel physically ill. Without real sunlight, she started to become delirious, convinced the fluorescent bulbs were irradiating her, giving her skin cancer. Sometimes it felt like she couldn't breathe. She would press her lips to the holes in the plexiglass and gasp, her heart bursting.

Whole days passed—or felt like they did—when she didn't get out of bed. But nor did she sleep. The tiniest of noises kept her awake. She imagined she could hear rats scratching under the bed, but never saw any.

Abbey knew about cam sites. She'd busted her ex-boyfriend on one once. Lee—a stoner creep who didn't think sending obscene messages to a naked stranger counted as cheating. But Abbey hadn't given a thought to the woman he had been watching on the screen. Had she been a prisoner too? Was Abbey listed on that same site? Maybe Lee would see her.

She was waiting for the toilet bucket to fill up. When it did, Shannon would have to come in, right? To change it. She would have a chance to escape. He might threaten her with the knife again, but this time she wouldn't hesitate. She strained over the bucket three times per day, desperate to fill it, careful never to spill a drop.

'I need a new bathroom bucket,' she told him, when it was three-quarters full.

'Fine.' He pushed some handcuffs though the slot. 'Cuff yourself to the bed. With both hands behind your back.'

She hesitated.

He reached for the light switch.

'Okay!' she said. 'Okay. I'm doing it.'

She sat down and cuffed her wrists together, the chain behind the leg of the bed. He made her show him how tight the cuffs were. Then he unlocked the door and brought in a new bucket.

Abbey had managed to lift the bed before. She had assumed she would be able to do so again, and slip the chain out from beneath the leg. But with her hands behind her back, she couldn't lift the frame. It was too heavy, and the angle was wrong.

Shannon had already put down the empty bucket and picked up the full bucket. He was grimacing, revolted by the sloshing fluid inside. It would take another month for her to fill another bucket and get another chance.

Abbey didn't think she would survive another month.

She lashed out with her foot. Shannon tripped over her and crashed headfirst into the concrete wall. The bucket tipped over and the lid popped off, spilling an ocean of sewage across the floor. Shannon landed in it, facedown, and didn't get up.

Abbey had watched him put the keys in his pocket. She stretched out her bare foot. She couldn't reach into his pocket. The opening faced away from her. She curled her toes around the rim of the pocket and pulled, trying to pull down his pants instead. His belt was too tight. But with a sound like popping corn, the stitches snapped. The pocket ripped open and the keys tumbled out, sending ripples across the fetid puddle.

Shannon stirred.

Panicking, Abbey tried to slide the keys towards herself. She managed to get them into her sweaty fingers, but she couldn't get the slippery key into the lock behind her back.

Shannon sat up, red-faced and dripping. His eyes focused on her, and lit up with a terrifying rage.

Abbey got the key into the lock, but it was too late. He punched her in the head. Sparks filled her skull. He hit her over and over until her ears rang. It was like the sky was falling. She couldn't even raise her arms to protect herself—when she tried, something tore inside her shoulder and the cuffs bit into her wrists until she bled.

So she went somewhere else. A woman named Abbey Chapman was being beaten to death, but she was no longer that woman. She knew things about the lives of many people—her mom, her brother, the president, Beyoncé and Shannon Luxford. How could she be sure she wasn't one of them?

When she came back into her body, Shannon was gone. The lights were out. Abbey was still cuffed to the bed, in a puddle of piss and blood.

This was the longest blackout yet, or maybe it just felt that way. Bruises swelled under her hair. Her eyes dried out and her tongue shrivelled. The room grew colder and colder. Maybe it was winter now, or maybe Shannon had turned up the air-conditioning to freeze her to death. Or maybe she had a fever.

She passed in and out of consciousness. Her dreams bled into reality. Sometimes she thought she was back in the Ohio Caverns, looking for her brother. Sometimes she knew where she was, but thought her mom was standing beside her bed, asking why she wasn't getting up. She tried to tell Mom about the handcuffs, but her throat was too dry and her lips too crumbly to make words. Eventually Mom gave up and went away. Abbey wept.

In a lucid moment, she decided Shannon was never coming back. She was going to die here. She was sure it had already been longer than three days without water.

Maybe she was already dead. She was a ghost. Soon she would meet her replacement.

Then the lights came back on.

Shannon came into the panic room, and unlocked the plexiglass door. He left it open for ventilation as he mopped the floor of her cell. He worked silently and carefully, like one of the queen's butlers. She was too weak even to speak. He was clean-shaven, with slicked-back hair and clothes that smelled of fabric softener. She was a pale, shivering husk, legs stained with her own shit. She was too ashamed even to look at him.

He bent down and uncuffed her.

She felt a rush of gratitude for this handsome man who was saving her life.

He left a bottle of water and a TV dinner on the floor, then he walked out and locked the glass door behind him.

'Thank you,' she rasped.

He looked at her for the first time, and smiled, showing perfect teeth.

'No sweat,' he said.

When he was gone, she crawled over to the meal. She took one gulp of the water, and immediately threw up over the clean floor.

•

The camera became her friend.

When she wasn't spreading her legs for it or gagging on something in front of it, she would talk to it. Tell it stories from her high school days. Like the time she had practised kissing on the bathroom mirror, and then seen the janitor cleaning it with the same mop he had just used to scrub the toilet bowls. She would tell it about Grandma Ivy, who would pretend to be deaf when telemarketers called and would leave her dentures in unexpected places as a prank. Ivy had been in hospital with emphysema when Abbey was abducted. Abbey sometimes prayed for her, and invited the camera to pray too. Being watched by strangers wasn't as bad as being alone.

She didn't tell the camera that she was a prisoner, and she never said anything negative about Shannon. She didn't know when he was watching the feed. Every once in a while he would come in and do something to the back of the camera, changing a battery, maybe.

But whenever she was performing, she could assume that people were watching. Strangers around the world. So this was her chance to get a message out. But it would have to be something Shannon wouldn't think was suspicious. She wouldn't survive another punishment.

She dropped clues into every performance. People must know she was missing by now. Maybe her face and name were all over the TV. Maybe Shannon was even a suspect.

'Hi, I'm Abbey,' she said with a flirty smile, before demonstrating each toy.

'Oh, Shannon,' she would moan, every time she pushed some horrid new object up her ass. He would think she was trying to curry favour. He wouldn't realise she was trying to make him a target.

When the police didn't barge into the panic room after

what felt like a week of this, she escalated things. She wished she knew Morse code, so she could stroke out a rhythm. She went to Google it. Remembered her phone was gone. In desperation, she scratched out a message on her own forearm with a fingernail. The angry red marks spelled out, HELP ME. She flashed it to the camera several times as she violated herself. She figured Shannon would be too busy watching her hands to notice the message further up her arm.

Unfortunately, her other observers didn't seem to notice either. Or maybe they noticed, but didn't care. She shut that thought down. No one would see a distress signal like that and just ignore it.

Would they?

Day after day, help didn't come. She was going to have to do something more dramatic. An SOS the audience couldn't overlook. But what she had in mind would almost certainly get Shannon's attention. There would be a punishment. Maybe a fatal one. She would only get one shot.

So she needed to build her audience before she tried it.

She threw herself into the performances. Her orgasms became more and more convincing. Even when she wasn't performing, she was performing. Smiling to herself, singing like a concubine, swaying her hips as she walked around the tiny room. She made her bed, putting her clothes away. Doing all the things that men don't realise they like, just in case someone was watching. She requested make-up and a hairbrush. Shannon gave them to her gladly, delighted by her newfound enthusiasm.

When she asked for a mirror, he stuck one to the outside of the glass. She couldn't touch it, but she could see herself.

She looked like a ghost. Once upon a time she had longed to be that thin. Long neck, thigh gap, ribs almost visible. She scrambled into the corner so the camera wouldn't see her cry.

She'd already composed and memorised the message. After she sent it, she might have to endure a period of starvation. If Shannon came in, she might even need to defend herself. She couldn't do that in this shape.

She started doing yoga in her cell. Plank, runner's lunge, warrior two. She did it naked, to grow the audience. She told Shannon she thought her breasts were getting smaller, and asked him for more food. 'Please—it's making me feel like less of a woman,' she told him.

He started cooking proper meals for her. Pasta with carbonara sauce. Caesar salads. Schnitzel. She wolfed them down, stronger every day. She thanked him with warmth which wasn't entirely fake. It was fucked up, how grateful she was for the food.

It was hard to tell when to do it. She had no way of knowing the size of the audience. Was she the most popular porn star on the internet yet? Certainly she was the hardest working.

Then one day Abbey noticed that she had started sleeping well. She looked forward to meal times. She had stopped fearing that she would never escape, and started accepting it. A tide of terror swept over her when she realised that in some part of her mind, this place had become her home.

It was time.

Shannon had left her a new toy—a dangerously huge silicon penis. Abbey held it up to the camera, hefting it, milking the suspense. Getting everyone's attention. Then she said: 'My name is Abbey Chapman. I've been kidnapped by Shannon Luxford. I'm being held prisoner in a two-storey house in Westbranch. Please help—he's going to kill me. My name is Abbey Chapman. I've been kidnapped by Shannon Luxford . . .'

•

This time Abbey was ready. She was strong, and she wasn't handcuffed to the bed. She had psyched herself up. If he switched off the lights and starved her, she could take it. But hopefully he wouldn't. Hopefully he would come in here to beat her or stab her—and she would kick him to death.

He did neither thing. He came in like everything was normal. He opened the slot and gave her a tray of stir-fried noodles, a new shade of eyeshadow and a cheerleader's uniform. Then he replaced the battery in the camera and left.

He hadn't seen the broadcast, she realised. A grin spread across her face. When the cops showed up on his doorstep, he would be completely blindsided.

She waited, tingling with excitement.

Hours passed.

Days.

The police didn't come, and Shannon kept behaving as though he hadn't seen her message. Abbey was adrift on a sea of confusion. Was it possible that no one else had seen it either? Or had thousands of people decided she didn't matter?

'What do you think this is?'

When the question came, she was sitting cross-legged on the bed with her eyes closed. Trying to imagine she was in a cornfield on a sunny day, nothing but yellow in every direction. She had taken a half-day meditation course on Spring Break, and it was really starting to pay for itself.

She opened her eyes, and immediately knew that Shannon had seen the video. He didn't just look angry. He looked hurt.

'I think this is a fucking prison cell,' she said. It was such a relief to drop the act.

'Fred saw your little message,' Shannon said. 'He told me about it right away. What did you think was going to happen?'

'Who is Fred?'

Shannon gestured at the camera. 'The guy you've been performing for this whole time.'

Abbey was confused. 'He's one of the people on the site?'

'There is no goddamn site, you stupid bitch. Did you really think I'd connect this camera to the internet? Fred mails outfits and toys to me. I record you, and mail the recordings to back to him.'

The dawning horror was too much to take. 'But . . . so he's paying you to . . .'

'No. It's a trade. He makes his own recordings and mails them to me. Everybody wins. And nothing touches the internet.'

Abbey couldn't speak. Her last hope, sucked down the drain.

'You're not even my type,' Shannon said, as though she should be ashamed of this. 'You're lucky Fred isn't into bruises. I'd love to beat the shit out of you right now.'

Instead, he turned out the lights.

•

'Tell me about Fred,' I say.

Abbey, Thistle and I are in the foyer at the FBI field office, waiting for her mom. Abbey won't go any deeper into the building, but at least we're out of the cold. Black clouds have gathered outside the window, blocking the moon. A storm is coming.

Abbey has been talking for so long that her voice is getting croaky. Back at the hospital, it took a couple of hours for her to tell us her story. A doctor eventually arrived in the parking lot, looking annoyed that she couldn't examine Abbey upstairs. Thistle and I were out of earshot for the examination, but Abbey says the doctor has given her the all-clear. As soon as we got to the field office, a trauma psychologist interviewed her. Thistle and I didn't hear any of that, either. Now we have Abbey back, and she's filling us in on the details we missed, in between sips of an electrolyte drink. The yellowish tinge is already fading from her skin.

Even after everything I've seen and done, Abbey's story has unsettled me. Maybe because I misjudged Luxford. I'd been hunting the wrong kind of monster.

'Shannon never told me Fred's last name,' Abbey is saying. 'Or anything else about him. And I basically stopped talking to Shannon after that. I'd given up. On everything.'

'But it wasn't long between your SOS and Fred telling Shannon, right?' I say. 'A few days at the most?'

Abbey shrugs helplessly. 'It was basically impossible to keep track of time in there. I don't know.'

'But not long enough for Shannon to mail something international,' I say. 'And you mentioned a cheerleader uniform, right?'

'Uh, yeah.'

'A foreigner wouldn't be into that,' I say. 'It's a pretty American thing.'

'Did Shannon mention his boss at all?' Thistle asks. 'Kenneth Biggs?'

'I don't think so.'

'How about Daniel Ruthven?'

'It was a fucking abduction,' Abbey says. 'There wasn't much small talk, okay?'

'When we found Shannon's porn stash,' I say, 'he went on the run.'

'Yeah, no shit. Left me to die.'

'Can you think of anywhere he might have gone?'

'He never mentioned a secret hideout, if that's what you're asking,' Abbey says. 'But I'd say there's a good chance he's with Fred.'

'You've been very helpful,' Thistle says. She squeezes Abbey's hand. Abbey looks down at Thistle's fingers. It's been a long time since she's had physical human contact, other than the beating.

'I'm afraid to sleep,' Abbey says, not letting go. 'I had dreams like this all the time. Getting rescued. How do I even know you're real?'

'There's a counsellor who can—'

'Abigail!'

A middle-aged woman has entered the foyer. She runs towards us, tears carving valleys through her make-up. Her handbag bounces so vigorously on her shoulder that a bunch of stuff falls out. She doesn't even seem to notice.

'Mommy!' Abbey cries. The two women wrap each other up in a desperate hug, like they're afraid a tornado or a flood will tear them apart.

Thistle tells Mrs Chapman that the trauma psychologist will have to speak to her about Abbey's long-term care, and that she will need to sign some forms regarding the flights. I'm not convinced that Abbey's mom hears or understands any of this.

Soon the psychologist reappears and takes over. Thistle nudges me, and we escape into the parking lot. It feels good to get outside, despite the frigid night air. All the grief in there was exhausting.

My Toyota is still at home. Thistle offers me a ride. As

we drive out, we pass a dark blue sedan in the parking lot. A Buick. I feel like I've seen it before, but it takes me a second to remember where. It's the one I saw at the cabin in the woods.

CHAPTER 30

I turn once. What is in will not get out. I turn again. What is out will not get in. What am I?

'I don't like not knowing the motive,' I say.

Thistle takes the exit towards my house. 'Control,' she says. 'Some men just like the idea of owning a woman.'

'Yeah. But if Luxford is our guy, why kill all those other people?'

Thistle drums her fingers on the wheel. 'He said Abbey wasn't his type,' she says finally. 'Maybe what he meant was, he doesn't like sex toys and outfits. Maybe he gets off on blood, pain, death. Maybe Fred's recordings are of torture, or murder.'

I squint. 'How does Biggs fit into this?'

'Biggs is in a different category altogether. He knew

Shannon. His death could have been connected to Hope's rape, like we said.'

'If Luxford gets off on murder, why rape Hope and all those other women at all?'

'A person can have more than one defect,' Thistle says. She only sounds half convinced, but she has no idea how right she is.

Thistle stops the car. I unbuckle my seat belt.

So does she.

It's after midnight. What is she doing? 'What, you want to walk me to my door?'

Thistle raises her eyebrows at me. 'We're short on time. You're telling me you're done for the day, just when we're getting somewhere? Have you joined a civilian consultants' union, and you only work nine to five now?'

Two dead bodies are concealed in my house. No, wait. Two and a half. It's hard to keep track.

'I get it,' Thistle says. 'You have a girlfriend.'

'I don't,' I say, taken aback. A girlfriend would be an excellent excuse not to let Thistle in, and I'm flattered that she thinks this is possible. But I don't want to be with anyone but her, and it's hard to pretend I do.

'It's okay,' Thistle says, but I can tell it's not. 'You don't need to—'

'I was just thinking about the mess. Come on in.'

I lead her up to the front door, my heart pounding. What am I doing? As I disengage the three locks, I wonder if I left any body parts lying around. I always clean up after myself—but what if I didn't, this time?

'Can you give me a second?' I ask.

Thistle smirks. 'Fine, go hide your porn. Be quick, though. I'm freezing my ass off out here.'

I think of the three frozen asses already in my kitchen, and slip inside. I switch on the lights and quickly scan each room. I'm looking for blood, bones, severed toes or fingers. There's nothing. Even the smell Shawn referred to seems to be gone. My leftovers are back in the freezer.

But my heart is still racing when I open the door to let Thistle in.

She looks around my living room with undisguised curiosity. I can almost see her girlfriend theory evaporating. Tattered clothes, abandoned coffee mugs, decomposing furniture—my stuff is everywhere, and no one else's is anywhere. No dining table, just a coffee table between the TV and the sofa. Thistle's thinking, *No woman would live here*.

She walks right into my kitchen and starts opening cupboards.

I run in after her. 'What are you doing?'

'You got anything to drink here?' she asks.

It's the first sign that she might be as nervous to be alone with me as I am with her.

'Vodka, maybe?' She reaches for the freezer with the bodies in it.

I grab her hand before she can touch it.

'You're my guest,' I say. 'Just relax. I'll get the drinks. How about Southern Comfort?'

'Sounds good,' she says, and walks back into the living room.

I let out a long, shaky breath, and grab a dusty, half-empty bottle my old roommate left behind under the sink.

'I'd make you a cocktail,' I babble, getting out the glasses, 'but I don't have any limes. That means no Alabama Slammers, no Scarlett O'Haras—'

'Straight up is fine,' Thistle says from the lounge room.

Out of her sight, I open the chest freezer. Biggs stares up at me through whitened irises as I grab some ice cubes and slam the lid. I wish I had something to cover him with.

I bring the glasses and the bottle to the coffee table. My hands are trembling slightly, making the ice rattle. It occurs to me that if she's drinking, she expects to be here at least a couple of hours. She wouldn't drive drunk, and neither of us can afford a cab.

Thistle pours us each a generous helping and clinks her glass against mine. 'Cheers.'

'Cheers,' I say. I take only the tiniest sip, but it still burns my throat.

'So,' she says, 'let's say Shannon is a thrill killer.'

'Let's,' I say. The sofa is small. The proximity to her feels dangerous, but there's nowhere else to sit. I sink into the cushions, wanting to be closer and further away at the same time. Like she's a fire. I want her warmth, but I'm afraid of getting burned.

'Let's also assume that he escalates, like most criminals,' Thistle says. 'He starts out by raping Hope. After successfully blackmailing her, he uses his new position as a TA to do the same thing to a bunch of other people.

He now has some power at the college and several young women under his control.'

'The blackmail angle shouldn't work,' I say. 'He committed crimes, and these women know about it. They should be threatening him, not the other way around.'

'It shouldn't work, but it does,' Thistle says. 'Remember, the victims probably aren't aware of each other. And we know from Hope and Abbey that he targets vulnerable, isolated women. If they speak out, they have no support network, and no proof that the sex wasn't consensual. None of them wants to get dragged into a public he said/she said, especially if nude photos and videos are likely to be leaked as part of it. And the guy looks like Superman. A lot of people would say the women wanted it.'

I nod slowly. 'As long as he doesn't push them over the edge by demanding too much when he's blackmailing them . . .'

'They keep doing it,' Thistle says. 'Right. And the longer they play along, the harder it gets to tell anybody.' She sips her drink. 'So then he escalates. He starts killing people. Single men who won't be missed. He kidnaps Abbey so he can swap videos with another killer, Fred.'

'Hold up,' I say. 'What if Fred is the killer? Shannon likes videos of murder, Fred likes videos of rape and imprisonment. So Shannon rapes, Fred kills, and they swap videos.'

Thistle takes a sip of her drink. 'Seems far-fetched. But maybe.'

Some would say a cannibal working for the FBI is far-fetched. I'm reluctant to discard the theory.

'So who's the blonde?' I say.

'She could be one of the people Shannon is blackmailing,' Thistle says. 'Maybe he makes her pick up victims for him. Or for Fred—whichever one does the killing.'

'Maybe she *is* Fred,' I say. 'It could be short for Winifred—or maybe just a code name.'

'Could be.' Thistle settles against the back of the sofa. It creaks ominously, and she leans forwards again.

'None of this tells us where Shannon is now, though,' I say. 'Or Fred. And we still don't know why those dates were highlighted on the wall planner, or where the bodies are.'

'Or why Shannon brought Biggs's severed hand back to the college,' Thistle says.

I clear my throat. 'Right.'

'We'll get there, though.' Thistle tops up her drink and holds the bottle over mine. 'More?'

'Aren't you driving soon?' I ask.

'You want me out of here.' Her voice is flat.

I don't know what to say.

'I figured you out, Blake,' she says.

My heart hammers my ribs. 'You did, huh?'

'Yeah. I believed you when you said I wasn't your type. But don't think I haven't noticed the way you've been looking at me these past few days. And clearly you haven't been pursuing anyone else.' She looks around at my derelict lounge room. 'You're just afraid of intimacy.'

Not what I expected. 'I've been trying to date,' I say.

'Stop lying to me,' she snaps. 'A guy like you would have a girlfriend if he wanted one.'

I try to work out if that was a compliment.

'I need you to make up your mind,' Thistle says. 'I don't have time for this.'

'I'm not afraid of you,' I say. Her anger is contagious. I rejected her to keep her safe, and now she's giving me hell for it.

'Bullshit. You're not as good a liar as you think you are, Blake. You were scared of having sex with me, so you told a stupid lie. When I still wanted a relationship, you told another one. You lied to me again just now, when you said you'd been trying to date. You're a virgin, and you're terrified of sex.'

My frustration and exhaustion and anxiety all bubble over. 'I'm not—'

'It's almost funny, given all the shit that *doesn't* scare you.'

'You're better off without me,' I snap. 'Can't you see that?'

We stare at each other in silence for a moment. She's confused. I'm on dangerous ground, but I can't stop myself. I'm just too tired to lie anymore.

'I'm a *bad person*,' I continue. 'I'm sick in the head, okay? The only decent thing I ever did in my whole life was push you away.'

'Oh, so this was for my own good?' She looks incredulous.

'You have no idea how much I wanted you. But you're

a good person, and you don't deserve to get stuck with an asshole like me.'

Tears sting the corners of my eyes. I blink them away.

Thistle is starting to look like she believes me, but that's only enraged her more. 'Did you ever stop to wonder if that was *my* choice to make? We both grew up in the same hellhole. You don't think I have problems too? I can't sleep without Ambien. I take stupid risks. I can't handle a normal job, or make friends with normal people. I have terrible taste in men, you included. I—'

She has no idea what problems are. 'You're the only person I've known for longer than a week who doesn't think I'm worthless,' I say. 'No one else cares about me, and I don't care about anyone else. If I hurt you, how the fuck am I supposed to live with myself? I'd rather live and die alone in this piece of shit place than take that risk.'

She stares at me, amazed.

'Sure, I'm afraid,' I say. 'But not of sex.'

She gulps down the last of her drink. Shrugs off her jacket.

'Prove it,' she says.

CHAPTER 31

I always follow my brother but you cannot see me, only him. You cannot hear him, only me. What are we?

It's not like I expect.

For one thing, no one gets bitten. Thistle pulls me off the couch and pins me to the floor, her hips on mine. Unbuttons my shirt one-handed while her other hand grips my hair. I couldn't bite her if I tried.

And I don't try. That's the other thing that shocks me. I let her hold me down as I lift her blouse, exposing her soft belly, and slide my hands up the smooth skin of her back, all the way to the nape of her neck. When she shivers and bends down to kiss me, the tang of Southern Comfort on her lips, it doesn't even occur to me to bite down. I just close my eyes, not wanting the moment to end, and at the same time needing more.

The sex itself goes wrong like all first times probably do. Thistle has condoms in her handbag but it's a while before she finds them. I fumble with one until she exasperatedly takes over, rolling it onto me while I stroke her bare thighs and wonder where her panties went. When she tries to kiss me again I tilt my head the wrong way, bumping my brow against hers. It takes a lot of shifting and wiggling to find the right angle before she can lower herself down onto me, the electric feeling making me gasp. We go slow, because every time we accelerate, we can't find a rhythm that suits each other. Her bounces don't match my thrusts, and the whole thing keeps grinding to a halt. Her knees and my ass both get rubbed raw by the floor.

But for the first time in maybe my whole life, I'm not thinking about food. Not thinking about anything, in fact. Timothy Blake has vanished, leaving only sensations. My hammering heart, the smell of her. The sweat everywhere except the scar tissue on her chest and throat, which stays dry and smooth. My hardness, her heat. Our ragged breaths. We stay semi-clothed—her black mesh sports bra, my dirty jeans knotted around my ankles—but, even so, there's a lot of flesh on display. And I don't want any of it, at least not in an unwholesome way. I've discovered a different sort of hunger. Maybe sex takes so much focus that there's no room for my addiction.

Or maybe it's about her. Maybe I want her more than I want to eat.

I finish much sooner than I intend to, throbbing and twitching as she clenches around me. When she rolls over,

I try to get her across the line, but I can't find the right spot. Eventually she nudges my clumsy fingers aside and works herself into a silent seizure, her teeth clenched, her brow furrowed. With her free hand she crushes mine. I watch, mesmerised.

Soon we're side by side on the floor, staring at the ceiling and breathing in unison, like a single creature with eight limbs. An octopus, legs tangled around each other. We lie there a long time.

'So,' she says finally, 'that happened.'

'Thank you,' I say.

'I didn't do it for you.'

We fall silent.

'I'm sorry,' I say, 'for pushing you away.'

She seems like she's waiting for something more.

Oh, right. 'And for lying to you,' I add.

'You should be,' she says, but I can hear the edge of a smile. 'It was a dumb thing to do.'

'Yeah.'

She rests a hand on my bare chest. 'Well,' she says, 'I guess you've made up for it. No harm, no foul.'

I stroke her shoulder for a minute, fascinated by the smoothness of her skin. Lightning flashes outside the window, thunder a few seconds later.

'You know, this doesn't have to be a thing,' she says. I hear a hint of nervousness in the implied question. 'If you don't want it to be.'

'I want it to be a thing,' I say. 'I really do.'

A pause.

'Do you?' I ask.

She lifts my hand to her lips, and gently kisses the spot where my thumb used to be. The contact sends a rush of warmth up my spine.

'Right now I'm happier than I've been in a long time,' she says.

'Me too.'

I love her. It's the first time I've ever allowed myself to think those words. Before, the hopelessness of the idea would have flattened me.

'Why me?' I ask.

She looks at me and grins. 'Fishing for compliments, much?'

'Maybe,' I say. 'But don't act like you didn't have other options.'

She leans closer, and nibbles my earlobe. 'You know, I used that app for a while—nTangle. But the guys I met, they always looked at me like I was a piece of meat.'

I can't help but glance towards the kitchen.

'You hungry?' she asks.

'No,' I say—and, for the first time ever, it's true. 'You?'

'I could eat.'

Her phone rings. I look at the clock. It says four am, but I never changed it when daylight savings ended, so it's five.

'Hold that thought.' She crawls over to her handbag. I admire the view.

She picks up the phone. 'Can this wait, Vasquez? I'm in the middle of something.' She shoots me a wink, which stirs parts of me I thought were done for the night.

Then her face changes. 'Say again?'

A pause.

'Okay. We'll be right there. I mean, I'll find Blake and be right there.'

She drops the phone. 'We gotta go,' she says. 'DNA came in. The severed hand we found? It doesn't belong to Biggs.'

CHAPTER 32

Two girls are born on the same day to the same mother, and yet they are not twins. Why?

'Run all that past us again,' I say.

'Certainly.' Dr Norman lays out all the DNA tests in a neat row on one of the morgue slabs. The numbers and graphs and percentages are meaningless to me.

Thistle's hair is still damp from the shower. She looks remarkably good for a woman who has had zero sleep. I don't think I've pulled up so well.

While Thistle was in my bathroom, the fear returned. I hovered outside the door, listening to the running water, picturing her bare feet on the worn surface of the tub and wondering if she could tell if a skeleton had recently dissolved in it. When it was my turn in the shower,

I worried that she was looking in my freezer rather than reading a follow-up email from Vasquez. When we got to her place, where she picked up a change of clothes, I wished I'd asked her if we could both shower there.

If this is going to work, long term, I need to do something about my house.

'This is the DNA test from the blood in the severed hand,' Norman says, pointing. 'It doesn't match *this* test, which is the cheek swab from Hope. But it does match the blood group we have on file for Kenneth Biggs—O positive—and it does match *this*, which is the DNA test from the blood on the wall planner at the dump.'

'So the hand doesn't belong to Biggs,' Thistle says, 'but it does belong to a middle-aged man, right?'

'Correct.'

'And all the other vics were in their twenties. Meaning there's an extra victim we don't know about yet. And it's possible Biggs is still alive.' Thistle sticks her hands in her pockets and whistles through her teeth. 'Lucky we didn't tell the family, huh?'

This doesn't make sense. I know it's Biggs's hand, because I cut it off his wrist. Unless the body in my freezer isn't Biggs. But, if not, who the hell is it?

I can't tell Thistle or Norman any of that. Instead I ask, 'Why would the perp put Biggs's wedding ring on some other victim's finger?'

'I don't know. Some kind of fucked-up ritual?'

'Any chance you made a mistake?'

Norman doesn't look offended. 'No.'

'What about the flap of skin from Gomez's house? Does that match anything?'

'Impossible to tell. The skin had been treated with a preserving agent I haven't yet identified. This prevented it from drying out or becoming brittle, but also wiped out any potential touch DNA.'

'So it could have been removed quite a long time before it was delivered to Gomez.'

'No more than a few weeks, I'd say. You can't preserve skin forever, no matter what you use.'

'What about the samples from Biggs's apartment?' I say. 'Hair and whatnot.'

'Those took a while to gather,' Norman says, 'and I'm still waiting on the lab report. I don't know what they do or don't match.'

'What are you thinking, Blake?' Thistle asks.

I'm thinking the body in my freezer sure looked like Biggs's picture. 'Maybe the hand came from Biggs's brother, or his cousin.'

'But it would have shared some DNA with Hope then, wouldn't it?' Thistle says.

'That's right,' Norman confirms. 'The hand was unrelated to her, except that they shared a common ancestor 200,000 years ago, like we all do.'

In that case, I can only see one other possibility.

'We need to talk to Gabriela,' I say.

•

As we drive through the early morning, I catch a glimpse of my face in the side mirror. I'm not a virgin anymore. I don't look any different, but something has changed beneath the surface.

When I turned thirty, nothing marked the occasion. I told no one, and since I had neither friends nor family, no one asked. Alone in my house, I lit three candles, stuck them in some guy's severed arm, and watched them burn. Thinking about how I was undoubtedly an adult now. Responsible for my own terrible choices.

This feels like that. I've become a man in yet another measurable way. But the change is bigger. Thistle just showed me that it might be possible for me to have a relationship. Maybe we already have one. But I need to become the guy she deserves.

When I get home I'll destroy the bodies in my house—and not by eating them. Reese Thistle's boyfriend wouldn't do that. I'm going to melt them in acid and pour them down the drain. Then I'll call Warner and tell her I quit. Today is the first day of my new life. I'm scared, but excited too.

Thistle and I drive in silence. I want to talk about last night, but I don't know what to say. Is it too soon to ask if we can spend tonight together, too? Hopefully she's wondering the same thing. I've almost worked up the courage to ask when we reach the apartment building, and the opportunity is gone.

We pull into a parking space and walk through the cold to the door. Different doorman—tall, black, balding, bearded, with triple stud earrings. We tell him the apartment number and he pushes the button without a word.

Gabriela answers: 'Hello?'

'It's Agent Thistle and Timothy Blake,' Thistle says. 'Can we come up?'

The door buzzes, and the doorman opens it for us. We ride the elevator up.

By the time we get to the apartment door, it's already open. Gabriela looks out at us worriedly, wearing a green and white kimono.

'Have you found him?' she asks.

'We'd like to talk inside,' Thistle says. 'Is your daughter home?'

'She got a call early this morning from a friend,' Gabriela says. 'She just went out.'

That's a rare stroke of luck.

'Kenneth Biggs isn't Hope's real father,' I say. 'Is he?'

Gabriela hesitates. 'He raised her, didn't he?' she says finally. 'That's real enough.'

Thistle and I share a glance.

'Hope gave us a DNA sample,' Thistle says, 'so we could identify her father's remains, if we found them. But if he's not her biological father, then that sample is misleading.'

'Did you find something?' Gabriela asks.

'We did,' Thistle says softly.

Gabriela staggers back as though she's been punched in the gut. Her face crumples and she moans.

Thistle and I step through the gap, and close the door behind us.

CHAPTER 33

I go up and I go down, to the sky and to the ground. I am present tense then past, let us take a ride at last. What am I?

'Does Hope know?' Thistle asks.

She and Gabriela are sitting on the sofa in the lounge room. I'm slowly making tea in the kitchen, out of sight, but not out of earshot. Thistle didn't explicitly send me in here, but I could tell from her body language that it was what she wanted. I used to be good at reading everyone except Thistle. Not anymore. It's as if the sex has made us telepathic.

'She has no idea,' Gabriela says.

If this is true, it means Hope didn't deliberately send us off-track when she gave us the DNA sample.

'Do you have to tell her?' Gabriela adds.

'Not exactly,' Thistle says. 'But now that we've found

your husband's remains, there are several ways she might find out. It might be a good idea to tell her yourself.'

'I can't,' Gabriela said. 'She adored Kenneth. It would destroy her to find out she wasn't his. And she would never forgive me.'

That may be true. But I can't imagine that Hope would be destroyed. Since the suicide attempt, she's become stronger than her mother realises.

'If he raised her,' Thistle says, 'she was his. Like you said.'

I bring in the tea on a tray I found, the sugar spoon balanced on the edge of a saucer like a seesaw. Gabriela picks up her mug and sniffs it. The aroma seems to wake her up, like smelling salts. Her eyes brighten a little, her spine straightens. But when she sips it, she doesn't react, even though I know it's hot enough to burn her tongue.

I should have made myself a coffee, to wake up. Still, I've never had such a good reason to be exhausted. It's hard not to grin, which would be deeply inappropriate in front of the grieving widow.

'Who was her biological father?' Thistle asks. The question is gentle, like she's a counsellor. But I know that she's really checking if we have a new suspect. This unknown man may have had more motive to kill Biggs than Shannon did, especially if he still had feelings for Gabriela.

'His name was Peter Rodman,' Gabriela says. 'He was with the immigration police.'

This surprises me. An undocumented immigrant falling in love with a border control agent would be bizarre, given how badly the latter usually treat the former, though it's mostly incompetence rather than cruelty.

Thistle is quicker on the uptake than I am. 'He offered you a deal?' she asks.

Gabriela nods. 'He found me, soon after I met Ken. He said there was no record of me in the system yet. He said if I did some things for him, he wouldn't file the paperwork.' She looks at the floor. 'He used a condom, but I suppose it broke, or he took it off.'

'Does he know about Hope?' Thistle asks.

'No. When I found out I was pregnant, I knew he would try to make me have an abortion. So I never called him.' Her eyes widened with alarm. 'You're not going to tell him?'

'No. Don't worry.'

She relaxes. 'That's good. He may want to meet Hope, but I don't want her to meet him. He is a bad man.'

'What about your husband?' I ask. 'Did he know?'

'He never noticed that the dates didn't add up,' Gabriela says, fingering the crucifix around her neck. 'We weren't married yet, and I was worried he, too, would pressure me to terminate the pregnancy. It seemed better to lie to my fiancé than to kill a baby.'

Out of the corner of my eye I think I see Thistle flinch. But when I look over, her sympathy-face is back.

'Later I realised I'd made a terrible mistake,' Gabriela continues. 'Ken was a good man. He would have loved Hope, and me, no matter what. But after he found out, he felt betrayed. I could have prevented that.'

'He found out?' I ask. 'When?'

'In May this year,' Gabriela says. 'I deceived him for almost twenty years. *That* was what hurt him.'

'May eighteenth?' I ask. That was one of the dates on the wall planner.

'I'm not sure. Why?'

'Never mind, I'm sorry. How did he find out?'

Gabriela looks at the closed curtains. 'Kenneth suffered from depression. He had good days and bad days, but after Hope tried to . . . well, he started blaming himself. Not just for leaving the gun safe open, but for her mental state. It was hereditary, he said. So eventually I told him. I wanted him to know it wasn't his fault.'

'How did he take it?' Thistle asks. 'When you told him?'

'Better than most men would have, I think,' Gabriela says, a bit defensively. 'He was angry. He wanted to know what else I had kept from him. Soon he realised there was nothing, and he cooled down. He asked me if Hope knew, and I told him she did not. Eventually he said he understood the choice that I had made, and that he didn't want to throw away our marriage because of it. But our relationship wasn't the same. He became withdrawn.'

Perhaps he committed suicide. Stripped off his clothes and walked into the woods. Weird way to do it, but possible. If that turns out to be what happened, I'll have a hell of a time explaining the severed hand.

Thistle's phone is ringing.

'Excuse me,' she says, and walks into the kitchen.

'How was he with Hope?' I ask Gabriela. 'Did they

drift apart?' Distance from family is a risk factor for suicide, and he would certainly have felt less close to his wife.

But Gabriela shakes her head. 'The opposite. It was as if the further he drifted away from me, the closer he became to her. To him, the genes didn't matter. She was his.'

It's like trying to solve two or three jigsaw puzzles at the same time, the pieces all jumbled together.

'He was a good man,' Gabriela says again.

Thistle grabs my shoulder. 'We gotta go. Now.'

CHAPTER 34

*I eat and grow, I die without air,
but I am not alive. What am I?*

It's impossible to find a park anywhere near Joseph and Francine Luxford's house. There's a car in every driveway and on every front lawn. The streets are thick with people. Seems like everyone in Houston is here.

Some of the protestors have signs with hashtags: #JUSTICEFORABBEY and #ENDRAPECULTURE are common. Others have longer messages, like: DON'T TELL MY DAUGHTER TO STAY HOME—TEACH YOUR SON RESPECT and WHAT KIND OF MOTHER RAISES THIS KIND OF MAN?

Apparently, since Shannon is nowhere to be found, his parents have become the target. As we drive, Thistle tells me that there was a story about Abbey on breakfast radio. It took the internet all of twenty minutes to find the address of Shannon Luxford's childhood home.

The #JUSTICEFORABBEY hashtag is trending, and more and more people keep showing up.

As Thistle and I push through the throng, I see that every type of protestor is here. There's the screaming guy who just wants someone to punch. There's the past victim, tears flooding down her cheeks. There's the shirtless party animal, his hairy nipples erect in the cold. There's the guy in the BLACK LIVES MATTER T-shirt, who hasn't yet realised he's at the wrong protest—or maybe he'll show up anywhere there are cops.

And there are plenty of cops here, dressed like they're ready to occupy a hostile country. Body armour, gloves, combat boots. Helmets with visors. Flash grenades and canisters of tear gas dangle from equipment belts. There are more assault rifles here than I've ever seen in one place. An armoured vehicle rumbles past, slowly nudging pedestrians out of the way. The sun is just peeking over the horizon.

'Is that an actual tank?' I ask.

'APC,' Thistle says. 'Come on.'

It's the wrong vehicle for the task. There are cars parked haphazardly on both sides of the street, and soon the APC gets jammed between them. It could probably push them aside, but not without scratching their paintwork and potentially ploughing into the crowd of pedestrians. The driver switches on the siren, as though that will get the parked cars out of the way.

A bottle explodes against the side of the APC. 'Bon voyage!' someone yells, cackling drunkenly.

'This is not safe,' Thistle shouts at me over the ruckus. 'If one person starts shooting, half these people are dead.'

She's not wrong. The Houston PD officers have clenched jaws and sweaty brows. The civilians are screaming at them, daring them to shoot, phones raised to capture the action.

We push through. Thistle keeps her badge in the air. Cops keep levelling their weapons at her—a black woman in a mostly white crowd—then seeing the badge and lowering them.

I'm not sure she's making the right call. It's only a matter of time before one of these knuckleheads mistakes the badge for a gun.

Finally we reach the Luxfords' house. Protestors are trampling the front garden and pounding on the windows and the front door of the house. A group of six are rocking the SUV from side to side, trying to flip it. The police haven't made it this deep into the crowd yet. They're too scared to leave their APC and their line of shields.

Now that we're so deep in the crowd, I realise that Thistle might be the only police officer within a hundred yards.

'The county cops will try to disperse the crowd with tear gas any minute,' she says. 'If Luxford's here, we have to find him ASAP.'

I look around. It's impossible. There must be a thousand people here, half of them with baseball caps over their eyes or bandanas covering their mouths. Even if

Shannon cares enough about his parents to come help them, we'd never know he was here.

'Put the badge down,' I say. 'These guys could turn on you.'

Thistle doesn't. 'Police!' she bellows. 'Step away from the vehicle!'

She radiates such authority that four of the six men rocking the car immediately put their hands up.

Someone else—a skinny meth head with a scraggle of chestnut hair—turns around and spits in Thistle's face. She barely flinches.

I grab the guy by the front of his tattered T-shirt and bare my teeth. He realises that I'm not a cop. Not someone who isn't allowed to hurt him. His eyes go wide.

'Blake!' Thistle snaps. 'Blake!'

I let the guy go. He slithers away into the crowd.

I nearly bit him, right in front of Thistle. It's dangerous for me to be here.

I suddenly realise that one of the screaming people is Joseph Luxford. He's standing on the lawn in flannelette pyjamas, his socks caked with mud. He's bellowing, 'Get the hell away from my house, you fucking animals!'

No one takes any notice. He just looks like another crazy protestor.

Leaving Thistle behind, I push through the crowd and grab Joseph. 'Is Shannon here?'

He screams at me, 'Get away from my goddamned house!'

'Hey! Remember me?' I step back so he can focus on

my face. 'Timothy Blake, FBI. If your son is here, he's in real danger. Have you seen him?'

'You're police,' he says, realising. 'Do something about these sons of bitches!'

'Where's your wife?' I ask. Maybe she'll be willing to listen.

Before Joseph can answer, I hear breaking glass and a cheer from behind me. A black man in an army jacket has smashed the lounge room window with a baseball bat. A white guy with a shaved head and a goatee is clicking a lighter.

Joseph sees. 'No!' he screams. 'Don't!'

The Molotov cocktail catches, leaving the sting of spilled gas in the air. The white guy hurls it through the smashed window. Smoke, underlit by the flicker of flames, pours out the window frame.

'No!' Joseph shrieks. 'Francine!'

Shit. I look back at the house, up at the top floor. A shadow flickers behind the window of that tiny bedroom, the one with the lock on the door.

'Is she locked in?' I ask.

'I just wanted to keep her safe,' Joseph stammers.

I shove him out of the way and push through the crowd towards the guy with the army jacket and the baseball bat. He's watching the flames with fading delight, as though he didn't expect things to go this far.

I grab the end of the bat. It feels like good quality, two or three pounds, mountain ash recently cleaned with rubbing alcohol.

The guy doesn't let go of the rubber handle. 'Hey, what the hell?' he complains. 'Fuck off, man.'

I look around. Thistle is nowhere to be seen. In the chaos, no one is watching. No phone cameras are facing me. So I yank the guy in and bite his wrist, severing the tendons that allow his fingers to clench.

He shrieks as he drops the bat. 'Holy shit! Jesus!' I'm already walking away with his bat. I force myself to spit out the blood, telling myself that I'm on a diet, and this time I'm gonna stick to it. Today is the first day of my new life.

I grab the lattice on the side of the house and start climbing. It's slow going, with the baseball bat in one hand.

When I'm a few feet up, Thistle sees me. 'Blake!' she yells.

'Francine is in there!' I shout. There's no time to explain further. I climb the ivy and creaking wood, the bat in one hand, splinters digging into the other. It's a long way down and, if I fall, I'm likely to get trampled to death.

I reach the window and peer through the glass, but I can't see anything. So I swing the bat one-handed.

The first swipe cracks the glass, but doesn't shatter it. Strike one.

The second blow knocks out a chunk not big enough to crawl through. Strike two. My left arm trembles from the strain of holding me up.

On the third swing, the glass disintegrates. I wrap my hands in my sleeves as I climb through the gap, but one of them gets sliced anyway. A warm flush of blood turns my sleeve the colour of red wine. I clench my fist tightly, trying to staunch the flow.

Francine is facedown on the floor. It's too soon for the smoke to have knocked her out—though I can smell it leaking through the bottom of the door—so she's unconscious for some other reason.

There. A spike of bone protruding through the skin of her upper arm. Maybe Joseph hit her, or maybe she tried to shoulder-barge the door. She probably fainted when she saw the injury, or felt the pain, or lost too much blood.

I can't carry her back out the window. Even if we managed to get through the frame without slicing something critical, she's too heavy to carry one-handed.

I hold the bat with both hands and ram it against the part of the door where the bolt was. No good. The bolt's on the outside, but the door opens inwards. The frame is too solid.

Instead I wedge the rim at the end of the bat's handle under the bottom of the door, and tilt the bat backwards.

There's a creak. I keep pulling.

The leverage forces the door upwards until the hinges snap. The door sags sideways. I rip it out of the frame and it topples over, narrowly missing Francine.

The smoke floods through, and I choke. It smells like bleach, as well as gasoline. The guy who threw the Molotov must have added some extra ingredients when he mixed it, turning the bomb into a chemical weapon. The smoke cloud is toxic.

I lift Francine over my shoulder, facing forwards rather than backwards so I can hold her nose and mouth shut. Breathing nothing is better than breathing bleach. Then I carry her out of the room and stagger through the smoke to the bathroom.

Holding my breath, I grab a hand towel and drench it with water. Then I use it to cover Francine's face—easier than keeping her nose pinched shut and her mouth closed with one hand.

The stairs look like a gateway to hell. Smoke flooding up them, fire glowing at the bottom. The heat dries out my face and hands. I close my stinging eyes and go by feel, fumbling for each step. I need both hands to keep Francine on my shoulder and to keep the towel over her face. My lungs are bursting.

The ground floor feels like an inferno. I can't open my eyes. There's crackling and spitting all around me. Luckily, I memorised the layout of the house the last time I was here. I bump into the kitchen bench, which helps me to orientate myself. I work my way around it, headed for the lounge room.

Broken glass snaps underfoot. I must be at the window. A shard of it punches through the sole of my cheap shoe. Soon I'm squelching in my own blood. For a second I worry about leaving so much DNA behind, and then I remember that for once I'm not committing a crime.

When we reach the front door I reposition Francine so I have a free hand to work the handle.

It doesn't turn. Locked. I fumble around, looking for

a latch or button. Can't find anything. Can't see. Can't breathe. Fucking Joseph must have locked the door when he went out there. We're trapped.

There's a mighty crunch, and the door bursts open. It hits me in the face and I tumble over backwards. Francine slips out of my grip. As I hit the floor tiles, I take an involuntary gasp of poisoned air.

'Blake?' a voice says. Thistle. 'Blake!'

I try to answer, but someone has turned my volume down to nothing. No matter how hard I push, the air in my lungs won't turn into sound.

'I've got you,' Thistle says, grabbing my shoulders. 'Can you hold on to me?'

I cough. 'Francine is . . .'

But then the whole world fades away to nothing.

CHAPTER 35

What do people pay for that
they never want to use?

Francine looks at me like one of those starving kids in the World Vision commercials. Resigned and hopeless. Seems to me that she has more reason to be optimistic than she did before. But I guess that house wasn't just her prison. It was her home.

'You saved my life,' she says flatly, without lifting her head off the hospital pillow.

I clear my throat. 'Tell me about Shannon.'

My voice comes out in an Alex Jones rasp. According to the doctor, I'll sound like this for a while. 'You shouldn't breathe bleach,' he said, like I was an idiot. At least I can still use my slashed hand. I'll have another cool scar in a couple of weeks.

This isn't the same hospital that Abbey was taken to.

It has nicer art on the walls, a bigger courtyard in the middle for exercise. More nurses, fewer patients. I gather that Francine had some kind of fancy insurance. They wouldn't even have treated me except that Thistle implied that I was a cop, injured in the line of duty.

'Where's my husband?' Francine asks.

'Talking to the police,' I say. 'They'll want to talk to you too.'

'About what?'

'About why you were locked in a room inside your own house.' I sink into a chair beside her bed.

'Joseph didn't know the building was going to catch fire,' Francine says. 'He was just trying to keep me safe.'

Against all odds, she *is* safe. The doctors have reset her broken bones, and thanks to the wet towel, she didn't inhale as much smoke as me.

'I'm not interested in arguing about the kind of man your husband is,' I say. 'I want you to tell me where Shannon's hiding.'

'I already told you. On Monday he dropped off some laundry—'

'And then he picked it up again. Didn't he?'

Francine says nothing.

'When I visited your house the first time,' I say, 'I didn't see a bag of clothes. Either dirty or clean. And the washing machine wasn't running. You don't have an outdoor clothesline. Therefore, he came back.'

'He's my son,' Francine said. 'Please. I can't help you.'

'If the police find him, he'll be arrested,' I say. 'If someone else finds him, things could be much worse. Next time it might be him trapped in a burning building. Or beaten to death by an angry mob.'

'I don't know where he is.' She says this as though she's trying to convince me it's the end of the matter.

'But you do know something,' I say. 'Don't you?'

She looks away, tears sparkling in her eyes.

'I saved your life,' I add. 'Are you gonna help me save Shannon's? Or are you happy to let him die?'

'He needed a ride,' she says quietly.

I sit down next to her. 'Where?'

'I picked him up from near his house. He said there was something wrong with his car.'

There was—the police were watching it. 'When was this?' I ask.

'Tuesday morning.'

Probably straight after he ran from us at the college. 'Where'd you take him?' I ask.

'Piney Point. He took the clothes and got into another car.'

'What kind of car?'

'Uh, it was grey. A hatchback. A young woman was driving.'

'A blonde woman?'

'No. She was Asian.'

'Young, you said?'

'Shannon's age,' she says defensively. 'Maybe a *little* younger. But not a child.'

'And then what?'

'And then they drove off.' She sniffs. 'He said he'd see me next week.'

'Well, he lied,' I say, getting up.

'All children lie to their parents.'

I can't believe she's still defending him. 'Look, the only way you'll ever see him again is if we catch him. If he contacts you again, you call us.'

She nods, but I can tell she won't.

•

'Okay,' I say, pacing back and forth across the hospital waiting room. 'Shannon is using his network to hide from us.'

'Shouldn't you be resting?' Thistle says. 'Your voice sounds like Batman.'

Anyone else who knows me would have asked why I'd risked my life to save Francine. They would assume I had an ulterior motive. But Thistle hasn't asked. She thinks there's a decent person hidden somewhere inside me.

Maybe there is. I had no selfish reasons to rescue Francine. I just did it without thinking. It's as if by believing I was good, Thistle *made* me good.

'I'm fine,' I say. 'All those women Shannon had naked pictures of? They're helping him. Whenever he needs a place to stay or a ride, he . . .' I think about it. 'In fact, I bet he took the grey hatchback. He probably told the Asian girl to report it stolen, but not until he had a head start. That would be the smart play.'

'Well, he won't stay off the radar long,' Thistle says.

'His face is all over the news now. Someone will spot him soon.'

She pats the seat next to her. I sit down.

'Sorry I hit you with the door,' she says. 'There was a lot of blood.'

Most of it probably belonged to the guy I bit. 'I'm fine,' I say again.

'You've earned a break. And we've exhausted all our leads. Why don't you let me take you home?'

'We're not done,' I say. 'We still don't know who the blonde woman is, or Fred. And we're not even a hundred per cent on Luxford's motive.'

'I know what it's like to not want to stop,' Thistle says. 'After I got shot—'

Her phone rings. She sighs, and answers. 'Thistle.'

She listens for a while, and then says, 'Got it, thanks,' and ends the call.

'We have a DNA match on the blonde hair from Biggs's car,' Thistle says. 'It belongs to Armana Black. Houston resident, with a past conviction for prostitution. Units out looking for her now.'

A name at last. I heave myself to my feet. 'Let's go.'

'I'm taking you home,' Thistle says. 'You need rest.'

'But—'

'You can talk to her when we bring her in. Okay?'

I nod. 'Okay.'

I do have things to do at home. But rest isn't one of them.

As we walk out, I glance through each door we

pass. Most of the patients are old, but there's nothing visibly wrong with them. Tubes go to their arms, but the more powerful drug is the TV flashing on the wall. The news babbles about another school shooting, this time in Missouri. The patients stare at the TV, anxious but motionless, somehow wound up and pacified at the same time.

As I pass one of the rooms, I see a young man. Most of his face is bandaged. Only one eye, his nose and part of his mouth are visible.

But I recognise him. He's one of the three guys who attacked me. The one who found a severed hand in my pocket, right before I bit his cheek off.

His eye focuses on me, and widens. He screams. The movement pops his stitches, turning the bandages pink.

Thistle turns to look, alarmed. 'Jesus,' she says. 'What's going on in there?'

'No idea.' I hustle her along the corridor. 'Let's get out of here.'

She slows down. 'Maybe that guy needs help?'

'A nurse was already in there,' I say.

'I didn't see a nurse.' But just at that moment, a nurse hurries past us and darts into the room with the screaming man.

'There, now he's got two,' I say. 'Let's go.'

She allows me to shepherd her into the elevator. I stab the button to close the door.

Thistle shoots me a sympathetic look. 'You don't like hospitals, huh?'

'Yeah,' I say.

My breathing doesn't return to normal until we're out on the freeway and the hospital has disappeared in the rear-view mirror.

•

My bathtub has never been so full.

Usually it's just one body at a time, and only the parts I can't eat without getting sick. Bones, brains, eyes, intestines. I cover them in a sulphuric acid-based drain cleaner—lye would be quicker, but only if I can heat it— then I let them melt away to nothing while I stand in the corridor to avoid the fumes.

Today the tub is a tangle of limbs, mostly with the flesh still on. Elliott, Francis and Biggs. Dissolving them will take hours. It would be so much easier if I just . . .

No. I don't do that anymore.

Thistle promised she'd call me if Vasquez managed to get anything off Luxford's computer—apparently the jumble of letters on the post-it note wasn't his password— or if anyone tracked down Armana Black, the woman whose hair was found in Biggs's car. I'm hoping she'll call me tonight, even if nothing happens with the case. Maybe just to check on me. I don't think I've ever had someone call just to check on me.

I use a wood plane to strip off the muscle and fat, then I smash the bones with a framing hammer. The smaller the pieces, the faster they'll dissolve. Carefully, dust mask on, I tip the jug of drain cleaner over them and watch them start to sizzle. I buy the cleaner from a different hardware store each time, and always pay cash.

These days, some funeral homes freeze the body with liquid nitrogen and vibrate it until dissolves into a powder. Then they bury the powder—it's supposed to be better for the environment than cremation. Maybe I could buy some liquid nitrogen next time, and—

No. There is no next time.

My hands are covered in blood. I force myself not to lick my fingers. Go over to the sink and scrub and scrub under scorching water.

My conscience is back. Thistle's voice in my head: *That blood's never gonna come off.*

'Sure it will.' I hold up my hands to the light.

I can still see it, she says. *Can't you?*

Biggs's head is still in my freezer. I'm keeping my options open. At the moment, my theory is that Shannon Luxford and Armana Black are working together, with Black possibly using the Fred alias. If there's not enough evidence against Black, a severed head hidden somewhere in her home would go a long way towards a guilty verdict.

Once there are no body parts hidden anywhere in my house, maybe I can get it professionally cleaned. Get rid of that bad smell, which is back. I could smell it from outside.

I've got nothing to do now. Normally I'd be eating. It's weird, having nothing to keep me occupied while the remains are dissolving. The boredom makes me hungry.

Going cold turkey is going to be harder than I thought. I'll take a walk, I decide. That sounds like something an adult might do. A non-cannibal, non-virgin adult with a girlfriend. I check the mirror—no gore to be seen—and get dressed.

I'm about to put the phone Warner gave me in my pocket when I hesitate. It's not a good time to do this. But there will never be a better one.

I dial.

Warner picks up herself, which is unusual. Her flunkies must be indisposed.

'Blake,' she says. 'What an unexpected surprise.'

'Is there any other kind of surprise?'

'I guess not.'

I can hear a man screaming in the background. The screams echo, like Warner is in a warehouse, standing quite a long way from the screaming man.

'I quit,' I say.

'I didn't quite catch that,' Warner says. 'Which gives you a second chance to decide what to say.'

'I quit.'

Dead air trickles down the line for a while. The screams have stopped.

'The FBI is not going to break me,' she says. 'I know about their little task force. If you've decided to help them, it won't go well for you.'

'That's not it.'

'Then what? You angling for a raise?'

'You were right,' I say. 'I don't have the stomach for this work. I thought I did, but I don't. I've dealt with the last of the clients you sent to me. But I don't want more.'

'Well,' she says, 'that is . . . disappointing.'

I can hear the man sobbing in the background.

'You don't need to send anyone after me,' I say. 'I'm not a danger to you. What little I know, I can't ever say.'

More sobbing.

'You let Indigo quit,' I say. 'The stripper you told me about, the one who hit a client. And nothing bad happened.'

There's a long pause, and for a second I wonder if she made that story up. Then she says, 'If I hear anything even resembling a rumour that you're helping the police look into my business, then what's happening to this guy will happen to you. And you don't want to know what's happening to this guy.'

'Understood,' I say. 'Thank you.'

Another pause. I hate talking on the phone. I can't read her at all.

'Are we done?' I ask finally.

'We're done.'

The line goes dead.

I exhale. That went well.

I check the pickling corpses—still too solid to go down the drain—and then walk out my front door and triple-lock it behind me. I stroll over and knock on my neighbour's front door. The dog starts barking immediately.

Eventually the door opens a crack. Shawn looks out. 'Uh, hi.'

I smile. 'I'm doing an early New Year's resolution,' I say. 'Feel like going for a run?'

CHAPTER 36

What word looks the same upside down and backwards?

'So it's like a fax machine?' I ask.

Shawn just laughs. 'Man, you're old.'

Actually, we're both in our early thirties, although you wouldn't know it to watch us run together. Shawn can jog uphill and hold a conversation at the same time. I can only talk on the downhill stretches, and even then I feel like I'm going to suffocate. Plus, my throat still hurts from the bleach. This was a terrible idea.

'I grew up,' I pant. 'In a house. With a fax machine.'

'Really? Did you have a typewriter, too?'

Actually, we did. There was a typewriter at the group home, although it was missing the letter L. I had to fill it in every time I typed my name.

I guess one of the rare benefits of poverty is the way it

connects you to the past. The poor kids of today live like the rich kids of the nineties, the poor of the nineties lived like the rich of the seventies, and so on.

'So it's not,' I pant, 'like a fax?'

'It's not *just* like that,' Shawn says, with the smoothness of someone who's explained this a lot of times before. 'Yes, you could use the app that way—take a picture of a document, type in the recipient's address, hit the "print and mail" button. But it has all sorts of applications. It's a fast, easy way to send custom postcards. Newsletters. Family photos. Christmas cards.'

This came up because I had asked Shawn if he used nTangle. Apparently he hasn't, but he works in app development too.

'Does anyone,' I gasp. 'Still send. Christmas cards?'

'My family does. Not yours?'

'No family,' I say, and spit on the ground. Then I remember the camping trip with my 'cousin'.

Shawn doesn't notice the inconsistency. 'That's a bummer, man. But hey—' he slaps me on the shoulder, '—maybe you'll have one soon. That woman I saw hanging around your house? She looked like a keeper.'

I feel an excited little kick inside, distinct from the heart palpitations which are slowly killing me.

We jog past a row of trees, turned into skeletons by the snow. The fog hasn't lifted. Car headlights struggle to penetrate the mist. It's a dangerous day to go running.

'What does she do, anyway?' Shawn asks.

'FBI agent.'

'Shit! For real?'

I nod.

'Man. She didn't look like one.'

I wonder what he thinks an FBI agent looks like. 'Well, she—'

'Your phone's ringing, bud.'

He's right. I didn't hear it over my pounding heart. I check the screen. 'It's her.'

'Be cool,' Shawn says, with a wink.

I answer the phone. 'Hi,' I say, trying not to sound like a panting dog.

'Blake. You okay?'

It's weird that we're still not on a first-name basis. 'Yeah. Just, uh, working out.'

Shawn gives me a thumbs up.

'Uh-huh.' Thistle sounds sceptical.

'What's up?' I gasp.

'We found Armana Black. Want to meet her?'

CHAPTER 37

The police call a man to tell him they have found his wife's body, and that he must come to the crime scene to identify her. When he arrives, they arrest him. Why?

'This is costing me money, you guys,' Armana Black says.

She has blonde hair cut short, with a tattooed neck and polyester clothes that are designed to look like leather. Maybe she cut her hair and added the ink when she heard the police were looking for a woman with long, blonde hair. She's also younger than I expected. Twenty-four, according to her licence.

I don't like going into the interview rooms. I'd rather see a suspect in their home or workplace, where their surroundings give me clues about them. And it's hard not to imagine myself on the other side of the table, being interrogated by two suspicious cops. It could still happen.

I may have turned over a new leaf, but old leaves have a way of blowing back onto the sidewalk.

The room doesn't look like they do on TV. Black is seated on a cheap sofa next to a coffee table. Thistle and I are on hard plastic chairs opposite her. There's no one-way mirror—just a camera in one corner, positioned to see the suspect's face. The resolution and frame rate are good enough to catch all the micro-expressions—a twitch at the corner of the lips, a widening of the eyes, a contracting of the pupils. Then computer software processes it to determine if the suspect is lying. But it's another deep-learning algorithm, and it's not good yet. I trust my instincts instead.

'Well, the sooner you answer our questions, the sooner you're out of here,' Thistle says.

'I know my rights,' Black responds, with the confidence of someone who doesn't. 'I get a free lawyer. And if you're not gonna charge me, you have to let me go within twenty-four hours. That's the fifth amendment.'

'It's the sixth amendment, and it doesn't specify a timeframe,' Thistle says. 'Texas state law says seventy-two hours. And the free lawyer only comes if we charge you.'

'Would you like us to charge you?' I add. 'We're happy to do that if it will speed this up.'

'I haven't done anything wrong,' Black says.

'You mean since last time.' Thistle flicks through a file. She's pretending that it's a rap sheet, but from this angle I can see that it's only an old consent form. 'I see here that you turned down a plea bargain when you were pulled in for solicitation last year.'

'They wanted me to testify against Charlie Warner,' Black says. 'Would you have done that, in my position?'

Warner runs all the brothels in Houston, so it's not too much of a coincidence that Black used to work for her. But it still makes me uneasy.

Thistle leans back in her chair. 'Tell us about Shannon Luxford.'

'I don't know who that is.'

'Uh-huh. You haven't switched on a TV today? Seen a newspaper?'

Black's throat bobs. We've caught her in a lie. 'Oh, yeah. The Crawdad Man, right? He killed all those women.'

At the latest press conference, Zinnen was careful not to accuse Shannon Luxford of being a serial killer, something we still can't prove. All we know for sure is that he abducted Abbey and raped Hope, he knew Biggs, and Biggs's phone trail dead-ended at the dump, as did the phone trails of all those overweight white men. It's not iron-clad. But the media has been happy to join the dots.

'Men,' Thistle is saying. 'His female victims survived, at least the two we know about. Are you at all worried about what they might tell us?'

'Why? I don't know those bitches.'

'You said we're costing you money,' I say. 'What do you do?'

'I run errands,' Black says.

'Like what?'

'Like whatever. Going to the post office. Picking up dry-cleaning, or takeout.' She glances at her watch. 'This is peak earning time, right here.'

She seems more anxious about this than about being under arrest, which makes her very smart or very dumb.

'Who do you work for?' I ask.

'Whoever. People hire me over the internet.' She looks at me like I wouldn't understand this. I wonder how old she thinks I am.

'It's called being an entrepreneur,' she adds.

I would have called it freelancing, but whatever. One of the nicest things about Texas is how far it is from Silicon Valley, but that distance seems to shrink every day.

'I assume you tell your employers about your criminal record?' Thistle says.

'If they ask,' Black says warily.

'Do these jobs ever require you to get in someone else's car?'

Black hesitates. 'Maybe. If I'm washing it, I guess.'

'In the past month, have you been in the car of someone who hadn't employed you?'

Black looks even more cagey now. 'I'm not sure.'

'If you have, it would make sense to tell us.'

'Look,' Black says. 'Sometimes you need to give a ride to get a ride, you know what I'm saying?'

'Elaborate,' Thistle says.

'I live outside the loop. Once or twice I've needed someone to take me home. A cab would have bankrupted me. But if I can find a straight dude with a car, I have another way of paying.' She glares at us. 'That's not illegal, by the way. No money changed hands.'

I wonder if she's telling the truth about that.

'These jobs,' I say, 'the paid jobs, are they recorded? You can tell us where and when each one was?'

'Why?'

Cards on the table time. 'Because the car of one of the Crawdad Man's victims turned up at a dump in Louisiana with your DNA inside,' I say. 'A witness can put a woman matching your description at the crime scene. Another witness saw someone—also matching your description—pick up a separate victim from his home.'

Black has gone pale. 'That wasn't me,' she says. 'I never visited any dump.'

'Let's say a man propositions you,' Thistle says.

'I never took any money.'

Thistle ignores this. 'He says it's his birthday. He's got some cash fresh from the ATM. You agree to help him out. But he has some weird role-play thing going on—he wants to pretend you're a giant. And he's rougher than you were expecting. So you panic. You do something . . . regrettable.'

Black looks from Thistle to me and back. 'This is all bullshit,' she says.

'Sex workers get treated like shit,' Thistle says. 'They get robbed, assaulted—'

'I'm not a sex worker anymore.'

'They get targeted by serial killers. Sometimes men do

things the hooker didn't consent to—they see it as theft rather than rape. It wouldn't be the first time a woman fought back, found herself with a dead body on her hands. And maybe a little extra spending money.'

'Jesus,' Black says. 'I didn't do anything.'

'Let's start on January ninth last year,' I say.

'Sure. Give me back my phone, and I'll tell you exactly what I was doing.'

It takes a minute to get her phone back from the front desk. We watch over her shoulder, making sure she doesn't erase anything.

She doesn't. And she works seven-day weeks—her movements look very well accounted for. On 9 January, the first day Biggs marked on the calendar, she was shovelling someone's driveway. On 13 February, the day before Valentine's, she was buying and delivering roses on behalf of disorganised husbands.

March 19 simply said, *hair*.

Thistle points to this. 'What was that?'

'Oh,' Black says. 'Yeah, that was a weird one. Someone wanted to buy my hair.'

A chill runs up my spine.

'Buy your hair?' Thistle repeats.

'Yeah. They wanted a natural blonde, at least ten inches, no split ends. When I got to her place, I recognised her, actually. Another one of Warner's girls, but she left before I did. I don't remember her name. It was a good gig, though. She paid three hundred bucks.'

'How much of your hair did she take?'

'All of it. She shaved me down to the scalp. She was very careful. I felt bad for her. I figured she'd just found out she had cancer. Why else would you be willing to pay so much for a blonde wig?'

'A wig,' I say.

'Yeah. I told her she could buy one from a shop, but she said she wanted to make it herself.'

CHAPTER 38

A car has two occupants. One is the father of the other's son. How?

'You want me to try to get a list of Charlie Warner's past employees?' Vasquez says, eyes wide.

'Right,' Thistle says.

For a moment, the only sound is the humming of computers and the whirr of the AC.

Vasquez stands up, glaring at us both. I know how he feels. I don't like the direction this case has taken either. If Warner hears that I've made this request, I'm a dead man.

'And how exactly am I supposed to do that?' he asks.

'You're keeping tabs on her already, right?' Thistle says. 'I figured you'd have one ready to go.'

'It's a highly sensitive investigation. Information like that is only accessible to people on the task force.'

'Well, we need it. Do you want to tell the director, or should I?'

Vasquez sighs. Rubs his face in his hands. 'Fine, I'll do it. But anything you find, you tell me first.'

'Done. How did you go with our suspect's phone?'

'Uh . . .' Vasquez sits back down and digs up a graph on his computer. 'Cell tower data doesn't take her anywhere near the dump site within the last three months. But it's possible she didn't take her phone with her when she went.'

'Or had it switched off,' I say.

'No. She's rebooted a few times, but hasn't left it switched off for more than a couple of minutes since she acquired it two years ago.'

'Can you see where she was on March nineteenth?'

Vasquez brings it up. 'Three addresses. One is her home, one is a shopping centre, and the third . . .' He types up a quick search. 'The third one is a condemned apartment building. Can't tell you which unit she was in.'

'How long has it been condemned?'

'Three years.'

Which means Black only *thought* she was visiting the home of the wigmaker. Or she was lying to us.

'Okay,' I say. 'What about her freelance career?'

Vasquez brings up Black's profile on the job site. 'She did all the jobs she said she did—at least, she accepted them, got paid for them and got excellent public feedback for them.'

'No doubt,' Thistle says drily. 'How about Luxford's computer?'

'Still nothing. The letters on the post-it note weren't the password, and I can't decrypt the hard drive without it. Any other ideas for what it might be?'

Thistle shakes her head.

'Show me the computer again,' I say.

Vasquez leads us over to one of the computers, which I recognise as the one from Shannon's place.

'It looks like he's used AES-256 to encrypt the hard drive,' he says. 'It's a symmetric encryption algorithm that uses a block cipher, so I'll never break it with today's technology.'

'But it was encrypted with current tech, right?' Thistle says. 'Luxford isn't a visitor from the future?'

Vasquez doesn't laugh. 'Decryption is always years behind encryption. That's what makes encryption useful for criminals, and a pain in the ass for us. But Luxford's ISP is cooperating, so we know he used Tor. You know about Tor?'

'Yes,' Thistle says.

'No,' I say, not wanting to appear too knowledgeable. I used to sell credit card numbers on the dark web.

'It's a secure web browser originally developed by the navy,' Vasquez says. 'Typically, when you're browsing with Tor, the only thing an outsider can tell is that you're using Tor. They can't tell what sites you're visiting or what you're doing on them.'

'The navy released it to the public, right?' Thistle says.

Vasquez nods. 'So they could use it without anyone knowing it was them. Anyway, Tor gets you to the dark web. Which is where you go if you want to tip off a journalist about NSA wiretapping. Or to buy drugs, or hire a hit man, or look at child pornography.'

'So what was Luxford doing?'

'I don't know. He accessed the dark web only twice, almost a year ago. My best guess, based on Abbey Chapman's testimony, is that he made a friend there, and then started swapping videos with the friend by mail.'

Fred.

'Why not keep using the dark web?' I ask.

'Because the cops might notice. We can't see what people are doing on the dark web, but we can tell they're on it. Whereas a USB stick in the mail isn't too suspicious. It might get X-rayed, but not read. We did find a USB stick, but it's encrypted too.'

I stare at the post-it note, still stuck to the computer. MTEDUFIHCRPFO. Impossible to remember, unless you've had plenty of practice memorising random letters. Easier to just write it down, like he did. But what for, if it's not the password?

'Bring up the login screen,' I say.

Vasquez does. 'We can't just guess,' he said. 'After two more wrong attempts, the hard drive will erase itself.'

Thirteen letters. I close my eyes and think back to the wheel cipher on Luxford's desk, back at the college. Thirteen discs. The configuration meaningless.

'What do you have in mind?' Thistle asks me.

'Hang on.' I didn't have time to memorise the order of the letters on every disc, and I only saw the wheel cipher from one side. But I think I have just enough. In my head, I rotate the discs, lining up the letters from the post-it note: MTEDUFIHCRPFO.

And there it is, on the row just above. A message in plain English.

I open my eyes. 'Try *show me the pain*,' I tell Vasquez. 'All one word.'

'You're sure?'

'I'm sure.' I look at Thistle. 'He used his wheel cipher. The thing on his desk.'

Thistle squeezes my shoulder as Vasquez types it in.

A message pops up: *Incorrect password. One attempt remaining.*

'Shit,' Thistle says. 'Sorry, Blake.'

'Was that upper case, or lower case?' I ask Vasquez.

'Lower case.'

'Try upper.' All the letters on the cipher were capitals.

'Really? If you're wrong, we lose everything.'

'Do it,' I say.

Vasquez looks at Thistle for confirmation. She nods. He genuflects and turns back to the keyboard. Types it in.

I hold my breath.

He hits Enter.

Welcome, Shannon!

'Mother of God,' Vasquez says.

'Ha!' Thistle slaps me on the back, grinning. 'You did it!'

I exhale, my hands shaking. It feels good to show off in front of Thistle. 'What's in there?'

Vasquez is bringing up a file directory. There are

hundreds of videos. He hesitates before clicking the first one.

'What?' I ask.

'A guy with an encrypted hard drive, a Tor browser and "show me the pain" as his password probably has some pretty bad videos in his collection,' Vasquez says.

'No shit,' Thistle says. 'You remember we found a young woman being held prisoner in his house?'

'I'm just saying, whatever this is, maybe you don't want to see it.'

The excitement has faded from Thistle's face. 'We have to.'

'I can get someone to transcribe it for you. These guys—' Vasquez gestures at the other desks, although they're all empty '—they're trained to watch this kind of thing. They get regular counselling to make sure it doesn't mess with their heads.'

Thistle looks at me.

I nod. Whatever it is, I'm sure I've seen worse. Done worse.

'We can handle it,' she says. 'Show us.'

•

Vasquez is right. It's bad.

Thistle and I walk out of Vasquez's office, our steps heavy. Ride the elevator up in silence. I find myself looking forward to even the meagre daylight outside.

Thistle looks shaken. So am I, although I didn't expect to be.

It wasn't the blood that got to me. I've seen plenty of blood in my life. It was the agony. The confusion. Hours and hours of screaming. People turned into animals by their own terror. And the eagerness of the gloved hands, which I assume belonged to Fred.

The videos confirmed our worst fears about what Shannon is into. But it didn't tell us anything about where he might be. And none of the people in the videos we saw—we watched a small sample of each one—look like any of the victims we know about. So either Fred isn't the Crawdad Man, or he's prolific. Or both.

'How does a person even *get* a fetish for that?' Thistle says finally.

'Maybe fetish is the wrong word,' I say. 'I saw some true crime on his bookshelf. He might have started out with slasher movies, and then moved on to reading about real killers, and now nothing shocks him except . . . that. Maybe he's addicted to being horrified.'

'I bet that'd be a real comfort to the victims.'

A terrified face flashes through my head. Echoes of a scream. I shake it loose.

We reach the doors. It's raining, the air not quite cold enough to turn the droplets into snowflakes. Thistle's car is a short walk away, but we're likely to be drenched.

'I don't think he's shocked at all,' she says. 'I bet he thinks it's funny. Like a school bully who laughs when he sees someone else getting beat up.'

This whole case is a mess. We have dozens of victims now, with less and less in common. Several suspects—Luxford,

Fred, Warner, the wigmaker—with unclear motivations and unknown locations.

The one thing we knew about the woman we were looking for was that she was blonde. Now we don't even know that. Armana Black said the woman who bought her hair was a brunette, but that it might not have been natural.

Thistle is evidently thinking along the same lines. 'I don't think Black has anything to do with those missing men,' Thistle says. 'You?'

'Just a hard-working entrepreneur,' I say, relieved by the change of subject.

'You think she was telling the truth about her ex-colleague?'

'Could be. You weren't wrong in there. Hookers are treated like dirt, and violence leads to violence. I can see one of Warner's girls snapping, and killing seventeen men.'

'With Luxford's help?'

'That's the part that doesn't make sense,' I say. 'He's a rapist, and she must have known it. Why would they team up?'

'Maybe they met some other way. Old friends? Relatives?'

'I don't think . . .' I trail off.

'What?' Thistle asks.

'What if she's one of the women he's been blackmailing?'

Thistle looks doubtful. 'There's a big difference between making someone give you a ride and making them kill seventeen people.'

'I meant the other way,' I say. 'She killed them, he found out about it, and he's been extorting her ever since. Maybe that's why Biggs doesn't fit the victim profile. Luxford made her kill him.'

'Why?'

'Maybe because Biggs knew what he'd done to Hope. I'm not sure.'

'Well, we'll know when we find him.'

We look out at the pouring rain. We're still huddled in the doorway like smokers.

'You remember last night . . .' Thistle begins.

'Yes,' I say immediately.

She grins. 'That's great, but I wasn't finished. You remember how I said I couldn't hold down a normal job?'

'Right. Me neither, for the record.'

'Well, I feel better about it now. At least I never had to sell my own hair to get by.'

I laugh. 'I'd buy your hair.'

'You would, huh?'

'Yeah. You've got great hair.'

She chuckles. 'How much? Maybe I'm open to it after all.'

'Fifty bucks.'

'Is that all?'

'Per strand. Just let me mortgage my house first.'

Thistle shoves my shoulder, smiling. 'All right, that's enough.'

I hug myself for warmth. Even standing near the closed door is cold. After a second, she puts her arm around me.

'Until Vasquez gets that list of Warner's ex-employees,' she says, 'there's nothing to do but wait.'

I nod. I can't think of any other leads to pursue.

After a pause, she says, 'My roommate is probably home. How about we wait at your place?'

The tub's empty. The stuff in the freezer is covered.

'Sounds good,' I say.

CHAPTER 39

What stinks when alive but smells good when dead?

The sex is better the second time. Less hurried, maybe. We make it to my actual bed, and we have the patience to get completely undressed, to kiss each other all over, to try a few positions and find each other's rhythm. It feels less like it's our only chance, now. Or maybe I'm just less scared that I'll lose control and bite her.

I wonder if it will keep improving forever. Surely not. It's gotta peak somewhere. We can't still be having the best sex of our lives in our eighties. Our hips wouldn't take it. Mine can barely take it now.

It's weird to think of Thistle as an eighty-year-old woman, knitting in a rocking chair on her porch. Weirder still to think of me beside her. But it feels more possible with every passing day. When we finally fall asleep,

I dream that we're on a little boat, out in Galveston Bay. The sun makes the sea sparkle. Thistle is reading a book, while I keep my eyes to the horizon, watching dark clouds creep in.

I wake up alone.

This is not abnormal, and it takes me a minute to remember someone is supposed to be here.

Thistle. When I fell asleep, her arm was across my chest and her legs were tangled up with mine. Now she's gone. I reach over to the other side of the single mattress. No one.

For a horrible moment I think I dreamed the whole thing. Last night, and tonight. Maybe Thistle still hates me. Or maybe she never existed. After our last case together she became my imaginary friend—perhaps she always was. I'm sane enough to know I'm crazy, but I'm never sure just how much.

No. The sheets are warm. She was here.

I roll onto the floor. Pull on a shirt and some pants—it's too cold to walk around in the nude—then I go looking for Thistle.

I open the bathroom door, only remembering half a second later that it would probably have been polite to knock first. But she's not there.

I check the bathtub, suddenly worried that I forgot to drain it. Empty. She hasn't fled after seeing eighty gallons of melted human. Or, if she did, she drained the tub first.

The clock in the living room says it's three am, so it's really four. I peer out the front window. Thistle's car is still here.

'Reese?' I whisper.

No answer.

The fear wells up from beneath me like groundwater. What if I hurt her? I'm a sleepwalker, partial to midnight snacks. What if I killed her?

I check the freezer. Lots of frozen meals past their sell-by. Bacon, hot dogs, mince. I rummage around, revealing a plastic sheet, Biggs's head beneath it. No sign of anybody else.

I hear something from outside. I cover Biggs and slam the freezer shut.

The sound came from the backyard. I tiptoe over to the back door. It's not locked—not even closed all the way. I widen the gap.

Thistle is sitting on the back step, huddled in her jacket, legs bare. It's stopped raining, but it's colder than ever. She looks up from her phone and smiles in the dark.

'Hey,' she says. 'Sorry—didn't mean to wake you.'

I sag with relief, and sit next to her. 'No problem. What's up?'

'Nothing. I wanted to see if my neighbour got my text about feeding my dog. I asked my roommate to do it, but she messaged late last night, saying she had to suddenly go to Memphis. A work thing.'

'Okay.'

'Phoebe says she'll be gone for a couple days. Want to stay over tomorrow night? My bed's bigger than yours.'

'Sure.' I wrap my arms around her. It already feels like a natural thing to do. She hugs me back. Our breaths shroud our heads in fog. I wonder if I should tell her how scary it was to wake up without her. Probably not. She might think that was alarming.

'You remember Ophelia Tynan?' she asks. 'From the group home?'

'Curly hair,' I say. 'Sucked her thumb until she was six.'

'Right. She had the bunk under mine, and she snored. Drove me crazy. I got so mad at her during the day, and she never knew why. I haven't thought about that girl in years. But you snore too.'

'I do?'

'Like an old dog. But it's cute, not annoying.'

'That's me,' I say. 'Cute.'

Thistle laughs. 'Well, give it time.' She stands up. 'Let's go back to bed.'

Then she stiffens.

'What?' I ask.

She releases me. 'What's that?' she asks, staring into the dead weeds of my backyard.

'What's what?' I ask, suddenly on guard. Could someone be watching us? My house is well secured, but my yard isn't.

'There.' She walks off the cold concrete and across to the dirt to a rough patch. It has fewer dead weeds than anywhere else, as though the earth has recently been turned. But I haven't done any gardening, ever.

I follow her. The bad smell gets worse as we approach. It was never coming from inside the house. No wonder leaving the back door open made it worse.

Jack Heath

Thistle bends down.
I see it at the same moment as she does.
Fingertips, sticking out of the dirt.

CHAPTER 40

You can break me without moving or even making a sound. What am I?

Later, I realised that I could have saved the situation. If I had crouched down alongside Thistle and helped her unearth the corpse, as though we were both discovering it, then that might have been okay. A normal person would have done that. But I just watched as she peeled back the tarpaulin, which had been hidden under a thin layer of dirt. As though I had already known the body was there.

'What the fuck?!' Thistle says.

'It's Daniel Ruthven,' I say.

It has to be. His head is gone, but he's the right height and weight, and it looks like he was skinned within the last few days, not long after his death. His raw, sticky muscles are still dark red rather than brown, and his fingernails have not yet become claw-like as the flesh receded. None of the Crawdad Man's other victims went missing recently enough to qualify.

Thistle slowly rises to her feet, looking at me. She doesn't ask me how I know whose body it is.

'What's he doing in your yard, Blake?' she asks.

'I don't know.' It's the truth, but it comes out sounding like a lie. I stare at the body. So much meat. If I washed the dirt off, it would still be edible.

'You don't know,' Thistle says softly.

I say nothing. Shannon Luxford must have dumped it here. He followed me home.

No, not Luxford. The wigmaker. Shawn's voice echoes through my mind: *That woman I saw hanging around your house? She looked like a keeper.*

At the same time I was planting Biggs's hand at the college, she was dumping Ruthven at my house. To implicate me, to intimidate me, to confuse the investigation.

'Okay,' Thistle says. 'Stay here. I'm going to call the FBI.'

She pushes past me and walks back into the house.

It takes me a moment to realise that she already had her phone in her hand. Why did she go inside?

I hear the freezer open.

I run back into the kitchen. Thistle is staring down into the freezer, eyes wide, knuckles white around the edge of the lid. She can only be looking at Biggs's severed head.

'Reese,' I say, 'this isn't what it looks like.'

'Jesus,' she whispers. 'You're the fucking Crawdad Man.'

'I'm not,' I say, my heart going into higher gear. 'I swear. Someone's trying to make it look like I am.'

'I wondered why this place was locked up like Fort Knox. I could tell the freezer was making you nervous . . . you said you were sick in the head. You even said you were afraid of hurting me. Oh God!'

She bends over, gagging. After three violent retches, she pukes onto the kitchen floor.

I rest my hand on her back. She shakes it off and backs away, flecks of vomit stuck to her chin. 'Don't touch me!'

I raise my hands. 'Thistle. I didn't do this. How could I? I've been with you the whole time.'

'Convincing me that Luxford was guilty,' she says. 'You knew so much about the case.'

'Luxford *is* guilty,' I say. 'He must have followed me home, got in here somehow.'

'Oh.' Thistle wipes her face with her sleeve. 'Okay. You're right. I'm sorry.'

She's only pretending to believe me.

'Please,' I say. 'Trust me.'

'I do,' she lies. 'Of course I do. I just lost it there for a minute. Don't worry, we can figure this out.'

She turns towards the coffee table, where her handbag still sits. I realise what she's doing a fraction of a second before she does it. She reaches for the handbag. I kick it off the table. A bunch of things skitter out across the floor—a wallet, some painkillers, a set of keys . . . and a Glock 17M.

We both dive for the gun. I push her fumbling hands out of the way and grab it.

'No!' she screams.

I scramble away from her so she can't snatch it out of my grip. She puts her hands up. She's shaking.

I don't point it at her, still telling myself I can fix this. I keep it by my side.

'Please believe me,' I say. 'Please.'

'I do believe you,' she lies. 'Of course I do. Just put the gun down and we'll talk.'

The vision of us as old people in rocking chairs fades away like smoke. Tears spring into my eyes. 'I can't.'

She changes tactics. 'You're sick, Blake. You need help. You don't know what you're doing.'

'I *am* sick.' My throat is closing up. It's hard to get the words out. 'But not in the way you think. I promise. I didn't kill that guy. Either of them.'

Another mistake. If I was innocent, I might have assumed the head belonged to the body in the yard.

'Put the gun down,' Thistle says. She's crying too. 'I don't have to call the police, okay? We can figure this out.'

She's trying to trick me. I force a smile. 'I can find the real killer. If I catch him, you'll believe me then, right?'

'I believe you now. We'll figure out what happened together. Okay? Just give me the gun.'

I realise her phone isn't in her hands anymore. My guess is that it's in her pocket, listening to this conversation. Either she decided to call 911 and wait for a few decades, or she's hit redial and called Vasquez. He'll be sending people here right now.

I pick up Thistle's keys off the floor. 'Where are you going?' she asks.

I should give her a fake destination, to buy myself some time. That would be the smart thing to do.

But I can't lie to her. Not now. Not when I'm so desperate to win back her trust.

'I don't know,' I say truthfully. Then I back away, out the door.

•

I'm driving aimlessly through the light and shadow of Houston by night. The AC blows warm air on my bare feet. I can hardly see the road through the tears.

I have to ditch Thistle's car. All police vehicles are low-jacked. Right now, I'm a blinking light on a digital map in someone's office.

But I won't get far on foot. Which means I need to ditch it somewhere where there are other transport options. Bus station. Airport. I can't fly anywhere, but it'll take them a while to work out that I didn't.

Or I could leave it unlocked in a bad neighbourhood with the keys on the seat. Get the cops chasing some joy rider for a few hours.

I could make someone pull over, use the gun to jack them. But assuming I don't get shot in the process—it happens—I'd be committing a pretty serious crime, which it would be tough to explain to Thistle. Later, once she realises that I'm innocent.

But you're not innocent, she says in my head.

'I am.'

You cut off Biggs's head and put it in the freezer.

'Yeah, but I didn't kill him. Or Ruthven.'

You cut off his hand and left it at the college. You ate parts of him. You—

'Once I find Luxford or his accomplice, I can prove they buried Ruthven's body in my yard. Then they'll get blamed for everything.'

My conscience falls silent, but I can tell she's not convinced. Thistle has seen the real me now. No matter who takes the rap, I can't undo that.

I pull over on the side of the I-60 and dig out the burner phone Warner gave me. It takes me a minute to switch on the data, and then another minute to register a burner email address. After that I google my way to the giantess forums Biggs was frequenting and create an account.

After scrolling through a ton of weird porn, I eventually find the comment I'm looking for. It's under a story about a shy man, seduced by a giant woman. *Anyone want to try this in real life? DM me.* Posted by SleepingBeauty321.

I check the profile. No photo, no bio, but a location: *Houston, Texas.* My hunch was right.

Without the resources of the FBI, the only way I'm going to catch the wigmaker is by using myself as bait. I send a short message: *I want to do this for real. I can pay.*

I wonder how similar that is to what Biggs wrote, before he died. Alone and scared, miles from the woman he loved.

Headlights flash in the corner of my eye. I turn my head and get a quick glimpse of the car before it smashes into the side of Thistle's Crown Vic.

CHAPTER 41

A plane crashes on the border between Texas and Mexico. Where are the survivors buried?

The world turns upside down, ground to sky and back again. My spine quivers like a freshly released bowstring. All the windows frost over immediately, except for the one right behind my left ear, which disintegrates. My organs swim around my torso, too loose in their moorings. The fluid in my brain whirls like my skull is a blender.

I black out, and dream of Thistle. She's sitting next to me in the shattered car, looking at the crumpled door. *Man*, she says. *The director's gonna have my ass for this.* Then she looks behind me and says, *Blake! Wake up!*

I open my eyes. Strong hands are grabbing me by the armpits, dragging me from the wreckage. I'm too dizzy to help. It's all I can do to keep the vomit down.

I find myself on my back on the freezing asphalt. The world keeps spinning, as though I were still trapped in a rolling car. When it steadies, I find myself staring up at Shannon Luxford.

'Mother*fucker*,' he says. I'm not who he was expecting.

I try to say something clever, but my jaw hurts. One of my teeth is loose in my mouth. I resist the urge to spit it out. A dentist can replant it if the root doesn't dry out.

Shannon raises a phone to his ear. 'Fred,' he says. 'I got the wrong one.'

There's a pause.

'Yeah, okay,' Shannon says. 'Thanks, man. I appreciate it. See you soon.'

He ends the call and lifts me up over his shoulder. I feel like Lois Lane. My ears are ringing and I think I might throw up. I'm helpless as he throws me into the passenger seat of his pick-up truck. Thanks to the bull-bar, the truck is almost undamaged.

Maybe he'll dismember me and throw me into a ravine. Maybe Thistle will eventually find my body. That will prove I'm innocent.

Luxford puts on my seatbelt and gets a roll of duct tape out of the glove compartment. He starts winding it around my torso, tying me to the passenger seat. I will my arms to move. My fingers wiggle, but my arms are too heavy.

I let out an involuntary groan as the tape squeezes my chest.

'Oh, does this hurt?' Luxford says. 'My bad.'

Then he punches me in the head. As my skull snaps sideways, I accidentally swallow the tooth.

'You don't even know what pain is, asshole,' Luxford says. 'Not yet.'

When I'm fixed firmly to the seat, Luxford starts binding my ankles. I try to kick him, but my feet move sluggishly. He pins them easily and keeps working, like he's putting a diaper on a squirming toddler.

This thought makes me realise that I've pissed myself at some point.

Luxford notices too. 'Goddamn,' he says. 'That reeks. Glad this isn't my car.'

'You got my message quick,' I slur.

'Don't know what you're talking about, man,' he says, and slams the door.

My upper arms are pinned to my sides, but my forearms can move. I think I could probably reach the park brake with my left hand. Useless while the car is already parked. But if we're taking a bend at speed, I might be able to crash the car.

I barely survived the first crash, though. A second might be a bad idea.

Luxford gets in on the driver's side. He drapes a coat over me, hiding the duct tape.

'My friend was expecting a hot, black, lady FBI agent,' he says. 'He'll be pretty disappointed when he sees you. I hope he kills you anyway. You really fucked up my life.'

It's hard to talk around my missing tooth. 'What does your friend do?' I mumble.

'He hurts people.' Luxford zooms back onto the highway, apparently keen to put as much distance between himself and the wreck as possible. My problem about being tracked by the cops seems to have solved itself.

'You pay him?' I ask.

'It's more of a sharing economy-type deal.'

I nod. The movement sends a wrecking ball through my skull. 'You traded videos of Abbey—and the other women—for videos of pain,' I say. 'Right?'

Luxford keeps his eyes on the road. He's trying to look calm, but a vein is bulging on his temple.

'Anything involving giants?' I ask.

He looks confused. 'You mean like the NFL team?'

'I mean actual giants.'

'Christ,' he says. 'You must have hit your head hard.'

'You met this friend on the dark web, right?' I say. 'You ever met him in person?'

He still says nothing, but I can tell the answer is no.

'Did your friend dump Ruthven in my yard?' I ask. 'Or was it you?'

His eyes narrow. 'Who's Ruthven?'

'The fat guy,' I say. 'The most recent fat guy.'

He shrugs, apparently bored. 'I don't know what you're talking about,' he says.

I can't think of a reason for him to lie about that. And he sounds truthful.

Which means that I've been investigating two separate cases all this time. One involves Shannon and Fred, sharing videos of rape and torture. The other involves a wigmaker and sixteen dead men. No connection, other than the fact that Shannon knew one of the wigmaker's victims.

'How long before they start looking for you?' he asks casually.

'They were already looking for me,' I say.

'Nice try.'

'It's true. I'm wanted for murder.'

He glances over at me. I hold his gaze.

'I cut off your boss's head with a bread knife,' I say. 'The FBI just found it in my freezer. Half the police force is looking for you, the other half is looking for me.'

The perplexed look on his face suddenly seems hilarious. I can't stop a mad grin from twisting my bleeding lips.

'You're *way* out of your depth, Shannon,' I say. 'You have no clue what's going on.'

He laughs uneasily and turns his eyes back to the road. 'You're a funny one,' he says. 'Maybe Fred will like you after all.'

We're approaching a bend. I reach for the handbrake. But Shannon slows down. I retract my hand before he notices it.

'First stop,' Shannon says.

A young woman is waiting out front of an apartment block, walking back and forth, stomping her feet in the cold. She's small, with dark hair and a fur-lined hoodie. As the car gets closer, I think I recognise her from one of the naked photos in Luxford's desk.

He rolls down his window. 'Hi, Macy.'

Macy digs something out of her pocket and thrusts it through the window. A driver's licence.

'I did it,' she says. 'But I need it back by tomorrow morning, okay? Before he notices that it's missing.'

Shannon studies the licence. 'Yeah, sure. No problem.'

Macy can tell he's lying. 'I'm serious,' she insists. 'I've done everything you ever asked, okay? If you don't get it back on time, he'll know I took it.'

She's scared, but not enough to have seen the news. She doesn't know that Shannon kidnapped a woman and kept her imprisoned for months. She certainly doesn't know he's a suspect in the Crawdad Man killings.

'Relax,' Shannon says. 'You'll get it back.'

Macy's eyes settle on me. 'Who's this?'

'He's no one.'

I could try to tell her what's going on. There's a chance that she could help me. But Luxford might kill her.

'I'm no one,' I repeat.

Shannon smirks. 'Good boy. See you around, Macy.'

He rolls up the window and drives off. In the side mirror I can see Macy pacing again, worried that he won't come back.

If he doesn't, she might tell the cops everything. She might mention me. Maybe they'll find us before Fred kills me.

'Who was she?' I ask, although I already know.

'Just a girl who owes me a favour,' Shannon says.

'Because you have naked pictures of her?'

'Right. I forgot that you'd seen those. She's nice, right?'

He doesn't mean her personality. 'How many girls owe you a favour?' I ask.

'Enough to get me this car, a fake ID and a few thousand dollars,' Shannon says. 'And a gift for Fred.'

'You mean me.'

'Not just you.' He slaps my knee. 'This is cool, right? Getting to talk man to man. No more pretending.'

The truck slows as it turns off the South Loop towards Kirby Drive, then into a grid of huge parking lots. The stadium on the horizon holds seventy thousand people, and contained even more during Hurricane Katrina. But there's nothing on right now, so the lot is deserted. Twenty-six thousand parking spaces—hundreds of acres of empty concrete. We drive through the darkness, past the stadium, towards the Astrodome, which is surrounded by abandoned construction equipment. They're renovating it—turning it into even more parking spaces.

A single car is parked alone in the moonlight. Hope Biggs steps out from behind the wheel.

CHAPTER 42

I have two bodies, joined in one. The more I stand still, the faster I run. What am I?

Shannon parks twenty or thirty yards away, making Hope walk stiffly through the cold.

'Just to be clear,' Shannon says, 'if you try to tell her where we're going, I'll kill her, then I'll kill you. Got that?'

There's no point appealing to his conscience. If he has one, he ignores it. Like me.

'If you do that,' I say, 'you have no present for Fred.'

'There are plenty more girls where this one came from,' he says. 'And I don't really need you at all. Don't try it.'

Hope opens the back door and climbs in behind Shannon.

'Hope!' he says. 'Glad you found a parking space.'

'Shannon,' she says. Neither begging for mercy nor

telling him to go fuck himself. She looks at me, and raises an eyebrow.

I try for a reassuring smile, but it comes out as a grimace.

'What happened?' she asks.

'Mr Blake was in a car accident,' Shannon says. 'Sit behind him, please.'

Hope slides across, out of my field of view. We have no way to communicate without Shannon knowing. I hear her put on a seatbelt. Shannon starts driving. We cruise across the acres of empty parking lot.

'Where are you taking us?' she asks.

'A hospital.'

'Why is Mr Blake taped to the seat?'

Shannon shoots me a sidelong glance as he turns back on to Kirby Drive. 'You two have met?'

The car is accelerating. It's almost fast enough for me to grab the handbrake and crash it. But now that Hope's in the back seat, I can't.

'My dad's missing,' Hope said. 'You might have heard. Mr Blake and his partner interviewed me.'

'I see,' Shannon says. 'Well, after his accident, I was worried about his spine. That's why I taped him to the seat.'

He says this with presidential confidence. Like he doesn't care whether she believes him or not.

'That's real nice of you,' Hope says flatly.

We take the on-ramp towards the South Loop. The pick-up zooms through the night towards Houston's outskirts.

'How much did you tell him?' Shannon asks Hope.

'Everything,' Hope says.

'Oh.' Shannon glances at her in the rear-view mirror. 'Nice to have it all out in the open.'

'Did you kill my father?' Hope asks.

Shannon grins at me. I wonder if he's about to repeat what I told him. About cutting off Biggs's head with a bread knife.

'Why would you even ask me a question like that?' he asks.

Then his chest explodes.

It's like the birth scene in *Alien*. The bullets must have flattened as they passed through Shannon's body. Bloody chunks of his bladder, lungs and heart splatter the windshield and the side window. Hope works her way up his torso methodically, putting bullets through his abdomen, his chest, his neck. I can hardly hear his screams over the deafening blasts of the gun right behind me. Finally she gets to his head. He stops gurgling as the window is flecked with grey and pink.

Shannon's dead foot presses down on the accelerator. I grab the emergency brake just in time. The engine complains and rubber squeals. Instead of zooming away, the pick-up goes into a skid. Hope unbuckles Shannon's seatbelt and tries to drag his twitching corpse into the back seat. She can only get him halfway, but it's enough to lift his foot off the gas. The vehicle slows, stops, stalls. Warning lights flash all over the dash.

I look around. Shannon's blood makes it hard to see through the windows, but it looks like no one's around.

Outside the loop, predawn. Ghost town. But someone will turn up sooner or later. We have to get this cleaned up, fast.

It's not until Hope grabs my shoulder that I realise she's been talking to me. My ears are still ringing.

'Hey,' she says. 'You okay?'

I nod. 'You?'

'Never better,' she says.

'Get his keys. Maybe you can use them to cut me loose.'

Hope gets out of the car and circles around to the driver's side door. When she opens it, the movement sends the red drips worming towards the road.

She grabs the keys from the ignition and slams the door, spraying me with blood again. I lick my lips without thinking.

Hope opens my door and starts hacking at the electrical tape with the keys. Punching holes, sawing, punching again.

'Are you gonna arrest me?' she asks as she works.

'I'm a civilian consultant,' I say. 'I don't arrest people.'

'But you're going to tell the police about this. Right?'

'I wasn't planning on it,' I say. 'Were you?'

'Honestly, I hadn't thought any further ahead than this,' she says. 'What was he going to do to us?'

'Nothing. But a friend of his was going to torture and kill us.'

Hope nods, satisfied. 'So what are *we* going to do?'

'We could tell the cops everything. You shot an unarmed man after voluntarily getting into his car, but given who he was and what he did to you in the past, you have good odds of a temporary insanity defence. You'd have to explain why you brought the gun with you in the first place, though. Do you have a concealed carry licence?'

'No. You sound like you have another option.'

'You can go home. Take a shower. Scrub your hands. Throw those clothes in someone else's trash. Go out for brunch with some friends tomorrow, somewhere public. Act normal. Pay with plastic. In a few days, buy some bullets to replace the ones you used.'

'What about you?'

'I can make Shannon disappear.'

'And his friend?'

'Him too.'

Hope nods again. 'Okay,' she says. 'Let's do this.'

She cuts the last piece of tape, and I can breathe again. I peel the severed strands off my clothes.

Hope holds out the gun for me to take.

'I don't want that,' I say. 'Wipe it clean, unload it, put it back in your dad's safe.'

Together, we lift Shannon's body and dump it in the tray of the pick-up. There's an old newspaper in there. I use bunched-up pages to scrub the windshield and the side window. The driver's seat is still soaked in blood. I'll have to live with that until I'm somewhere safe.

'You really think we'll get away with this?' Hope asks, as I throw the bloody newspaper into the tray and close the lid.

'You will,' I say. 'If I get caught, I won't turn you in.' Not that anyone would believe me anyway, a wanted criminal blaming this young woman for murder.

'Have you done anything like this before?' Hope asks.

'No.' The truth. The things I've done were much worse than this. 'But it'll work.'

I drive her back to the stadium parking lot. The sun is rising as I let her out near her car. As I'm pulling over, my phone beeps. I check the message.

Text me your address, sweetie. I'll pick you up at dusk. Bring $500 cash, and be ready for an unforgettable night. X—Sleeping Beauty

'Problem?' Hope asks.

'No problem.'

She opens the car door. Hesitates. The cold air flows in.

'Did he really kill my dad?' she asks.

It would give her closure, believing that she'd avenged her father's death. If I tell the truth, the guilt might overwhelm her.

But Shannon was a bad guy, who intended to kill us both. And if tonight goes the way I think it will, everything will be out in the open soon.

'No,' I say.

Hope looks up at the lightening sky, blinking away tears. Blood dribbles from the corner of the open car door, like sand through an hourglass.

Typical, Thistle says in my head. *You'll lie to save your own skin, but not to give anyone else any peace.*

'Don't worry,' I say. 'I think I know what happened to your dad. By tonight, I'll be sure.'

CHAPTER 43

I have a ring but no hands. I have many voices but no mouth. What am I?

After Hope is gone, I search the pick-up.

I find several thousand dollars in cash. A gun, which I don't touch. A small padded envelope with an address written on it. Shannon's handwriting. No name. The envelope is empty, but about the size you'd choose for a USB stick. I'm thinking that's Fred's address.

Too far away to check out right now. I have a lot to do before my rendezvous with the wigmaker—AKA Sleeping Beauty, AKA the Crawdad Man.

I drive to a strip mall, find a public bathroom and wash the blood off my face. Shannon's blood and mine, swirling together down the stainless-steel drain. The mirror is scratched to shit, but I can more or less make out the damage from the crash. A black eye, a broken nose, a split lip. Not a bad disguise, all up. But if I don't straighten my nose, I won't be able to breathe through it when it heals.

I pinch the bridge and wrench it sideways. The sparks shoot up my nostrils like coke, making my eyes water. Then I stagger out of the bathroom.

The wigmaker knows what I look like. She followed me home after I visited the college, and dumped a body in my backyard. The busted-up face will help, but I'll need a haircut, too.

The strip mall has a twenty-four-hour drug store. I spend some of Luxford's cash on a pair of scissors, a pack of disposable razors, some shaving cream and condoms. The young woman behind the counter serves me without looking up from her phone, the blue glow of the screen highlighting the powder on her cheeks.

I raid a charity donation bin for some clean clothes. They're better quality than you'd think. In Texas, people throw things away not because they're ruined, but because they shouldn't have bought them in the first place. The problem tends to be a lack of closet space.

I find a white shirt and a Blues Brothers-style dark suit. No belt, no tie, but the clothes look like they'll fit well enough that it doesn't matter. I take them back to the bathroom and start cutting my hair.

Going on the run is easy for me. This is how I used to live—off the grid. I can't imagine a spoiled rich kid like Shannon Luxford stealing second-hand clothes and shaving his head with a disposable razor in a public bathroom. I wonder what his plan was. How long would Fred have protected him?

The sun is up when I walk out of the bathroom. My old shoes are still bloodstained, but I figure I can go to the supermarket without arousing suspicion. I walk in and grab a basket, taking the aisles one at a time. I pick up paper towels. Two bottles of refrigerated water. Some meat-tenderising powder. A hammer, just in case. I don't know how to use Luxford's gun, but I know how to use a hammer. I pay cash.

It takes me a few hours to clean the pick-up. I pour the meat tenderiser into one of the water bottles and shake it until the mixture thickens. Then I pour the fluid onto the bloodstained parts of the seat, rubbing it into the cloth with my fingertips.

When I'm done I sit on the back seat, waiting for the tenderiser to break down the proteins in the blood. I don't know what I'm going to do about the body under the cover in the tray.

I assumed you'd eat it, Thistle says in my head. *I hear that's your thing.*

'I don't do that anymore,' I say.

Because you're too busy having sex with me, right? Thistle says dryly. *That was the plan? Tell me, at what point in the future do you picture me forgiving you?*

'When you realise I didn't do anything wrong.'

She just laughs. It's a sound with no joy.

•

I didn't text Sleeping Beauty my real address. I told her to collect me from a random apartment building in East Houston. The pick-up is parked in one of the visitor spaces out front. Now I'm watching the sun go down.

I didn't eat Luxford. I used his cash to buy a mattock and a shovel from a hardware store, then I drove all the way up to Huntsville State Park. I spent hours digging a deep hole way off a trail. Then I got him out of the trunk, dragged him to the grave and lowered him in.

I even said a few words before I refilled the pit. Trying to prove something, I guess, though I'm not sure what, or to whom.

Not long to wait now. It's safe to make a call. If the FBI traces it, they won't get here before the wigmaker does.

I reassemble my phone and dial Norman. She picks up straightaway. 'Hello?'

'Dr Norman, it's Timothy Blake.'

'Mr Blake. What can I do for you?'

Her tone throws me. If she's heard that I'm wanted for murder, she does an excellent job of hiding it. Maybe no one thought to let her know.

'Hello?' she says.

I wanted to tell her that I'm not guilty. Get her thinking about the things that don't add up. Things that Thistle might be too enraged to see. But if she really hasn't heard, I can ask her something else that's been on my mind. 'I had a question.'

'Shoot.'

'That flap of skin from Gomez's house. You said it had been preserved somehow.'

'That's right. But not with formaldehyde—something odourless.'

'It got me wondering if the killer might have preserved the rest of the victim, too. Do you know if it's possible to stuff a human being?'

'With what?' I can hear noises in the background. A male voice, maybe her husband. Clattering dishes. She's having an early dinner. Strange to think of her having a normal life outside that icy room I always see her in.

'Whatever taxidermists use,' I say.

'No,' she says. 'Separated from the body, skin eventually shrivels and goes scaly, no matter what you pickle it in. A stuffed person wouldn't last more than a few weeks.'

'Why doesn't that happen with animal skin?'

'It does, but the fur covers it.'

'Huh. Thanks, doc. It was just a thought.'

She chuckles. 'Your thoughts are always amusing, Mr Blake. Is there anything else?'

I feel like I should say goodbye to her. We've worked well together. And even if I don't get shot by police over the next few hours, it's possible that I'll be the Crawdad Man's next victim.

'No,' I say. 'Have a nice night.'

'You too, Mr Blake.'

The line goes dead.

I dial Thistle. The call goes straight to voicemail.

'You've called Agent Reese Thistle. Leave a message.'

Beep.

'It's me,' I say. 'I'm using myself as bait. The Crawdad Man is the wigmaker, and she's about to pick me up. You can follow the signal from this phone. Do me a favour, and catch her before she kills me.'

I pause.

'Listen, I'm sorry,' I add. 'There's a lot of things I should have done differently. But thank you for ... for being who you are, I guess. I gotta go.'

I end the call.

I put the phone on silent. Then I wrap it in two condoms.

A few years ago I tried to swallow a big chunk of meat that turned out to have a shard of bone in it. It got stuck halfway down my throat, and I panicked. I thought I was going to die. I wondered how long it would be before my roommate eventually smelled something from my room. He'd bust down my door to find one and a half corpses. The headline would be: CANNIBAL CONSULTANT CHOKES TO DEATH ON VICTIM.

I spent three terrifying minutes punching myself in the solar plexus, and eventually managed to hack the chunk back up. I knew it had been a narrow escape, so I taught myself some tricks to suppress my gag reflex.

I take a few deep breaths, and then I put Charlie Warner's phone in my mouth. It's a small phone, but it still seems way too big once it's actually in my mouth. But I just picture the ocean, the grey water lapping at the shore in Galveston, and push. As the phone goes further and further down my oesophagus, I clench my left hand into a fist. I'm not sure why that helps, but it always does. Before I know it, the phone is gone, and I'm gasping for air. Then I wipe the drool off my chin, grab five hundred dollars from Shannon's stack, and get out of the car.

I don't want Sleeping Beauty to know which car is mine. She'll see it parked in a visitor space and get suspicious, realising that I don't live here. I walk a few feet away, rubbing my palms together in the cold.

A song is stuck in my head.

Standing on the corner with a dollar in my hand, honey
Standing on the corner with a dollar in my hand, babe
Standing on the corner with a dollar in my hand
Standing here waiting for the Crawdad Man . . .

Headlights on the horizon. She's here.

CHAPTER 44

What eight-letter word contains every letter?

Gomez wasn't wrong—she is beautiful. Long eyelashes, long neck, full lips with a faint gloss. As she rolls down the car window, she flashes me a perfect smile, like a movie star meeting a fan.

'Hey, handsome,' she says, like she means it. 'Come on in out of the cold.'

She's not wearing her blonde wig, and I realise that I've seen her before. Not just in the corridor outside Biggs's office. I saw her at the cabin in the woods, flirting with the nervous black man.

The hair threw me, so I didn't recognise her at the time. Hopefully my lack of hair throws her, too. I should have figured all this out way earlier.

I hurry over to the car and get in. The seats are supple leather. The radio plays Norah Jones, soft enough that

I can only just hear the upright bass under her smoky voice.

'Nice to meet you, Hank,' the woman says. Her eyes are wide and sky blue.

I shake her hand. 'Nice to meet you, Sleeping Beauty.'

She laughs. 'Oh, no. I'm Cindy. Sleeping Beauty is waiting for you. You'll meet her soon enough.'

'Oh. Okay.'

I look out the window. No flashing lights, no sirens. Thistle must not have heard my message yet.

Cindy reaches over, and touches my cheek with her knuckles. She has a French manicure.

'You're hurt,' she says, with what sounds like genuine concern.

'You should see the other guy.'

She beams. 'Oh, you're a fighter.' She puts her hand on my knee. 'I like that. Strong, brave. A good man to have around.'

I hope her hand doesn't move any higher. She'll realise she doesn't interest me. She's not Thistle.

'Are you nervous?' she asks. 'It's okay to be nervous.'

'A little,' I admit.

'It's funny, isn't it,' she says, 'what scares people and what doesn't.'

'What scares you?'

She sighs, a long stream of air from pursed lips. Even her breath smells sweet. Peppermint.

'Intimacy,' she says.

'I used to have that problem.'

'Really? Tell me, how did you overcome that?'

'A woman kind of overcame it for me,' I say.

'Aha.' She winks at me. 'This woman. Is she still around? It's all right if she is.'

'No. I screwed that up.' But maybe I can fix it. You're the key.

'I'm sorry.' She squeezes my knee. 'Don't worry. You'll find Sleeping Beauty very forgiving.'

We drive further and further east. Eventually the car crosses the border into Louisiana. The sign says: BIENVENUE EN LOUISIANE. Cindy takes a turn towards the dump.

'Is this where she is?' I ask.

'No, sorry. This is just a precaution.'

She does exactly what she must have done with Biggs. We drive through the gate—it opens automatically for her car, like Gomez said—and she leads me over to the shipping container full of archive boxes. The one where I found Biggs's blood.

He must have been nervous at this point. Maybe even getting scared. Wondering if he'd made a terrible mistake, one he couldn't come back from.

Cindy unlocks the container with her own key. We walk into the darkness. She turns on the little desk light.

'I need to borrow your phone,' she says. 'It's a privacy thing. Sleeping Beauty is old-fashioned—she doesn't like cell phones. We'll come back here to pick it up, after. Okay?'

I wonder if Sleeping Beauty is Cindy's alter ego. You can't tell if someone is crazy just by looking at them, but the way the light casts a shadow across half her face, revealing only one unblinking eye, makes madness seem possible.

'I left my phone at home,' I say.

She smiles patiently. 'Come on.'

'For real,' I say. 'I don't like being beholden to it.'

She holds my gaze, her pupil huge in the dark.

'I have to check,' she says. 'Do you mind?'

I spread my arms and legs wide, like a frequent flyer about to get tested for explosives.

She slowly runs her hands up and down each of my legs, gently squeezing. Then she touches my arms, my chest, my hair, my back. Finally she cups my ass and my crotch.

'I apologise,' she says.

I clear my throat. 'No problem.'

'Come with me.'

If I had a phone, I guess she would have left me alone in here while she hid it somewhere else at the dump. That must have been what happened to Biggs. He would have waited, alone in this dark container, more and more convinced with every passing second that this was all wrong.

Until he decided to leave a message behind.

I look at the spot on the wall where the calendar used to be. Suddenly I realise what he was trying to do. The dates were a message. A code so basic that even a non-professor could decipher it. I can't believe I didn't figure it out sooner—it's just like Tyrrell and his 88 tattoo.

Twelve dates, one per month. Twelve numbers.

9, 13, 19, 15, 18, 18, 25, 7, 1, 2, 2, 9.
I, M, S, O, R, R, Y, G, A, B, B, I.

•

Cindy drives me back towards Houston. Thistle must have heard my message by now. Where are the sirens? Why isn't every squad car in Texas converging on us?

On cue, my phone starts to buzz inside my stomach.

I cough with surprise. The vibration turns my guts to water. I don't know whether I'm going to throw up or shit myself.

'Are you okay?' Cindy asks, alarmed.

I clear my throat. 'Fine,' I gasp.

The phone keeps buzzing. I clench my pelvic floor. *Don't call me*, I think. *Track the phone!*

'You don't look fine,' Cindy says.

I thump my chest. 'It's just . . . anxiety.'

'Okay.' Cindy touches my arm. 'Ride it out. Just listen to your breaths, okay? In and out.'

The phone stops. I exhale shakily.

'That's it,' Cindy says. 'Nice and slow. You're doing great. Relax your shoulders.'

I loosen my muscles. I should have worked out how to turn off the vibration before I swallowed the phone. Another call, and I could be in deep shit. Maybe literally.

'Thanks,' I say.

'Of course.'

'You've dealt with something like that before?'

'I used to get panic attacks,' Cindy says. 'One time

I hurt somebody. I didn't mean to—I just lashed out. So I taught myself some calming techniques.'

It all clicks together. She's the one Warner told me about. The sex worker who hit a client, and was allowed to quit. Sindy with an S.

'Did it help?' I ask.

'Not as much as leaving the situation did.' Sindy looks at me. 'I do hope you don't want to leave?'

'No,' I say.

'Great.'

She takes the turn-off towards the cabin in the woods.

When I was homeless, and starving, I'd sometimes have out-of-body experiences. People would walk past me, and for a second I would *be* them, glancing at my expensive watch as I strolled to my high-paying job as a consultant or hedge fund manager. Sometimes I would see myself out of the corner of my eye, a hairy, sunburned ruin in faded rags. But most of the time I would be invisible. That lawyer or executive would look right at me and see an empty patch of sidewalk.

Now, as Sindy parks the car in front of the log cabin, I have another dissociative moment. For a second, I'm that jittery black man with the horn-rimmed glasses, and Timothy Blake is watching us from the bushes. I look, but don't see him. Nor do I see any sign of the police coming to arrest Sindy and vindicate me.

'Something wrong?' Sindy asks, as we get out of the car.

'No. Nice place,' I say, looking at the cabin as though I haven't already examined it inside and out.

'Thanks. My father-in-law built it, and when my husband died, it became mine.'

'I'm sorry. About your husband.'

She bows her head. 'Thank you.'

As we walk up to the door, she says, 'Just letting you know, my hobby is taxidermy. The house is full of animals. I've been practising since I was a little girl, so I'm used to it, but it can be jarring for newcomers. I didn't want to surprise you.'

'I like surprises.'

She inserts the key into the lock, and touches my arm. 'I bet,' she says, smiling.

She opens the door and switches on the light. My gaze immediately flicks to the wolf. Sindy has done a great job. Even knowing that it's long-dead, I can't shake the feeling that it might move.

Sindy looks me up and down. 'You're the first guy not to react,' she says.

'I'm just frozen with terror,' I tell her.

She smiles at the false modesty. I listen for sirens. Still nothing. We could be the last two people on Earth.

'Can I get you a drink?' Sindy asks.

Bad idea. 'No, thank you.'

'You sure?' she says, still headed for the kitchen.

'I don't drink,' I say.

'Ah.' She turns back. There are any number of reasons someone might not drink. Religion, health, taste. But in Texas, people always assume you're an alcoholic.

'I have to tell you something,' Sindy says.

'I'm all ears.'

'She might not wake up.'

'What do you mean?'

'One day, the right man will come.' Her eyes are bright, but sad. 'He'll touch her in just the right way, and she'll be roused. But that man may not be you.'

'I understand,' I say, though I don't.

Sindy takes my hand. 'Are you ready to meet her?'

Madness in her gaze. She can see reality from where she's standing. But she doesn't live there.

I remind myself that she's not going to kill me. At least not yet. The man with the glasses made it this far. So did Biggs, I'm pretty sure. So I say, 'Yeah.'

Sindy peels back the rug, revealing the trapdoor. She unlocks it and lifts it up, revealing a square of blackness.

'Come on down,' she says, like a game show host. Then she walks into the dark.

CHAPTER 45

If you skin me I won't weep,
but you will. What am I?

The room under the house is lit only by an old-fashioned lamp in the corner. It's a low-watt bulb, and a sheet of lace has been draped over it to darken the room still further.

My heartbeat accelerates. Nothing good ever happens in a basement. The animal part of my brain is yelling, *Get out get out don't go down there get out!*

Sindy switches on one of those fake fireplaces, which is rigged up to a car battery. As the flickering glow falls across the room, I see a padded armchair in the corner next to a hat rack and a gilded mirror. There's a basin and a garden hose. But most of the room is taken up by a giant bed.

And lying on the bed is a giant.

The rational part of my brain has always been a little slower than the instinctive part. For a moment I've stepped off the edge of the real world and fallen into wherever Sindy lives. So my first thought is, *She's real. Holy shit, the giantess is real!*

She's at least eight feet from head to toe, but everything is perfectly in proportion. It's suddenly hard to tell if she's huge or I'm tiny. It's like I've gone down the rabbit hole and eaten the caterpillar's mushrooms. My perspective is so distorted that I miss the last step and stumble into the room.

Sleeping Beauty has a huge mane of slightly curly blonde hair fanned across the pillows. Eyes almost as big as baseballs stare up at the dark ceiling through half-closed lids. Her glossy red lips are ever so slightly pursed, as if she's waiting for a kiss. The satin sheets of her bed are pulled back halfway, exposing huge breasts clad in lacy purple lingerie. Her enormous hands are by her sides, upturned, a foot away from her gargantuan hips. Huge feet are tenting the sheet down the other end of the bed, as far apart as her gigantic shoulders. I've heard yoga people call this 'corpse pose'.

I walk closer, entranced. So much meat. A feast like this could keep me going for months.

But the scent isn't quite right. I can smell perfume, shower gel, conditioner. The faint aroma of make-up. But there's no odour of sweat, or skin. She's fake.

'You can leave your clothes on the armchair,' Sindy says. I had completely forgotten she was in the room. 'I'll leave you two alone.'

Remembering Thistle's idea of the sex doll brothel,

I touch Sleeping Beauty's upper arm. Maybe it's silicone. But it feels completely real. As Sindy walks back up the stairs I peel back the sheets, baring her huge thighs, knees, shins. I can see a thatching of pubic hair through the sheer fabric of the panties. The underwear must be custom—no store would sell anything so big. Sleeping Beauty's calves have been shaved. I can see the hairs, cut back to almost nothing. I can even see a nick behind her knee.

I touch the cut, marvelling. Then, running my fingers around the area, I find something else. The same thing that Biggs must have noticed, before he ran into the woods, naked and screaming in terror.

Stitches.

They're tiny, done with immense care. When I peer under the giant's calf, I can barely see them. They're the same colour as her skin. Now that I'm looking for them, I can see them elsewhere—on her hands, her hips, her neck. No wonder this place is poorly lit.

This looks and feels like real human skin because it *is* real human skin.

This is where the sixteen missing fat men went.

I remember what Dr Norman said: *Separated from the body, skin eventually shrivels and goes scaly. A stuffed person wouldn't last more than a few weeks.* So Sleeping Beauty would need regular grafts. Some patches are a little smoother than others. Newer. A ragged-edged circle under her armpit is especially smooth and soft. I'm guessing that's Ruthven. The newest victim. I wish he'd had an identifying mark, like a mole or a tattoo. But if he had, she probably wouldn't have used that part. If he had enough tatts, he wouldn't have been a target at all. Weird to think that some ink might have saved his life.

I wonder how many of Sindy's clients have fucked this thing, not noticing that it was a patchwork of human corpses.

I wonder how many *did* notice, and continued anyway.

Are you kidding me? Thistle says. *Most people would have done what Biggs did. Run screaming into the woods. Had a heart attack. You think some of those guys realised they were fucking a dead body, and kept going?*

I think of the guilty, disgusted look on the last client's face as he left this building. 'Yes,' I say.

That's nuts, Thistle says.

'People are nuts.'

Not everyone is a psychopath like you, Blake. Don't you think you might be overgeneralising from your own experience?

'I'm not a psychopath,' I say. 'There's a difference between a person who ignores his conscience and a person who doesn't have one.'

Is there? Thistle sounds doubtful. I remember again what she said about Luxford, when I said he might not have a fetish for pain. *I bet that'd be a real comfort to the victims.*

The timeline is coming together in my head. Sindy quits her job with Warner. She knows how to seduce a man, but doesn't like getting fucked. She discovers the giantess forums somehow—maybe via her deadbeat husband?—and asks She's Alive to make a giant doll she can pimp out. But they can't, so Sindy hatches a plan to make men screw each other instead of her. She uses nTangle to target men with plenty of flesh and therefore plenty of skin, all the same shade. Her taxidermy skills are good enough to turn them into a doll. She buys hair from Armana Black—and maybe some other women—to make a wig for it, and one for herself.

Sindy uses the giantess forums to find clients. But one of them, Biggs, realises what she's done and flees in terror. He dies of a heart attack in the woods, and I take the body before she finds it. This leads to an FBI investigation, which she tries to derail by planting one of the bodies in my backyard.

What happened to her husband? Maybe some of the oldest skin is his—or maybe he's already been replaced by fresh grafts.

The trapdoor opens.

Sindy comes back down the stairs.

She's holding the hunting rifle.

•

I put my hands up immediately. 'Whoa, hold on.'

Sindy levels the gun at my head. 'You want to tell me who you really are?'

She's dropped the soothing, sexy shtick. Now she's just an angry, scared person with a gun. I'm close enough that she won't miss, and far enough away that I can't grab the rifle. Right in the danger zone.

'I'm no one,' I say. 'My name is Hank. I'm just a guy who wanted to bang a giant. A real one.'

She cracks the stock open, showing me the shell casing inside. Then she snaps it closed and points it back at me.

'No you're not,' she says. 'If you were, you'd already be doing it. You're a cop.'

'I'm not a cop. A cop wouldn't have paid you, right? That's entrapment.'

'Holy shit.' Her eyes widen. 'You're that fucking FBI agent. I thought you looked familiar.'

'I don't know what you're talking about, lady. I was good to go—but that's not a giant. It's a dead animal. A bunch of dead animals.'

'You said it,' she says. 'Animals. Sorry, asshole, but giants don't exist in real life. Nor does Santa Claus, in case you were wondering. Now that you've brought the police to my doorstep—'

Thistle's here. I try not to look relieved. 'Police?'

'Drop the act. Here's what's going to happen. You'll walk out of here. I'll stay in the house, but I'll be watching you through my scope. You're going to convince your cop friends to leave. I don't care how you do it. But if they're not gone in five minutes, I'm going to start shooting. You first, then them. I reckon I can get all of them before one gets me.'

I need to stall her. Give the police some time to case the house. Give Thistle a chance to figure out how to save me.

'Is that how you killed all these "animals"?' I ask.

Sindy holds my gaze. 'They died humanely.'

'What kind of animals were they?'

'Dangerous ones. They were hunting me as much as I was hunting them.'

'I doubt that,' I say, thinking of Ruthven. 'I think they were just lonely.'

She jerks the gun upwards. 'Come with me,' she says, and backs slowly away up the stairs.

I don't follow her.

'Just so you know,' she says, 'I don't think the people outside are even sure anyone's home. My plan B is to lock you in the cellar and shoot the first person who approaches the front door. Then all the others. Once they're dead, I can come back down and kill you.' She looks me up and down. 'You have lovely skin, by the way.'

I don't, but it's an effective threat. Two days ago I was a virgin. By next week I might be part of a sex doll.

I slowly climb the stairs.

When we get to the front door, Sindy stands behind it. I can see a van parked outside in the dark.

'Remember,' she says. 'Five minutes. I'll be watching.'

The cabin has two windows. I wonder which one she's planning to shoot from.

'Give me ten,' I say. 'I don't know what I'm going to say.'

'You'll think of something,' she says, and opens the door.

I walk out of the house slowly, my hands up. The door creaks closed behind me, but doesn't click. She's keeping it ajar.

At that moment, four people get out of the van—and I realise that they're not my salvation.

Charlie Warner hops down from the passenger seat. Sariklis and Tane—the guy who accosted me at the courthouse steps—clamber out of the back of the van, both holding guns.

Maurice Vasquez gets out of the driver's seat.

CHAPTER 46

What gets bigger the more you take away?

My first thought is that Vasquez is a hostage. But the other explanation makes much more sense.

'I told you not to take the case,' he tells me.

'You did,' I say. 'It seemed suspicious at the time.'

It didn't. But I'm at a hell of a disadvantage. Sindy is pointing a gun at my back. The three men are pointing guns at my front. The only person not holding a gun is Warner. All I can do is bluff. Act like I knew this was coming.

'I always liked you,' Vasquez says. 'This is nothing personal.'

Warner cuts him off. 'For me it is,' she says. 'You took advantage of my good nature, Blake.'

'Is that right?' I say.

'You said you were quitting, and I let you,' Warner says. 'You said you wouldn't tell the FBI what you knew.

Immediately after that, I get a call from Vasquez, telling me that you're looking for a blonde woman in her early forties. Later he calls again, and says you want a list of my old employees.'

'He called you straight away, huh?'

Vasquez doesn't look embarrassed. 'You're not in a position to criticise,' he says.

'He did,' Warner says, ignoring him, 'because he understands loyalty.'

The irony of a traitor being praised for loyalty seems to be lost on everyone.

'I wasn't after you,' I say, because it's the truth, and I can't see another way out of this. 'I was pursuing a lead in the Crawdad Man case.'

'That's interesting,' Warner says, 'because you appear to *be* the Crawdad Man. My boys have had a look around your house, where they found two of his victims—victims I certainly didn't give you. And even though Vasquez tells me that you never received the list of my ex-employees, he was able to trace your phone to where Indigo lives now. Sindy—the very stripper-turned-hooker-turned-liability I was telling you about a few days back.'

Snowflakes fall through the beams of the van's headlights. Clouds of condensation obscure the faces of Sariklis and Tane. I wonder how they got to my house before the cops did.

'I'm not the Crawdad Man,' I say. 'Sindy is. She planted evidence in my house. She's—'

'I'm sick of your bullshit, Blake,' Warner says. 'It's

time for you to die. Painfully and publicly, so my other body-disposal guy will think twice about crossing me. But if I spread the word that you're the Crawdad Man, the cops will think it's a vigilante killing.'

Spread the word? Apparently she hasn't heard that the police already think I'm the Crawdad Man. Vasquez must not have told her—I'm sure Thistle called him.

Warner shakes her head wearily. 'Honestly,' she says, 'you almost ruined everything. If that FBI agent hadn't called Vasquez directly, we wouldn't have been able to contain the story.'

I'm not wanted by the police after all. Vasquez intercepted the message. That explains why Dr Norman acted so normal on the phone. It takes me a second to work out which FBI agent she's talking about, and another second to realise what 'contain' might mean.

'Where's Thistle?' I ask Vasquez.

'That was a shame,' Vasquez says. 'I always liked her, too.'

It's like a punch to the guts.

I look at Vasquez's face. There's no comfort in it.

'She's dead?' I ask.

'Not my fault,' he says.

The shadows get darker even as the headlights go blinding. The blood roars in my ears like a hurricane. It feels as though the ground is sinking under my shoes. Like I'm in a slow-moving elevator.

Thistle is dead. Thistle is dead. Thistle is dead.

I want to kill someone. Maybe myself, maybe everyone else, maybe God himself. Thistle was the only person in this wretched city worth saving, and now she's gone. My heart is ripping itself in two. If I had a button that could end the world right now, I would push it.

But I don't. So I'm going to have to kill everybody one at a time, and Vasquez is closest.

'You motherfucking son of a bitch!' I scream, charging towards him.

He steps back, startled. I lunge at him, teeth first. I'm almost at his throat when he pistol-whips me in the side of the head. The world tilt-a-whirls and I go down like a bag of rocks. I try to grab his legs, but my vision is swimming. I'm going to throw up. *Thistle is dead.*

'Oh.' Warner's voice seems to come from a long way away. 'He had a thing for her?'

'Yeah, from day one,' Vasquez says. 'She liked him, too. They both thought they were hiding it well, but they weren't.'

'What did she see in him, I wonder?'

'Beats me. He sure isn't *my* type.'

I manage to roll over, looking up. Vasquez is pointing his gun at me.

He looks at Warner. She nods.

'Goodbye, Blake,' Vasquez says.

'Hey, asshole,' I rasp, 'you know what a dead man's switch is?'

He hesitates.

I could have figured out that he worked for Warner. I could have written a letter detailing that, and all the other dangerous things I knew about her organisation.

I could have mailed it to myself over and over, so if I ever died, someone would eventually find it in my mailbox. I could have hidden something in my house or my car or a storage unit, so it might take years to surface.

I didn't do any of that. And I don't really think the possibility will stop him from killing me. But it might make him uneasy for the rest of his life.

'Nice try, Blake,' he says, and pulls the trigger.

The gunshot splits the darkness.

A cloud of pink mist explodes out of Vasquez's head. He falls over like a bowling pin. *Thud*.

Warner has the quickest instincts. She dives for cover behind the van.

Sariklis and Tane are still looking at me, as though I might somehow have made Vasquez's skull burst with telekinesis. Sariklis says, 'What the f—' and then a rifle round punches through his heart. There's a wet *thunk* as the bullet hits the side of the van. He staggers, gulping like a fish.

That gets Tane moving. He ducks behind the van.

I scramble sideways, getting out of the line of fire. Sindy hasn't shot me yet, maybe because I'm on the ground and unarmed, but that could change at any moment. I manage to crawl over behind Sindy's car as another shot rings out. Warner is screaming orders at Tane, but it doesn't sound like he's listening.

I get to my feet, keeping my head low.

'If you're not gonna fucking fire, then give me your goddamn gun!' Warner roars. 'Tane? Tane!'

From here, I can see what Warner can't—that Tane is facedown in a puddle of sleet and blood.

I run into the forest, looking for better cover. I need to get a head start. Whoever survives this will be after me soon.

What's the point? says someone in my head. It's not Thistle's voice. She's gone. This is all me. *Just let them kill you. You're cursed.*

Another gunshot. Nothing hits me, but the sound distracts me enough that I forget about the pit trap. I step into it for the second time this week, my foot plunging through the camouflage. This time I'm too dizzy to save myself. I tumble right into the foul-smelling hole.

And keep falling. This trap is way deeper than it needs to be to snare a deer. My feet hit a layer of something sticky, and then the freezing water beneath. The pit has filled up in the recent rain. The water is clogged with debris, big mushy lumps. Maybe wood, gone spongy after soaking up the water. I stifle a scream as my whole body is swallowed. Soon my head is under. I can't see. Can't breathe.

I thrash wildly around in the water. I can't swim upwards. The surface is completely covered by chunks of ... something.

Suddenly I realise what I'm drowning in. My whole brain shuts down. *Don't think about it.* I try to find the edge of the pit, but everything I grab turns out to be a loose piece. *Don't think about Sindy flaying her victims.* Finally I catch hold of something solid. Part of a tree root, connected to the wall. *Don't think about her dragging the skinless bodies to this pit.*

I haul myself up, lungs bursting, heart pounding, until my head is above the surface of the water—but that just means that it's surrounded by floating flesh. I still can't breathe. I keep climbing, shoving the mush aside.

Insects are crawling all over my cheeks. A worm wriggles up my right nostril. And then, finally, air.

I take a deep breath, and fight back an ocean of vomit. Then I keep climbing. My feet trample rotting muscle and bone. My fumbling hands find a sturdy piece of weedy dirt near the top. I drag myself up.

Finally my legs are free. I scramble up and over. I'm covered in mud, blood and slime. I look like a golem. The Earth itself, come to life.

The worm is still in my nose, tickling my brain. I pinch the squirming end and pull it out, resisting the urge to sneeze.

The voice is back. Not Thistle. I think she's gone forever. *Couldn't you have just eaten your way out?* it says.

'I'm not hungry,' I mutter. When Thistle was alive, love pushed out the hunger. Now grief has replaced them both. It feels like I will never be hungry again.

Through the trees, I can see Charlie Warner slumped against the side of the van. She's taken a round through the stomach. The front of her shirt is soaked with blood. Her face is pale, twisted in pain. One of her hands spasms in her lap. The other is underneath her leg, maybe clamping a second injury.

Sindy walks down the wooden steps into the clearing, wrapped in a heavy coat, cradling the hunting rifle. She's a hell of a shot. By my count, it's taken her only four rounds to kill three people and wound one more.

She slowly approaches the van. She can't see Warner from where she is. Probably wants to make sure everyone's dead.

She stalks around the edge of the van. Spots Warner.

'Hey, boss,' she says. I can barely hear the words. My ears are still ringing from all the gunshots.

'You ungrateful bitch,' Warner wheezes.

'I always thought you might come looking for me.'

'Wasn't looking for you,' Warner says.

'I always liked your hair,' Sindy says, and levels the gun at Warner's heart.

Warner shifts, freeing her hidden hand. I see the compact Springfield XD-S a split second before she shoots Sindy through the head.

The rifle falls from Sindy's grasp. She crumples to the ground. In the darkness, it looks as though she's evaporated, leaving only a puddle of clothes. Like a Jedi.

'Blake!' Warner shouts, her voice hoarse. 'I know you're there.'

She doesn't, so I stay silent. I want to kill her. But even if I had a weapon, that wouldn't bring Thistle back. Maybe I should just run—except I have nowhere to go.

Then she says something else.

'If you get me to a hospital,' she says, 'I'll cancel the order. I'll save the FBI agent.'

CHAPTER 47

What goes up when rain comes down?

If a doctor restarts your heart after a flatline, that means your heart never actually stopped. All the parts of it were just unfocused. Twitching all at different times, instead of one coordinated *thump*. Like the first time Thistle and I had sex, the rhythm wrong, our hips out of sync.

Too long in that state, and you die. Your brain, starved of oxygenated blood, curdles in your skull. But if the defibrillator gets there first, it shocks the confused cells, forcing them into line. Uniting them to a common goal.

'She's not dead yet,' Warner continues. 'At least, probably not. Vasquez told her to keep what she knew about you to herself, in case other people at the FBI were compromised. Then I sent Tyrrell to her house. But I can call him off. There might still be time.'

A minute ago my heart wanted a dozen different things,

but none of them very much. Now it's desperate for just one thing.

Save Thistle.

'Make the call,' I yell.

'Get me to the hospital first,' Warner says.

I emerge from the shrubbery. If she shoots me, she shoots me.

'Jesus,' she says, staring. Covered in mud, blood and scraps of flesh, I finally look like what I am. A demon.

'Make the call,' I say.

'Hospital first,' she says.

Snarling, I grab her and drag her into the passenger seat of Sindy's car. The van has too many bullet holes and smears of blood. The car is unlocked, but I don't have the time or the tools to hotwire it. I run over to Sindy's corpse and dig through her pockets until I find her keys.

By the time I get back to the car, Warner's eyes are closed.

'No!' I slap her. If she dies, so does Thistle.

Warner's eyelids flutter. She looks at me. 'Jesus,' she says again.

I dig her phone out of her pocket and press it into her hand. 'Make the call,' I say. I turn the key, and the engine grumbles.

Warner swipes to unlock the phone, leaving a smudge of blood on the screen.

'Take me to the hospital,' she says.

'I'm doing it! Make the fucking call.' I floor the accelerator. The wheels spin in the dirt for a second before the tread catches and the car lurches back up the driveway.

When I glance over, Warner appears to be swiping through her contacts. Looking for Tyrrell, I hope.

'Put it on speaker,' I say. 'I want to hear every word you say.'

She mumbles something. My ears are still ringing.

'What?' I say.

'I'm calling him,' she says. 'I'm doing it. Just get . . .'

She's blacked out again. Her skin is deathly white. It's surreal to see someone so terrifying look so helpless. Charlie Warner has killed dozens of people, and ruined the lives of many others.

The phone is ringing. I shove her shoulder. Her head thunks against the window, and she gasps.

'Stay awake,' I say. 'If Thistle dies, I'll eat you alive. You understand? I'm not being figurative.'

The phone keeps ringing for a while, and then cuts out.

'He's not picking up,' she says unnecessarily.

'Try again.'

She fiddles with the phone as the car hurtles down the highway. After what seems like way too long, the phone starts ringing again. I'm clenching my remaining teeth so hard it feels like they might fracture.

The phone keeps ringing.

Warner's eyes are closed again.

'Hey!' I backhand Warner across the face.

She looks at me through bleary eyes. 'Dad?'

I never wondered about Warner's early life, and I'm not going to start now. 'I'm not your dad,' I say. 'Focus.

You have to call Tyrrell. Tell him to stop what he's doing immediately.'

The phone keeps ringing for a while, and then cuts out again.

'Try again,' I say.

Warner looks out the window. 'This isn't the way to the hospital,' she says.

She's right. But she's too weak to do anything about it.

Soon we reach Thistle's house. It's a one-storey, two-bedroom place with stucco walls and a small lawn out front, ripped to shreds by her dog.

Tyrrell's car is parked a few houses up. I'm too late.

'No!' I unbuckle my seatbelt and leap out of the car, leaving it in the middle of the street with the engine running.

I run up the path to the front door. Try the handle. It's unlocked.

I sneak in. Tyrrell is here. I don't want to spook him, especially if he has Thistle. The floorboards creak under the synthetic rug, and I wince. I listen for breaths or footsteps, but I can't hear anything over my racing heart.

She might still be alive. Maybe. Tyrrell might be the kind of killer who takes his time.

I grit my teeth and shake my head, trying to dislodge the image of Thistle bound to a chair or stuck in a bear trap. Then I creep further into the house.

Photos of people I don't recognise line the walls. Thistle's not the type to fill the house with photos of herself. An umbrella stand with a lone umbrella is up the other end of the hallway, too far from the door to be practical. I move down the hall towards it. The bedrooms are to my right, the living area to my left. Both bedroom doors are open. Through the gaps I can see bookshelves, nightstands, a sliver of a bed. I've never been in Thistle's bedroom, so I don't know which one is hers. But one of the rooms has no books on the shelves, which doesn't seem like her. I slip into the other one.

The heavy curtains are drawn. The bed is a single, with lavender sheets. A dream-catcher hangs from the lamp on the nightstand. The books on the shelves are new-agey—angels, tarot, the healing power of crystals. This isn't her room.

I go back out. As I'm about to turn towards what must be Thistle's bedroom, I notice something in the living area. From this angle I can see Tyrrell on the sofa, watching TV with the sound off. I wonder if he knows that Warner was on her way to kill me.

He sees me at the same moment as I see him. He jolts in his seat.

'Christ, Blake,' he says. 'What happened to you?'

'It's a long story,' I say. 'The FBI agent—have you dealt with her yet?'

'No,' he says, getting up. 'Still waiting for her to get home.'

I can't tell if he's being truthful. Would he watch TV if he was lying in wait? Would he stick around if he'd already killed her?

I didn't think to take the Springfield from Warner before I came in. Stupid. Now I'm defenceless.

Tyrrell gestures at the TV. 'Care to join me?'

He knows that I'm on Warner's kill list. He's trying to get me into a vulnerable position.

'No thanks,' I say. 'Boss lady sent me here to tell you to call it off.'

'Oh, she did?' He doesn't believe me.

'You weren't answering your phone. Come on, we gotta get out of here. Warner's been shot. We need to get her to a hospital.'

'Okay. Let me grab my things.' His hand goes out of sight behind the sofa cushions.

I grab the nearest object—the umbrella in the stand—and throw it at him. It misses, but it throws off his aim. When he pulls the trigger of the Walther in his hand, a puff of plaster dust bursts out of the wall behind me as I run at him, reaching for the gun.

He backs away, but trips over the coffee table. Another bullet hits the ceiling. I jump on him and grab his wrist, crushing it until the gun slips from his fingers.

He pounds me with his other fist. My brain quivers like Jell-o. I lose my grip on him, and he throws me off.

He scrambles towards the fallen gun. I'm still on the ground. It takes me a split second to realise that he'll almost certainly get to the gun first, and that even if by some miracle I end up with it, I don't know how to use it. So I grab the umbrella instead.

He snatches up the gun and whirls around. Takes aim at my head.

I take aim at his, and push the button on the umbrella.

The spring-loaded mechanism clicks, and the spiked tip goes straight into Tyrrell's eyeball. He shrieks, flailing as blood and vitreous humour pours down his cheek, and then he disappears from view as the canvas of the umbrella unfurls. I give the handle a shove, and the screaming stops.

'Reese!' I call out, as Tyrrell hits the ground with a thud.

Silence descends upon the house.

'Are you here? It's okay. It's Blake.'

Nothing.

She's not dead, I tell myself. *She's hiding. She thinks I'm the Crawdad Man.*

'Don't shoot me, okay?' I say. I check the kitchen, because it's closest. Then the laundry. The bathroom. No sign of her.

Finally I check the last bedroom.

It's empty, and not just of people. Thistle's clothes are gone. Her books. Her viola.

There's a handwritten note on her bedside table. I guess Tyrrell didn't notice it. He probably thought the other bedroom was hers. Without Thistle's stuff, it just looks like storage.

Phoebe,

I'm sorry to leave like this. You've been a good friend to me. I hope I'll see you again—but not anytime soon.

It's nothing you did. I made a mistake. Actually, mistake doesn't cover it—I screwed up so badly that I can't be a cop anymore. That guy I told you about, he turned out to be a criminal. You have no idea how bad. And if I'm not a cop, I don't know what I am. I need to go somewhere while I figure that out.

I wanted to stay until you got back from Memphis, to say goodbye. But the thought of another night in this city makes me feel sick. I can't be here right now. Please understand.

There's a month's rent in the Apache Tears. You know what that means, right? I hope that gives you enough time to replace me. Helen is looking after Junie until you get back.

I'm really sorry. I'll miss you.

Reese

P.S. I'll ask my old colleagues to watch the house. If that guy comes to the door, don't answer.

A teardrop lands on the note. I brush it away with my thumb, and walk out of the room. I find myself looking at the dead man with an umbrella stuck in his head, without really seeing him. Part of me is aware that I'm in a house where shots were recently fired, and the police are probably on their way. I can't stay. But I don't know where else to go.

I'm a missing persons investigator, but for the first time, I'm clueless. Thistle could be anywhere. Even if I somehow found her, there's no way I could convince her to trust me again. It's over.

Eventually I wipe down the door handles, the umbrella, and the parts of the floor I might have touched with my hands. No time to mop up my muddy footprints. I leave Tyrrell where he is. I don't touch the crystal healing book, which almost certainly contains a month of rent. Apache tears are a kind of volcanic glass.

By the time I get back to the car, sirens are in the air, and Charlie Warner is dead.

CHAPTER 48

I can turn back time, resurrect the dead, make you smile, make you cry. I form in an instant, but last a lifetime. What am I?

The highway cuts a ghostly ribbon through the forest. My headlights turn the trees grey, like headstones. I've showered, but I can still feel the dead all over me. The heater roars, drying out my eyeballs. The radio is cranked up as loud as it goes, so I can't hear myself think. It doesn't work.

Without Thistle, I can't change. But without Warner, I have no one to eat. The hunger will slowly drive me crazy.

I could turn myself in. Confess to everything I've done. Die by lethal injection. Or maybe hobble out of prison an old man, penniless in a futuristic city I don't understand, Reese Thistle a distant memory.

That's the less appealing of my two options.

I still can't hear Thistle in my head. Instead I have Hope's voice: *Let me give you some advice, Mr Blake. If you ever want to kill yourself, put the gun to the side of your head, not the front or the back.*

That's the more appealing option. I have Warner's Springfield. My aim isn't good, but it's good enough. There's just one more thing I have to do first.

The turn-off is so well hidden I nearly miss it. I brake hard and narrowly avoid flipping the car. I spin the wheel and send the car bouncing down a dirt road. It seems impossible that anyone could live so far from civilisation. But according to the navigation software on my phone, this is the right way. I resist the urge to double-check the address on the envelope, hand-written by Shannon Luxford.

I've chosen my last meal. Fred.

And then I'll stop, I tell myself. *This is the last one.*

'. . . *found dead at a remote homestead near Beaumont, Texas*,' the radio says. '*Police have confirmed that they believe there is a connection to the double homicide in West Houston.*'

Quick work. I guess they found Warner's body—I just left it in the street—and followed the phone trail back to Sindy's cabin, where they found a dead FBI agent and around twenty other bodies, some of which had been stitched together. Glad I'm not the one who has to deal with the fallout.

The field office director comes on the radio. '*We're pursuing several leads*,' she says. '*We urge anyone with information to come forward.*'

That's code for: *We're shitting ourselves.*

The news anchor is back. '*The victims' names have yet to be released,*' she says, barely managing to keep the glee from her voice, '*but the details of the case have been described as "disturbing".*'

Even when my own body is eventually found, it's unlikely that the police will connect any of this to me. Warner's gun is probably untraceable. I only killed one of the many, many victims, and any trace of me will be buried by the sheer volume of DNA from other people. Once all the bullets have been counted and the guns examined, the cops will probably announce that all those people killed each other.

Some will suspect it isn't true. But an open case of this magnitude would look bad for everyone. Better to blame the victims and declare the case closed.

Maybe Thistle is listening to the radio right now. Maybe she'll follow the case from afar, and eventually realise that I wasn't the Crawdad Man.

But that won't help. It wasn't the body in the back yard that destroyed our relationship. It wasn't even the head in my freezer. It was the look on my face. She knows me now. Nothing can undo that.

Another turn-off. This narrow trail isn't on Google Maps, and would be easy to miss. But there's a rotting wooden sign, for the mailman.

'*My next guest is Professor Raquel Solar from Louisiana State University,*' the anchor continues. '*Professor, these latest shootings bring this year's gun death toll to seven hundred and twelve in Texas alone. Is it time to talk about gun control?'*

Another voice comes on. *'We've done nothing but talk, Susan. Compared to other countries—'*

I turn off the radio. A house is visible through the trees.

It's nothing like Sindy's cabin in the woods. It's a sprawling two-storey building, with probably five or six bedrooms. A big white pick-up is parked right in front of a two-car garage. Electric lights are switched on—it's off the grid only in the criminal sense. I bet there's hot water, too. Someone is living a good life out here.

More lights come on as I stop the car and kill the engine. Automated security lights, I think.

As I get out of the car, the front door opens. A man in jeans and a knitted sweater steps out—he's friendly-faced but muscular, like a young Matt Damon.

He approaches me, sneakers crunching on the gravel. 'Shannon?' he says, extending his hand.

I shake it. 'Fred. Nice to finally meet you in person.'

'Likewise.'

He has a firm handshake. I won't be able to overpower him—I'll have to take him by surprise.

He looks me up and down, assessing. He clearly doesn't know what Shannon looked like, but I'm older than he would have expected. The shaved head and the broken nose helps, though. I could be anybody.

'Thanks for letting me crash here,' I say.

'No problem, man. Stay as long as you need. We gotta look out for each other, right? Come on in.'

Finally he turns away, walking towards the house. I reach behind my back and grip the hammer. I've never killed someone in cold blood before. But I need this. One last monster to eat.

'The other guys love your videos, man,' Fred says, without looking over his shoulder. 'They're really looking forward to meeting you.'

I let go of the hammer and let my shirt fall back down to cover it.

'The other guys?' I say.

ACKNOWLEDGEMENTS

Thank you to my endlessly accommodating family, especially Venetia, Mum and Dad. This book couldn't have happened without your support.

Thanks to the amazing teams at Allen & Unwin, Bolinda Audiobooks, Booked Out Speaking Agency, Curtis Brown Literary Agency, Hanover Square Press and ICM Partners, who made *Hangman* such a success and took a leap of faith on an even more disturbing sequel.

Thanks also to the talented translators who helped Timothy Blake go global. I'm so sorry about all the wordplay in the riddles.

Particular thanks to Charles Bonnot, Luke Causby, Clare Forster, Angela Handley, Natalie Hallak, Peter Joseph, Dan Kirschen, Ali Lavau, Nadia Farah Mokdad, Christa Munns, Kathleen Oudit, Jane Palfreyman, Christopher Ragland (the wonderfully sinister voice of Blake) and Ben Stevenson.

Thanks to Sarah Bailey, Jeffery Deaver, Gregg Hurwitz, Gordon Reece, Ben Sanders and Emma Viskic for writing such terrific noir and for recommending *Hangman* to your greedy fans.

Thanks to all the readers who took a chance on *Hangman* and then, instead of demanding that the author be institutionalised, submitted riddles and volunteered to have characters named after them in the sequel. Sorry I couldn't use everybody! Apologies to Shannon Luxford, who's a very nice person in real life.